Edge of Eden

By Nicholas Proffitt

GARDENS OF STONE
THE EMBASSY HOUSE
EDGE OF EDEN

EDGE
OF EDEN

NICHOLAS
PROFFITT

BANTAM BOOKS
NEW YORK • TORONTO • LONDON • SYDNEY • AUCKLAND

EDGE OF EDEN

A Bantam Book / June 1990

Grateful acknowledgment is made for permission to reprint the following: "Since I Met You Baby" by Ivory Joe Hunter, © 1956 UNICHAPPELL MUSIC INC. (Renewed). All rights reserved. Used by permission. "Stayin' Alive" by Barry Gibb, Robin Gibb and Maurice Gibb © 1978 Gibb Bros. Music. All rights reserved. Used by permission. "The Duke of Earl" by E. Edwards, E. Dixon, and B. Williams, copyright © 1961 (renewed) by Conrad Music, a division of Arc Music Corp. Reprinted by permission. All rights reserved.

Library of Congress Cataloging-in-Publiction Data
Proffitt, Nicholas, 1943–
   Edge of Eden / Nicholas Proffitt.
     p. cm.
   ISBN 0-553-05763-4
   I. Title.
   PS3566.R643E36   1990
   813'.54—dc20   89-18056   CIP

Published simultaneously in the United States and Canada

Bantam Books are published by Bantam Books, a division of Bantam Doubleday Dell Publishing Group, Inc. Its trademark, consisting of the words "Bantam Books" and the portrayal of a rooster, is Registered in U.S. Patent and Trademark Office and in other countries. Marca Registrada. Bantam Books, 666 Fifth Avenue, New York, New York 10103.

PRINTED IN THE UNITED STATES OF AMERICA

RRH   0 9 8 7 6 5 4 3 2 1

For Paine and Lucia, who followed the game.

Ngatia ciathii hiti cieragara.
When lions have gone, hyenas dance.

Gutiri mundu utangituika wa ndigwa.
There is no man that cannot become an orphan.

—KIKUYU PROVERBS

Edge of Eden

Part One

KIFARU

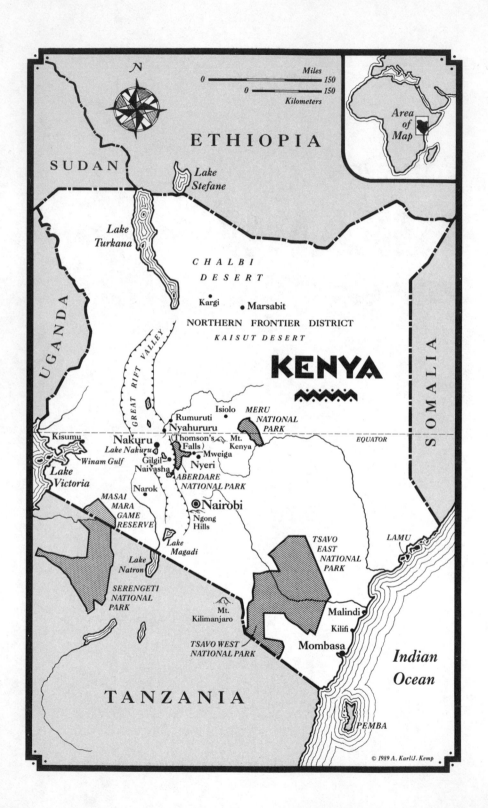

N

© 1989 A. Karl/J. Kemp

Miles
0   150
0   150
Kilometers

Area
of
Map

ETHIOPIA

SUDAN

Lake
Stefane

Lake
Turkana

CHALBI
DESERT

Kargi   • Marsabit

NORTHERN FRONTIER DISTRICT

KAISUT DESERT

KENYA

UGANDA

GREAT RIFT VALLEY

Isiolo   MERU
Rumuruti   NATIONAL
Nyahururu   PARK
(Thomson's)   Mt.
Falls)   Kenya   EQUATOR

Kisumu

Nakuru
Lake Nakuru   Mweiga
Winam Gulf   Gilgil   Nyeri
Naivasha
Lake
Victoria   ABERDARE
NATIONAL PARK
Narok

MASAI
MARA   ⊙ Nairobi
GAME
RESERVE   Ngong
Hills

Lake
Magadi

Lake
Natron   TSAVO
EAST
NATIONAL
PARK

SERENGETI
NATIONAL
PARK

Mt.
Kilimanjaro   Malindi

Kilifi

TSAVO WEST   Mombasa
NATIONAL PARK

Indian
Ocean

TANZANIA

PEMBA

SOMALIA

LAMU

1

Whatever it was, it had been dead for some time. Peter Odongo, already husbanding clues, knowing there would be too few, was certain of that much even before they found it. His nose told him.

At first he thought it was compost he was smelling, the spongy mat of rotted vegetation which lay on the forest floor like a rough-napped rug, but as they pushed closer there was no mistaking it. That educated nose of his had led him to too many sad discoveries in the shantytowns behind River Road in Nairobi and in the foul alleys of the Mathare Valley for him to confuse that smell with anything else for long. But not even a precocious nose could tell him exactly what had died, and the old woodcutter who had made the find earlier that morning had not ventured close enough for a positive identification.

Another fifty meters along the trail, which was nothing more than an animal track, and Odongo could see for himself. The carcass lay directly on the path, blocking it. A serval, its face glossy with blood, left off feeding and eased away as the two men approached, watching them over a shoulder as it went, looking more annoyed than alarmed. Larger cats—lions down from the moor above the tree line, or perhaps a leopard—had already come and gone. The abdomen had been torn open and the viscera scooped out and eaten, the spot marked by black blood splotches and gobbets of suet. Both haunches and most of one shoulder had been chewed away. Peter's escort, a ranger from the National Parks Department, slung his ancient carbine and ran toward the pile of bones and collapsed flesh. "Don't touch anything!" Odongo shouted after him.

The ranger, a local man, dim and excitable, ignored the instruction. Using both hands, he pried open the beak-shaped mouth, fished beneath the rough, sandpapery tongue, and held up his prize. "See! It is here, Inspector! Just like the others! Do you see?"

"Yes, I see," Peter said with a nod and a resigned sigh. "Bring it here."

Like a dense dog oblivious to his master's displeasure, the grinning ranger trotted over and dropped a small, smooth, whitish object into Odongo's upturned palm.

No longer worried about prints, Peter rubbed it briskly between a thumb and two fingers, like a coast Arab working a string of worry beads. He was no zoologist, but he knew what it was: an incisor tooth of a spotted hyena, *Crocuta crocuta*. Two months ago he would not have known that.

Sticking to procedure, he slipped the tooth into a small plastic bag, then put the bag into a larger evidence satchel. He took a notebook and a stub of pencil from a pocket of his khaki safari jacket and approached the carcass with caution, as if it were a beached torpedo which might yet blow without warning. He wet the tip of the pencil with his tongue, found a blank page and, in a neat hand, entered: *Diceros bicornis*. Two months ago he wouldn't have known that either.

It was a black rhinoceros, although the granulose hide was the same dingy gray color of all rhinos. The animal was small, even for a black, which invariably ran smaller than the whites. The big horn would have gone about four pounds, five at most. Hardly worth their effort, he'd have thought.

Peter squatted in front of the ruined head. Staring back at him was a bullet wound, its rimming flesh puffed, the hole itself caked with maggots and black flakes of dried blood, a transfixing third eye centered between small, almost hairless ears, just above where the short back horn should have been. The front horn was gone too, hacked from the prehensile upper lip with a casual expertise.

Like most Africans, Odongo was not sentimental about animals. It was his official duty these days to be outraged by their slaughter, but if he had any feeling about them at all it was a vague fear; the larger ones invariably wanted to eat you or to trample your crops. Nor did he cherish them. In fact, he was embarrassed by them. Those people, mostly foreign and mostly white, who saw animals as the African's "priceless heritage" were often the very same people who associated wildlife with an inherent savagery.

Yet there was something touching about this particular animal's pathetic and desecrated face, a resigned acceptance that went with the unanswered plea in those lusterless eyes. Despite its daunting mass, the rhinoceros, with its comical, beaked face, had always struck Peter as the most vulnerable and sympathetic of beasts. And it was this, not sentiment, that now led him to say: "Poor *kifaru*. Who did this to you?" The glassy eyes, no wider than a wart hog's, held no answer.

Peter borrowed the ranger's field knife and spent five minutes digging in the wound, soiling his hands and cuffs, finally prying out a misshapen, mushroom-headed slug. Using tweezers, he dropped the bullet into another cellophane bag, deposited it in the evidence satchel, then straightened and began a quick walk around the carcass, not really expecting to find anything, almost overlooking the arrow.

It lay deep inside the animal, inconspicuous among the bones in what was left of the hindquarters. It must have been fired into the haunch and then fallen into the cavity opened by the scavengers. He pushed up a sleeve and, grimacing, stuck an arm into the carcass to retrieve it.

The arrow was hand-forged, with a bamboo shaft, an iron tip with barbed tines, and three striped fletching feathers from a bird Peter could not identify. He sniffed the point, but the stench of the rhinoceros was so overpowering that he had to carry the arrow a considerable distance away before he could conduct a valid test. When he tried again he detected a faint scent of dogbane. It didn't make sense, he thought. Why bother with a poisoned arrow if you were going to shoot the beast between the eyes with a large-bore rifle? He shook his head and entered the anomaly into his notebook.

Peter parked the ranger under a tree to keep him out of the way, then began to comb the immediate area, moving in a series of expanding circles, using connecting animal paths where he could, hacking through the dense bush with a *panga* that badly needed sharpening where he could not. It was hot, sweaty work and he did not feel the forest's wet chill. Down below it was a bright morning, or at least it had been when he'd started out, but there was little evidence of it here on the mountain. Now and then there would be a minute tear in the dank blanket of bush and mist, giving Odongo a tantalizing glimpse of light-struck valleys and open glades before the foliage and the fog closed in again. Once, across the valley separating the ranges, he saw the snaggle-toothed peak of Mount Kenya—Kirinyaga, the Ostrich Mountain, as the locals called it—proud and cold and wrapped in its own gray cloak of cloud.

He worked quickly but carefully, fearful of bumping into an animal but spurred on by his discovery of the arrow. Aside from the hyena's tooth and the bullet, he had not expected to find anything more in the way of physical evidence. He never had before during the two long months he'd spent on the case.

Two hours later, his excitement had burned down to cold ash. He was just thinking about the rest of his day—a four-kilometer hike to the road, check in briefly with the district and provincial police at Nyeri, then two more hours driving the ninety-five miles back to Nairobi to brief the Assistant Minister on his lack of progress—when he found the next anomaly, or rather his nose did.

His circling had taken him back to the main track when he picked up the scent again. It was the old familiar smell, but it was not coming off the dead rhino; he was more than a hundred meters upslope from the carcass, and the wind was wrong. It was coming from higher on the mountain. He started for it at a quick trot, then stopped, turned around, and went back for his escort.

Peter found the ranger asleep under his tree, his mouth open in a leaf-rattling snore, his rifle flat on the ground beside him. He kicked the man's foot. The ranger lumbered to his feet without apology.

"Didn't you tell me you were at park headquarters this morning when the woodcutter came in to report a dead animal?" Peter asked.

"*Ndiyo, bwana,*" the ranger confirmed in sleepy Swahili.

"Did he say anything about a second animal?"

"*Hapana, bwana,*" the ranger said, shaking his head. Then he came fully awake and reverted to English. "Second animal?" He checked the path up and down, as if he might somehow have overlooked a prostrate elephant. "What second animal?"

"Never mind. Come. We're going on."

The ranger, his rifle at the ready, went ahead as they followed the twisting path up through "wait-a-bit" vines and tendrils of fog, moving even more slowly than the incline or the overgrowth or the masking mist dictated. The park ranger, a Kikuyu supposedly imbued with all the innate curiosity of his tribe, seemed uncharacteristically hesitant to plunge into a new adventure. He was a gate ranger, selected for his job because he had good English for the tourists, not a Field Force ranger trained to deal with poachers who were armed and who might well be waiting beyond the next turn. Peter knew what must be going through the ranger's mind. Clearly, the man had not anticipated anything more stressful than a walk in the woods when he'd volunteered to guide this brusque policeman from Nairobi. That, and perhaps a chance to impress a man who could put him on the path to promotion with a word to the warden. But new developments now only made him nervous; the woodcutter definitely had not mentioned a second animal.

Odongo, too, was experiencing a reluctance at odds with his earlier excitement. A clammy uneasiness seeped into him, leaving him damp with sweat despite the bracing mountain air. He identified the feeling almost at once. Fear. Strong and primal. As silly, but as real, as a child's fear of the dark.

It was not so surprising. Peter Odongo was a son of the western shore, of Lake Victoria. He did not like forests and he especially did not like this forest, the great equatorial rain forest of the Aberdare Range, the once and final refuge of Mau Mau. This was a Kikuyu forest. A Kikuyu forest watched over by the Kikuyu god Ngai, who was said to live atop nearby Mount Kenya. A Kikuyu forest filled with Kikuyu spirits.

Peter Odongo, who was not a Kikuyu, could feel them all around. They tracked him through the trees, teasing ghosts who darted into and out of shimmering pockets of ground fog, there one second, gone the next. He could swear he had just now seen Dedan Kimathi, the Mau Mau commander hanged by the British twenty years ago, vanish behind an akokanthera tree, a tangle-bearded apparition draped in uncured animal skins, emaciated and covered with sores from living on a fugitive's diet of roots and bark.

Odongo reined in his stampeding imagination. He was an educated man, a rational man . . . a Luo man, he chided himself, not some superstition-riven bushman. He was even a Catholic man of sorts, taught by the Consolata Fathers that the only ghost was the Holy Ghost. Ashamed of himself, he shouldered his way past the ranger on the tight trail and picked up the pace, still following his nose.

They found the source of the smell around the next bend, in a large and pleasant glade. This time the ranger held his ground; he stood rooted in place, gripping his carbine tight, his eyes wide, riveted on the thing in the tree.

It hung by its ankles, tied with sisal rope to a sturdy branch of a tree at the edge of the clearing. Odongo saw the nude pink body, trussed and strung up like a game trophy, bristling with arrows that had the same striped fletching as the one in his satchel, and his first thought was: "A *mzungu!* Mother of God, they've murdered a white man!"

Then he looked more closely at the patch of tight curls planted in the loose, flapping scalp like black peat, and saw that it was not a white man at all.

Peter quickly closed his eyes and tried his policeman's trick, pulling down the blinds inside himself, shuttering up his heart and stomach so they would not betray him. It was a trick he had mastered early on in his service with the Kenya Police, one that left him cold and detached, his emotions in quarantine, the complete professional. It had earned him the reputation as a shockproof investigator back when he worked homicide. It was a handy trick for a policeman, perhaps even indispensable, but it was not one that everyone could learn.

Peter Odongo had learned it, but it did not seem to be working. He took a deep, shuddering breath and walked slowly toward the thing in the tree, keeping his eyes aimed at the ground, telling himself that it was not because he could not face what he'd just seen, but because it was sound procedure. He was simply checking for evidence, making a mental note of where he stepped so that he could back out in his own tracks without riling the scene of the crime. It made such perfectly good sense he almost believed it.

He stopped and looked up only when he was nearly on top of it, almost butting heads with it, the dangling pink face upside down, looking as though it had been turned inside out, level with his own. It would have been looking right at him if it had had any eyes.

✽　　✽　　✽

Inspector Peter Odongo, his nerves calm, his policeman's trick working at last, stood off by himself on the lip of the wide glade, making notes and watching with disapproval as the locals—a mixed herd of policemen, Field Force rangers, and minor district officials—trampled the crime scene.

It was their lack of professionalism that bothered him, more than a genuine concern for the evidence; he'd given the area a thorough going over in the hour it had taken them to respond to his radio call. Aside from the arrows lodged in the subject's body and the bongo-hide quiver he had found lying against the tree, the only other piece of evidence to be had was safe, tucked away in his tunic pocket.

Now the others circled the corpse cautiously, reluctant to get too close to it, murmuring among themselves in voices muted with awe and an unmistakable undercurrent of fear. Not even the older men had seen anything quite like this, not in twenty years, not since the dark time of the Emergency. Even standing apart from the mob, Peter could hear one of the men make the comparison, give voice to it, whispering the words almost breathlessly—*Mau Mau*—like an incantation from an ancient, forbidden religion.

They gave Peter plenty of room, sidling glances his way but keeping their distance, seeming to prefer even a dead man's company to his.

Odongo understood. He was the outsider here, the *bwana* from Nairobi who could make trouble for them if he decided to criticize them in his report. And, of course, he was even more of an outsider than that; he was a Luo, a Nilote among the Bantu, most of them Kikuyu along with a handful of their Meru and Embu cousins. Dislike and resentment seemed to come off their turned backs in shimmering waves, as palpable and as pungent as their peculiar body odors.

Without warning, a surge of anger rolled through Odongo, an anger without definable cause or target, yet so sudden and profound that it momentarily checked the flow of blood to his head, leaving him nauseated and causing him to sway slightly. He had to take a number of deep breaths before his dizziness passed. When it had, he slapped his notebook shut with both hands in a vicious motion. The noise made the others involuntarily straighten and turn his way. "So where are your fucking officers?" he thundered, glaring at them. "Are they coming or not?"

They all looked at one another without speaking, until a voice piped up: "No officers were on seat when we logged your message, sir." The group parted to reveal a middle-aged police sergeant in a woolly pully, a regulation blue police sweater with leather patches at the shoulders and elbows. The rest of his kit consisted of loose khaki shorts and knee-stockings, a uniform more suited to the climate of his garrison at Nyeri, nestled at a comfortable 2,000 meters in the trough between the

Aberdares and Mount Kenya. The sergeant put out his chin and added, without fear and with a large measure of pride, "I was the ranking sergeant on seat when you radioed, sir. I am Sergeant Wakiru."

"And did the ranking sergeant on seat think to let the district commissioner know about any of this?" Odongo asked in a tone that framed his doubts.

"The DC he is coming, sir," the sergeant said, the hurt plain in his voice. "I rang round to him myself."

Peter nodded and the motion seemed to drain some of his anger. "All right. But we can't wait for him any longer. Cut this . . . this man down. He's been inconvenienced long enough."

They went about it gingerly but not gently, not wanting to touch the thing. One of the rangers spread a large canvas tarpaulin below the body while a constable, a knife clamped in his teeth like some long-ago pirate from Lamu, shinned up the tree and scooted along the branch to cut the ropes. The corpse dropped onto its head with a hollow, sickening sound, collapsing in segments and winding up on its back, the least of the indignities it had suffered.

The ranger below, his face an ebony grimace of distaste, daintily picked up a corner of the tarp with two fingers and gave a quick flip of the wrist. The sheet billowed briefly, then settled over the remains. The five arrows, stuck in the dead man's chest like so many tent poles, pushed up the canvas to form a musty mausoleum.

Once the body was out of sight the men seemed to relax a little. They huddled in groups of three or four, whispering animatedly, speculating about the murder, still marveling at the gruesome inventiveness of it. Every now and then one or another of them would glance over at the canvas-covered lump and fall silent.

The district commissioner arrived twenty minutes later, accompanied by four bodyguards armed with automatic weapons. His escort, neither soldiers nor policemen as far as Odongo could tell, fanned out around the perimeter of the clearing to secure the site. The DC himself, looking like one of his colonial predecessors in his one-piece safari suit and pith helmet, stopped in the middle of the glade and doubled over, his head down and his hands on his knees, laboring to catch his breath. He was an obese man, unused to physical exertion, and his official Range Rover was way back on the road, four long kilometers down the mountain.

Odongo waited politely for him to collect himself, then said, "The subject is over here, Commissioner, if you'd care to have a look."

The DC raised his head, blinked watery eyes until they focused, and puffed: "Ahhh . . . there . . . you are, Inspector. By . . . all . . . means. Lead the . . . way."

Peter waited until the commissioner was standing beside him before dropping to one knee and flipping back the canvas. The sudden bloom of smell was like an unexpected blow to the solar plexus. How odd, he thought, not for the first time, that the smell of a dead man should be no different from that of a dead beast. As an educated and rational man, he knew, of course, that meat was meat, but he'd always felt that somehow there should be a distinction.

"What we have is an African male of as yet undetermined age and tribe," Odongo began, his eyes on the body, his voice steady and matter-of-fact. "Five arrows, probably dipped in a poison of some kind, have penetrated the upper torso. He has been skinned, his nose and tongue have been cut away, and all his teeth have been extracted. Very symbolic. But I don't know why they picked out his eyes, unless they meant to . . ."

Odongo was talking to himself. The commissioner was pedaling backward, issuing horrible gagging sounds, in such a hurry to get away from the thing on the sheet that he stumbled and fell heavily, losing his pith helmet and landing on his amply-padded backside. He scrambled over onto his hands and knees and began to vomit.

Odongo stood and raised his eyes to the forest's canopy, watching a white-whiskered Colobus monkey while he waited for the retching noises behind him to stop. The others, who did not get many opportunities to see the powerful humbled, were not so considerate: they gawked at the helpless official with open delight, not troubling to hide their grins, the recent near-mutiny of their own stomachs conveniently forgotten.

Peter waited until the noises stopped, then went over to help the man to his feet. The DC's legs were still wobbly and a chain of mucus dangled from the second of his chins. He was embarrassed but still too rattled to try to hide it. "I'm a politician . . . not a policeman," he apologized between famished gulps for air. "I'm . . . I'm not accustomed to these things."

"Of course you're not," Peter said in a soothing voice, genuinely sympathetic. "Here, come sit for a moment." He led the commissioner to a mossy stump well away from the corpse, handed him back his pith helmet, and bellowed: "Wakiru!"

The sergeant presented himself with a foot-stomp and a salute of such panache he could have learned it only in the colonial army, the old King's African Rifles: pouter-pigeon chest, nose in the air, palm turned out the way his English officers had taught him some thirty years before. "Sir!"

"Form a detail to carry the subject to the road," Peter said. "Leave the arrows just the way they are and make sure no one touches the shafts. When you get the subject to Nyeri, get on to Nairobi and tell them I want a fingerprint man and a ballistics expert sent up right away. And by right away I mean this afternoon." He handed the man his evidence satchel. "They are to do the arrows in the body first, then everything in this bag. The bullet to be checked is in there as well."

"But, sir. We have people in Nyeri who can do the things you require."

"Just ring up Nairobi, Sergeant," Odongo said in a flat voice, his inspector's voice.

"Sir!" Sergeant Wakiru executed yet another exaggerated salute and trotted off.

The district commissioner was up, rocking gently on the balls of his feet, testing his legs and his composure. Finding them reasonably solid, he nodded in the direction of the departing Sergeant Wakiru. "What do you have besides the arrows and the bullet?"

"The quiver . . ." Peter said, reaching into his pocket and bringing out a plastic packet, ". . . and this."

The DC took the packet and held it up to a thin ribbon of light snaking through the low-riding clouds, shaking it, trying to make out what was inside. Then, with a small sigh of recognition, he dropped his arm. "So. Another one."

Peter nodded. "It was in the dead man's mouth, wrapped up in his severed tongue and stuffed halfway down his throat. I'll carry that one back to Nairobi myself."

The district commissioner, looking queasy again, handed it back without comment.

"We found another one under the tongue of the poached *kifaru*," Odongo said. "They are the same. Everything about this one is the same as the others."

"Not quite the same," the district commissioner said in a solemn voice. "They've never killed a man before. At least not in my district."

"People who butcher animals the way they do are capable of anything," Peter said. "You saw him. That skinning job was the work of professionals. I'll have to wait for the medical examiner's report to be absolutely certain, but I think they skinned him before they shot him full of arrows."

Suppressing a shudder, the commissioner leaned over to look again at the packet in Peter's hand. "Are you sure it's a hyena's tooth?"

"Quite sure," Peter said, putting it back in his pocket. "One of the tearing teeth."

The commissioner surreptitiously ran his eyes around the edges of the glade, as if he expected one of the slope-backed beasts to come bounding out of the trees at him. Momentarily reassured, he turned back to Odongo. "I still don't get this business about the teeth," he said. "Where do they come from? What is their significance?"

Peter shrugged.

The commissioner did not see the gesture. He was looking past Odongo, a reflective, faraway look in his eyes. "I know, of course, that there are many hyenas in these mountains," he said quietly. "But I was raised in Kamba country, on a *shamba* near Machakos, a small farm at the edge of the Kapiti Plains, and I've always thought of *fisi* as a plains animal, a savanna animal."

Peter Odongo, watching two of Sergeant Wakiru's men run a stout carrying pole through the knotted ends of the canvas tarpaulin, then lift their load with a grunt, merely shrugged again and said: "There are hyenas anywhere there is something to eat."

2

Had it a window, Peter Odongo's office in Jogoo House, the Ministry of Tourism and Wildlife, would have looked out onto the bustle of Harambee Avenue. Instead, as his friends from the Central Police Station remarked on their infrequent visits, it was a dark, airless cell, more suitable for a common criminal than a full inspector of the Kenya Police.

His office was no smaller than the Assistant Minister's water closet, Peter would tell them with a stoic smile, an accurate barometer of his status within the ministry. His friends, those few colleagues brave enough or foolish enough openly to be his friends, would laugh with sympathy, secretly thankful they had not been the ones loaned out to Wildlife to look into the recent rash of game code violations, even more thankful they had not been born Luo. The only thing standing between Inspector Odongo and a brilliant career, they agreed among themselves, was his tribal affiliation.

Peter was in his tiny office by seven the morning after his safari to the highlands. He worked until noon on his report, sent it upstairs with a messenger and, skipping lunch, went off to the racecourse at Ngong to see one of his informants, a track tout connected with a minor smuggling ring. He found his man clocking time trials, but all he got was a tip on a sure thing in Sunday's third race, which meant that one of the politicians had a horse running and the fix was in. Peter gave the man a little something to put down for him and left.

When he got back to Jogoo House, sixty shillings poorer, he found a new stack of paper on his desk: three reports, all relating to the dead man on the mountain, and three messages, all from the Assistant Minister, asking to see him the moment he returned.

He riffled through the reports—ballistics, prints, the medical examiner's findings—skimming a bog of bureaucratic verbiage written in painful English to get to the summarizing paragraphs, astonished at the speed with which they had been done and delivered. Nothing like a human skinning to spark a little interest, he thought. When he finished his reading, he pulled an outsize manila envelope labeled "Aberdare National Park" from his file drawer and went out to catch the lift.

An aluminum tag fixed to the bulkhead limited the elevator's capacity to eight, but a dozen people crowded aboard on the ground floor and five or six more squeezed in as the car made its agonizingly slow ascent, stopping on every floor. A white man was trapped in the center of the human press. Peter could see the *mzungu* trying to hold his breath against the pungent odor of Africans who'd refused to assimilate the European habit of regular bathing. As the white man's face got redder, Peter's grin got bolder.

Peter disembarked on the top floor and walked the long corridor to the Assistant Minister's corner office, passing room after identically furnished room: a table, two chairs, and two stamp *bwanas*. The stamp *bwanas* sat slumped in their seats, reading or dozing or staring vacantly at walls that were bare but for a retouched color photograph of President Jomo Kenyatta, the Mzee, the "Old Man," father of the nation, looking dignified in a blue pinstripe suit and clutching his trademark, a jeweled fly whisk. In the middle of each table was a single ink pad and an assortment of rubber stamps.

As much as Peter Odongo had resented his unexpected and unwanted transfer to Wildlife two months before, he was glad to be a policeman, glad to have a real job. Every government building in Nairobi was cluttered with these so-called stamp *bwanas,* bright young men who, like himself, had been awarded scholarships to Nairobi University to prepare for careers in government service, and pumped full of heady expectations. But unlike himself, so many of them had merely graduated to the discovery that there were not enough meaningful jobs to go around. Guaranteed government employment regardless, they soon found themselves sharing tiny offices and trivial tasks, taking turns in putting their gratuitous mark on the endless parade of paper that accompanied every official transaction, their bitterness and disillusionment growing with each boring hour, each thwack of the stamp.

The secretary in the Assistant Minister's outer office, a young, high-breasted Kikuyu girl, was thumbing through a glossy Italian fashion magazine, studying the photographs and advertisements with a face-screwing concentration. Looking up to find a mere police inspector there, she took no trouble to mask her annoyance at the interruption. She brusquely ordered him to have a seat and, taking the magazine with her, went in to tell her boss he was there. When she returned, it was back to Roma and Milano. Another fifteen minutes passed before she checked her wristwatch and pointed at the door. Peter tucked his envelope under an arm and went in without knocking.

The Assistant Minister came around his desk to greet him with a smile, a gleaming rift in a perfectly round face that was an incandescent, almost metallic black, even blacker than Peter's own long, dark face. The purity of the man's blackness was underscored by the vanilla suit he wore, an English suit matched with a French shirt, Italian shoes, and a Swiss watch. And parked in the lot outside, Peter knew, was the Assistant Minister's new German automobile, an early Christmas present from his Belgian wife. The Assistant Minister for Wildlife was a walking advertisement for the European Common Market.

"Inspector Odongo! How good to see you again!" he said, offering a friendly handshake. "So sorry to keep you waiting. Please. Sit and be comfortable."

Peter took one of the chairs facing the large teak desk and waited, his envelope in his lap, a wariness in his eyes, unconvinced by the man's tone of hearty goodwill.

The Assistant Minister went back behind his desk and sat down. His palms pressed together in front of his full moon of a face, he looked at Odongo over steepled fingers. Beneath his emotionless and appraising eyes, the benign smile lay on his lips like a tool left on a window sill, something he had used once and forgotten to put away. His desk was perfectly clean except for a copy of Odongo's report and an executive toy of some kind, an elaborate maze with steel balls.

The silence lengthened, became uncomfortable, before the Assistant Minister leaned forward to tap Peter's report with a stubby, but manicured, finger and said: "Interesting. Very interesting, indeed."

Peter did not know how he was supposed to respond, so he did not.

"Most interesting of all," the Assistant Minister went on, "is the way you've managed to reach so many conclusions while in possession of so few facts."

"Theories, Minister, not conclusions," Odongo corrected, politely. "It's true I don't have much hard evidence at this point, but what I have lends itself to certain assumptions. I thought you might like to hear them."

"Oh I do, Inspector, I do. But what I'd really like to hear about is how you reached these assumptions."

"It's all in my report, sir."

"Yes, yes," the Assistant Minister said, his impatience showing. "But why now? For two months your reports have been so conservative, so shy of conjecture. Now this." He waved at the paper with a brushing backhand, as if to sweep away its contents. "Why the sudden change?"

"Sheer accumulation," Peter said. "Except for the death of a human being . . . and I realize, of course, that murder is a major exception . . . yesterday's incident in the Aberdare Forest fits a pattern. It was just one more episode among many, but I felt there were now enough of them to make assumptions. So I made them."

The Assistant Minister sighed and turned long-suffering eyes to the picture of the Mzee on his wall, a photo similar to those hanging in the offices of the stamp *bwanas,* except it was larger, almost life-size, and over his blue pinstripe suit the President was wearing a luxuriant black and white mantle made from Colobus monkey skins. Odongo noticed that the portrait was inscribed.

"I'm afraid you're going to have to make those assumptions again for me, Inspector," the Assistant Minister said, his smile home again, his tone kind. He placed a thick hand, palm down and fingers splayed, on top of Odongo's report. "This here is all police jargon . . . *subjects* and *perpetrators* and *modus operandi* and the like. . . ." He gave a helpless shrug. "I'm an administrator, not a policeman."

Peter remembered the Nyeri district commissioner saying, "I'm a politician . . . not a policeman," and decided that the DC was by far the more honest of the two.

"What is it exactly that's giving you so much trouble?" Peter asked, his condescension ringing even in his own ears. He realized his error even as he made it and the look on his superior's face confirmed it. The Assistant Minister reacted as if he had been shot, going stiff in his chair. The smile that had never quite reached his eyes—eyes now half-lidded with fury—vanished without a trace. Peter gripped the arms of his chair and waited for the explosion. He could almost read the man's mind: "Cheeky Luo bastard."

Instead, after a long and pointed pause, the Assistant Minister said, "No trouble, Inspector. No trouble at all. I just thought that this might be a good time for us to talk, in plain and simple language, about where we stand in this case."

"Yes, sir. Of course."

"Good." He fixed Peter with another cool, lingering look, then pulled a pair of reading glasses from the breast pocket of his ice-cream–colored suit, put them on, and gave his attention to the report in front of him.

"Why don't we begin with this most recent incident," the Assistant Minister said, glancing idly at the top page of the report. "It says here that you received a radio message early yesterday morning from the chief warden of Aberdare National Park, informing you that a local woodcutter had discovered a dead animal inside the park, in the Treetops Salient. So you dashed off straight away." He looked at Odongo over the tops of his half-glasses. "Is this woodcutter a suspect?"

Odongo shook his head. "No, sir. I had a long talk with him at police headquarters in Nyeri and it's obvious that he was just in there collecting wood. He wasn't going to report the animal at first because he was afraid he would be put in jail for being in the park. But then he was even more afraid not to report it. Someone might have seen him, and he didn't want us to think he was a poacher."

"When you first received this message, did you have any reason to think you were going up there to see anything more than a dead animal?"

"No, sir," Peter said. "I expected nothing more than a routine poaching. There had been five poaching incidents in the park in the previous week, and I had asked the warden to keep his rangers away from any new discoveries until I'd had an opportunity to look them over." Odongo paused, then added, "I'd been having some trouble with his people with regard to evidence. They tend to pick up and play with everything they see."

"What sort of evidence are we talking about?"

Odongo stood, rummaged in the pocket of his tunic, and scattered a fistful of teeth over the desk top, rolling them out with a dramatic flourish, as if they were dice in a game of chance.

The Assistant Minister picked one up. "All of these came from Aberdare National Park?"

"Yes, sir."

"They are similar to the ones from Tsavo." It was a flat declaration rather than a question.

Peter nodded. "And from Meru."

"So you think we're facing a single gang of *shiftas,* I suppose?" the Assistant Minister said. "The same bandits in all three parks?"

"No doubt," Peter said emphatically. "I have a box full of these teeth in my file cabinet, like business cards."

"And now they've moved to the Aberdares."

"Yes. Sometime in the last week or week and a half."

The Assistant Minister tossed the tooth back onto the desk and settled back in his chair with a sigh of leather. "All right then, Inspector," he said. "Tell me what we know, or think we know, about these outlaws."

"To begin with, we know they are professionals," Peter said as he used the flat of his hand to sweep the teeth to the edge of the desk, then into his pocket. "Well-organized, well-equipped, well-financed professionals."

"How can you be so sure they aren't locals?"

"Locals—meat and skin poachers—almost always use silent methods," Odongo said. "Pits, traps, bows and arrows. Only professionals can get guns, and the gang we're talking about is better armed than your Field Force ranger sections. They used Kalashnikov AK-47s and American M-16s in the Tsavo and Meru parks. I've just seen the ballistics report on the bullet I recovered in the Aberdares. It was a 7.62 NATO long round, fired from a G-3, the German assault rifle."

"Was it now?" The Assistant Minister sounded skeptical. "How can that be? Not even the Army has G-3s. Only the GSU has that weapon." The General Service Unit was the nation's elite paramilitary force, and Jomo Kenyatta's palace guard.

"Well, these poachers have at least one," Odongo said. "And apparently they don't care if we know they have it. They wouldn't have left that bullet for us to find if they did."

The Assistant Minister shrugged. "Perhaps they were just careless."

"Not careless," Peter said firmly. "Arrogant."

"Just for the sake of argument, let's say that they are locals," the Assistant Minister said, "amateurs who somehow got their hands on one or two modern weapons. Perhaps they found them, or stole them, or even bought them on the black market. Regrettable as it is, such things do happen."

"Yes, sir, they do. But that's not what happened in this case. What I think happened is that—"

The Assistant Minister put up a hand to stop him. "Think? What you *think*? Don't tell me what you think. Tell me what you know."

"Sir, if you would let me fin—"

"Didn't you say, not a moment ago, that an arrow is the mark of an amateur? And weren't poisoned arrows found in the rhino and the human victim? It's right here in your report."

Odongo bit his lip and tried to control his anger. The Assistant Minister was playing the devil's advocate, trying to be sure that sloppy thinking and deductive shortcuts had not contaminated the analysis. Odongo could understand that. What he didn't understand was the man's dogged belligerence. He seemed offended by Peter's whole approach.

"The dead man was indeed a local poacher," Odongo said, tossing the minister a bone. "He shot the rhinoceros with an arrow tipped with a poison which normally takes about twelve hours to work. He was trailing the animal, waiting for it to die, when he was jumped by the professionals. They butchered him as a warning to others to stay out of the park."

The Assistant Minister was staring at him. "Remarkable," he said, shaking his head in mock admiration. "You got all that out of six arrows, two hyena teeth, and one ballistics report."

"In a manner of speaking, yes, sir, I did." Peter leaned forward in his chair and a jerky animation infused his voice and hand gestures. "Look, sir, the use of modern weapons tells us that these are men with ample resources. The hyena's tooth left in the victim's mouth is a calling card, one that tells us that this is the same gang that was operating in Meru park a month ago and in Tsavo East the month before that. The fact that they are moving about the country tells us that they are not simply out to put a bit of meat in the cook pot; meat and skin poachers usually stay fairly close to their *shambas,* and they almost never cover the kind of distances we're seeing in this case. I've no doubts at all, Minister. We are dealing with a very well-organized, highly professional poaching ring here." Peter paused, then said in a puzzled tone, "But surely you must have come to a similar conclusion months ago. Wasn't that why you asked us to loan you an experienced investigator in the first place?"

"I asked for police assistance because my minister told me to ask for it," the Assistant Minister said with a shrug. "Personally, I thought that my Field Force rangers could, and should handle it."

"Oh."

There was a short silence before the Assistant Minister said, "Even if we agree that this is the work of professional poachers, what makes you think the murder victim was a local poacher? And how could you know the motives of his killers?"

"On your first question, the answer is guesswork," Peter promptly conceded, "but guesswork based on evidence. The dead man carried no food and had no other belongings with him, so I think he is a local man, from Nyeri, or Mweiga, or one of the *shambas* along the edge of the park. We brought in some of the area chiefs and headmen to look at the body, but because of the disfigurement of the face, we haven't found anyone who can identify him. But the poisoned arrows say he's a poacher. So does the quiver made from the hide of a bongo, a protected animal for years now, even before the ban on hunting."

"Who says the quiver and arrows were his?" the Assistant Minister asked. "Who says they didn't belong to his killers?"

"The only fingerprints we found on the arrows belonged to the murder victim," Odongo said. "And while I do not have hard evidence for you, Minister, my *theory* is that he didn't shoot himself."

This time, the Assistant Minister did not let it pass. "Don't be impertinent, Inspector. I'm warning you."

"Yes, sir. Sorry, sir."

The Assistant Minister was watching him again, peering over the tops of the half-glasses with appraising, knowing eyes. Here it comes, Odongo thought. He was surprised it had taken this long. He waited for the question, wondering what form it would take this time. He'd heard so many variations, from the idly curious to the aggressively hostile. Before he could hazard a guess, it came. "Odongo. That is a Luo name, isn't it?"

With an inward sigh, Peter said, "Yes, Minister, it is."

"Mission schools?"

"Yes, Minister."

"Kenyatta University College . . ." Peter started to shake his head. ". . . or Nairobi University?"

"Yes, Minister."

"Full scholarship?"

"Yes, Minister."

The Assistant Minister was nodding along to the rhythmic beat of the exchange. Peter somehow doubted that this man, an assistant minister and a fast-rising star in the ruling KANU party, had taken the time or the trouble to investigate his background. That he hadn't had to was what made it so hard to take. Was he so easy to classify, to pigeonhole, Peter asked himself? Yes, of course he was. He knew that while he was not a typical Luo man—the typical Luo man was planting crops or tending his herd or throwing a gill net over the waters of the Winam Gulf right now—he was all too typical of a certain subclass of Luo man. With four key clues—his age (thirty-four), his years in government service (eleven), his job classification, and his rank—this Kikuyu minister could deduce almost everything about his life.

"The Luo are quite a clever people, aren't they?" the Assistant Minister said.

Just how, Peter asked himself, was he supposed to answer such a question? With the arrogant-sounding truth? "Yes, and especially compared to Kikuyu baboons." With a self-effacing lie? "Oh, not really, sir. We just work hard."

It didn't matter. Peter knew that by "clever" the Assistant Minister had not necessarily meant intelligent, or wise, or anything complimentary. He meant it in the same way *mzungus* meant it when they referred to Africans or Asians as clever. They meant too clever by half.

"No more than any other, sir," he said in answer to the Assistant Minister's question.

Another silence, the longest yet, fell across the room like a shadow. Odongo was not sure what, if anything, that meant. He did not really know the Assistant Minister. Until now his dealings with the man had been limited. There had been a long, friendly chat when he was first assigned to the ministry, but after that he had been left largely on his own, with explicit instructions not to bother the Assistant Minister unless he had a dramatic development to report. As there had been few dramatic developments, he had met with the man only twice in two months, when the poachers shifted their operations from Tsavo to Meru, and again when they left Meru. He had been waiting to hear back on his request for a third appointment—to inform the Assistant Minister that the gang had resurfaced in the Aberdares—when this latest incident occurred.

"I spoke to your superintendent at the Central Police Station this afternoon," the Assistant Minister said. "Now that a man's been killed, the police will be taking a much greater interest in this case."

"I'm sure we will," Peter said.

"I suggested to him that he might want to take you off the investigation now." The Assistant Minister was watching Odongo carefully, looking for a reaction. When he saw none, he added, "Nothing personal, of course. I merely thought he might want a homicide expert to take over.

I'm telling you this now in case you hear any gossip. I wouldn't want you to misinterpret my intentions."

"No, sir."

Odongo resisted the impulse for a moment, then caved in. "Ahh . . . may I ask what the superintendent said?"

The Assistant Minister smiled. "He said that until two months ago, *you* were his homicide expert, and that he could not think of a better man for the job. He also said he still doesn't understand why you were taken from him and loaned to this ministry."

Because the *senior* superintendent does not like Luos, Peter thought. And because of that last case he had worked on.

"Anyway, he said he'd like to confer with you sometime in the next day or two," the Assistant Minister was saying. "The way we left it was that you would continue working here under my supervision, but he'd like you to keep him apprised of your progress. And you are to send copies of your reports to me to him as well."

"Yes, sir."

"Good. Now let's get back to business, shall we?" the Assistant Minister said. He stood and walked around the desk to straighten the photo of the Old Man, then went back to his chair. "Let us say you've convinced me that he was a local poacher. What makes you think he was killed as a warning to others?"

"Because of the way he was mutilated," Odongo said, an odd excitement in his voice. "Everything was symbolic of the poacher's world. His nose, a rhino's horn, was cut off. His teeth, an elephant's tusks, were extracted. Even his skin, a leopard's pelt, was peeled from head to toe. . . ."

Odongo was completely unaware of the gruesome portrait he presented. He was smiling broadly, almost laughing, as he detailed these atrocities, so delighted was he with his penetrating insight into the minds of the murderers. It was not a lack of feeling or sensitivity on his part so much as an almost childlike sense of pleasure and satisfaction in doing the work and doing it well. He had missed homicide work a good deal more than he had let himself admit. Nevertheless, he would have been appalled and embarrassed if he'd been able to see himself.

The Assistant Minister clearly did not know what to make of Odongo's performance. With a visible effort, he pulled his eyes away from the police officer's obscenely happy face and hurriedly thumbed through the report, trying to locate a more constrained account of the killing.

"What about the tongue and the eyes?" he finally asked.

"Ah, those are more traditional messages," Odongo said, still smiling. "Gouging out the eyes is a warning to others against seeing anything if they happen to be wandering about the forest. And cutting out the tongue, of course, means do not talk about anything you do happen to see."

The Assistant Minister seemed impressed. He also seemed to be catching Peter's fever. He tapped the report and said, almost eagerly, "You say here that you think they skinned him before they used the arrows. . . ."

"Yes, sir. And I was right. I saw the medical examiner's report just before I came upstairs. The subject was very much alive when they skinned him."

The two men sat there, grinning at each other across the desk.

Finally, the Assistant Minister said, "Well, Inspector. I'm beginning to see why your superintendent thinks so highly of you."

"Thank you, Minister."

"All right. Let us assume that all your theories are correct. How do you suggest we proceed from here?"

Odongo took a deep breath and said, "I've been giving it a great deal of thought, and I . . . uh, do you mind if I smoke?"

"Not at all."

"Thank you, sir." Peter pulled out a packet of Roosters and fished in his other pocket for his Bic lighter. The look on the minister's face could not have been more horrified if he'd undone his fly and pulled out his penis. Before he could pollute the room with the cheap, foul-smelling cigarette, the Assistant Minister produced a packet of Benson and Hedges and said, "Please, try one of these."

"Oh, why yes, thank you." Peter took one and allowed the Assistant Minister to light it with a gold-plated Dunhill.

"As I was saying, I've given it some thought and I think we must do something quickly. If the poachers stay with their usual timetable, we at least know where they will be for the next three weeks. In the Aberdares. But that's rough country, all mountains and dense forest, and it will be very difficult to find them and bring them to justice. So I propose that we put together a team of men to hunt them down, men who are as at home in the bush as the criminals are. I don't think policemen will do; they aren't trained to operate in the bush. Nor the Army. We need something special, something completely different, a team made up of expert trackers and hunters. They would have one mission and one mission only, to track these bandits and catch them in the act." Peter sat back in his chair, puffing contentedly on his Benson and Hedges.

The Assistant Minister picked up one of the steel balls from the toy on his desk and began tossing it up and down in one hand, staring at Odongo all the while. Finally he nodded. "Not a bad idea, Inspector, but you are not the first to come up with it." He leaned forward conspiratorially. "I shouldn't be telling you this as it's still very much a secret, but we already have a special Anti-Poaching Unit. At the moment it's deployed in . . . well, no need to go into that. And we're in the process of forming additional APU teams to be dispersed among those parks and reserves where poaching has been the worst. A second unit is in the final stages of training now and should be ready for action in about six weeks. As soon as it is, you can have it."

Secret? Peter almost bit through his tongue to keep from laughing. The experiment had been common knowledge at Central Station for weeks. He not only knew the APU existed, but that it had already proved a failure. Which was not surprising. It had been hastily manned with rejects from throughout the park system, Field Force rangers recommended by their wardens who, predictably enough, volunteered those men they most wanted to be rid of. Once in place the APU had adopted a static outpost strategy, setting up a permanent base camp from which it sent out daily foot patrols armed with outdated .303 Enfields. The poachers knew where the rangers would be at night, and which trails they would have to use when leaving the outpost during daylight hours. The APU had been hit by a number of ambushes.

"Six weeks isn't soon enough, sir," Peter said. "We only have three."

"You don't know for certain that they will move in three weeks. And if they do they'll just pop up elsewhere. Bringing them to justice will be the new team's first assignment."

"We can't wait, sir. We must move against them now. Once the short rains start our chances diminish drastically."

The Assistant Minister laughed good-naturedly and threw up his hands, bowing to the younger man's determination. "Oh all right, all right," he said, still smiling. "You win. I'll have the APU—the one that's already operational—shifted to the Aberdares straight away."

"You don't seem to understand," Odongo said. "I don't want it."

The Assistant Minister stopped smiling. "You're right, Inspector. I don't understand. What *do* you want?"

"We need men with special talents," Odongo said. "These poachers hunt the animals. We must hunt the poachers. We should hire ourselves a professional hunter, the best we can get."

"A professional? You mean a *mzungu*? A white hunter?"

Peter shrugged. "They are the most experienced at this sort of thing. We need someone who knows the Aberdare Forest and who knows how to lead other men."

The Assistant Minister was staring coldly at him. "You realize, of course, that the kind of white man you speak of, the kind who knows the Aberdare Forest so well, undoubtedly got to know it by hunting down our freedom-fighter brothers during the struggle for *Uhuru*."

Peter thought himself as patriotic as the next man, but he didn't know if he would go so far as to call the Mau Maus freedom fighters. He nodded, anyway. "I understand your feelings perfectly. I would take pains to find a younger man, one who wasn't old enough to have been involved in the way you mean."

The Assistant Minister was frowning. He shook his head. "No, I think not. We don't want, we don't need, that sort of man. Use our own rangers. That's what they are for."

"Judging by their performance, I couldn't begin to tell you what they are for," Odongo replied bitterly. "Your Field Force rangers had their chance at Tsavo, then again at Meru, and they failed. They never laid eyes, much less hands, on a single one of those thugs."

"They didn't have much to go on," the Assistant Minister said pointedly.

"They had enough," Peter said. "They were told where to look and still could not find them. And when they discovered that the poachers were equipped with automatic weapons, well, I don't think they looked very hard."

The Assistant Minister stopped juggling the steel ball. "I warned you, Inspector. I cannot tolerate insults to this ministry."

"And I cannot tolerate sloppy field work," Odongo said, his voice rising. "I must have confidence in any field force I decide to use. And I have no confidence in your rangers."

"But you *do* have confidence in mercenaries? Led by some *bwana mkubwa* white hunter?" The Assistant Minister shook his head sadly. "What you are proposing means bringing outsiders into official government business. It goes against protocol."

Peter snorted. "How can you concern yourself with petty bureaucratic protocol when our national interest is at stake here?" he asked.

"What do you mean by that?"

"I mean that these *shiftas* are striking at the heart of our economy. Kenya is not blessed with gold or tin or chrome or oil. All we have is wildlife. Wildlife brings in tourists and tourists bring in foreign exchange. Killing an animal is no different from robbing a Barclays Bank."

"Are you telling me my responsibilities?" the Assistant Minister inquired softly, incredulously. Then he lifted his voice to a shout: "I am the Assistant Minister for Wildlife!"

Peter resisted the impulse to yell back: "Then act like it, goddammit!" He knew how perilously close he was to being sent packing back to the Central Police Station. Whereas only the day before he would have given anything for just that, he now wanted to stay on this case more than he wanted anything. What had begun as a simple incident of poaching had evolved into a full-blown homicide, and if he went back to Central now it wouldn't be to work homicide. The senior superintendent would stick him behind a desk writing procedural manuals.

So he tried a different approach. "Of course, Minister. I did not mean to give offense. It is just that I am afraid that if we don't catch these people very soon there will be a scandal."

"Scandal? What do you mean, a scandal?" The minister's eyes flew involuntarily to the side wall, to the photograph of Mzee, as if he'd already been called onto the State House carpet to explain.

Stifling a smile, Odongo said, "Now that there's been a murder how long do you think we'll be able to keep it out of the newspapers?"

The minister went perfectly still. "Are you threatening to go to the press if I don't agree to let you organize this private team of yours?" he asked, his voice sharp-edged.

"No, of course not," Odongo said quickly, trying to look insulted. "But two dozen or more people saw the body. Another dozen or so in the police network know the details, from the forensics team to the lowliest constable in Central Province. By the time I made it down from the mountain the news was all over Nyeri headquarters." Peter spread his hands in a gesture of helplessness. "The horrifying way in which the subject was mutilated makes this a highly sensational case. People, being people, are going to talk about it."

"We know how to keep things out of the newspapers," the Assistant Minister said.

"Those controlled by the government or party, perhaps," Odongo agreed. "But not the others. Not for long."

Droplets of sweat beaded up on the Assistant Minister's forehead. He did not speak for a time, then he asked: "So who would lead this mercenary unit of yours? Do you have a man in mind?"

Odongo leaned forward earnestly, careful not to let the triumph he was feeling show. "No I don't. But it shouldn't be too difficult to find the kind of man we need. Ever since the hunting ban, many of them have retired or are out of work. We should have a large pool to choose from."

"I still don't like it," the Assistant Minister said. "It makes it look as if we have to ask our former oppressors for help whenever we have a problem."

"Whoever the man is, I will make certain he understands that he answers to me," Peter said quickly. "Just as I answer to you."

"That is very important," the Assistant Minister said. "They ran the show so long they still think it's their God-given right."

"Then I have your permission to proceed?"

The Assistant Minister sighed, and nodded. He pointed a finger at Odongo. "But listen carefully, my young Luo friend. Until now you have worked without much supervision. That time has ended. I want to be kept informed of every detail of your operation. I want daily reports from both you and this *mzungu* hunter of yours. If you've nothing to report, I want a report saying you have nothing to report. Do you understand?"

"Yes, Minister."

"Just be sure that you do. That will be all, Inspector. You may go."

Odongo gathered up his manila folder and left the room quickly and quietly, practically on tiptoes, anxious to be away before the Assistant Minister had a change of mind. As he reached the door, he heard a sharp snicking sound behind him, the click-click-click of steel balls rolling through a maze.

3

Miles and miles of bloody Africa.

His voice sounded small and lost, even in the long hush that was daybreak, even to him. He would not even have known that he'd spoken the words aloud if the herd he was watching, a mix of kongoni and Tommy, had not abruptly quit grazing to cock a collective ear, poised to bolt. But the savanna itself, still cool and damp after its slumber, from the foot of the hummock where Adrian Glenton lay with the rising sun at his back, to the horizon, had been spooked.

Miles and miles of bloody Africa.

How often, Adrian wondered, had he heard his father or one of Pate's old settler friends, say that? The expression was hoary, as old as the white man's tenure in Africa, and it was almost always uttered with ambivalence, a sardonic union of affection and exasperation, the one no less heartfelt than the other. Pissed or sober, first generation or third, hunter or farmer or both, the emotions at play in their voices were always mixed. Just as they had been in Adrian's.

The herd had agreed that it was safe to go back to their breakfasts, but one of the hartebeests assigned itself sentry duty, taking up its post on top of an eight-foot-high kopje, a rocky mound similar to the one Adrian occupied. As if on a prearranged signal the other animals, their tails switching once again but their ears still perked, dropped their heads and resumed feeding.

Adrian slowly raised the glasses and swept the veldt as the first, best light of the day, a tracking light, began to separate reality and shadow. As if by magic a lion, still and watchful, turned into a large rock. A rock became a sleeping Thomson's gazelle. All over the endless plain of the Masai Mara things were being transformed into the shapes and attitudes they would keep for the rest of the day.

Adrian drew an open fan with the glasses, working up in widening arcs. He skimmed the chin-high line of thorn growing around the water hole then abruptly stopped and swung back. A tick bird, *askari wa kifaru,* "the rhino's guard," was bobbing along the top of the bush like flotsam in a choppy sea.

A few seconds later a rhinoceros, a big black, lumbered out from behind the thicket wall, the tiny tick bird perched on its fat rump. Strictly from habit, Adrian Glenton's pulse quickened and his mind raced with calculations: distance and angle, windage and droppage. Broadside like this, he had his choice of brain, heart, neck, or lung shots. All he needed was a rifle.

The technicality deflated him. Any of his heavy rifles, from his Holland and Holland .375 magnum to his antique .470 Nitro Express, would have done the trick, but they were back in Nairobi, locked away in a gun safe in accordance with the new law of the land. Another reminder of how the hunting ban, more than a year old now, had changed his life.

In the beginning, the changes had seemed more cosmetic than cosmic, touching merely the edges of his life, not the core. He had taken solace in the comfortable familiarity of daily routines and rituals that went largely unaltered: the early risings and retirements, the looking after of men and equipment, the bush-proven techniques he used to track game. There were still the gin-and-lime sundowners before his camp shower and the whisky sodas around the fire after supper as he charmed the clients with his polished repertoire of lore and lectures, seeding his tales of close shaves in the bush with solid information about dozens of species, everything from their more quirky mating habits to the size, shape, and consistency of their stools. Even his uniform had stayed the same; he wore a sweat-bleached khaki safari jacket and long cotton trousers on this chilly, late September morning, and scuffed chukka boots.

Those were the several similarities. The difference was singular: while he still went out before dawn each morning to scout game for the paying customers, today's client carried a camera instead of a rifle. In a stroke of Mzee's presidential pen, Glenton had been transformed from a hunting guide into a tourist guide, from a universal folk hero—the "great white hunter"—into the equivalent of a domestic servant, a nanny and nursemaid. The difference, as profound as it was simple, was that nothing ever died anymore.

It wasn't that he needed the blood to make it work. Like most professional hunters, Glenton had believed in preserving animals; none of them wished to see a species become extinct, if only for the sake of their bank balances. It was just that the guaranteed absence of blood took the edge off. Like a bloodless bullfight, the safari had become a ceremony stripped of dignity, for the hunted as well as the hunter. The new law rendered a man's livelihood, and his life, silly.

The big companies, Archer's and Ker-Downey and the like, had made the adjustment without undue agony; the cost of big game hunting was such that photo safaris accounted for the bulk of their trade anyway. So had the best free-lancers, hunters like Eric Rundgren and

Bunny Allen, Glen Cottar and Mike Prettijohn. They retired, or agreed to manage coffee or sisal estates for rich owners, or set off for unenlightened places like Botswana and the Sudan where big game hunting was still legal and where governments in need of foreign exchange were more than willing to swap the most choice concessions in return for help in starting up a safari industry.

In debt and unsure of the future, Glenton had considered the Sudan, tempted by offers from colleagues to throw in with them in this venture or that. But in the end he had declined. He just couldn't bring himself to leave home, to leave Kenya, even when it meant having to go to work for one of the bigger tour companies as a bush expert. His reasons were not hard to find. All he had to do was open his eyes.

Adrian lowered the binoculars and watched the Mara open up under the sun's warming hand like an expectant, trembling virgin. The Lorogoti Plain lay naked and exposed, belly up, a tawny expanse of flats and swells stretching away to the Soit Ololol Escarpment, a proud bosom that seemed to rise and fall in the unstable morning light. He could see the dark coursing veins just below her skin, the Talek and Mara rivers sneaking toward a rendezvous. Adrian shut his eyes, and when he opened them again he was on the shore of a golden ocean, its surface dotted with armadas of grazing herds: zebra and giraffe, topi and gazelle, wildebeest and antelope, and a herd of elephant lying at anchor in the shallows along the river's edge like a fleet of great gray galleons.

It was a sight he had seen a thousand times, maybe more, and it never failed to move him. This was country as God had meant for it to be at the Creation, and at times like this it was easy for him to entertain the illusion that he was alone in it. He had never been out of Africa, but he envied no man. No man but the younger version of himself.

His eyes misted and he had to bite his lip to keep the unexpected surge of emotion from making a total fool of him. The Masai Mara, all tarted up in dawn's flamboyant rags, had done it to him again, he thought sheepishly; had turned him, Adrian Glenton, a man without poetry, into a sentimental twit. When the sun was high enough to throw its hard light full on her painted face, he told himself, the Mara would be nothing more than what she was, what she would always be. Just a few more miles and miles of bloody fucking Africa.

And as for this lingering ennui, this persistent pining after yesterday and the old rules . . . hell, even under the old rules he couldn't have potted the rhino this close to a water hole.

The black hadn't gone far. It browsed peaceably, working its slow way along the outer edge of the thicket, reaching up with its beak-shaped mouth to pull off leaves and twigs. On the rhino's rump, the tick bird also was preoccupied with food. It hopped about in tiny circles, hunting and pecking for vermin.

The rhino was a temperamental and unpredictable animal, dangerous to an unarmed man, but Adrian was not worried. The creatures had notoriously bad vision and even worse hearing, and while they did possess a highly developed sense of smell, he was a good fifty or sixty yards downwind.

This one was a decent-size male, close to three tons, Glenton estimated, with a fine front horn. It would be worth at least half a roll of Kodachrome to the members of his tour group back at Mara River Camp. His headman Chege would be turning them out of their camp beds about now, while the rest of the boys brewed tea—or coffee more likely, since most of the clients were American—and got ready to hurry them through breakfast so they would be on schedule for the early morning game run.

Glenton was staying with the group at River Camp, just outside the reserve boundary, but he was doing the scouting for three different parties, each booked by the company into accommodations tailored to fit their various wants and means. One group was at the pricey Governor's Camp, where the wines were vintage, the flatware silver, and the table linen linen. Another was staying at Keekerok Lodge, less luxurious but far from basic. The last group, fourteen people all told, was at Mara River Camp, the least expensive and most primitive of the three but the one which put the tourist in closest touch with "bush Africa," Adrian Glenton's Africa. That was why he had elected to sleep and take his meals there.

All three tours, anxious to get their money's worth, were waiting for him to call in his game report.

Adrian slipped the radio from its belt case, checked to see that it was set to the correct channel, and raised it to his mouth. At that moment the rhinoceros, as if it had seen the move and wished to register a protest, pointed its rear directly at Adrian, hiked up its tail, and urinated straight back between its hind legs in a hissing stream, as thick and as strong as something from a fire hose. For punctuation, the animal moved a few steps to one side and, its bum still aimed at Adrian, emptied its bowels. Then it scattered the steaming dung with its back feet to mark the water hole.

Adrian lowered the radio and laughed. The rhino didn't hear him, but *askari wa kifaru,* the rhino's guard, did. The tiny bird flew up with a chatter, sending the rhino charging off upwind with a thunderous "HUMPF!" The kongoni and Tommy followed suit, the herd flying apart from the center, its shards scattering in an eruption of bounding, blurred shapes.

Adrian laughed again and called in his game report.

He gave them the lions at Aitong even though he had not been there this morning; he'd seen a black-maned male and two females near there the previous evening, working the edges of a massive wildebeest herd, and it would be a day or so before they moved on. He gave them the pair of cheetahs he'd spotted late yesterday afternoon near the Mara River bridge, close to the Tanzanian border, hoping they would still be in the area. And he gave them the pack of hyenas on the north bank of the Talek River, near Fig Tree Camp, on the opposite side of the wildebeest herd from the lion pride. He did not give them the rhino. *Kifaru* had marked this water hole for the two of them. It would have been a betrayal somehow to bring outsiders into it now.

That should keep them happy, Glenton thought. Tourists, especially the Yanks, had a fondness for carnivores. It would also keep them busy. The sites were far enough apart to keep them on the hop until curry time. After lunch, all three of the company's tours would be returning to Nairobi.

The thought of Nairobi, or "Nai-robbery" as Pate, ever the up-country provincial, still called it even now that he lived there, depressed Adrian. He was not looking forward to the noise and stench of too many cars and too many people, or to the small, lonely caretaker's cottage that waited for him like an open grave.

He glanced over the veldt again and decided he had been too hard on the old whore. The Mara was beautiful. The sight of her now filled him with contentment, and suddenly he felt better than he had in weeks. The stomach-knotting tension, a cold bedmate of late, lifted, and he thought he might be able to grab a bit of kip before he had to join the group at lunch and help get them ready for departure. He briefly considered his Land Rover parked at the base of the kopje, then decided to sleep right where he was, in the sun, with the Mara's soft breath on his face.

Rolling onto his back, Adrian grinned up into a sky that was already as blue as a peacock's throat, and said out loud: "Just another shitty day in Paradise."

He was awakened by a distant drone of engines. When he rolled over he saw their dust; four rooster tails, coming fast. He checked the sun and was surprised to see that it was almost eleven o'clock. He had slept for more than four hours. He also saw that the black rhino was back at the water hole.

Within minutes, two of the combis, painted in black and white stripes to make them resemble zebras, were in position around the animal, and the other two minibuses were sneaking in from behind. Adrian raised the glasses and read the logos stenciled on their doors. Two from Abercrombie and Kent; one from UTC, the United Touring

Company; one from Adrian's own outfit. Even at this distance, he could hear the distinctive sound of hungry tourists on a kill, a blend of excited human gabbling and the irksome whirr of motor-driven cameras.

The rhinoceros was glaring balefully at the intruders, swinging its ponderous head from side to side, fixing one, then the next, with beady, malevolent eyes. Adrian focused the glasses and saw that it was all a front; the beast was shuffling its feet in confusion, frightened half to death. The rhino, an animal nearly as vocal as a porpoise, issued a string of short squeals, a sign of the fear it was feeling.

"For God's sake, bugger off and leave the poor bastard be," Glenton muttered, not sure whether he was speaking for the animal or himself.

He checked his outfit's combi and saw that it carried a group from River Camp. The stout American lady with her nose to the window had sat across from him at supper last evening. Mrs. MacReedy from Cincinnati. Her husband, who had not made the African trip, manufactured toilet bowls. Glenton, afloat on his fourth whisky soda of the evening, had referred to Mr. MacReedy as "the Crapper of the colonies," and Mrs. MacReedy had taken offense.

The tourists were taking turns on the camera platform, their upper bodies poking through the roof hatch. They took their snaps and sneaked a few extra frames while those waiting below clamored for their turn in indignant English, American, French, German, and Italian. Judging from the volume of their whining, they were having the time of their lives.

The radio chirred, and when Adrian picked it up he found himself on with the UTC guide, a Boer named Vanderbyl whom he knew casually from the Muthaiga Club in Nairobi. He could see the man waving to him through a window of the combi.

" 'Ullo, Glenton. Woot are ye doing there, mun? 'Aving yer mornin' wank, yeese?"

"Yeese, mun," Adrian agreed amiably, mimicking the man's thick Afrikaner accent, undiluted by a decade in Kenya. "How in hell did you find us?"

Vanderbyl laughed. "One of the balloons out of Keekerok spotted the beast and put the word out on the net. Ye weren't going to keep it all fer yerself now, were ye, mun? After all, we're one big 'oppy fam'ly, eh?"

"One big happy family, my arse," Adrian murmured, cutting off the radio in disgust. Kenya had gone to hell. New hotels and lodges going up faster than termite mounds after a rain. Coastal resorts printing up their menus in German, French, or Italian. And the combis. Most of all the bloody combis. Their tracks crisscrossed the Masai Mara like scars. The reserve's animals were becoming so used to humans they were going tame. And what did the tour companies need with bush trackers? With hot-air balloons and hand-held radios, a blind man could find game.

"*Wa kifaru*," he muttered, addressing the rhino. "Don't just stand there, you big twit. Go get the bloody bastards."

As if it had heard him, the rhinoceros chuffed once and charged the nearest minibus, one of the Abercrombie and Kent combis. It caught its target broadside, the force shattering the plexiglas windows on that side and scooting the vehicle three feet sideways. Adrian heard the screams of the tourists inside and saw a man sticking halfway through the top hatch drop his video camera and fling out his arms, holding on for dear life. Without hesitating, the rhino charged again, lower this time, hooking its large horn under the chassis frame and flipping the combi over as easily as a fry cook turns a meat patty.

Adrian was on his feet and scrambling down the side of the kopje, running toward a scene of utter confusion. Two of the minibuses had already started up and were quickly backing out of harm's way. Their passengers clawed for space at the windows, wildly snapping pictures of both the overturned van and of Adrian, an apparition that seemed to have materialized from out of nowhere.

The UTC combi was carrying a Game Department ranger for just such an emergency and he poked his rifle out the window and fired a shot. Even at near point-blank range it missed the rhinoceros by a good four feet. "*Hapana!*" Adrian shouted as he ran. "No! Don't shoot!"

The ranger fired again and, astoundingly, missed again. Vanderbyl wrestled the weapon away from him, worked the bolt frantically, and got off three hurried shots of his own. All three hit the animal in the side, the impact points marked by geysers of dust. The rhino fell to its knees, then fought its way back up. It teetered there on shaky legs, drooling blood, then wheeled and disappeared into the heart of the thicket.

The Abercrombie and Kent tourists were just beginning to work themselves free of the overturned van when Adrian got to them. Vanderbyl was already there, and the two of them helped people out through windows and doors that now opened skyward.

Several of the women passengers were crying, but except for a few cuts and bruises it did not appear that anyone had been hurt. The man who'd been trapped in the roof hatch when the van went over was on his feet and limping about, telling anyone who would listen about his broken back. That he could move at all, much less with such apparent ease, told Glenton that it was nothing quite so dramatic.

On the presumption of color—he was the only white man among the combi crews—Vanderbyl took charge, herding still shaken tourists into the undamaged vans in that booming voice Adrian remembered from the Muthaiga Club; whether ordering up a Pimm's, berating a slow waiter, or propositioning a married woman with her husband across the room, Vanderbyl never spoke in less than a shout.

The loading went smoothly until the Yank with the bad back was at the door of Vanderbyl's combi. "Hey! My camera!"

"Don ye wurry, mun," Vanderbyl said reassuringly. "We'll bring it along." He switched the ranger's rifle from one hand to the other and took hold of the man's arm to lift him into the van.

"Fuck that noise, Jack," the tourist said, shrugging off Vanderbyl's helping hand. "We're talking about a two-thousand-dollar movie camera." He strode off toward the wrecked combi, his "broken" back completely forgotten.

Then everyone wanted to go back. They piled out and ran to retrieve their cameras and bags, their Nikons and Leicas, their Gucci and Pucci, rifling through the debris like Taureg women picking through an ambushed caravan. Adrian saw the UTC driver and the ranger exchange disappointed glances.

When they had retrieved their valuables, the passengers, physically and emotionally spent, meekly reboarded the combis under Vanderbyl's reproving Dutch gaze. When the last one was aboard he gave a thumbs-up signal and the other vans cranked their motors and started for home.

Vanderbyl had made a space for Adrian on the long bench seat of the UTC combi. He grinned and called, "Come on then, mun. Yer curry'll be gettin' cold."

Adrian did not move. "My Land Rover's parked behind the kopje," he said. "Besides, haven't you forgotten something?"

"Woot's that, mun?"

Adrian pointed at the thicket. "There's a wounded rhino in there."

Vanderbyl's grin faded and his face, fair as a Scot's, darkened slightly. "And it kin bloody well stay in there."

Adrian just stared, saying nothing. After a moment Vanderbyl cleared his throat and said, "I hit him good, mun. He's bled to death already fer sure. Leave him be. The Game Department lads can pick him up."

Adrian shook his head. "That's not the way it's done."

"It's the way I'm gonna do it," Vanderbyl said.

"Bloody hell," Adrian said quietly. "You shot it, you finish it."

Vanderbyl slid over to the end of the seat and tossed the rifle to Adrian, who had to react quickly to catch it. "You finish it, mun," he said, grinning. "You're the *fundi*."

The Game Department ranger started to protest the donation of his rifle, then caught himself before he said anything that might remind anyone that he was supposed to be the *fundi*, the expert, and that it was his job to go in after the rhino.

Vanderbyl waited to see if he would get an argument from Adrian. When none was forthcoming he pulled the door shut and turned to his driver. "*Endelea!*" The combi sped off, bouncing over the veldt and leaving Adrian just as they had found him, alone with the rhino.

He still had his radio, and the ranger's rifle, but he made no effort to call them back or to stop them. Strangely enough, he was not all that unhappy to see them go. They had ruined his morning and his mood with their intrusion and now, with them gone, he had a chance to salvage something of both. Unwittingly, Vanderbyl had handed him a legitimate excuse to ply his trade.

In normal circumstances he would have taken a cigarette break just then, giving Vanderbyl's three bullets a chance to work on the rhino, time to break him down. But Adrian did not want this big black to suffer any longer than it had to. They had shared a special moment and he felt an affinity for the animal.

The ranger's rifle, an Enfield .303 that looked as if it predated the Great War, was too small for rhino and dirty to boot. Adrian was not surprised; standards had gone to hell in the two years since control of the National Parks Department, autonomous since independence, had been turned over to the government. He checked his ammunition supply and found the chamber empty and a single cartridge in the magazine. It didn't matter; with a wounded rhino lying up in heavy cover, a man rarely got more than one shot anyway.

He chambered the round, then located the place where the rhino had gone down. Squatting beside a pool of blood, he saw that it was full of bubbles and had a pinkish cast. One of Vanderbyl's shots had clipped a lung.

Glenton followed the blood spoor to a chest-high hole in the bush, the rhino's tunnel, but stopped twenty meters short to study it. He never lingered too close to the edge of thick growth; if an animal were suddenly to break cover there would be no time to react.

The rhinoceros was directly downwind, which left Adrian with a couple of options. He could use the wind to his advantage by coming in from the rear, or he could give *kifaru* the wind and make a frontal approach. Neither alternative appealed to him. A flanking stalk would be safer but more time-consuming; he would have to enter the thicket farther along the line and then guess where the rhino was lying up before he could work out the proper angle of interception. Tackling the beast head on, trailing it along its own path, would be faster, but potentially fatal. And there was the limited stopping power of the Enfield to consider.

Thinking about it, he realized that he had already made his decision. If he had been willing to let the animal die a slow death, he would have left with Vanderbyl and the others.

He went in through the hole. Once inside, he stood still for a few minutes to adjust to the change in light, then went ahead cautiously, bent at the knees, his body a straight line from the waist up, holding his rifle across his chest.

It was tedious going. A foot forward, a pause to listen, another foot, another pause. Thorn-studded brambles begrudged his every step, tearing at his clothing and body and leaving both ripped in a dozen places, but although his senses had never seemed sharper, he could not feel the scratches. All he could feel was the blood pounding in his veins, and the vast satisfaction of knowing that the long layoff had not dulled the skills of a lifetime. He felt fine. No, better than fine. Wonderful. He had not felt this good, this alive, in months. If he could have seen himself from without, he would not have been the least surprised to see that he was grinning from ear to ear. Christ how he'd missed it!

But Adrian Glenton's soaring feeling of exultation, of pure joy, did not survive. In the end there was no dramatic resolution, no last-second, life-preserving shot, perfectly placed to drop the charging rhino at his feet. No charge at all.

Glenton found the rhino sixty or seventy meters into the thicket. He heard it well before he saw it, that high-pitched squeaking noise rhinos make when they are dying. The creature lay on its side with its nose in the air, a sure sign that it was choking on its own blood. It turned to look at Adrian but didn't even attempt to rise. It just lay there, bleeding from the mouth and making the squeaking noise. Despite their size, and all that armor, rhinos had glass chins. They did not have that reserve of energy and determination that made many other animals resistant to bullets.

He made short work of it, raising, sighting, and firing in one smooth motion, shooting the rhino in the side of the head midway between the eye and the ear. A clean brain shot.

The squeaking noise stopped.

On the long rear seat of the combi, Mrs. MacReedy was being comforted by her friend and traveling companion, Mrs. Plante. Each of Mrs. MacReedy's shuddering sobs elicited a soothing "there, there dear," from Mrs. Plante. It was like a bad music hall skit, Adrian thought uncharitably, one that had been playing for more than three hours now. The six other passengers stared out of the windows in stony silence, their sympathy for Mrs. MacReedy long since exhausted.

The reason for Mrs. MacReedy's seemingly unassuageable grief was not the rhino's savage assault on the Abercrombie and Kent van, although that too had given her quite a scare. She was upset because of something she had witnessed earlier, when the tour group followed Adrian's lead to the hyenas. It was then she discovered that Africa was something altogether more than Disneyland without proper plumbing. To her horror, she had seen a hyena eat a baby wildebeest still swaddled in the placenta of its birthing sac. With the labor-weak mother and Mrs. MacReedy both looking on, the hyena had broken the newborn calf's back with a single snap of its powerful jaws, and then gobbled it down in one gluttonous sitting.

For a few hours, so precious in hindsight, Mrs. MacReedy had been shocked into silence. She had not wept then, or even later, when the rhinoceros seemed bent on murdering them all. No, she had waited until she had a captive audience, when the group had started on the four-hour drive back to Nairobi.

Adrian flinched as yet another sob ricocheted through the combi, cursing himself for electing to ride with the clients instead of driving himself back in the Land Rover. He was in a foul mood, and the noise wasn't helping.

It had been a day of violent mood swings—up and down, down and up—a wild ride that had left Adrian feeling edgy and short-tempered, down for good. The euphoric feeling he'd had while stalking the wounded rhino had died along with the animal. With that one crashing shot his joy had turned into a bilious anger.

It all had been so unnecessary, he thought. That was the tragedy of it. The reserve ranger had panicked. One shot into the air would have frightened the animal off. And that bloody Boer! Vanderbyl was no professional, but he should have known better. And if he'd had to shoot he could at least have gone about it properly. You always went for a vital organ, for the quick, clean kill; you didn't just bang away.

The late sun, skipping like a laser off the dish of the Longonot Satellite Station, blinded Adrian, although it did not seem to bother Chege behind the wheel. They were only a few miles from the road that would carry them up the Kikuyu Escarpment and on into Nairobi. Adrian wasn't sure he would make it. He commandeered the rearview mirror to check on the two women in back. Mrs. MacReedy was dabbing at her eyes and snuffling. Mrs. Plante was patting Mrs. MacReedy's hand and cooing. The tableau, a profane pieta, had not changed shape all through the dusty drive to Narok and across the floor of the Rift Valley.

Now there was a pair for you, Adrian thought. Early in the safari it had become obvious, made so by Mrs. MacReedy's incessant reminders, that Mrs. MacReedy was wealthy and that Mrs. Plante was not. Mrs. MacReedy had let everyone know that she was bankrolling Mrs. Plante's holiday in exchange for her companionship. Mrs. Plante had paid for her passage in full, with a hundred humiliations, but she had gotten back as much of it as she could. There was the time Mrs. MacReedy trapped herself in the one-hole thunder box behind their tent and Mrs. Plante left her there for the best part of an afternoon, pretending to be asleep and unable to hear all the cries for help. And the time, scarcely more than an hour after Adrian had warned the group about the deadliness of the green mamba, that Chege found a harmless green snake in the ladies' tent and Mrs. Plante told him to leave it there; it was coiled on Mrs. MacReedy's pillow when she came in from her very first bush shower, a traumatic experience in its own right.

Watching the sly, satisfied look on Mrs. Plante's face as she held the hand of her distraught benefactress, Adrian doubted whether their friendship would survive the trip back to Cincinnati. He had watched the two of them work each other over for four days now. The hyena could have taken lessons.

Adrian made it to the bottom of the escarpment, even a few miles up, but no farther. They were just passing a quaint roadside chapel, built by the same Italian POWs who had built the road, when Mrs. MacReedy snuffled once too often. Adrian, who had just turned around in his seat to tell them about the chapel, blew up. "God's holy trousers woman! Quit your bloody fucking sniveling or I'll run you back straight away and feed *you* to the bloody fucking hyenas!"

There was a moment of stunned silence in the combi, then a scattering of applause. Glenton turned and faced the front. Behind him the clapping faded away to silence and the silence held; no more talk, no more sobs. The mirror was still turned in Adrian's direction—Chege never used it; he said it took the sport out of driving—and he saw that Mrs. MacReedy had fainted, or wanted everyone to believe she had. Her mouth was open, her eyes were shut and her head lolled on its fat stem. Mrs. Plante had stopped patting Mrs. MacReedy's hand and was staring at the back of Adrian's head with the same rapt look of worship and self-satisfaction that a Masai herdsman gives his prize bullock.

Adrian's tantrum had not changed his mood; if anything, it had sealed it. It had not been much of a job, but it was the only one he had. And there was little doubt that it was gone. The MacReedy woman was just the sort to lodge a formal complaint. And Tubby Jenkins, Adrian's immediate supervisor, had been looking for an excuse to give him the sack. Adrian exhaled heavily; it looked as if he'd be giving the Sudan a go after all.

The rest of the run into Nairobi was completed without another word from anyone. The van crept through the rush-hour traffic and pulled into the firm's underground garage on Mama Ngina Street a little after five o'clock. Without waiting to see if Mrs. MacReedy would survive her ordeal, Adrian hopped out and started for the dispatcher's office.

He made it less than halfway before he was intercepted by Tubby Jenkins. "Ah, there you are, Glenton. So what is it you've done this time?"

Adrian stared at him. Was it a rhetorical question, or was it that Mrs. MacReedy had not fainted after all? Perhaps she had been in a telepathic trance, beaming her outrage on ahead. "What do you mean?"

"I was rather hoping you could tell me," said Jenkins, a short, round man whom Adrian had known, and disliked, for more than half of his thirty-five years, ever since they had been at school together at Gilgil.

"Look, Jenkins, if you have something to say, say it," Adrian said wearily. "If not, I'm off to the Norfolk for a drink. And I need the drink a sight more than I need to be standing here playing at riddles with you."

"All right then," Jenkins said pleasantly. "There's a policeman waiting to see you. In the dispatcher's office."

"A policeman? To see me?"

Jenkins smiled and nodded.

"What's it about?"

"Haven't the foggiest, although he did mention something about working with the Wildlife people. He's a *watu*, as black as the ace of spades. Perhaps his sister is preggers and he's looking for the responsible party." Jenkins laughed, and went off to help the clients with the unloading.

Glenton continued slowly toward the dispatcher's office, trying to think why a native bobby working for Wildlife would want to see him. Had someone, Vanderbyl perhaps, rung them up from Keekerok to report him? Were they going to give him shit about finishing the rhino rather than leaving it for the Game Department? The shooting had been wholly justified of course, but with all the changes in regulations lately, who could say how they might interpret it? Whatever it was, he did not need the aggravation. It already had been one bitch of a day.

The dimly lit garage, filled with exhaust and an echoing bedlam of banging hammers and dropped spanners, seemed like a living entity to Adrian. It was as if he were in the belly of some massive beast, one that had already devoured him and now threatened to digest and absorb him body and soul.

He felt a sharp and sudden pang of longing for the quiet simplicity of the bush. With a desperation that shook him, he wanted to be back on his kopje with the sun coming up behind him. Just him, and the herds, and miles and miles of bloody Africa.

4

"Mr. Glenton?"

"That's right."

"I am Inspector Odongo of the Kenya Police."

Inspector Odongo of the Kenya Police was not in uniform. Like Adrian, he wore a khaki safari suit, but any resemblance ended there. Where Adrian was dirty and rumpled, the African was starched and creased, scrubbed clean as a *toto* going off to the first day of primary school.

"Frightfully sorry, Inspector, but you shan't find that dreadful woman's body here," Adrian said in his best English squire's accent. "I minced her up and posted her to America. Still, it was only a month ago and the way the post is, you can probably catch her at the GPO if you're quick about it."

Odongo did not laugh, or even crack a smile. There was no sign of bewilderment in his dark face; he recognized the joke, he just hadn't found it amusing. Which made him a man of unusual discernment, Adrian decided, suddenly embarrassed by his own foolishness.

"I had to shoot the rhinoceros, Inspector," Adrian said seriously, in his normal voice. "It was wounded and in pain and a threat to any tourist who might have stumbled across it before the Game Department got round to doing something about it. I don't know what Mr. Vanderbyl told you, but I don't see that I had any choice in the matter."

This time the inspector clearly was bewildered. "I don't know what you are talking about, Mr. Glenton," he said.

It was Glenton's turn to be confused. "If it's not that then what . . . what can I do for you, Inspector?"

"You could give me a moment of your time," Odongo said. "Mr. Jenkins said we could talk here." He closed the office door, motioning to Adrian to take a chair, then sat himself down in the wooden chair behind the dispatcher's desk.

The office was tiny and cluttered. Wildlife pictures and airline calendars with enticing scenes of Kenya covered three walls. The remaining wall was glass, offering a view of the garage. Through it, Glenton could see Tubby Jenkins and the MacReedy woman standing next to the combi, deep in spirited conversation.

Without preamble, Inspector Odongo said, "I have been told that you speak Swahili. What about tribal languages?"

"I get along well enough in Kikuyu, Masai, and Kalenjin," Adrian said, wondering what this was all about. "But no Luo, I'm afraid."

The inspector's face seemed to deflate a little, leaving a deep crease down each side of his mouth. "Can you also tell me which village I come from?" he asked quietly.

Touchy bastard, Glenton thought, pretending to study the man's face. He knew just enough about the Luo to say: "'Hmmmm, a small fishing village on the Kavirondo Gulf of Lake Victoria. Somewhere near Kisumu, I'd say."

"We call it the Winam Gulf," the inspector said, "and almost every village in the area is a small fishing village somewhere near Kisumu."

Glenton laughed and took a wild guess. "All right then. Dunga." It was the first place that popped into his head. He had once found a bottle of homemade gin in a tiny Asian *duka* there, when he was coming back by boat from a long safari in Uganda, the last three days of which had been dry. The stuff had tasted awful, and his client, an American who liked puns and Kipling, had christened it "Dunga Gin."

Inspector Odongo was staring at him oddly. After a long moment he said, very seriously, "That is correct." And after another long moment, "We need your help, Mr. Glenton."

Adrian had trouble making the abrupt transition. "Hullo? Oh, I see. Uh, who is we? The police?"

The inspector nodded. "And the Ministry of Wildlife. We are working together on this problem."

"What exactly is the problem?" Adrian asked.

Odongo told him, beginning at the beginning, two months before, with the dramatic rise in poaching in Tsavo and Meru, where five rhinos, two leopards, and twelve elephants had been killed, through the incidents in the Aberdares, including the murder of the local man, to the decision to create a special anti-poaching unit. The murder victim had been identified: a Kikuyu named Mwangi, one of two brothers who had a *shamba* on the edge of the park. The Mwangi brothers were well known to the local population as small-scale poachers who sold illegal game meat to butchers in the nearby town of Mweiga. According to neighbors, the two men had crossed into the park four days before Odongo found the body. Mwangi's brother had not been seen since, which raised the specter of a second murder.

"We know it's an inconvenience, that you'd have to take a short leave of absence from your job here," Odongo said in conclusion, "but

I'm sure that your firm will understand that it is for the good of our nation."

Glenton had listened attentively, without interrupting. When Odongo finished, he asked: "Why a special unit? Why not use Field Force rangers?"

"We did," Odongo said. "They did not perform well. They managed to locate the gang only once, in Tsavo, when a Field Force patrol walked straight into an ambush. The poachers had automatic rifles, the rangers had old bolt-action rifles. The rangers ran away." The inspector hesitated, then said: "Also, I suspected collusion between the gang and one or more of the rangers. Each time the rangers set up an ambush, the poachers killed an animal at the other end of the park, as though they knew. I wasn't able to prove anything, but . . ." He shrugged.

Adrian was grudgingly impressed by the policeman's candor. Until now, he hadn't thought much of Odongo. When he first looked at the man, all he had seen had been the ankle boots made out of genuine leather rather than pressed cardboard, and the safari suit that was several cuts above the kind one had made in a day by the Asian tailors in Muindi Mbingu and Biashara streets. He had checked the man's hands, noted the absence of calluses, and written him off as yet another "missionary boy," bright enough more likely than not and essentially useless when it came to anything at all practical. But any civil servant with big enough balls to talk about official corruption with a total stranger merited a second look. For the first time, Adrian began to adjust to the idea that he might legitimately consider the policeman's offer. "All right, that's why a special unit," he said. "But why me?"

"You come very highly recommended," Odongo said. "I made the usual inquiries—the safari companies, former members of the Professional Hunters Association, that sort of thing. The same names kept coming up and yours was among them. I did not say why I wanted a hunter, only that I wanted the best."

"There's one or two better."

Odongo consulted a small notebook. "Four, actually," he said. "Two declined to help, one is in hospital, and one has left Kenya for Rhodesia, where he will no doubt be using his skills to hunt men rather than animals."

Glenton had heard talk that Simon Packenham had taken a commission in the Rhodesian Army, to teach tracking to Selous Scouts. "That is precisely what you are asking me to do, isn't it?" he said. "Hunt men rather than animals?"

Inspector Odongo shrugged, but he was watching Adrian's face closely. "There are men and there are men," he said.

Glenton met the African's steady, unblinking stare, then nodded and said, "Yes, I suppose there are."

He looked out to the garage where Mrs. MacReedy, along with her Sancho Panza, Mrs. Plante, was still in conference with Tubby Jenkins. Mrs. MacReedy, gesticulating wildly, was doing all the talking while Tubby did all the listening, his face bunched with a solicitous concern. Every now and then, Jenkins turned to glare in the direction of the dispatcher's office.

Adrian decided then and there to accept Odongo's offer. While he did not take time to analyze them, his reasons were both practical and philosophical. His most immediate concern was to beat Tubby Jenkins to the punch. He'd be damned if he would give that fat little shit the satisfaction of sacking him. Besides, the case intrigued him; that business with the hyena's teeth was fascinating. But more than anything, if he took this job he would be back where he belonged, out in the bush, with a rifle in his hand instead of a radio, free from the combis and the hot-air balloons and the tourists. It was a crude philosophy, but deep down Adrian believed that a man was what a man did. If he were a clerk he would have the soul of a clerk, and if he were a king he would have the soul of a king. In his haste to shed an image of himself as a glorified nursemaid to those with more disposable income than sense, he shunted aside the thought that there might be a corollary: if a man hunted, he would have the soul of a killer.

The decision made, Adrian felt suddenly giddy. It was all he could do not to laugh out loud. This was not the time to show pleasure. Odongo was waiting for an answer, and there was some bargaining to be done.

"This anti-poaching unit of yours," Adrian said. "Who's to control it?"

"You would. But you would clear everything with me."

"And who do you clear things with?"

"The Assistant Minister for Wildlife."

"How large a team do you have in mind?"

Odongo shrugged. "How many men do you think you would need?"

"How many men are there in the Kenya Rifles?" Adrian said with a snort. "Aberdare National Park is big, bloody big. It must be two hundred square miles."

Odongo consulted the small notebook. "Two hundred and twenty-eight square miles. And we can't afford to hire the army."

Adrian smiled. "Just as well; they would only get in each other's way. So how many men can you give me?"

"Six."

"Six!" Adrian couldn't believe he had heard him correctly. "How in bloody hell am I supposed to comb two hundred and twenty-eight square miles of mountain and rain forest with six bloody people?"

"As best you can," Odongo said calmly. "That is all the Assistant

Minister will authorize." He paused before adding: "If you have a specific reason for needing more men, you can draw from the Field Force ranger sections in the area."

Adrian was silent for a moment, then asked, "Do I get to choose the six?"

When Odongo hesitated, Glenton said quickly: "That is a condition. Unnegotiable. I choose the six."

"Five," Odongo said. "I forgot to tell you that the six includes yourself."

Adrian stared at him for a long moment, and then started to laugh. After a few seconds Odongo began laughing too. They laughed and laughed until they were helpless in their chairs, tears rolling down their faces.

Finally they had to stop to catch their breath. Wiping his eyes, Adrian asked, "What does the job pay?"

Still chuckling, Inspector Odongo said, "We can pay you four thousand shillings a month."

That was more than five hundred dollars American, Adrian figured, more than he was making now, and he wouldn't have to put up with the Tubby Jenkinses and Mrs. MacReedys of this world.

"Make it six thousand. I expect I'll catch these poachers in a week or two, then where will I be?"

"Four thousand five hundred."

"Five thousand."

"Agreed." Inspector Odongo put out his hand and Adrian shook it.

"Now, how about the men?" Adrian asked.

"We will pay each man seven hundred fifty shillings a month. It's more than fair; we pay our Field Force rangers only four hundred a month."

"You pay your rangers to go into the bush after common poachers, not proven man-killers. Fifteen hundred."

"Nine hundred."

"One thousand."

"Agreed." The inspector put out his hand and they shook again.

"When can you start putting your team together?" Odongo asked.

"I'll start first thing in the morning. It will take a week. I have a good idea who I want but I'll need some time to collect them."

"That's fine," Odongo said. "It will give me some time to gather the equipment you'll need, weapons and radios and the like. I also have to arrange for a base of operations in the Aberdares. Perhaps the park warden can give us a building in his headquarters compound in Mweiga."

Adrian shook his head. "Too much in the public eye," he said. "There's a place just outside Mweiga. Aberdare Ranch. Have you heard of it?"

"No."

"It's a private rhino sanctuary owned by a wealthy Yank who's rarely on the premises," Glenton said. "It's isolated and it runs right along the edge of the park. There are some guest cottages we might be able to use. The manager is an old friend of mine."

"All right," Odongo agreed. "You go ahead and make the arrangements. Unless I hear otherwise, I'll meet you there one week from today, in the late afternoon."

They shook hands once again to seal the bargain and the policeman left, giving the anxiously waiting Tubby Jenkins a polite nod on his way out. Adrian quickly followed, brushing past Jenkins without so much as a glance.

"Hold on a moment, Glenton," the startled Jenkins called after him. "I'd like a word with you."

Glenton turned and smiled, his eyebrows lifting as if he had just noticed the man. "Ah, there you are, Tubby," he said, deliberately using the hated nickname from their school days at Gilgil. "Just the man I want to see. I'm afraid that I shall have to resign my position here without notice. It's a bother I know, but the government has enlisted my services for a bit of hush-hush work. Sorry, but duty calls."

Before the flabbergasted Jenkins could respond, Adrian added, "I'll be round one day soon to pick up what I'm owed. Till then, it's been a real experience working with you. Ta."

Whistling the Colonel Bogie March, he strode jauntily out of the garage and up into the street, into a failing light.

In the evenings a jacket and tie were required at the Muthaiga Club, so Adrian hurried home to bathe and change, wanting to catch his father before Pate sat down to his customary early dinner. He arrived at the club a little after six-thirty.

The Muthaiga Club was a low, rambling structure, painted pink and set in a lush tropical garden. It had a spacious bar and dining room, a main lounge and several smaller ones, and, overlooking the swimming pool and the golf course, there were rooms to let, by the day, week, month, or year.

In older, some said better days, "the Club" had held a special spot in the hearts and minds of the white population. For the Nairobi set it was a refuge and a playground, a place where the cares of work were forcibly checked at the door and where one could relax with one's own kind. For the up-country settler it was the first stop on a safari to Nairobi, a place to greet old friends and meet new ones, where one could catch up on the latest gossip in a land where gossip was a currency that purchased full hospitality at any provincial farmhouse. The picnics, parties, balls, brawls, and romantic peccadilloes of that bygone time had long since passed into legend, but a few artifacts survived: some sepia photographs; a handful of Kiplingesque characters, "flanneled fools at their wickets"; one or two flesh-and-bone fossils who had somehow managed to resist time and tropical disease. Now and then someone like Beryl Markham, the aviatrix and author, might pop in, though she did not often leave her home on the grounds of the Ngong racecourse. And if you wanted to tap her remarkable store of lore, it was whispered, you had to catch her rather early in the morning, before she began drinking.

Adrian had his own early memories of the club. Of games on the lawn, croquet and "run fox run." Of towering giants in broad-brimmed hats and knee boots, carrying whips. Of the day his father had introduced him to Alan Black, the famous ivory hunter who was shy as a bongo, so reclusive that once, on one of his rare trips to England, he booked every room in a hotel so he wouldn't have to make small talk with other guests.

Most of all he remembered coming in from Nakuru for an agricultural show and arriving at a ball in a carriage Pate had hired for the occasion, cuddled with his mother under a lap robe against the cold July night. It was 1954 and Kenya was caught up in the Emergency, but not even the specter of Mau Mau could spoil the occasion. That evening, just a month before she died, was one of the clearest memories he had of his mother. How lovely she had looked to her eleven-year-old son that night as she hummed along to the strains of a waltz drifting out from the dance floor, her face flushed from the cold and anticipation, as pink as the flamingos back home on Lake Nakuru.

There was a row in progress at the desk when he arrived, and it was several minutes before he was able to sign in. One of the members' wives was trying to get in unescorted, and it seemed that, at the behest of her estranged husband, her name had been scratched from the roster of associate members. The woman was drunk, and in a nasty mood.

"Then check again, you fool," she was saying to the desk clerk, a bearded, turbaned Sikh. "You've obviously made a mistake."

"I am very-very sorry, *memsahib,* but my instructions are very-very specific. I must honor the member's desires."

"Don't talk to me about the member's desires. I could tell you things about the member's desires that would curl your greasy hair."

Adrian and the Asian exchanged a glance. The problem did not come up as often as it once did, but it did come up. Full membership in the club was restricted to men. Women could be granted auxiliary membership, but the unspoken rule was that signing privileges did not necessarily go to a member's wife; they went to the woman "under your roof." The practice was a holdover from the time when there were as many mistresses as wives. It helped to keep the two separate, and it kept blood off the club's carpets.

"I'm only going to ask you this once more," the woman said, slurring her words slightly. "Are you or are you not going to let me in?"

"I am very-very sorry, madam."

"But not as sorry as you're gonna be, you cheeky chut," she said with a snarl. "I just happen to be a *very-very* good friend of the manager of this establishment. It's back to the Punjab for you."

It was a testimonial to the Sikh's training that he did not leap over the desk to throttle the woman for calling him a "chut," which was shorthand for "chutney eater," a racial slur still in vogue among the old settler class.

The desk clerk said nothing; he just regarded her coldly but politely, until she turned on stiletto heels and stormed from the club.

Adrian took her place, stepping up to the desk to sign the register. "Good evening, Mohinder," he said, as if he'd neither seen nor heard anything out of the ordinary.

"Good evening, Mr. Glenton. Will you be joining us for dinner?"

"Yes, I think so. I'm looking for my father."

The Sikh shot a cuff to check his wristwatch. "You will find him in the lounge, sir. He will be going in to dinner in fifteen minutes." Like an old rhinoceros, David Glenton was a creature of unswerving habit.

"Yes, I know," Adrian said. "Thank you, Mohinder."

"Not at all, sir."

Adrian made straight for the main lounge, for the padded chair in the corner farthest removed from the bar. Pate liked a toddy before supper, but he didn't like sitting in the bar; too many "A's" to suit him—Africans, Asians, and Americans. Here they were just three months away from Independence Day, the fifteenth anniversary of *Uhuru*, and it still rankled him that the club had been forced by law to take in nonwhites, and by economic necessity to take in Americans.

Earlier, Adrian knew, his father had come down to watch the retired army officers beat Retreat and then moved to the lounge where he had one of the waiters fetch him a White Cap, or as Pate and his unreconstructed colonialist friends still called it, a White "Chap." He would nurse his lager until it was time to go in to supper. After dinner he would return to the lounge for a cup of Earl Grey tea. On the stroke of 8:15 he would retire to his utilitarian room overlooking the golf course to read for thirty minutes before putting himself to bed. It was a routine that had not varied in two years, not since he'd lost the place at Rumuruti and moved into the club.

For all the club's masculine prejudice, the lounge had a feminine feel to it. Worn oriental rugs were scattered across the parquet floor.

Overstuffed chairs and sofas were covered with floral-pattern slipcovers, and the wicker furniture was painted in pastels, mostly pink. The sewing salon effect was muted only by the art: prints of hunt scenes, and soldiers in the uniforms of wars long since won or lost. And a moth-eaten head of a male lion, a less than defiant reminder of who was king of this chintz jungle.

Adrian found his father sitting alone, his face hidden behind that morning's *Daily Nation,* the Aga Khan's newspaper.

"Hullo, Pate."

"Hah?" The newspaper came down with a noisy rustle. "Oh, it's you. Back from the Mara, are you?"

"So how have you been getting on?" Adrian asked, taking the chair across from him.

"Hah! The bloody power's on the bung again. Off and on like a randy dog who's found a bitch in heat. The Tana River station's silting up again, I suppose. Mucking up the bloody turbines. Bloody baboons can't do anything right."

"For Christ's sake, Pate. Keep your voice down." On the far side of the room, Adrian saw, the Vice President was reading the most recent overseas edition of *Newsweek,* only a week old.

"Hah!"

There was something unusually wild and angry in Pate's eyes this evening, and Adrian studied his father carefully, searching for any new evidence of deterioration. He did not see any, but then he could only see what was on the outside, nothing of what was happening within.

Pate's decline in the past two years had been startling. It was as if, in leaving the farm, his roots had been pulled up, leaving him to wither and die. The physical rot had been marked. His hair had thinned and gone white, almost overnight it seemed, along with his mustache and eyebrows. The skin of his face, once tight and weather worn, had loosened and begun to crumble, like meat boiled too long on the bone. His hands, once strong and capable, now trembled, and his deep, timbrous voice, while still loud, had become shrill and cranky. In two short years, he had become an old man.

Adrian was equally alarmed by the change in his father's personality. David Glenton had been a man of quiet confidence and authority, a taciturn man who, when he did have something to say, was heard with respect, and whose counsel was sought and taken. Now he had become garrulous, full of blustery pronouncement and hidebound opinion. He had turned bluff and querulous, constantly complaining about something or other, most likely the state of the state, railing on about how nothing in the country, or the whole bloody continent for that matter, worked the way it once had.

The transformation pained Adrian, but he understood how it had happened, and why. The fact that he had never actually lived on the Rumuruti farm had not prevented him from sharing his father's sense of loss and outrage.

They had used the same tactics at Rumuruti that they had used the first time, thirteen years before, when they took the farm at Nakuru. A slow, steady, grinding process that, in the end, proved inexorable. In both cases it had begun the same way, with a car bearing Government of Kenya plates pulling up the driveway just before lunch.

David Glenton never did meet the African who eventually got the Rumuruti farm. All he knew at the time was that the man was a powerful politician, one of Mzee's cabinet chiefs. The man's aides did all of the negotiating, telling Glenton that their minister greatly admired the farm and wished to buy it, quoting a figure thirty percent below true market value. Pate politely informed them that the place was not for sale at any price, and they left.

They came back a month later. And the month after that. Each time the offer was a little less than the time before. In the meantime things began to go crook on the ranch. Laborers, some of whom had been with Pate for thirty years, since the early days at Nakuru, started to leave without explanation. Cattle raiders, never a problem in the past, began culling the herd, and the police seemed unable to stop them. An outbreak of rinderpest hit the herd, then anthrax and bovine leptospirosis. It was no better on the administrative front. Pate was in town every other day, sorting out problems with permits.

He went to see the district officer. Then the district commissioner. Then the province commissioner. Finally he went to old friends in Nairobi who still had some connection with the national government. None of them could, or would, help.

The trouble at home went on. Lions, infrequent visitors normally, appeared on the farm in startling numbers and began killing calves. Pate's headman, a Dorobo who'd been with him since Nakuru, was killed by a mamba which somehow got into his bed. A mysterious fire burned up the servants' quarters.

After a year of it, David Glenton sold. At six shillings on the pound. He got rid of his furniture in a lawn sale and moved into the Muthaiga Club in Nairobi, a changed man.

Adrian had always thought that Pate might have been able to handle it had it been the first time. But now he wondered how strong his father really had been after Nakuru, where the story had been much the same. Perhaps he really gave up then. Losing Bushbuck Farm had been the decisive blow, at least for Adrian. His mother was buried there. And the grandfather he never knew. His father had thought about moving them when he bought the ranch at Rumuruti, but then he had remembered how hard Jonathan Glenton had worked to build Bushbuck Farm, and how deeply Clare Glenton had loved it. And so he'd left them there. The care of the two graves was the only thing he had insisted upon as a condition of the sale.

Pate had that look in his eye. He was glaring across the lounge at the Vice President. "Is that man working?" he asked in a carrying voice. "If he's working, I shall report him. It is against the rules of the club."

"He's just reading a magazine, Pate, that's all."

Unappeased, David Glenton continued to stare across the room. "Then why does he have a briefcase? He was supposed to check it at the door. How did he get it past Mohinder?"

"Pate, he hasn't opened the briefcase," Adrian said with a sigh. "He's just reading his magazine."

"He was supposed to leave the briefcase with Mohinder," David Glenton insisted.

"Oh for Christ's sake!" Adrian said with exasperation, suddenly tired of pampering the old man. "The man is the Vice President! Who knows what kind of papers he's got in there! It could be state secrets, or plans for a coup, or a bloody girlie magazine! Whatever it is, he is not going to bloody well leave it with anybody, especially Mohinder."

David Glenton did not argue. He sulked, and continued to watch the man the same way a marabou stork watches a dying animal.

Adrian suddenly felt as though he were suffocating. All he wanted to do now was to finish his business and leave, to get away from the Muthaiga Club and from his father, both of them relics of a Kenya that now seemed a part of prehistory.

"What I came to tell you," he said, "is that I won't be visiting you for the next week or two. I'm going up-country."

"Oh? Where? Anywhere near Rumuruti? If so, why don't you pop in and see what the baboons have done to the old farm—"

Adrian quickly cut him off. "I'll be in the highlands, doing a little control shooting for the government."

"The government! Hah!"

"I just wanted you to know."

From a pocket of his waistcoat, David Glenton pulled a pocket watch, a fine piece with elaborate scroll work, and a script inscription that read: "To a loving husband, DG, from a devoted wife, CG."

"Well, if you're going away, then you should dine with me this evening. It's almost time to go in."

Adrian had planned to stay for dinner, but now he just wanted to be gone. "Sorry, Pate. But I'm off at first light and I still have a lot of things to do. Pack and all that."

"Oh, very well. Come see me when you get back then. By the way, what will you be shooting?"

"Hyena."

Not knowing which he felt most—affection, guilt, or relief—Adrian stood, gave his father a little pat on the shoulder, and walked away.

He was almost to the reception desk when the lights went out. There were groans and shouts and the scurrying sounds of waiters rummaging for flashlights and candles. The last thing he heard as he groped his way to the door was his father's voice cutting through the darkness: "Hah! The *nation builders* just stopped pedaling!"

5

There was a shorter way to the Magadi road, but Glenton left Nairobi by way of the western suburbs. With the parched prospect of the Rift Valley ahead of him, he wanted to enjoy the cooling caress of the Ngong Hills as long as he possibly could.

When seen from a distance, the Ngongs looked more like the bony knuckles on a fist than soothing fingers. According to Masai legend, they were just that: knuckles, *Ngongo Bagas*. They belonged to a giant who had terrorized their ancestors. The ants, the Masai's allies, had piled loose dirt over the sleeping ogre, covering everything but his knuckles. According to another version, the hills were the dirt God flicked off his fingers when he finished the Creation.

He turned at Dagoretti Corner and went through the leafy suburb of Karen, named for the Danish noblewoman Karen Blixen who had written a lot of lovely nonsense about colonial Kenya under the pen name Isak Dinesen. He joined the main road west of Kiserian, passing a modest memorial to Denys Finch-Hatton, the Baroness Blixen's largely imagined lover and nowhere near the hunter her husband Bror had been, and finally crawling to the top of the Ngong watershed, 7,000 feet above sea level.

At the crest, Adrian stopped to savor the view and smoke a cigarette. From here all the way to the white soda lake at Magadi, more than a hundred kilometers, the road dropped down in three giant steps as it ran the scoured floor of the Rift. Here was Kenya in all her contradictions: beautiful and ugly, vast and cramped, inviting and aloof, timeless and immediate, pastoral and dangerous, impatient and indifferent. It was her indifference he found most alluring; she was immune to men and their boastful deeds.

Adrian restarted the Land Rover and went swooping down the escarpment in a stomach-tossing series of laborious ups and exhilarating downs. At the foot of the first step the little trading crossroads of Olepolos sat baking on a bed of brown grassland and whistle thorn. Several miles farther on was the turnoff to Olorgesailie, the site of the Leakeys' paleontological digs. The turnoff to Olorgesailie was marked with a Parks Department sign pointing the way to the national monument, and by a rude collection of souvenir stands run by Masai women dressed in full tribal raiment. Adrian pulled up to them and rolled down the window. But before he could speak, he was mobbed by an army of women and children, all of them yelling and shoving curios through the window at him: beaded bracelets and necklaces, hide shields, and the short, down-sized tourist version of the Masai spear.

"I am seeking a man, not trinkets," he said quickly, in Masai, afraid they would put out his eye with a spear. "Does anyone among you know Joseph ole Kantai of the Ilkeekonyokie section? Another name that dwells within him, his elder name, is Senteu, the same as the good son of the Laibon Batiany."

"*Uui,*" they exclaimed, intrigued that this *Ilmeek,* this alien, spoke the language of Maa, but disappointed at losing a customer. "I know him," one of the women said shyly, "but he moves from kraal to kraal and one never knows where he is from one day to the next. If you keep south you will see the *moran* on the road. Ask them. They will know where he is."

He thanked her and left quickly, before he felt obliged to buy something. He drove only two more miles before he saw the *moran.* The warriors were standing on the shoulder of the road, signaling for him to stop.

There were five of them and they were magnificent, lithe as gazelles and haughty as lions. Their hard, muscular bodies were slathered with a red ocher and they used the same mud to plaster down plaited hair. Beaded necklaces and bracelets and earrings, strung by adoring girls, adorned their ears, necks, wrists, ankles, and arms. They wore scarlet togas, and carried buffalo-hide shields and long javelin spears. They approached Adrian's window with their hands out, palms up, crying out in Swahili, in voices which managed to be mendicant and arrogant at the same time: "*Shilingi! Shilingi!*"

"*Hapana shilingi,*" Adrian snapped back, so disappointed in them that he rattled on in Swahili. "No money, hear? I am not a tourist and I don't want to take your photograph."

They just laughed and switched into Masai so they could talk about him among themselves. Adrian heard himself called *l'Ojuju,* the Hairy One; while he was not particularly hairy, it was one of their pet terms for white men. He heard *Ilmeek* again, alien, a sobriquet applied to any non-Masai, black or white. He even heard his old favorite, *Iloridaa enjekat,* "he who confines his farts," a reference to his European clothes, which, unlike the Masai's Roman-style toga, did not allow the wind to bear away bad odors.

He let them have their fun a moment longer, then said in rapid Masai: "I see that since you are no longer permitted to hunt lions, you hunt tourists instead. You wait in ambush for them beside the road, then you let them take your picture for money, for *shilingi*. You should be ashamed of yourselves. You are supposed to be warriors, not merchants."

Their lean faces, nearly as fine-featured as a Somali's, changed in a heartbeat. For a moment Adrian was afraid he had gone too far, that they were going to drag him from the Land Rover and pin him to the ground with their long spears.

"Who dares to speak to us this way?" one of them said, his eyes hot and murderous.

"A circumcision brother of the elder Senteu, Joseph ole Kantai," Adrian said firmly, "and perhaps of your own father as well." The rank was all honorary, of course, but any port in a storm. Then, with a reckless, gambling bravado, he said: "And one who has killed more lions than you've fucked girls."

One *moran,* their self-appointed spokesman, laughed and nodded, relaxing his grip on his spear. "I think I've heard of you, *l'Ojuju,* and it's true, you have killed many lions," he said. "But it is also true that you got your lions with a rifle while I got my girls with a spear." He opened his toga and grabbed his dangling penis.

They all laughed and Adrian joined in. Then, as long as they were in a good mood, he said, "I'm searching for Joseph ole Kantai. Do you know where he is?"

They did, and told him, and waved goodbye when he left. Driving on, Glenton was haunted by the picture of the *moran* with their hands out, using them for begging bowls. The pride that had kept them from adapting to modern times did not seem to work against more subtle forms of corruption, he thought.

He knew he was guilty of romanticizing the Masai, but he couldn't help it. It was in his genes. In all their scattered empire, the English always had a soft spot in their otherwise stony hearts for the proud, the primitive, for those who gave them the most headaches. The Pathan. The Zulu. Even, although they would never admit it, the bloody Boer, a wog same as the rest as far as they were concerned. Kenya's whites, of mostly sturdy British stock, were no different. They loved the Masai for their beauty, their courage, their refusal to be changed.

Today's Masai were little different from those who had first arrived in Kenya in the fifteenth century after migrating up the Nile. With their togas, short fighting swords, and helmetlike haircuts, the *moran* still showed the Roman influence on the Nilotes and Hamites of Northern Africa.

It was hard not to love them, Adrian thought. What formidable fighters they had been, the only ones who had been capable of stopping the seemingly unstoppable, the inexorable advance of the Zulu from the south. Besides, how could you resist loving people so independent that they died if you kept them in jail for any length of time? Colonial magistrates had been forced to fine Masai sinners rather than impose prison terms; to do otherwise was to hand down a death sentence.

But pride had a price. In refusing to accept the *Ilmeek* English and their largess—from police protection to modern medicine—the Masai had been left behind. While the others, especially the Kikuyu, prospered and proliferated, the Masai were thinned by civil war, and one disease after another. In 1869 it was cholera contracted from their up-country cousins the Samburu. In 1880 it was smallpox. Today it was syphilis. And when Whitehall finally returned Kenya to its native people in 1963, the Masai, who had refused to take part in the long political process, were in no position to claim a fair share. They had left it to the Kikuyu to suckle at the British teat, to go to British schools, to clerk in colonial administrative offices, to learn *Ilmeek* ways. Now these same Kikuyu who had once run from the Masai *moran* in terror to hide behind British skirts, were running the nation, Maasailand included, wielding *Ilmeek* laws to win what they had never been able to win on the field of battle, shoving the Masai onto ever more barren pastures.

Like Joseph's kraal, Adrian thought when he found it. It was a typical *engang*, a collection of grass-and-dung huts surrounded by a thorn fence designed to keep wild animals out and livestock in. There was no one in view when he stepped into the compound; the sun was right overhead and the women and elderly, and those *totos* too young to be out tending goats, were indoors. Even some of the livestock had been brought in out of the heat and away from the flies. Adrian's nostrils filled with distinctly Masai smells: dung, urine, curdled milk, and cow's blood.

The *moran* had said that Joseph's hut would be fifth in the ring, counting clockwise from the kraal entrance. Finding it, Adrian called Joseph's name. A moment later the hide flap over the doorway was pushed aside and Joseph emerged blinking into the intense sunlight. His expression did not change when he spotted Adrian. He merely said: "*Keserian ingera? Keserian ingishu?*" How are the children? How are the cattle?

It was a traditional Masai greeting, acknowledging the value the Masai placed on their children, custodians of the future, and their livestock, the basis of all wealth, prestige, and power. Adrian, a man with neither children nor cattle, gave the traditional reply nonetheless, saying they were well.

Joseph just nodded and, still without expression, said: "Tell me four great wonders."

Adrian answered: "A calabash, which does not drink the milk that is in it. A snake, which moves without legs. Water, which, though it has no legs, still travels. A stool, which has legs, but still cannot walk."

Joseph shook his head sadly and said in English: "You're such a dipshit."

Adrian laughed and embraced him. "A dipshit, huh?" he said, stepping back to look at his friend. "I should never have let you go on safari with Americans. You've spent too much time away from the Masai."

"A calabash which does not drink the milk that is in it, eh?" Joseph countered. "You've spent too much time among the Masai."

It had been more than a year since Adrian had last seen his friend, not since that final hunt. Joseph looked fit but more tame than Adrian remembered. Perhaps it was because the warrior braids were gone, along with the beaded ornaments and the body paint. Joseph's hair was cropped short now, as befitted a mature and responsible man, a junior elder of the tribe.

Otherwise he looked much the same, Adrian thought. With his narrow nose and high cheekbones he was still a handsome devil, despite the Masai custom of extracting the two middle teeth from the lower jaw. All he had on was a pair of shorts with "Michigan State Athletic Dept." stenciled on them, and his chest and stomach were ridged with muscle. Adrian looked at Joseph's haircut and said, "I see you survived the *eunoto* ceremony."

Joseph nodded sadly. "*Aiya*. I sat on the same cowhide I sat on when I was circumcised, while my mother shaved off my hair."

"How are you finding elderhood?"

"Boring," Joseph said, then, switching to Masai, "and about to get worse." He gave the Masai equivalent of a sigh, a slow blink. "My old fire-stick elder and the others are unhappy with me. They are after me to choose a wife. They say it's time for me to take up my responsibilities. They want me to settle down."

"That's what they want. What do you want?"

"What I can't have," Joseph said with a shrug. "I want to be a *moran* again. I want to live in the warrior *manyatta,* sharing stories and girls with my brothers. I want to be back in the bush, in the feasting camp, away from this talk about responsibility and respectability. I want to turn back time."

Adrian nodded with sympathy. No one, he knew, had more thoroughly enjoyed, or fully lived, the carefree life of the Masai *moran* than Joseph. The fourteen years that Joseph had spent in the warrior class had been the most exciting years he would ever know.

Even among *moran,* that tribe within a tribe, he had been something special, a young man with all the qualities most prized by the Masai. He was good-looking. He was exceedingly, some said foolishly, courageous. He was polite and generous. He was a gifted orator. So it was no surprise when the boys of his age-set elected him *Olaiguenani,* the one who presides over the circumcision group's meetings and represents them in discussions with their fire-stick elders, the sponsors who'd kindled the fires which had heated the circumcision knives. Later, as a full *moran,* he'd been chosen by the elders to be the *embika,* the leader of the warriors' kraal, charged with maintaining discipline and punishing troublemakers.

It was only after he began working for the white hunters, picking up their strange, alien ways and neglecting his tribal duties, that he fell out of favor with the elders. He hunted animals besides lion, the one true King of Beasts, and, as every right-thinking Masai knew, the only one worthy of hunting. He ate wild game meat, not just beef. And he was always going off somewhere with *l'Ojuju,* the Hairy One, when he should have been tending to his responsibilities at home. When the elders had enough of it, and of him, they had stripped him of his titles.

Until then, and even after, he had been arrogant as only a Masai *moran* could be arrogant. Adrian had heard a wonderful story about just how insufferable the younger Joseph could be: once, when one of his elders innocently remarked "lend me your ear," Joseph had snatched up his spear, sliced off an earlobe, and handed it to him.

Thinking about it, Adrian couldn't help smiling. "Well, before you marry and settle down," he said, "would you like to be a *moran* again for a short while?"

"How?"

"I'm putting together a small team, half a dozen men, to hunt down a gang of poachers in the great Aberdare Forest. I want you with me."

"What would I do?"

"What you do best. Seek and destroy. Hunt."

"I have never hunted in forest. That is Kikuyuland."

"Hunting is hunting," Adrian said. "Besides, I'd also want you to be my second-in-command. I need someone strong to keep the others in hand."

Joseph idly scratched at his right ear, the one missing a lobe. "This hunt of yours," he said in English. "Will there be killing?"

"I don't know," Adrian said. "Possibly. Probably."

Joseph looked around the drowsing kraal. From the nearby huts came everyday sounds: the bleat of a kid, the clatter of a pot, a mother's lullaby, the splatting hiss of a urinating animal. He turned back to Adrian, shooed the flies away from his face, and said: "Fucking A."

Adrian was back in Nairobi by midafternoon, and he had recruited the second man for his team by nightfall. That was how long it took him to comb the grog shops of Eastleigh and find the man he was looking for, a Liangulu he knew only as "Tembo."

Tembo was no young man, somewhere between fifty and seventy, but Adrian had used him before, despite his ironclad rule against carrying drunkards on safari. It was no mere coincidence that the Swahili word for elephant was *tembo;* no one knew elephant the way Tembo knew elephant.

Adrian knew he was taking a risk, that he might well be wasting one of his precious choices, but he told himself that it took a poacher to catch one. The Liangulu had been a small enough tribe to begin with, one devoted almost exclusively to the poaching of elephants, and in the late 1940s and early 1950s it had essentially been wiped out in a country-wide campaign to stamp out poaching. Tembo's father and seven brothers had been shot to death in the space of a year. Since then, Tembo had seemed bent on finishing the job on the family's menfolk, with *pombe,* the cheap, yeasty homemade African beer.

Adrian found him in a *pombe* shack on Juja Road, curled up in a corner on the dirt floor and snoring so loudly that he drowned out the noise of the jets taking off and landing at Eastleigh Air Force Base. Adrian settled up the man's bar bill, slung him over one shoulder, and carted him out to the Land Rover.

Chege lived in the Eastleigh district, in Nairobi South B, one of the poorer public housing projects, and Adrian took the comatose Tembo there. Obligingly, Chege said he would be happy to keep Tembo for a day or two; he seemed less curious about Adrian's fume-shrouded cargo than about why his *rafiki,* his friend, had quit the company. Adrian put him off with a promise to explain it some day, and asked him to clean Tembo up. If and when Tembo dried out, Chege was to tell him that a job was waiting for him in the Aberdares. He left five hundred shillings with Chege, half for him, for his trouble, and half for Tembo, as bait, along with directions to Aberdare Ranch. Then he went home, had two stiff whisky sodas, and fell into bed.

Just after sunrise the next morning he was back at the wheel of the Land Rover, heading northwest on A-104, toward Naivasha, Gilgil, and Rumuruti. He had lied to his father about not going to Rumuruti.

He fairly flew down the Kikuyu Escarpment, driving like an African, taking the hairpin turns much too fast, dodging smoke-belching buses and recklessly overtaking *matatus,* the overcrowded vans which were the primary mode of transportation for the *wananchi,* the common folk. The *matatu* operators, whose own recklessness was substantiated by their fatality statistics, were menaces, but they were not without a certain humor; they gave their ramshackle vehicles cutely apt names like "Shake, Rattle and Roll" and "Stairway to Heaven."

He was retracing the last leg of the drive back from the Mara. It was only two days ago, but already Mrs. MacReedy and Tubby Jenkins were faintly recalled goblins from a childhood nightmare. The Rift was on his left this time, spectacular as ever. He passed the chapel built by the Italian prisoners and zoomed by the turnoff to Narok and the Mara without a glance in their direction.

Despite being one of the most heavily used highways in Kenya, or more likely because of it, the road between the Narok cutoff and Naivasha was a national disgrace, a pitted and treacherous gauntlet with great chunks of paving missing from the shoulders. Even so, Adrian put the accelerator pedal to the floor and kept it there, pushing the Land Rover at one-hundred-twenty kilometers per hour on the straights, as fast as it would go. He bounced on the hard bench seat, hanging onto the wheel as if it were electrified, with his arms straight and his elbows locked, his entire body shaking and his ears aching from the incessant rattling and the engine whine.

Yet he was smiling, pleased with how well things seemed to be going. His recruiting was ahead of schedule. By tonight he would have his team nearly completed. He had Joseph as his adjutant, a tough and vicious disciplinarian, the key to the team. He had Tembo for the elephants. And today, in Rumuruti, he would sign up his childhood playmates, Damon and Pythias, Dorobo hunters who knew forests the way Tembo knew elephants, and who could double as experts on leopards. And, of course, he had himself as the *fundi* on rhino.

By this time tomorrow he would need only one more recruit, someone with an intimate knowledge of the park and the *shambas* on its boundaries, someone who knew the people and who could provide the team with sound intelligence. Which meant a local Kikuyu, most likely. Adrian did not relish the idea of filling one of his few slots with a stranger, but he had no candidate of his own. He decided to ring up Inspector Odongo from Naivasha, to start him looking for someone.

When he reached the outskirts of Naivasha, fifty-five miles from Nairobi, he turned left onto South Lake Road and began circling the lake, hunting for a telephone. He passed up the first few logical choices, the Lake Hotel and Safariland Lodge, and kept on going, not quite sure why. He simply didn't feel like stopping just yet. It was a candescent morning. The light was catching the tips of Lake Naivasha's whitecaps. The papyrus isles were adrift on the breeze, and the African punters were poling the bass and tilapia fishermen out to the reed beds.

He was now in part of what, in earlier times, had been called Happy Valley, heartland of the old settler set, Pate's crowd. His too in a way, since he had childhood memories of visiting several of these farms. He passed Fisherman's Camp, following the detour around Inner Lake and Kongoni Farm. Out of pavement now and shimmying over a washboard dirt road, he went through Ndabibi Estate, former home of Gilbert Colville and his infamous dog. The ghost of Colville's dog was said still to haunt the big white house on the edge of the lake, the Djinn Palace, where Lord Erroll had lived before he was shot to death one evening in Nairobi after dining at the Muthaiga Club with his young mistress, Lady Broughton, and her elderly husband, Sir Delves.

That had been early in 1941, two years before Adrian was born, but he still remembered the disapproval in his mother's voice when she recalled how the scandal, and the ensuing murder trial of Sir Delves, had eclipsed even the Battle of Britain as the topic of conversation at the Muthaiga Club. The popular Sir Delves had been acquitted to great cheering, and that randy cad Lord Erroll had been mourned by few; only a dozen or so Happy Valley wives, and Colville's dog. Every year on the anniversary of Lord Erroll's death, the ghostly dog was spotted on the grounds of the Djinn Palace, dragging a ghostly chain.

Adrian did not stop to make his call anywhere along the lake shore, though he still knew people on these farms. Instead, he completed the circuit, crossing the Gilgil River and rejoining the main highway. And since he was already well on the far side of Naivasha, he decided to press on to Gilgil and telephone from there.

Off to his right, some twenty miles away, Adrian could see the eastern slopes of the Nyandarua Mountains, more commonly called, by whites and Africans alike, by their old name, the Aberdares. While he had spent little time in them as a child, those graduated foothills and shadowed peaks had been a constant, reassuring feature of his boyhood's landscape, a cool promise on a hot day. But now he could not look upon their silhouette without a prickling sense of foreboding. Black clouds hung suspended over the far peaks like rotted breadfruits, a sure sign that the short rains would be early this year.

There were a few Masai herds grazing along the roadside, but not as many as there once had been. This high stretch of the Rift, from the extinct Longonot volcano in the south to the Laikipia Plateau just above Nyahururu (formerly Thomson's Falls), had been part of greater Maasailand until the British used the treaties of 1904 and 1911 to force the tribe out of the highlands and down onto the sandy southern regions. This was some of the most prized and productive ranch land in all of Africa, much too good to waste on the primitive Masai and their stringy cattle. That was how most government officials (most of them Kikuyu) saw it anyway, much the same as the colonial administrators before them.

He telephoned from the office of the Agip station near Pembroke House, his old school. Facing the window as he dialed, Adrian had a view of the playing fields. On the far pitch two teams of boys in striped jerseys were engaged in a hot game of rugger, while on the near field, the one closest to the petrol station, another group played football. Adrian could hear their faint shouts as they lined up for a corner kick, and it brought back his own glory days in goal.

Aside from the time spent at games, which he'd been good at, Adrian's years at Pembroke had not been especially happy. Unaccustomed to the company of white boys his own age, he had been almost pathologically shy at first, then merely restless and bored. The boys from big cities like Nairobi and Mombasa were cliquish and snobby, even though the truly top families sent their sons to boarding schools in England, not Pembroke. And while these boys were far more knowledgeable than Adrian in the ways of the flesh, they were remarkably ignorant when it came to the really important things: hunting and tracking. His fellow provincials from the farms of the White Highlands were as quiet and standoffish as he was, adrift in a sea of homesickness. One of them, a boy from an isolated ranch near Archer's Post in the Northern Frontier District, had tried to solve the problem of his loneliness by going home one holiday and returning with his Samburu gunbearer. The headmaster had sent the bewildered warrior home straight away.

Boarding a mere forty kilometers from the farm in Nakuru, Adrian had been luckier than many of his classmates, able to spend his holidays and weekends at home. It made school bearable. Then Clare Glenton died and everything changed and nothing was bearable.

Pate had grieved hard, even harder than Adrian, who did not think it was possible. At first his father had thought to drown himself in whisky, and Adrian, on mourning leave from school, had helplessly watched him try. When Pate sobered up only to find himself still alone, he began to spend less time on the ranch and more on outside things. He joined a farmers' vigilante group which was helping the British Army hunt down Mau Mau terrorists, and volunteered for all the missions they would give him. When he wasn't chasing Mau Mau he devoted his time to his second business, Bushbuck Safaris Ltd., until then a mere sideline, a way of indulging his love of hunting while bringing in extra income. He would do anything, it seemed, to be away from Bushbuck Farm and its memories of his wife.

Whenever Pate was out in the bush with a hunting client or chasing Mau Mau, and that became most of the time, Adrian stayed at Pembroke on holidays and weekends. He had lost his mother, and for all practical purposes his father as well. If it hadn't been for the Hudsons, the family's closest friends, he didn't think he would have gotten through it. "Uncle" Vic and "Auntie" Jeanne Hudson became Adrian's surrogate parents, and his salvation was in the time he spent at their ranch in Rumuruti, the same ranch Pate bought after independence, when the Hudsons, unwilling to accept the new reality, gave up and repatriated to England.

Bad days. Not the sort to mellow slowly into treasured memories of the old school, or a fondness for Gilgil itself. Even without his personal experience, Adrian doubted he ever would have felt much nostalgia for Gilgil. While surrounded by perhaps the finest grazing land in the country, it was a bleak garrison town, distinguished only by the endless rows of barracks belonging to the Kenya Army and to the National Youth Service. He had never been able to understand how the town could ever have been known as "Swinging Gilgil" to the Happy Valley crowd. These days, the Agip station was one of the livelier places in town.

It took ten minutes and nearly as many tries before the Gilgil operator managed the double miracle of keeping Nairobi and Jogoo House both on line while the switchboard connected him with Odongo's office. "Hullo, Inspector. Glenton here."

"And where is here?" Odongo asked in a wry voice. "From this end, it sounds as if you're speaking from the bottom of a hole."

Adrian laughed. "You aren't too far off, Inspector. I'm in bloody Gilgil. Just ringing to let you know that I should have our anti-poaching unit recruited by the end of the day."

"Excellent news, Mr. Glenton."

"All except one," Adrian added, going on to explain his need and asking Odongo if he could find him a reliable Kikuyu to serve as a liaison between the APU and the local Aberdares population. Odongo promised to look into it. "Ring back later this afternoon or this evening. I should have someone for you by then."

"That would be super," Adrian said. Then, not expecting anything, he asked idly, "Any developments since our chat?"

"Yes. My collection of hyena's teeth is growing," Odongo said. "The warden was on last night to report that he's found another fine specimen for me. This one came with a leopard, a female who seems to have lost her coat."

"That's unfortunate," Glenton said. "It can get cold in the mountains at night."

"Which is why we must hurry if we are to make things hot for our friends. You go on and finish your work and I'll find you a good Kikuyu, assuming there is such a thing."

"Right-o," Adrian said with a chuckle, ringing off.

Anxious to be shut of Gilgil and dogged by an odd sense of urgency, Adrian took only time enough to have the station attendant top up both internal tanks and fill the jerry cans strapped to the rear bumper, then he was under way again.

The turnoff to Thomson's Falls and on to Rumuruti was just beyond the fringe of Gilgil, but Adrian did not take it. Instead, he passed the turn and went on toward Lake Elmenteita. As with his dawdling ramble around Lake Naivasha, he couldn't explain it, and it wasn't until he reached the outskirts of Nakuru, a hundred miles from Nairobi, that he knew with any certainty where he was going.

* * *

Nakuru was no longer the sleepy, up-country market town he re-membered. Many of the things that had given the place a distinct, frontier flavor were still intact—the wide High Street lined with squat buildings and a covered walkway, with room enough to turn a wagon and a full span of oxen; the side streets which ended without warning, petering out in the open grasslands of the Rift—but the town had grown like a stubborn weed in the forty years since its heyday as capital of the White Highlands, and even more in the four years since Adrian Glenton had last seen it.

Inching through the town in low gear, Adrian was shocked to see how crowded and dirty it had become, choked with dusty African markets and Asian *dukas* flogging everything from soap to samozas. That crystalline and invigorating highlands air, once famous for its restorative power, now was full of sooty particles from traffic and factories. Farm animals ran loose, and naked children played in the dust and in the puddles that collected in the potholes. Even the Stag's Head Hotel, where the Glentons had often gone for Sunday lunch, seemed sad and dilapidated; just outside the entrance, a drunken Afri-can lay unconscious in a pool of his own vomit.

The din was enough to crack marble. Vehicles of every sort, their horns in full cry, clogged the center of town, and people swarmed like *siafu* ants along walks and streets and jammed the dusty square that served as a bus and *matatu* terminal. They came in all shapes, sizes, tribes, and types. Young Kipsigis girls with silent infants strapped to their backs in slings fashioned from *kangas*. Kikuyu city spivs in their pegged pants and point-toed shoes, on the lookout for easy money. Wide-eyed Masai men standing like crested cranes with one foot propped on the opposite knee, leaning on their spears and trying, without much success, to look unfazed and unimpressed by the bustle of Kenya's now third-largest city.

Thanks to the season and the 6,000-foot elevation, the day was dry and cool, but windy, and a fine dusting of soda blew in from Lake Nakuru. Adrian got through town as quickly as traffic permitted, only to find himself ensnared in a long line of lorries making for the industrial area, for the flour mills, or the blanket factory, or the Union Carbide plant, or the plant where they extracted natural insecticides from the dried flowers of pyrethrum daisies.

With a curse, he joined the rest of the mob and hit his horn, leaning on it for almost a minute before acknowledging the futility of it all. He cursed again, rammed the gearbox into four-wheel drive and pulled out of the queue, jumping the berm to cut across open grassland. He drove in a mindless rage, abusing the vehicle and himself as he jounced across the rough terrain, not quite sure what it was that was fueling his anger.

Then, directly in front of him, filling the windscreen, was the promise of asylum: the Menengai Crater. The extinct volcano had been one of Adrian's favorite places when he was a boy and he aimed straight for it. When he reached the base of the cone he circled until he found the dirt road that led to the top, then started up. It was a steep but simple climb for the Land Rover, and he was on the rim, nearly 7,500 feet above sea level, in no time at all.

Switching off the engine, Adrian got out and let a deep and blessed silence, spoiled only by the metallic pinging of the cooling motor, envelope him. He fished a packet of Embassys from his pocket and lit one. Only then did he begin to relax.

The view was spectacular in any direction. He could see across to the opposite side of the caldera, eleven kilometers away, and down to the bottom of the wooded crater itself, four hundred meters from rim to floor. Deep within the crater he saw steam jets and a small band of giraffe. Looking south he had a fine view of the Solai Valley and of the town he had just battled his way through. From this lofty vantage, Nakuru looked like the quaint, quiet village he remembered.

Below the town was Lake Nakuru, a dark ring with a pink aureole: thousands upon thousands of flamingos. And beyond that was Lake Elmenteita, and the curiously shaped hill that the older whites in the area still called "Delamere's Nose," presumably because it reminded them of the rather prominent proboscis of the late Hugh Cholmondeley, third Baron Delamere and Kenya's most famous European settler. But perhaps it was only because Lord Delamere had owned that land.

Once, when he was a boy, Adrian had heard Pate refer to Lake Nakuru as "Delamere's Nose," and when he asked why, his father had said, "The lake is shaped rather like a nose, wouldn't you say? And when the flamingos settle just so, it brings to mind the burst veins in a drunkard's nose. Now you aren't old enough to remember old Hugh, of course, but I can tell you . . ." And Clare Glenton had interrupted in a laughing but no-nonsense voice: "That will do, Pater dear. You know as well as I that Lord Delamere was a great man."

Adrian could hear her soft voice, could see her lifted brow and pursed mouth as she called David Glenton by his pet family name, which a young Adrian had irreverently shortened to Pate. His mother always said it through her nose, giving it the full treatment, pronouncing it "Pay-tuh." In a rather lame attempt to retaliate, his father had tried calling her "Mater," but it never took. Even in fun, Clare Glenton could not be mocked.

For the first time since climbing the crater Adrian let his gaze wander to the southeast, and quickly found the farm. It was just one indistinct multicolored patch among many in the earth's quilt, but it was as readily identifiable as his mother's voice in a crowded room. He wasn't at all surprised to discover that his eyes were damp, but he blamed it on the wind in his face.

And, also for the first time, he finally knew why he was here, even though he had a job to do and should be getting on with it. Going to see Pate at the club . . . his loop through the once familiar farms on Lake Naivasha . . . his anxiety to get out of Gilgil, only to pass by the turnoff to Rumuruti—he understood now that all of it had been part of a curious, cautious stalking maneuver, a prelude to the past.

Wiping his eyes, he climbed partway down into the caldera and began picking handfuls of *Saintpaulia,* the common African violet. When he had enough, he set them carefully on the seat of the Land Rover, cranked the engine, and began his descent.

It took him nearly an hour to get down the volcano, work back through the northern outskirts of the town, and reach the farm. He passed by the main gate and continued along the dirt road running parallel to the farm. Off to his right was Hyrax Hill, the former home of Mary Selfe and now a museum for the New Stone Age and Iron Age artifacts discovered on the place. Mrs. Selfe had donated the house as a memorial to her son, an airman killed in the Second World War.

He drove another ten minutes before coming to the gate he wanted. When he was through and had closed it behind him, he continued across open grazing land toward a tree-studded kopje. Parking at the bottom of the hill, he gathered up his flowers and began to climb.

It wasn't a proper cemetery. Just the two graves, set in a shaded clearing in the center of a copse, with a fine view down the valley. One was marked with a tall obelisk. A bronze plaque fixed on the base read: "Here lies Jonathan Glenton, who was born in Liverpool, England, on May the 4th, 1893, came to Kenya on September the 14th, 1912, and died on the Fields of Flanders, France, on September the 9th, 1918. He loved, and he faithfully served, his God, his King, his Country and his Family. May he rest in Peace."

The other marker was a small whitewashed slab, as plain and as straightforward as the woman under it, simply reading: "Clare Griffiths Glenton, born Mawingo Farm, Nanyuki, January 3, 1923, died Bushbuck Farm, Nakuru, August 8, 1954."

6

Robbie Lewis had once been told, by an especially odious male colleague, that a man could always tell when a woman had been well and truly loved the night before. There would be a bloom on her cheeks, a liquid calm in her eyes, and a general air of contentment and well-being about her. He had called it "that fresh-fucked look."

Robbie, wearing nothing but a *kanga* and sitting on the veranda of her house in Muthaiga with a pot of coffee and a month's worth of newspapers and magazines piled on the table in front of her, fit that description this morning, only she called it "that fresh-filed look."

She had started on this week's file yesterday morning at the hotel in Mogadishu, written most of it in the airport departure lounge with her Olivetti on her lap, and had finished it off in the air. Once back in Nairobi, she had gone straight from the airport to the Reuters office and sent her file on to *Newsweek* in New York. By the time she got home to Muthaiga, the newsdesk was already calling to confirm that they had received a clean, ungarbled copy.

All was right with Robbie's world. Her Nigerian take-out had run as an overseas cover while she'd been in Somalia; her Ogaden "duel in the desert" story was finished and filed; she had had a hot bath and a decent night's sleep, in her own bed; and if the BBC World Service could be trusted, which it normally could, no new wars, famines, coups, or plagues had wracked black Africa while she had slept.

She poured herself another cup of strong Kenya coffee and read again the hero-grams that had been waiting for her in the *Newsweek* incoming basket at Reuters:

9/18/78. Multithanks for your top-notch files from Lagos. Great stuff. Wineburg/Overseas.

9/19/78. Nigeria files superb. Giving you six columns in domestic mag. For space reasons, Overseas killed you for this week, but will revive you at even greater length next week. Thanks again for classy files. Rogers/Foreign.

9/21/78. Well done! On to Somalia! Klinger/Newsdesk.

More of the same would be coming in later today, after everyone had a look at the Ogaden file. She wasn't preening. It was just that the Ogaden stuff was even better than what she had sent them from Lagos. Five days in the desert with the Western Somali Liberation Front. Constantly on the move, hiding from Ethiopian warplanes. An ambushed convoy with two dead Cuban advisers. Poisoned water wells, the brainstorm of a Soviet general in Addis Ababa. Entire villages turned into mounds of white ash by napalm. Laughing children using bomb fragments for toys. Somali women wailing over the shattered bodies of their husbands. It was a surefire combination: Big Picture Politics, Bang-Bang and Ooga-Booga. Her editors, who thought tragedy was not being able to find a taxi on a rainy night in Manhattan, would eat it up.

But that was last week. Today there was nothing she had to do. No overbooked flight to fight her way onto. No waiting around a seedy office, or an even seedier hotel room for word on this travel permit or that interview with the Third Deputy Assistant Minister of Bullshit. No dinner alone in some land without food. She could read a book, or putter in her garden, or wander down to the Norfolk pool, or cajole one of her male colleagues into buying her lunch at the Muthaiga Club, which was only fifty yards behind her house and fifty years behind the times.

Robbie stretched languorously, almost losing her loosely but strategically tied *kanga*, which was no more than a single piece of colorful printed cloth. She wanted, no, she *needed* a long stay at home, and she was determined to get it even if she had to use up some of the vacation time coming to her.

She started in on the pile of papers, reading closely, looking for good story ideas, for a thumbsucker, an analysis piece she could do from Nairobi. Idi Amin, the Clown Cannibal of Africa, was up to his old tricks next door in Uganda, but there was nothing spectacular enough to justify yet another scare story slugged "Demented Dictator" or "The Dark Continent's Darkest Hour." Amin was Ooga-Booga journalism at its best, or worst; but even her seemingly insatiable editors, who rarely passed up a chance to pepper Africa stories with their unique brand of liberal racism—"it's so sad, and such a shame"—were getting tired of him. She would have to find something else.

After an hour, her "fresh-filed" feeling was gone, its place usurped by a depression so deep it numbed her. In the short time she'd been away, the African beat had gone on. In Uganda, Idi Amin slid deeper into lunacy. In the Horn, Ethiopia and Somalia waged a dirty desert war over the scorched wasteland called the Ogaden, from which she'd just returned. In the Central African "Empire," Emperor Bokassa I, having taken one hundred million dollars from his poverty-stricken country's treasury to pay for his coronation party, economized by having his cook fix him meals fashioned from human body parts. And down south, white men killed black men for Rhodesia and black men killed white men for Zimbabwe. Day after dismal day, week after wretched week, the same bad news, the same sorry story of a continent in crisis.

Robbie loved Africa, but it was breaking her heart. It constantly delighted her and just as reliably dismayed her, and she never knew which it would do next. As always, on this latest trip there had been moments both wonderful and terrible.

Scene One: She is in line at the Lagos airport, behind a fat lady who has her ticket between her teeth, a live chicken in one hand and a goat on a leash in the other. When the lady reaches the Nigeria Airways counter, the ticket agent plucks the ticket from her mouth, and the ensuing conversation takes place:

Agent: "No goats."

Woman: "No goats? What do you mean no goats?"

Agent: "I mean no goats."

Woman: "Since when no goats."

Agent: "Since two days ago no goats." With an officious flourish, he produces a piece of paper. The woman leans close to read it, then nods with resigned acceptance.

Woman: "You're right. No goats."

The woman drops the leash and shoos the goat. The goat does not move. She tries again. The goat does not move. She begins beating the goat with the live chicken, swinging the hapless bird by its feet in wheeling roundhouses. There is a moment of pandemonium, full of flying feathers, squawks and bleats. The dazed goat moves off, to wander loose around the airport. The woman, clutching her boarding pass in one hand and the stunned chicken in the other, strolls on to the departure lounge.

Scene Two: She is in the back of an ambulance, a Land Rover three-quarter-ton truck with a canvas cover, jolting through the desert night beneath a rising, pumpkin-colored moon. There is no road, not even a recognizable track. The floor of the truck bed is littered with wounded guerrillas, a dozen men in all. Each new bump is followed immediately by their moans and screams. Robbie is not an unwelcome presence; in fact, if it wasn't for her they would not be on their way to Somalia, to the hospital in Hargeisa. The guerrillas have very few vehicles and they must conserve them for important missions, like ferrying American reporters around the front. It is not frivolous, the officers say; favorable news stories about their cause might persuade Washington to give them aid, and then they can buy more trucks. Usually, the officers tell Robbie, the badly wounded are taken to Hargeisa on the backs of camels, and few survive the trip. Even by Land Rover the journey takes six hours; six hours of moaning and screaming; six hours of Hell. One of the men has advanced gangrene and the stench from his rotting leg fills the truck, permeating everything. By the time they get to Hargeisa, only seven of the twelve wounded are still alive. Unable to get the smell of rot out of her clothes, Robbie burns them.

That was Africa, Robbie thought. A mixed bag. Humor and horror. Farce and folly. She loved it, she hated it, and she did not know how much more of it she could take.

"Memsaab." Alphonse, her house man, was standing at the veranda door. "Telephone please, *memsaab.*"

Lost in thought, Robbie had not heard it ring. "Thank you, Alphonse," she said, going inside to take the call.

It was Samwel Mbituru, a reporter for the Kenya African National Union paper. "Roberta, have you seen this morning's newspaper?"

"Don't call me Roberta. Just because I was born with it doesn't mean I've got to lug it around the rest of my life."

"It is a very nice name. But please, have you seen this morning's paper?"

"Sammy, you'll probably never talk to me again after I say this, but the truth is that I hardly ever read the KANU party paper. I find it Byzantine, bombastic, and boring."

She heard Samwel's almost girlish giggle. "If you think reading it is boring, try writing for it sometime," he said. "But I wasn't talking about my newspaper; I meant the *Daily Nation.*"

"Yeah. I went through it only a minute ago."

"Did you see the item about the murder in the park?"

"What murder in which park?"

"Aberdare National Park. It was a short piece, saying only that the authorities found a body, a local poacher."

"Must have missed it. So what's the big deal?"

"I think you should look into it."

"Now why would I want to do that, Samwel?" Robbie said. "*Newsweek* isn't interested in local murders, unless somebody were to knock off Kenyatta, of course."

She heard his horrified gasp. "Roberta! You mustn't say such things. Not even on the telephone. Particularly on the telephone." There was a short pause down the line. "I merely thought you might find it interesting, that's all."

Robbie sighed. No one was as congenitally conspiratorial as an African journalist, unless it was a French journalist.

"Why might I find it interesting?"

Another pause, longer than before. "I don't want to talk about it on the telephone. Can we meet somewhere?"

"Sorry Sammy," Robbie said. "Wild horses couldn't drag me into town today. I just got back from a month's swing through West Africa and the Horn and I plan to spend today getting reacquainted with my own house."

"May I come to your house then?" he said, and when she hesitated, he added, "I think it might be a story for you."

Robbie closed her eyes. The last thing she wanted was a story, any kind of story, much less a local Ooga-Booga story. "Oh, all right, come on over."

Sammy was at the front gate within the hour. Her *askari,* who would let Jack the Ripper onto the grounds with a salute just because he was white, would not admit a brother African until he had cleared it with the *memsaab.* Racism operated on many levels in Africa.

"Sammy! Want some lunch?" Robbie said as he stepped up onto the veranda.

"No, *asante sana.*"

"You sure? I've taught Alphonse how to make an authentic Philly cheesesteak; he makes 'em better than Pat's King of Steaks, even better than Jim's on South Street. I'm going to have one, maybe two."

"No, no thank you."

She shrugged. "Suit yourself, but you're missing a bet. I even have real Cheez Whiz pigeoned in from the States."

Now that he was here, Robbie was no longer put out with Samwel for nagging her into thinking about work on her first full day home. Like so many expatriates, she had discovered that it was much more difficult to make African friends than she had anticipated, and Sammy was one of the few she had. He was well educated and a competent journalist, even if he did work for a paper that was little more than a KANU party house organ. He was also a valuable source, privy to the jealousies and intrigues among government officials. It was nice to know such things even if she never wrote about Kenya politics. Few in the Afrika Korps hack-pack did; no one wanted to run the risk of pissing off a big shot and getting booted out of the only comfortable, English-speaking base in black Africa.

Sammy also amused Robbie; it was always good to see him, if only to see what he was wearing. Short and homely, he was nonetheless every inch the dandy when it came to his clothes. Today, he had on a dark blue suit, flaming red suspenders, and a black silk shirt. A red-and-blue polka-dot cravat was at his throat, and a red flower in his buttonhole. His two-tone shoes, blue and white, reminded Robbie of a late 1950s DeSoto. Crowning this sartorial statement was a wide-brimmed white hat with a bright red band. He looked, Robbie thought, like a North Philadelphia pimp.

"Well at least sit and have some coffee with me," she said.

Sammy didn't move. His eyes probed the garden, lingering for a beat on William, her gardener, who was busily raking up violet petals from the jacaranda trees, then moving up, above the privet hedge, settling at last on the house next door.

"Could we go inside to talk?" he said.

Robbie smiled. African journalists were conspiratorial *and* paranoid.

The house next door belonged to Dada, who was the widow of Ndugu, Jomo Kenyatta's closest friend. Just how close was evident in the honorific name Mzee had bestowed upon him. In Swahili, *ndugu* meant brother, as in "Brother of the Nation." Ndugu's one and only wife, by default, became *dada,* "Sister of the Nation." As far as anyone knew, Ndugu hadn't been the Old Man's real brother, but rather his *ndugu wa kupanga,* his "brother by arrangement." Both he and Dada— she was widely thought to be the more intelligent of the two and, over time, became the more powerful partner—had served the President as ministers without portfolio and had lived at State House. Dada had been permitted to stay on there after her husband's death, but her relatives lived in the Muthaiga house, which was patrolled night and day by plainclothes General Service Unit troops and Rhodesian Ridgeback dogs. Robbie remembered the day Dada's family had moved into their newly finished house from their home *shamba* outside Thika, pulling up in a convoy of Army trucks loaded down with cooking pots and mattresses, even a few goats and chickens. They had looked like a family of Okies fleeing the Dust Bowl.

Dada's house was a typical example of what Robbie called "Third World A-Go-Go" architecture; a huge, layer-cake, peach stucco monstrosity, out of place among Muthaiga's predominantly English country-style bungalows. She had never been asked in, but she suspected that the interior was just as bad, or worse, all done up with the same expensive bad taste that one saw in so many of the Asian homes, with blocky uncomfortable furniture, wild colors and fluorescent overhead lights, or maybe one of those tassel-shaded lamps shaped like a nude, pissing cherub.

Samwel was raptly watching the guards play cards on the third-floor balcony, their machine guns resting on the ledge.

"They have no idea who you are," Robbie said. "And Dada only comes to visit once a week. On Thursdays."

"Humor me," Samwel said.

"I know what you're up to, you sneaky shit," she said with a laugh. "You're just trying to whet my appetite with all this cloak-and-dagger stuff. But okay, we'll go inside."

Samwel grinned and Robbie looped her arm in his and led the way into the sitting room. She had changed into bleached Levi's, a ratty old Temple Owls short-sleeved sweatshirt, and Birkenstock sandals. With Sammy in his fop's togs and Robbie dressed like an American teeny-bopper, they were definitely an odd couple.

Alphonse had her cheesesteak ready and she gnawed on it while Samwel decorously sipped a cup of tea. "Now then," she said once they were settled and Alphonse was out of the room. "What's so newsworthy about a dead poacher in the Aberdares?"

"I'm not sure."

"Not sure?" Robbie said. "Then what's all this mystérioso shit."

Samwel was staring at her. "Do all American women curse the way you do? It's most unladylike. You're not at all like a British lady."

"I'm not a goddamned lady, I'm a foreign correspondent," she said. "And I'm sure as hell no horse-faced, horse's ass British lady. Now what do you mean you're not sure?"

Sammy shrugged. "When I saw the story in the *Nation* this morning, I thought it might make a good story for us, too. It happened in Kikuyuland, after all, in the heartland of KANU's constituency, and we like to focus on news in that area. So I rang up the Kenya Police. Normally they are most cooperative with my newspaper, but when I mentioned this case I got . . . how do you call it? . . . the runaround. They would tell me nothing beyond what was already in print, and when I persisted I was threatened."

"What kind of threats?" Robbie asked, growing interested in spite of herself.

Samwel shrugged again. "The usual . . . if you know what is good for you, you will discontinue your inquiries . . . that sort of thing."

"So what did you do?"

"I have a good source at District Police Headquarters in Nyeri, so I rang him. He told me there was talk of a poaching gang running wild in the park, a big one, and that all of the district officials were quite agitated about it. He said that the man who was murdered was brutally tortured before he was killed, that he'd been disfigured in some kind of ritualistic way."

"Disfigured how?"

Samwel told her while Robbie's cheesesteak lay half-eaten on her plate. She was definitely interested now. "So the victim was a poacher killed by his own gang," she said. "Your basic falling out among thieves."

"No, no," Sammy said quickly. "The chap who was murdered was a local man. How do you say it? . . . small potatoes. He went into the park with his brother, who is still missing, and the gang caught him and killed him."

"As a warning to others not to poach on the poachers?"

Sammy's face lit up. "That's it!" He was getting excited himself. "Anyway, several animals already have been killed by this gang. A *kifaru*, a rhinoceros. And a leopard. Those were the two most recent. And there are rumors going around Nyeri that this same gang has killed dozens of other animals in the past several weeks, in Tsavo East and in Meru."

Robbie waited for Samwel to go on, but he seemed to have finished. "What else did you find out?" she prompted.

"That's all. But just as I rang off, my editor comes over to my desk and says to me, and I quote, 'discontinue your inquiries.' The exact same words the police had used. They called him and told him to stop me. I'm sure of it."

Robbie sat back, disappointed. "Real interesting, Sammy, but I still don't see anything in it for *Newsweek*. It sounds like cops and robbers in the woods, nothing more."

"I know, I know," Samwel said impatiently. "But you must understand how these things work. On something like this it's all in the voices, the gestures. There is something big going on, something the authorities are anxious to conceal. I would stake my life on it."

"So tell your editor to go fuck himself and go for it."

Samwel winced, then smiled. "I said I'd stake my life on it, not my career."

Robbie smiled back. Samwel had once told her that he did not expect to be a journalist all his life, that he wanted to get into politics someday. If he kept his superiors happy, he'd told her, KANU might put him up as the MP from Muranga.

"If it's such a great story, why are you so anxious to give it away?" she asked. "To me?"

Samwel pulled a red silk handkerchief from the breast pocket of his suit jacket and dabbed at his lips. "You are my friend and I wanted to make you a gift of it," he said with a disingenuous smile. "Besides, it is too dangerous for me. Only the foreign press can touch it."

Robbie laughed, an unrestrained, almost girlish laugh. "Sammy, you'll make a perfect politician some day. The Frank Rizzo of East Africa. You're such a bullshit artist."

He giggled happily and said, "I still have a few sources that my superiors do not know about, like my policeman friend in the Nyeri HQ, and I could pass whatever they tell me on to you. Think about it."

Robbie picked up her sandwich, which was stone cold, and chewed on it absentmindedly, thinking about it, as Sammy had suggested. She had spent all morning looking for a story that would keep her home, and perhaps this was it on a plate. In itself, it was not a story of great interest to the average American reader or, more to the point, to the average American editor. But ever since the ban on hunting, and the subsequent rise in poaching, she had been searching for a peg on which to hang a take-out, perhaps even a cover, on endangered species. She could almost see the tag-line now: "The End of the Game: Africa's Vanishing Wildlife." It would make a perfect *Newsweek* cover, with lots of color pictures of sweet imperiled animals accompanied by tear-jerking text. The idea had been sitting on her back burner for a long time, just waiting for an excuse to happen, and a poacher war might provide that excuse. Properly played, such a story could keep her off that midnight plane to Booga-Booga for up to a month. Maybe longer.

"Okay, Sammy. I'll toss it to the crocodiles in New York and see if they swallow it."

"Wonderful," Samwel said, beaming. "It will make a good story. We will make a good team." He stood, smoothing out his creases.

"Okay, see what you can dig up," she said. "I'll check with the police. Let's see if they give me the same bullshit they gave you. Any other suggestions on where I should start? The East African Wildlife Association maybe?"

"No, go to the power," Sammy said, setting his hat at a rakish angle. "See the Assistant Minister of Wildlife if you can; he's the official responsible for anti-poaching efforts. He also can clear it for you to talk to others, like the park warden."

"Fine," she said, showing him out to the veranda. "I'll see what I can do." They parted with a handshake at the foot of the porch steps and she watched him sneak across the lawn to the front gate. He was fussing with his broad-brimmed hat, using it to screen his face from any curious eyes that might be watching from Dada's house next door.

Robbie was in and out of the Assistant Minister's office in less than half an hour, her notebook full and a dazed look on her face. She had never met such a friendly, charming, and cooperative government official in all her eighteen months in Africa. The man was a Tastykake, a real sweetie pie.

She rode the elevator to the bottom of Jogoo House and stepped out into a dank, dimly lit hallway. She consulted her notes and went to the left, counting doors. At the third door on the right, she stopped and knocked.

"Come." The voice was deep and forceful.

Robbie opened the door and went in smiling. "Inspector Odongo? I believe you're expecting me."

The man's face said otherwise. He was sitting behind his desk staring slack-jawed at her. He broke off to look down at the slip of paper in his hand, then stared at her some more.

Did she have the wrong office? "The . . . umm . . . the Assistant Minister called you a few minutes ago to ask if you would see me?" she prompted, ready to apologize.

"You are not Robert Lewis of *Newsweek* magazine," he announced.

"You're absolutely right, I'm not," Robbie said with a grin. "But I am Roberta Lewis of *Newsweek* magazine. Friends call me Robbie."

The policeman scrambled to his feet. "I'm so sorry," he said, plainly embarrassed. "Please. Let me get you a seat." He excavated a chair from one corner of the tiny office by sweeping a stack of papers onto the floor, and set it down beside his own behind the desk; there was no room in front of the desk. They were so close together their knees were almost touching.

"The minister has asked me to cooperate fully with you, Miss Lewis," he said. "So how may I help you?"

Robbie, who had on the Ralph Lauren brushed-denim outfit she always wore to official interviews, carefully crossed her legs, trying not to kick Inspector Odongo in the shin or give him a peek up her skirt, and flipped open her notebook. "The Assistant Minister has filled me in on the murder, and on the poaching gang you're after," she said, "and I hoped you might tell me in more detail how this special anti-poaching unit of yours plans to go about catching these people."

Inspector Odongo was staring openmouthed at her again. He seemed to be having difficulty breathing. When he finally spoke, his voice was a hoarse croak. "H-He did *what*? He told you *what*?"

Puzzled, Robbie started to repeat it, but Odongo held up a hand. "I heard you, Miss Lewis. I'm just finding it hard to believe that that idiot told you these things."

"Oh?" Robbie said, startled herself; she had never heard an African civil servant call his superior an idiot before. A more common experience was the underling who gushed about the nobility of his boss. "Well, I thought it was nice of him. He was quite helpful."

"To you, perhaps," Inspector Odongo said, an edge to his voice. "But not to me, and not to our mission."

"I think he's just anxious to show that his ministry is doing something about the poaching problem in this country," she said, surprised to hear herself defending a bureaucrat. "I really don't see what you're so upset about, Inspector."

"I'm upset because if you write a story it will undercut our effort even before it gets under way," Odongo said softly. "The poachers would hear of it; your magazine is sold on the street here. They will know how many we are, and what we are doing. They might decide to shift their operation elsewhere, and then we will have to find them again. At the very least, the element of surprise will be lost."

Robbie started to say something, but Odongo held up his hand to stop her again. "Look, Miss Lewis. I don't mean to be rude, but this is our best chance to corner and catch these people and I cannot have meddling foreign journalists ruining that opportunity. These men we're after are not mere poachers any longer, they are man-killers."

"I'm well aware of that, Inspector Odongo," Robbie said testily; she did not appreciate being called a meddler. "But your activities would just be a lead-in to a bigger story on the poaching problem and how it relates to the larger issue of endangered wildlife. My editors are planning to do a major cover story, and that takes time. I wouldn't have it in print until at least a month from now. Whatever you're doing should be done by then."

The inspector heard her out with pursed mouth and hooded eyes, full of suspicion. When she finished, he said: "Perhaps it will be, perhaps not. It makes no difference. I know how you journalists work. You poke into things and ask questions. Each person you talk to will be another person who knows what is going on. The chances of information leaking out multiply accordingly." He shook his head. "I am sorry, Miss Lewis, but I cannot help you."

Robbie just shrugged and began flipping back through the pages of her notebook. "Hmm, let's see now," she murmured, as if talking to herself, then she began to read snippets of her notes. "A six-man team . . . led by a former professional hunter named Glenton . . . base of operations, a private game sanctuary at Mweiga called . . . hmm, let's see, ah, here it is . . . Aberdare Ranch. . . ."

Odongo interrupted. "You can't use it."

Robbie made a show out of turning to the first page and scrutinizing it. "Hmm, can't seem to find where the Assistant Minister says anything about being off the record. No, uh-uh, nope. Looks to me like I can quote directly." Robbie looked up at the scowling policeman and gave him her sweetest smile.

"I don't know what he could have been thinking of," the inspector said mournfully, his tone conceding defeat.

Robbie felt a sudden sympathy for him. His reasons for not wanting a journalist nosing around made sense. Much more sense, really, than the publicity-hound Assistant Minister's indiscretions. Not that it cut much ice with her. Odongo had his job to do, she had hers. But she did feel sorry for him.

"Inspector," she said gently. "You know what we say about loose-lipped politicos like the Assistant Minister back where I come from?"

"What?"

"His brains are in his ass."

The inspector gaped for a moment, then let loose with a bellowing laugh, nodding to himself and spluttering, "Yes, oh yes."

She waited until he wound down to a chuckle, then said: "Look, Inspector. I think I know a way out of our dilemma if you're interested."

Inspector Odongo grew instantly serious. "Yes, I am very interested."

"Okay, here's the way it reads to me. You don't want me blowing your anti-poaching operation and I need to have more details from you if I'm going to write a sexy story, right?"

"Uh, right."

"All right then, let's cut a deal."

"Cut a deal?"

"Yeah. You know, a trade-off. For my part, I'll go ahead and start gathering stuff for the harmless part of the story, talk to the animal preservation groups and the like, but I'll hold off on your part of it until you catch these creeps. In other words, I won't go poking into things and asking questions."

Odongo was watching her warily, but he couldn't help smiling when he heard himself quoted with such precision.

"And for my part?" he asked.

"You deal me in on your operation," Robbie said. "I get informed about everything that goes on. I get full access to the men on your team, especially this Glenton guy. I get to be there when you bring in the poachers. And I get it all on an exclusive basis."

Inspector Odongo took almost a full minute to think it over, then he nodded.

"Terrific!" Robbie said, slapping her notebook shut and showing him a mouthful of perfect white teeth. "You nail the bad guys and I'll write a story that will make you a goddamn international hero. Bambi's bodyguard."

The inspector smiled uncertainly, shaking his head in amazement.

"So that's our deal," Robbie said. "Any questions?"

"One," Odongo said. "Do all American women curse the way you do?"

7

Rumuruti was a town at the edge of things. It lay in a kind of no-man's-land between two very different worlds, the high grassy plain of the Laikipia Plateau and the horizonless desert of the Northern Frontier District. From the airy plateau, the NFD looked like Hell's forge. From the parboiled desert, the Laikipia was a cool glimpse of Heaven itself. The tiny town sat sandwiched between them like a girl on a porch swing with two suitors, unable to make up her mind and wondering where her destiny lay.

The elegiac sense of homecoming that Adrian had felt in Nakuru was long gone by the time he got to Rumuruti. That was not so surprising; he had less of an emotional investment in Rumuruti. By the time Pate had taken over the Hudsons' farm early in 1964, less than two months after independence, Adrian had been out on his own for nearly a year, living in Nairobi and single-handedly running Bushbuck Safaris Ltd., struggling to build it into a full-time business. So while his memories of Laikipia Farm were good ones, they were associated more with the Hudsons and the African staff than with his father.

His meandering pilgrimage had meant a late start out of Nakuru and he had spent the night in Nyahururu, at Thomson's Falls Lodge, the old Harry's Hotel. He had telephoned Odongo from there to learn that the inspector had been true to his word; he had found a Kikuyu, one of the Field Force rangers from the park, a man who came highly recommended. Adrian had gone to bed early, immediately after supper, but he awakened tired, kept up half the night by the roaring of the Karinaru River spilling over the falls at a rate of twenty thousand gallons per minute.

Now, yet again, here he was trespassing on what once had been Glenton land, sneaking in through the gate farthest from the main compound and rocketing down the dirt road leading to the African *boma*.

From the look of things, not much had changed in the two years since he had last seen the place. Despite Pate's bitter speculation about what the new owner had done to it, the farm looked to be in good nick. The fences were mended and all the posts were straight; the gates hung properly on their hinges; and, judging from the condition of the meadow, the sprinklers still worked. The true test, of course, was in the crop, and those cattle that Adrian could see from the road seemed to be in excellent shape.

He was halfway to the laborers' settlement when he saw that he was not going to make it undetected. Another vehicle, a Land Rover as old and dented as his own, was cutting across the pasture to intercept him. It pulled to a stop in front of him, blocking the way. A white man cradling a double-bore shotgun got out and stood in the road.

Adrian braked and poked his head out of the window, but before he could say anything, the man called out: "Step out, laddie, and let's have a look at you. But *pole pole,* eh?"

Adrian killed the motor and got down slowly, *pole pole,* keeping his eyes on the man. If you could dress an elephant, he thought, here was what you'd have. The man was not young, sixty or sixty-five, but powerfully built. He stood well over six feet and weighed perhaps seventeen stone. He wore a short-sleeved safari jacket, baggy shorts, a sweat-stained, floppy-brimmed hat and canvas plimsolls with no socks. Despite his size, his head was too big for his body, and his ruddy face, devastated by smallpox scars, made Glenton think of mince. In his hands, which were as big as the rest of him, the shotgun looked like a harmless toy.

"Now then, laddie, just where the bloody hell might you be goin'?" he said, holding the shotgun so that it was loosely aimed at Adrian's groin. "This ain't a bloomin' game park, you know."

"And good day to you too, Mr. Wilkinson."

The man squinted and came closer, but he did not lower the shotgun. "Do you know me then?" he asked suspiciously.

"Yes. And you know me. Adrian Glenton. David Glenton's son."

The man squinted even harder, then smiled and exclaimed. "I'm buggered if it ain't! So, all growed up, are you? When I last saw you, you was what? . . . twelve? . . . thirteen?"

"And on holiday at the Hudsons'. You came to supper."

"So what brings you back here, laddie? And why didn't you stop by the house? I'd have shouted you a cup'a. Kettle was just beginnin' to boil when I spied your dust."

"I'd tell you, but it's rather difficult trying to talk with my balls in my throat," Adrian said, only partly in jest. "Mind pointing that thing somewhere else?"

"Oh, sorry," Jock Wilkinson said with a laugh. He raised the shotgun, resting the muzzle on his shoulder.

"I didn't go by the house because I didn't think I knew anyone at the house. Are you staying there now?"

"That's right," Wilkinson said with a dispirited sigh.

"What of your own farm?"

"Gone, laddie, same as yours. Not long after your father sold out, them bloody Wabenzis from Nai-robbery came sniffing round my place. And after seein' how they did him, I'm afraid I didn't put up much of a fight."

Adrian did not have to ask what a Wabenzi was. That was what Kenya's poor called the privileged elite, the monied few who rode about in Mercedes saloon cars, a symbol of power all across the continent. The literal translation of Wabenzi was "men of the Mercedes-Benz." The Wabenzi were modern Africa's newest tribe, as real as the Wakamba or the Watusi.

"It reminds me of what J. M. Kariuki used to say, before he was assassinated," Adrian said. "Kenya has become a nation of ten millionaires and ten million beggars."

Wilkinson hawked and spat. "Don't go quoting that Kuke bastard to me, laddie. I was chasing his Mau Mau arse round the Aberdares when you were no bigger than a dik-dik's dick. He was just another bleedin' sot Kikuyu, same as the rest."

Adrian did not agree, but he didn't argue. He changed the subject. "So what are you doing on our, er, on Laikipia Farm? Have you bought it?"

"It's Uhuru Farm now."

Adrian made a mental note to tell Pate; it would give him something more to complain about. Vic Hudson had poured his life into making a go of the ranch and Pate had honored his friend's hard work by keeping the original name.

"And no, laddie, I haven't bought it," Wilkinson said. "I just manage the place. Been runnin' it about a year now. Ever since I come back from the bloody U.K. I thought you'd have heard all about it."

Adrian shook his head. "I didn't even know you had sold your place, much less gone to England. My father didn't know either. Or at least he didn't tell me."

"The bloody wog who took my place brought in a chappie of his own to run it for him, so the missus and I decided to move back to the U.K.," Wilkinson said. "Back to the Midlands after forty years in this country. And what do I find there? Land prices too dear for anyone but a bleedin' lord. No work to be had, even if I knew anything besides farming. Shiftless bastards tellin' me not to worry none, tellin' me to kick off me bloody boots and go on the dole." Wilkinson's voice shook with indignation. "Lasted all of six months, I did."

Adrian nodded in commiseration. It was a familiar enough tale by now, but that, and the fact that Wilkinson should have known better, did nothing to dilute his sympathy. Too many of his friends had suffered the same disillusioning experience.

The white exodus touched off by *Uhuru* had been followed by a slow but steady return flow when those who had panicked and left discovered what was waiting for them in England, or Australia, or New Zealand, or South Africa. Many of them had been second- or, like Adrian, third-generation Kenyans who had never even been to England on holiday. It had not taken them long to conclude that they had pitched up on an alien shore. They simply could not cope with the climate, the cuisine, the prices, the manners, anything. They even had difficulty with the language, speaking, as they did, a hybrid colonial *patois* liberally salted with Swahili and Hindi words which provoked blank stares from Britons so long removed from the glory days of the Empire.

But those had been minor aggravations. In the end, what invariably defeated Kenya's white emigrants was claustrophobia, the overwhelming conviction that every last square inch of that miserable, suffocating little island was in use. People who had grown up with the sweeping distances of the Great Rift Valley came back from London complaining of severe headaches and blurred vision, caused, so they claimed, by their gaze constantly slamming into things, terrace houses, or office buildings, or one bloody thing or another.

That, and the absence of Africans. It was something they had trouble putting into words, if they even deigned to try, but Adrian knew what they meant. It was a great irony, a great joke, but the truth was that they had missed the very people they were running away from. They missed the sight, the sound, even the smell of Africans. The sing-song chanting of a work gang. The unchained laughter of gossiping *ayahs*. The tangy smell of woodsmoke in the early evening. The pure joy in life that had surrounded them all of their lives. They may not have chosen to take an active part in that life, but it had always been there for them, like a warm hearth.

Some of Adrian's homesick friends had taken to wandering the streets of London's Notting Hill, where so many immigrant Africans and Asians—as the Indians were called in East Africa—lived, just to be in familiar surroundings. Many of those who tried resettling in white-ruled South Africa, where there certainly was no dearth of natives, came back. Even the unreconstructed found apartheid a bit too much for them, a sterile and impenetrable barrier between them and the powerful life force of the African.

It had been as bad, if not worse, for their parents and grandparents. If anyone should have known better than to try to leave Kenya, it had been those of Pate's and Wilkinson's and Victor Hudson's generation, most of whom had been born in Africa just before, or just after, the Great War. But some of them had left, and some had returned, and some who remained in England, like Uncle Vic, only did so because they died before they could get back. Of a broken heart, Aunt Jeanne insisted.

It wasn't until they were back in Hull or Blackpool that they remembered exactly what it was that had brought them, or their fathers before them, out to Africa in the first place. They had come looking for nothing less than Eden, Eden in the here and now; a paradise regained for those with sense enough to abandon the failed promise of England. And, for a while at least, they'd found it. Sweeping, untrodden landscapes. Air untainted by the grimy stacks of Birmingham and Sheffield and Manchester and Leeds. Great herds of the Lord's own creatures running free. And no restrictive class system to keep a man tethered to the circumstances of his birth. It was a country where a man's children could grow up free and healthy, and he himself, with a bit of luck, an understanding banker, and some half decent weather, could grow rich. There were cooks to do the cooking, houseboys to do the cleaning, *ayahs* to nurse the children, field hands to tend the crops, *mchungas* to herd the cows, *syces* to groom the horses, gun-bearers to bear the guns. In Kenya they could live like gentry, but without the snooty airs that went along with the closed country life in England.

It was inevitable, Adrian supposed, that the experience of those early settlers, like the pioneer experience of the American West and the Boers' Great Trek across South Africa, would assume mythical trappings. Like the Indian Raj, or the antebellum South, Kenya—or "Keen-ya" as they called it—must, indeed, have seemed like Paradise before the Fall.

Never mind—until it was too late—that the Africans of "Ken-ya" were simultaneously mapping an Eden of their own, one free of British magistrates with their powdered-wig laws, and Christian missionaries with their powdered-face God. Their vision of a new, African Eden was rooted in the heady notion of independence, of freedom, of *Uhuru,* a conviction that if the white serpent could only be driven from the garden then Paradise would surely follow.

The ensuing clash between two cultures unable to agree even on how to pronounce the battlefield's name, put paid at last to the white myth called "Keen-ya." Like the Raj before it, it stood no chance against the overboiling of native hopes and expectations. The Brits— despite his English bloodline, Adrian considered himself African, not British—never did twig to the idea that their very presence in East Africa was their original sin, that racism was their apple, and history their serpent.

Since that time, of course, both Englishman and African had fallen from grace, had been expelled from the Garden. The white Eden, founded on colonialism, had collapsed beneath the weight of a historical tidal wave. The black Eden, founded on the golden apple of *Uhuru*, had grown wormy with corruption and mismanagement.

Even had they known what would happen, Adrian believed, many of the whites who left at the time of *Uhuru* would have come back chastened, convinced that even Eden after the Fall was better than the U.K. They were not running the show in "Keen-ya" any longer, but they still could, and did, feel superior. Like Pate, they could sit in their clubs and tell "wog" stories, and say "I bloody well told you so" each time something went wrong. Besides, their money went farther in Kenya.

Jock Wilkinson was still talking. "This chappie I manage for ain't a bad sort, really. . . ." Then, remembering who he was talking to, he quickly amended, ". . . for a bloomin' highwayman that is, of course. Everyone knows he pinched this land from your family. What I meant is that he comes up to examine the books two or three times a year and leaves me be the rest of the time."

"I know what you meant, Mr. Wilkinson," Adrian said with a rueful smile. "No need to tread lightly. The subject is not the same exposed nerve for me as it is for my father."

"So how is the old warrior?"

"Getting older."

Wilkinson sighed. "Ain't we all, laddie. Ain't we all."

They fell silent, out of things to talk about. Wilkinson watched the cattle, taking quick inventory. Adrian was gazing off to the north, down into the devil's anvil of the Northern Frontier District, where columns of dust rose from the desert floor.

Wilkinson followed his gaze. "That'll be Simon Evans. He works the tourist trade now, runnin' camel safaris into the NFD."

When Adrian did not respond, Wilkinson said: "You still ain't told me where you was goin' to, laddie. To the African *boma*, looks like."

"I'm looking for two Dorobo brothers, Damon and Pythias. They're twins, about my age. Have you heard of them?"

Wilkinson was nodding. "Best bloody trackers I ever saw. Besides, with names like that how could I not hear of 'em?"

"My mother gave them those names when they were *totos*, maybe five or six years old," Adrian said. "They were always together, and she couldn't pronounce their Dorobo names."

"Fine woman, your mum. Wasn't much she couldn't do. I'd see her now and again when she came up to visit the Hudsons. Ah, green monkey disease, wasn't it?"

When Adrian did not respond to the question, Wilkinson cleared his throat and said, "So them two Dorobo boys was at Nakuru with you?"

Adrian smiled. "The three of us were inseparable when I was growing up. Most of what I know of hunting I learned from them. Their father was our headman at Bushbuck Farm. Here too, until a couple of years ago. He was killed by a mamba."

"I remember."

"Are they still here?" Adrian asked. "The brothers, not the snakes."

"One of 'em is," Wilkinson said, "but I couldn't begin to tell you which. Never could keep them straight."

"Pythias has a scar on his upper arm where it was sliced through to the bone. I put it there. I was nine and they were trying to teach me to throw a spear."

"Let's go find out, shall we?" Wilkinson said. "You can follow me, though I imagine you know the way well enough."

The two men went back to their Land Rovers, and drove the remaining three miles to the African *boma.* The *boma* was home to close to a hundred people, most of them wives and children of the ranch laborers. While the inside staff lived in the main compound, in cement-block servants' quarters next to the owner's house and the overseer's cottage, Wilkinson's place now, those who did outside work, which consisted mainly of tending the herd, lived in the *boma,* a self-contained, miniature village, with vegetable gardens, a *duka,* and a small school. There also was a garage shed where bush mechanics kept the ranch's machinery and vehicles in working order.

They checked in with the headman, who was new to Adrian but quickly became all smiles and handshakes when he saw that the stranger was escorted by *Bwana* Wilkinson, more than happy to dispatch someone to fetch whomever Adrian wanted.

It turned out to be Pythias.

The Dorobo recognized Glenton from fifty yards away and came running, his arms out, exclaiming in English: "Adrian! Adrian! You are here!"

Wearing silly grins, the two men, both of them sporting streaks of gray in their hair, embraced and began pounding on each other, suddenly boys again. The Dorobo, barely five feet tall, more than a foot shorter than Adrian, still looked like a boy.

"So, you have come to claim your brother," Pythias said happily in Kalenjin, the language of the Dorobo.

Adrian pushed up the African's sleeve and ran a finger across the scar on his arm. "Why not? You must belong to me. You bear my brand."

Pythias laughed. "You became a great hunter, my brother, but it is a good thing there are rifles. Otherwise you would have died from hunger long ago."

"Mr. Wilkinson tells me that Damon is no longer here," Adrian said, switching to Swahili so Wilkinson could follow along. "Where has he gone?"

Pythias grew solemn. "North. Into the Turkana country."

"But I can't imagine one of you without the other. Did anything happen between you? Did you quarrel?"

Pythias shook his head. "If only we had. Quarrels can be undone, but what he has done cannot be," he said sorrowfully. "He has fallen in love. With a Turkana woman."

It was all Adrian could do not to burst into laughter. Careful to keep his tone serious, he asked, "A Turkana? How did they meet?"

"He was out hunting hyrax when he came upon one of their camel trains. He passed time with them and started talking to this girl. . . ." Pythias sighed. "Four days he spent with them."

"And now he's gone to live among her people?"

"He had no choice; she would not come here. And who can argue with a Turkana woman? That's what happens when the men of a tribe treat their women equally. But what do you expect from men who aren't circumcised? Luo men are not circumcised either, but even they do not treat all women as if they were their mothers. The Turkana are strange."

"They are also nomads. Do you know where in the Turkana country he went?"

"He's told me where the clan camps at different times of the year, but I've had no word from him in nearly a year. The smell of pussy has made him forget his friends, his brother."

"Has he married her?"

"Not yet, I think. Their marriage process is long, three years or so. Partly because brides are expensive and it takes a man a long time to gather enough animals for a dowry. Also, the man and woman must wean their first child before they are married. The Turkana are very strange."

Adrian wondered how a Dorobo could acquire enough camels or cows for a wife. The Dorobo were hunters, not herders. Even their name, which came from the Masai *il-torrobo*, meant "poor man," or "person without cattle."

"Well, I hope she was handsome at least," Adrian said.

Pythias shrugged. "If you like small asses." Then, after a pause, he admitted, "I never met her. But I saw her when I went out to the Turkana camp to try to talk Damon out of it." He sighed and conceded reluctantly, "She did have good tits, I guess, and those welts they raise on their bodies are said to make fucking more exciting."

Wilkinson, who had been listening, gave a sage nod and said in English: "Cicatrice decorations. Body bumps, I call 'em. And they do make the old humpy-pumpy more exciting, by Christ."

Adrian and Pythias both stared at Wilkinson in surprise, then dissolved into laughter. The big man's reddish face went even redder. "I was a randy young bucko meself once," he said defensively. "I wasn't always an old fart."

"Neither was I," Adrian chided him, "but I don't know a thing about body bumps."

Wilkinson grinned sheepishly. "In younger days, I spent a bit of time in the Sudan, among the Nuba."

"I won't let on to your missus if Pythias won't," Adrian said. Then, with a sly smile, he said: "He couldn't very well bandy it about if he weren't here, now could he? So how would you feel about me borrowing him for two or three weeks?"

"You bein' serious now, laddie, or are you still having me on?" Wilkinson asked.

"Quite serious," Glenton answered. He turned to Pythias to explain: "I've taken on a hunting job for the Ministry of Wildlife. If you fancy a change of scenery, I'd like you to come along as my chief tracker. The job pays one thousand shillings a month."

"I don't care what it pays," Pythias said. "It would be an honor to hunt with you again. It would be like old times." He turned to Jock Wilkinson with imploring eyes.

"Is your work caught up, laddie?" Wilkinson asked. "Have you taken care of that big *simba* I told your headman about? I don't want to go findin' any more dead cows on that section."

"*Ndiyo, bwana. Simba* is gone."

"Got a permit to pot a bothersome lion, did you?" Adrian said.

Wilkinson snorted. "A bloke's got to pay too much bribe money to get a permit these days, laddie. Besides, you don't need a permit just to talk some sense into a lion, do you?"

"I talked to *simba* hard," Pythias said, still in English. "She left."

"Then I suppose I could spare you for a week or two."

"*Asante, bwana. Asante sana.*"

"I have a place for Damon as well," Adrian told Pythias in Swahili. "Do you think we can track him down?"

The Dorobo shrugged and said, "I can track anything that moves." Simple truths did not add up to arrogance.

"More to the point," Adrian said with a smile, "when we do find him can we pry him loose from this Turkana woman of his?"

Pythias shrugged again and said, "Who knows?"

Wilkinson used his floppy hat to mop the sweat from his face, then plunked it back on his balding head. "The NFD is no country to trifle with, laddie. By all rights, you should be going in convoy with at least one other vehicle. Afraid I can't offer to go with you," he said, "but I can see to it that you have the proper provisions. How are you fixed?"

Adrian closed his eyes and ran through the checklist in his head, ticking the items off aloud: "Petrol, two spare wheels, spare fan belt and hoses, puncture repair kit, patches, full set of tools, tow rope, winch. I keep all those things in the Land Rover anyway. But I'll need some bottled water, tinned food, and medical supplies."

"And a rifle, laddie. That's *shifta* country you'll be goin' through."

Adrian shook his head. "Mine are locked away. Law of the land, you know."

"Not for country folks, it ain't," Wilkinson said. "I've five or six on special permit and I'll shout you one. But for God's sake don't lose it or let an army patrol catch you with it. Do, and it's my arse. Now let's go along to the house and I'll get you the things you'll be needin'."

Adrian turned to Pythias and said, "Why don't you get your things together and I'll pick you up here in about an hour."

The Dorobo nodded happily, his face nearly disfigured by his smile. He turned to trot away, then stopped and came back to tell Wilkinson: "When I talked to *simba* I had to talk very hard to get her to go away and leave us alone. So hard that I talked her out of her skin. Would you like to have it for the floor of your house?"

8

They came up out of the semiarid valley and into a lush and verdant landscape. Kikuyuland. As they climbed, the country changed colors, going from yellow to brown to a dozen shades of green. The dry bushland and flat-topped acacias of the low veldt fell away, yielding first to the blood-red flame trees and purple jacarandas of the foothills and then to the green coffee trees and banana palms of the highlands.

Adrian had set a circuitous course for Turkana country, driving south from Rumuruti rather than north, as far south as Mweiga on the eastern slope of the Aberdares. He had to arrange for a base camp before doing anything else.

Aberdare Ranch sat by itself on a shelf of the Aberdare Range. It was a big property, twenty-five thousand acres, and as mist-bound as its namesake, with one entire side sharing a common border with the park. The main residence was in a copse of trees on the side opposite the park. Glenton found Stephen Hone there on the veranda, just sitting down to his afternoon tea.

Hone looked up as Adrian got out of the Land Rover. "Isn't it odd how you always turn up at exactly half past four, just in time for tea and biscuits?" he said, as if it had been days rather than months since he had last seen him. Then, spotting Pythias, he added, "Tell your chappie there that if he's clever enough to find the kitchen, my cook will get him a bowl of *posho*."

"You've just told him. He speaks English," Adrian said, slapping the dust from his clothing. "And to hell with your bloody tea and biscuits. I need a beer. *Baridi sana.*"

Hone translated the order into Swahili for the servant who was pouring tea: "A beer for the gentleman. Very cold."

While Pythias trailed the houseman inside, Adrian came up the steps and dropped into a chair made of thorn branches. The veranda looked out over an immaculately kept lawn, then a brushy depression, affording a sweeping view of the mountains beyond, dark and brooding under lowering clouds.

"From the look of that sky the short rains will be early this year," Adrian said conversationally.

"I dare say you're right," Hone agreed, leaning over the glass-topped table between them to spoon sugar onto a biscuit, then stuffing the whole thing between chipmunk cheeks. Grains of sugar dusted the corners of his mouth.

Stephen Hone was a short, round, balding man in his mid-sixties. Physically, he reminded Adrian of Elmer Fudd in the Bugs Bunny cartoons that the Voice of Kenya aired on the telly in the afternoon. He had pink skin, smooth and hairless, and the doughy, unformed features of a pudgy infant. He did not look at all like the sort of man who had once had a price on his head. Fifty thousand shillings to be precise, offered by the Mau Mau general command in the waning days of the Emergency.

A retired British Army officer turned white hunter, Hone had been one of the masterminds behind the "pseudos," Kikuyus loyal to the crown and trained in infiltration techniques who disguised themselves in the long tresses and tattered rags of the Mau Mau and, posing as fugitives, joined the bona fide Mau Mau gangs that had operated in these very mountains. The intelligence passed on by the psuedos had been instrumental in turning the tide for the colonial government. Not that it mattered in the end; the uprising had done its job, persuading Whitehall that perhaps the time for independence talks had come.

Adrian, a mere boy when all of that was happening, had not met Hone until much later, when the Mau Mau ringleaders were either dead by way of a high rope or sanctified by high office, after Kenya became free. Stephen Hone, a hero to the white community, anathema to the black, had gone back to professional hunting for a time, but the years of chasing Mau Maus through the forest had taken their toll and, feeling his age, he had gone into semiretirement. Adrian had worked with him on a half dozen safaris over the years, on a subcontract basis, supplying the customers and a pair of young legs, while Hone provided an unmatched knowledge of the Aberdares and its game. They got on well together, and when the hunting ban ended their professional relationship, they remained close. About the time Adrian took his job with the tour company, Hone signed on to manage Aberdare Ranch for its wealthy American owner, a preservationist with a passion for rhinos. It was a comfortable arrangement, providing Hone with a modest income and giving him a home in his beloved Aberdares.

The servant returned with Adrian's beer, poured it into a pewter mug and left as silently as he'd come. The beer was colder than the Brits normally served it, but still too warm for Adrian, who had picked up a taste for ice-cold beer from his American clients. But it was wet and he was glad to have it. He drank it down in two greedy gulps while Hone munched contentedly on his sugared biscuits.

"Stephen, I've a favor to ask," Adrian began.

"Mmmm. I know. A police chappie rang up this morning to see if you had been in touch yet. Wanted to send up a lorry load of equipment."

"Ah, did he, ah, tell you what I have in mind?"

"In a roundabout way. Seemed like a decent enough sort. Odongo, his name was. Yes, Inspector Odongo. Must be Luo, yes?"

"Yes. I don't know him well, hardly at all really, but I think he's all right. A bit humorless but very professional." Adrian shrugged. "Who knows. He may even be competent."

"A competent public servant," Hone said musingly. "That would be a marvel, wouldn't it?"

When Hone did not volunteer anything more, Adrian took a deep breath and asked: "So what did you tell him?"

"That I'd be in the dog box if I let your chaps use this place and my Yank owner got wind of it."

"Yes, I suppose you would," Adrian said, trying to keep his disappointment from showing. "Well, no bother. We'll just make other arrangements. The park warden may be able to find a place for us in his headquarters."

"No need for that. I gave my permission. You can use the guest cottages over by the forest guard post. On the Treetops Salient."

Adrian exhaled with relief. "Thank you, Stephen."

"Just keep your people out of trouble and out of sight," Hone said. "It shouldn't be too difficult. The guard post is vacant most of the time and when there is someone there he's usually fast asleep."

Adrian nodded. "Thank you again. It's good of you."

"Don't mention it, old man. If there are poachers on my flank I want them disposed of before they jump the ditch and have a go at one of my rhinos."

"Don't worry," Adrian said. "I'll have them in irons within a fortnight at most."

"Yes, I dare say you will," Hone said, grinning. "Well, shall we be off to inspect your accommodations? The china's not exactly Wedgwood, but there's pots and pans, and towels and bedding. All the comforts of home."

Adrian laughed. "Most of my boys are used to sleeping on the ground, and they wouldn't know a fork from a cleft stick. But I would like to see the lay of the land."

"Lay of the land," Hone repeated, amused. "What a vulgar expression. But then most of your clients were Yanks, weren't they? I rather fancied European nobility myself. Gave one an excuse to fill the chop box with pâté rather than catsup."

Adrian could see Hone sprinkling sugar over foie gras. He laughed again and said, "You always were a snob."

Hone cast a disdainful eye over Adrian's Land Rover and insisted on using the ranch vehicle, a shiny new Toyota Land Cruiser. Skirting the ranch's airstrip, they bumped along a dirt road for half an hour before pulling up to a collection of modest cottages. There were three, arranged in a triangle, with a cottage at each of the points. Each house had a patch of freshly cropped lawn out front, girdled by a white picket fence. At the center of the triangle, equidistant from each bungalow, was a natural swimming pool, apparently fed by an underground spring. The overflow ran down a sluice for forty yards before emptying into the man-made ditch that separated Aberdare National Park from the maize and banana *shambas* on its eastern border.

"Well what do you think?" Hone asked with a smile as the two men got out of the Toyota. "Will it do?"

"A bit posh for my bunch, don't you think?" Adrian said. "I'll have the devil's own time of it getting them off their bums and out into the bush."

Hone laughed and started for the nearest bungalow, but Adrian was already striding away in the opposite direction, toward the game ditch.

Designed to keep the park animals out of the cultivation on the adjoining *shambas*, the ditch was roughly wedge shaped, eight foot wide at the top and nearly as deep, and all strung with a light wire fencing. On the whole, the ditch served its purpose, although now and then an elephant, finding the maize and banana trees on the opposite side too enticing to ignore, would use its tusks and weight to undercut the dirt banks and collapse the walls. The ditch wouldn't be much of a deterrent for a man either, Glenton saw at a glance. It would be merely a moment's work to scramble down one side and up the other. A moderately nimble man could leap it.

The Park Department's guard post was about fifty yards away and Glenton made for it, following the wire.

The post, nothing more than a dilapidated wooden shack made of weathered planking, was empty, and judging from the accumulation of dust and cobwebs, had been empty for a time. Adrian nodded in satisfaction and walked back to where Hone waited.

"Vacant?" Hone asked.

"Yes."

"Thought it might be. The warden should be able to keep it that way for you if it's prying eyes you're worried about."

"I'll have a word with him."

"Good. Now let's have a look at your new quarters, shall we?" Hone said, leading the way past the swimming pool. "I do hope you've brought along your bathing costume."

They spent the night at Aberdare Ranch, Adrian in one of the several guest rooms in the main house, Pythias on a spare cot in the servants' quarters, and were on their way by first light.

They went north on Highway A-2 along the front of Mount Kenya, catching a rare glimpse of Batian, Nelion, and Lenana, the mountain's three spiked peaks, clear of the usual morning cloud cover. As the road twisted, the snowcapped summit, the second highest in Africa at 17,058 feet, seemed to be moving, on their flank one moment, dead ahead the next.

For the first time in a long time, Adrian was in a fine mood. He had enjoyed a good visit with an old friend, a good supper, and a good night's sleep, uninterrupted by dreams of squawking tourists and squawking radios. For the first time in a long time, he felt as if his days had purpose.

His mood was buttressed by the grinning Pythias, perched like a small bird on the other end of the seat, impervious to the Land Rover's jolting ride, sunning himself in the glow of his own surprise reunions: with Adrian, his childhood friend; with the dense Aberdare rain forest, as natural and secure an environment for a Dorobo hunter as a mother's womb; and, soon now, with his brother Damon.

They passed Naro Moru, staging area for climbers intent on assaulting Mount Kenya's dozen glaciers, and went through the town of Nanyuki, crossing the Equator. Adrian thought of Rebmann and Krapf, the German evangelists who had brought the first reports of Mount Kenya back to London in 1849, only to be laughed down by members of the Royal Geographic Society, who could hardly have been expected to swallow the story of snow on the Equator.

From Nanyuki the road curved east, hugging the base of Mount Kenya until it broke through the high-country wheat on the north slope, a landscape as richly yellow as the sunflowers in a Van Gogh, and began its steep descent to the foot of the escarpment. Coming out of the wheat, Glenton could see deep into the Northern Frontier District, a stygian backdrop, as dramatic and as melancholy as the mountains of the moon.

As always, the first sight of the NFD fired Adrian with an excitement and an anticipation that was almost sexual, as though he were at the portals of a bridal chamber. Stretching before him was Kenya's last virgin wilderness, uncontaminated by the tourist-chasing, make-a-quid mentality of the rest of the country. For the next day or so, however long it took to find Damon, there would be no towns to speak of, no traffic, no crowds, no noise. Only Africa. Miles and miles of bloody Africa. Africa as his father and grandfather had known it.

The sense of separateness, of entering into a unique and vaguely ominous world, was heightened at the border post just beyond the little town of Isiolo. Adrian signed the log book, listing his destination, expected length of stay, and planned exit point. If he failed to sign out within twenty-four hours of the time he had noted, the rangers would launch a search.

The pavement ended at Isiolo. From the checkpoint to the Ethiopian border, a distance of nearly three hundred miles, A-2 was no more than a corrugated dirt track, hard and dusty in the dry months, soft and slick in the wet. The NFD did not get much rain, only a dozen or so inches a year, but what it did get often came in one or two torrential downpours, sending flash floods roaring through the *luggas* and washing away the camel paths that masqueraded as roads.

Thunderclouds were massed overhead but Adrian was counting on the rains holding off for another fortnight. That would still be early—the rains normally started in early November—but it would give him time to complete the job. Once the rains began, the difficulty of the APU's task would multiply tenfold.

Once past the NFD checkpoint, Adrian and Pythias saw two or three zebra-striped combis, loaded with tourists, but they all turned off around Archer's Post, bound for cozy lodges in the Samburu and Shaba game reserves. After that, they had the road to themselves. The rattling of the Land Rover, moving at top speed over the rut-ribbed road, discouraged conversation, and after a few shouting tries they gave up and turned to the passing scenery, watching for game with the expert eye of men who hunted for a living.

One did not see the same sheer numbers of animals in the Northern Frontier District that one did in such places as the Masai Mara, but for a supposedly empty region the NFD teemed with game. There were the usual species, albeit in far lesser numbers, but also wildlife found nowhere else in the country: long-horned beisa oryx and long-necked gerenuk, reticulated giraffe and blue-shanked Somali ostrich, and the rare Grevy's zebra, whose size and distinctive markings made it a favorite target of poachers. In the NFD, one did not have the feeling of being overwhelmed by nature's bounty, Adrian thought. Each animal seemed more of an individual, distinct and precious.

There was plenty of game, but few people. After passing a few Samburu out with their herds, they went mile after mile without seeing another human being. The NFD did indeed appear to be empty, but Glenton knew that several hundred thousand people wandered this blistered landscape, more than a dozen tribes large and small, most of them nomadic herders dependent on cattle, sheep, goats, donkeys, and camels for their survival. The Turkana lived on the western and south-ern shores of Lake Turkana. The Boran and the Gabbra ranged along the Ethiopian border, in the Chalbi Desert northwest of Marsabit. The Rendille kept to the Dida Galgalu, the Plain of Darkness. And the northeastern region was Somali country. The Samburu, cousins of the

Masai, lived between Isiolo and the Kaisut Desert, the region through which Adrian and Pythias were now passing.

And there was another frontier "tribe" to keep in mind: the *shifta,* armed gangs of bandits, most of them Somali, who often preyed on solitary vehicles using the Isiolo-Marsabit road. After a series of fierce skirmishes in the late 1960s, the Kenya Rifles, assisted by the British Army, had loosened the *shifta* choke-hold on the NFD, but some gangs remained, and they remained armed and dangerous. Adrian reached down to feel under the front seat, checking to see that Jock Wilkinson's double-bore shotgun was where he could get to it in a hurry.

In this place it could take all day to travel fifty miles, but they made good time. No vital parts fell off the Land Rover and, miraculously, they suffered none of the usual tire punctures. Not that it was easy going. The ceaseless jouncing threatened to turn internal organs into paste and a fine dust drifted around the passenger compartment, coating everything. By ten o'clock it was 110 degrees outside, and felt like twice that inside the Land Rover. The heat did not appear to bother Pythias, but sweat ran down Adrian's face in rivulets, giving his dust-covered features the look of a tribal mask.

It was midafternoon by the time they reached Marsabit, the last, and only, real town on their route, 215 miles from the Isiolo border post, nearly 300 miles from Aberdare Ranch. They stopped at the Marsabit Lodge just long enough to top up the petrol tanks and get a drink—a Tusker beer for Adrian, a lemon squash for Pythias—relaxing in the cool shade of the densely wooded mountain that rose incongruously up from the arid plain.

Resuming their journey, they drove west out of Marsabit without even a dirt track to guide them, navigating by means of a sagging but still hot sun. Instead of slowing them down, the absence of a road made things easier. This section of the Chalbi Desert was as level as a billiard table, a sun-cracked, smooth hardpan with only the odd volcanic hill on the horizon to give its flatness perspective. Full-blown mirages appeared and disappeared—shimmering lakes, palmy oases, snow-dusted mountains—mocking in their cool clarity. Large white cakes of pure salt were strewn over the desert floor like ice floes on an arctic sea. The only other blemish was the Land Rover's own wake, two lonesome tire tracks stringing out behind.

The oppressive heat continued into the late afternoon, but Adrian was no longer encased in a sweaty film; a hot wind blew, drying perspiration as quickly as it beaded up. Driving in a kind of torpor, lulled by the absence of a proper road, he idly surveyed the Chalbi and wondered how people managed to live in such a land. Water, he knew, was not the problem; water was there if one was willing to dig for it. The problem was grazing. Camp too long in one spot and the herd destroyed the root system; there would be no new growth when the rains finally came.

They stopped for the night at Kargi, a village of sorts on the maps, but in reality little more than a water hole and a hostel for camels. They slept on air mattresses rolled out on the roof of the Land Rover. The temperature had fallen nearly forty degrees since noon, and they wrapped themselves in the traditional Dorobo *karos,* a blanket made of hyrax skins. In the morning they patronized a local tea shop for a breakfast of milky tea and *maandazis,* the triangular cakes that tasted like unsweetened doughnuts, and were under way by nine o'clock, on a line with Von Höhnel Bay at the southernmost tip of Lake Turkana.

In his journal of his 1888 expedition with Count Teleki, Ludwig von Höhnel had described this land as something "flung from some monstrous forge." After two hours, Adrian, steering around pieces of petrified wood forty million years old, had seen nothing to contradict that impression. They drove for another hour before Pythias, who'd been keeping track of the sun ever since they'd left Kargi, broke his silence. "Soon now," he said.

Adrian stifled a smile, wondering just what "soon now" meant to the Dorobo. Once, years ago, he'd been camping alone in the bush north of Rumuruti and was just fixing himself a lunch of bangers and beans when he looked up to find a Dorobo watching him. He had no idea where the man had come from or how long he'd been standing there, but he invited the Dorobo to eat with him. When they finished, the Dorobo asked Adrian to let him return the kindness, to come back with him to his camp and have supper. Adrian, on the trail of a trophy-size lion, hesitated; he did not wish to be rude, but there was a time factor to consider. "How far is this camp of yours?" he had asked. "Not far," the Dorobo replied. "How far?" Adrian insisted. "Not far," the Dorobo said again, shrugging. "Two, maybe three days' walk."

But even as Adrian replayed the memory the land began to change, subtly at first, then dramatically. The hardpan gave way to soft sand, then spotty brush, then denser bush. Shoots of mustard-hued grass grew up between the rocks, and suddenly there were birds in the sky, bulbuls and superb starlings. A handful of doum palms and tamarinds popped up on the horizon, sure signs of water. Adrian glanced at Pythias and shook his head. He prided himself on having a sixth sense when it came to such things, but Pythias was blessed with at least seven.

The next sign of life was a camel train. At the head of the string, walking next to the bell-camel, was a Turkana dressed more appropriately for war than for shepherding duty. A hippopotamus–hide shield was slung across his back and he carried an eight-foot-long, leaf-bladed spear. A knobkerrie fighting stick, held by a thong around his waist, and a nasty-looking wrist knife rounded out his arsenal. But the truly remarkable thing about him was his coiffure. His hair was piled high in a beehive, with a thin reed arcing up out of the stack and plunging back in like a single-banded rainbow. The whole elaborate edifice was slathered with a caking of bright blue clay. Adrian slowed and steered directly for the head of the train, using the shiny blue hairdo as a beacon.

The herdsman reacted as if he were under attack. Jerking the bell-camel to a stop, he rapped the beast across the back of the knees with the shaft of his spear, bringing it down to a kneel. The creature collapsed in stages—nose first, rump last—folding up like a chair, all edges and angles. One by one, the trailing camels followed suit. The Turkana took up a fighting position behind the bell-camel, unslinging his hippo shield and propping it on the beast's back. He held his spear high and cocked, and waited stoically for the Land Rover.

Adrian stopped at what he judged to be a safe distance, using the average Masai's skill with a spear as a gauge; this Turkana's throw might reach, but not with accuracy. He turned to Pythias and said in English: "Do you want to talk to him, or shall I?"

"You," Pythias answered quickly. "He scares the shit out of me."

"He scares the shit out of me, too," Adrian said.

He thought about the shotgun, then quickly dismissed the idea and stepped down from the Land Rover unarmed. Holding up a hand, palm out in what he hoped would be taken as a gesture of peace, he began to walk slowly toward the hunkered camel. When he was near enough for a lethal throw, the Turkana shook his spear menacingly. Adrian stopped in mid-step.

The Turkana spoke first, in Swahili. "I have no quarrel with you, English. You can go in safety. But I will kill the Rendille pig with you. He will not steal any of my camels."

Adrian sighed. He felt as if he had stepped into one of the Chalbi's mirages, into a reflected image from an earlier time. He wasn't sure if it was 1978 or 1878. "My companion is not a Rendille," Adrian said.

"Then I will kill the Samburu pig with you. We also have cattle nearby. He will not steal any of our cows."

"He is not Samburu, either," Adrian said.

"What is he then?"

"Okiek. Dorobo."

After a pause, the Turkana said, "Tell him to come out and stand where I can see him."

After a pause of his own, Adrian turned and signaled for Pythias to join him. Pythias got down from the Land Rover and approached slowly, his reluctance plain in every step.

The Turkana lowered his spear and started to laugh. "You are right,

English. He is Dorobo. Only the Dorobo are the size of children even when fully grown. I understand now. You are hunting lion and you have brought him with you to use for bait."

Pythias went stiff at the insult, rising up on tiptoes to his full five feet, but he said nothing; he was still too intimidated by this fearsome-looking warrior.

Adrian shook his head. "No, I am not hunting lion. I am hunting a man, a Doro . . ."

The Turkana was not listening. He had stopped laughing and was squinting at Pythias, trying to get a better look at him. He stepped out from behind the camel and ventured a few paces closer, his eyes growing wider with each step. When he was less than a dozen yards away he moaned, dropped his spear and shield with a clatter, and threw himself face down in the sand.

As Adrian and Pythias watched in amazement, the Turkana slithered on his stomach the last few yards to reach Pythias, touched his forehead to the Dorobo's bare toes, and cried in a strangled, barely audible voice: "Forgive me! I didn't know it was you. How could I have known? Don't kill me! Please!"

Completely unnerved, Pythias jerked his foot away, spun about, and bolted for the Land Rover.

Adrian reached down and pulled the warrior onto his feet. The Turkana was rubber-legged and Adrian had to hold on to him to keep him from going down again. The man was plainly terrified.

"What's this nonsense?" Adrian asked sharply, trying to penetrate the man's fear, at a loss to understand it. He was unsettled himself; Turkana warriors didn't frighten easily. "Why are you acting so foolishly?"

The Turkana blinked several times, like a man coming out of hypnosis. He gazed at the Land Rover, then down at his own body, as if he couldn't believe he was still in one piece.

"That man . . . ," he said, pointing a quaking finger in the direction of the Land Rover, where Pythias sat with the doors locked and the windows rolled up, ". . . is not a man."

Adrian, who still had the Turkana by the shoulders, gave him a shake. "Talk sense."

"He's not a man," the Turkana insisted. "He's a spirit."

Adrian laughed, so surprised that he reacted in English. "A spirit? What are you talking about?"

The Turkana couldn't have answered Adrian's question had he understood it. He was staring at the Land Rover, mesmerized. "The man he once was was killed by a lion. Torn to pieces. I saw him. I helped bury what was left of him." He pointed once more. "That man is a spirit. That man is dead."

"Don't be daft," Adrian said. "Did he look dead to you? You touched his foot. Did he *feel* dead?"

The Turkana pulled his eyes away from the Land Rover and faced Adrian. "Who are you to say what a spirit can or cannot do?" he asked indignantly. "Spirits can make themselves solid if they choose to. All I know is that man is dead."

Adrian opened his mouth to curse the Turkana's bloody obstinance, then closed it with a snap, suddenly realizing what the man was telling him.

"This spirit," he said quietly. "Did you know him well when he was a man?"

The Turkana nodded. "He was betrothed to the daughter of my mother's brother."

"Did he have a scar on his arm? Here?" Adrian touched himself on the arm.

"No. No scar."

"Did he ever mention having a brother?"

"He often spoke of a brother. He said his brother was a great tracker, a great hunter, even better than himself."

"And did he mention that this brother was also his twin, a man who looked exactly like him?"

The Turkana stared at Adrian for a moment, letting the revelation sink in. "I don't believe you," he said, wanting to desperately.

Adrian shrugged. "See for yourself." He waved to the Land Rover, gesturing for Pythias to join them.

Pythias rolled down a window, poked his head out just long enough to yell *"Hapana, bwana,"* and rolled it up again.

Adrian turned to the Turkana and said, "See? He's afraid of you. Would a true spirit be afraid of a mere mortal?"

"Who knows?" the warrior said sensibly. "I've never met one before today." He had stopped trembling, an indication that his fear was beginning to fade. His sarcasm was another.

Adrian picked the man's spear off the ground, handed it back to him and said, "Wait here." He went to the Land Rover and, after a lengthy and heated argument, conducted entirely through a slightly cracked window, came back with Pythias in tow, leading the Dorobo by the arm, half escorting him, half dragging him. He pushed up Pythias's shirtsleeve and said, "Look at this man's arm."

The Turkana, who was keeping a prudent distance between the two strangers and himself, leaned forward cautiously for a quick look, but he did not relax his grip on his spear.

"Was the man you knew marked in this way?" Adrian asked.

The Turkana shook his head.

"And would you agree that this is an old scar and not a fresh one?"

The Turkana nodded.

Pythias, still unsure about what was happening, looked from one man to the other, a premonition beginning to cloud his face. "You are talking about Damon, aren't you?" he said. "This man knows my brother. Something bad has happened to my brother. What is it?"

When neither man answered, he faced the Turkana. "What made you act that way? Did you think you were seeing a ghost?"

The Turkana nodded. *"Ndiyo."*

"My brother is dead," Pythias said. It was a statement, not a question.

The Turkana nodded again. *"Ndiyo."*

"How did he die?" Pythias asked calmly.

"Like a Turkana. With courage," the warrior said. "He went out alone to track a lion which had killed one of our cows. The animal ambushed him."

Adrian put a comforting hand on Pythias's shoulder, but the Dorobo shook it off and sat down on the ground, turning so that he was sitting cross-legged with his back to the two witnesses. They could not see his face and he made no noise, but his shoulders were shaking.

The Turkana met Adrian's stricken look. "You spoke the truth, English," he said, shaking his head. "Your friend is no spirit. Spirits cannot cry."

9

Duke, Duke, Duke
Duke of Earl . . . Duke, Duke
Duke of Earl . . . Duke, Duke
Duke of Earl . . . Duke, Duke
As I . . . Walk through this world
Nothing can stop . . . The Duke of Earl

Robbie Lewis turned up the volume on her cassette player and sang along with Gene Chandler as she poured herself a Bloody Mary from the thermos propped on the dash of the office Peugeot.

The music took her back to when she was fifteen and singing doo-wop with the gang outside the Melrose Diner on the corner of 15th and Snyder. She watched the herd of wispy-bearded wildebeests grazing peacefully on the wide plain in front of her and said aloud: "You're a long way from South Philly, Roberta Angelina D'Agostino." Silently, she lifted a toast to the girl she used to be.

It was a little before six o'clock and Robbie was parked near the Athi River, on the cusp of a gentle rise in Nairobi National Park, just ten minutes in real time from her center city offices in the Hughes Building on Muindi Mbingu Street, but an aeon removed in spiritual time. The cylindrical tower of the Kenyatta Conference Center, poking up through a morning haze on the horizon, and a light plane doing lazy loops over Wilson Airport were the only signs of the modern, discordant world outside the park.

She had been waiting at Mbagathi Gate, motor running and resident's parks pass ready, when the ranger came to open up, and he had let her in early. She had ridden into the park on a magical carpet woven out of silver threads, the first thin streaks of daylight, even while the tour company combis were still parked outside the downtown hotels, the guides herding their flocks through breakfast. For a while at least she had the park to herself.

It still amazed her that this calm and silent place was right next door to the rowdy city. An oasis in the middle of Babel, she thought.

Robbie had spent many an early morning here in the park during

her first few months in Kenya, enthralled by the light and space of
Africa after nearly two years of being locked in the dim dungeon that
was London, her first overseas post. She did not come all that often
anymore, but she had an eight o'clock appointment this morning with
Inspector Odongo, at the animal orphanage by the main entrance.
Besides, she was fidgety. She had passed a restless night and had been
up early, before the servants. She had thrown on jeans and a pullover,
mixed up a batch of Bloody Marys, and sallied out in predawn darkness,
catching her *askari* by surprise, asleep in his guard house by the gate.

Nairobi National Park was the smallest of the country's eleven national parks and reserves, just forty-four square miles. It was fenced on
three sides to keep wildlife out of the city's streets, although now and
again there would be reports of a leopard carrying off someone's
dog. The south side was wide open, merging with the seamless veldt.
The last few days of September, coming at the end of the long dry
season and just before the short rains, were an excellent time for game
viewing. The Athi was a generally dependable source of water and the
park was almost always full. One could find most everything except
elephant, which kept away for reasons of habitat: there was a paucity of
large, bushy trees within the park, and they had to cross a vast, treeless
plain to get there.

It was a pleasantly cool and cloudy morning, typical of the season.
Darker clouds loitered over the rounded tops of the Ngong Hills, but
they had been there for days now without dumping rain. They rumbled
and glowered, flexing like schoolyard bullies, all talk and no action. But
any day, from now until mid-November, they would quit their bluster-
ing and deliver.

> *Since I met you baby*
> *My whole life has changed*
> *Since I met you baby*
> *My whole life has changed*
> *And everybody tells me*
> *That I am not the same*

Robbie helped Ivory Joe Hunter carry the melody, adding a throaty
contralto, her voice both smooth and raspy at once, as if someone had
taken a coarse-grained sandpaper to it. It was a cabaret voice, un-
trained but practiced, good enough to have helped pay her way through
four years at Temple University. She had been the "chick singer" in a
six-piece band that had stubbornly insisted on playing oldies-but-goodies
during the heyday of Beatlemania. Back then, of course, the "oldies"
hadn't been all that old.

How long ago it all seemed. How long ago it all was. In some ways she hadn't changed much. Physically, hardly at all. At thirty-one she still had the same sinewy, athletic body she'd had at eighteen—"great ass, no tits; I give her an eighty," Joey Caputo would announce whenever she walked by—and the same smooth complexion and olive coloring. She still wore her crow-black hair rather short and combed straight back from the temples, the wings joining in back to form what, in the neighborhood, they had called a "duck's ass."

But in other ways, she had changed a great deal. For one thing, she had tamed her brassy South Philadelphia accent; or rather, her "Sowf Fuh-luff-ya" accent. She hoped that none of her former neighborhood playmates would accuse her of getting an "addy-tood," but she no longer said "yous" when addressing more than one person, as in, "Yo, guys! So what do yous wanna do ta-night?" When she wanted to, she could even stop herself from hailing people with "Yo!" If the guys could hear her now they wouldn't believe their ears. She was "bee-yoo-dee-ful!"

For another, she had become something of a sophisticate. She had experienced worlds never even imagined by Kitty Bono or Polly Carbone or Mary Petronelli or any of the other girls with whom Robbie used to sneak into the movies to study Kim Novak or Ava Gardner and then ape their every mannerism. Robbie had met the Queen of England. She had even—"Yo, Ma! You better siddown for this!"—met the Pope!

Temple University was not then, nor would it ever be, a finishing school, but the transformation of Roberta Angelina D'Agostino into Ms. Robbie Lewis had begun there. Temple was known, then as now, as a "peoples' university," a polite way of saying that it was for students whose finances ruled out more costly schools in the area, like Penn, or Haverford, or Bryn Mawr. Heavily supported by the state, it was a commuter college with a low tuition, the cheapest ticket in town.

If it hadn't been, Robbie might not have been able to go to college at all. She had fantasized about someday attending Penn, but while her grades at South Philadelphia High School were good, they were not quite good enough for a full-ride scholarship to an Ivy school. Her father, a former beat cop forced to take a medical retirement after being savagely beaten by a gang of hoodlums, supported his family on a disability pension. A year at Penn came to more than his annual income.

Temple's low fees, along with what she made singing, had been the answer for Robbie, but hers had not been the typical collegiate experience. She awoke each day in the same modest Snyder Avenue row house where she had lived all her life and rode the subway to campus. When her classes—journalism was her major, English Lit her minor—were done for the day, it was home for a few hours of studying, then off to wherever the band was playing that night, if they were lucky enough to have a gig.

And her experience certainly was not typical of student life in the 1960s. While her college years coincided with the crucible years of campus unrest—1965 to 1969—it was as if the sixties never happened. Not to her, anyway. She was a juvenile delinquent in her day, but never a hippie. She wore pedal pushers and tight black leather pants, but never a Hopi skirt or a dashiki. She listened to the Del Vikings and Dion and the Belmonts and Frankie Lymon and the Teenagers, but not The Doors or The Beatles or Jefferson Airplane. She had been a child of the fifties all the days of her life, a child of South Philadelphia.

In its espousal of old-fashioned values, its emphasis on family and church, its insistence on personal loyalty and neighborhood nurturing, South Philly had been a place out of time. In the predominantly Italo-American neighborhoods of South Philadelphia, young men did not march against the war in Vietnam, they marched to it. They did not take over campus administration buildings, they took jobs on the docks. They did not keep faith with their black brothers in Philadelphia, Mississippi, they kept an eye on the niggers across Broad Street right there in Philadelphia, PA. In South Philly there were no "sit-ins" on the lawn at Dow or DuPont, only bocci on the grass in Marconi Plaza or Roosevelt Park. No love-ins or be-ins or happenings, just confession on Saturday and communion on Sunday and the occasional funeral Mass for a native son coming home from Vietnam in a box. All that South Philly knew of the sixties were silver chalices and gold star mothers, and Roberta D'Agostino—doo-wop queen and onetime member in good standing in the ladies' auxiliary of the Snyder Avenue Stilettos—had been no different.

Temple had been Robbie's escape hatch, her way out. It surprised her friends—she surprised herself a little—when she actually used it. They knew of her effortless coups in the classroom, of course, but she had been as wild and as reckless as any of them. She threw up in the street when she got drunk. She swore like a stevedore. She "went all the way" with half the boys she dated. She even boosted a car once as a favor to Vinnie Massamino, her "old man" in the Stilettos and a dead ringer for South Philly's own Fabiano Forte, better known to the rest of the world as Fabian.

Robbie had just turned eighteen when she enrolled at Temple, and she had been out of control for five full years already, a source of pain and embarrassment to her invalid father and devout mother since the night of her thirteenth birthday when a police officer—Pop's former partner—brought her home after she was caught stealing parts from a city bus parked in the SEPTA trolley yard. Her despairing parents were resigned to seeing her end up like her two older sisters, both married to "made" men, *goombas,* street soldiers in Angelo Bruno's mob family.

The same thought had occurred to Robbie, and perhaps it was that which started her thinking seriously about breaking out. Her sister Gracie, the quiet one, was a widow at twenty-seven, her husband Frank found in the trunk of a Lincoln parked under the ramp of the Ben Franklin Bridge, shot through the eye with a silenced .22. Her sister Rosalie, the busty one, who'd had a body like Gina Lollabrigida's at eighteen, was a thickening mother of three at twenty-five. She would be a fat-assed mother of six by thirty-five. By forty-five she would be an old crone right out of some dusty Calabrian hill village, complete with a mustache and a different set of rosary beads for each day of the week.

But more likely it was because she had led a double life all along. Her strong academic record was not due strictly to a natural brilliance; she had studied in secret, anxious that her pals not find out, often starting on her homework at one or two o'clock in the morning, after being out with the guys. And she read constantly, poetry mostly—Sara Teasdale, Edna Millay, and Emily Dickinson—their images as sharp as diamond-tipped drill bits, boring to the core of her, forcing her to examine emotions she would never admit to having on the street. Robbie had even tried writing the stuff herself, her poems conjuring up shining cities made of glass and romantic heroes who wouldn't dream of rolling up a pack of Luckies in the sleeves of their T-shirts or larding their hair with grease. She put her poems in a notebook and put the notebook under her mattress, and grabbed at Temple's offer of a small scholarship stipend as if it were a life preserver.

But rescue was not so easy as that. Day by day and inch by inch, she grew apart from the friends of a lifetime. They were not equipped to discuss Spenser's innovative use of allegory in *The Faerie Queene;* she was not equipped to debate the merits of this or that brand of disposable diaper.

When she graduated, she made it a clean break, leaving not only the campus but also the neighborhood. Her first job was with the *Newark News*. Newark, New Jersey, was not very far from Philadelphia, just ninety minutes up the turnpike, but she and her new friends spent their weekends in New York, and her visits to South Philly became less frequent. Then stopped. She still kept tabs on how the Phillies and the Flyers were doing, but that was the limit of her allegiance.

The *News* was by far the more feisty of Newark's two big dailies, and Robbie, who quickly gained a reputation for being rather feisty herself, did well there. With her background it was inevitable that she would be assigned to cover the city's sizable Italian community, and it was just a matter of time before she began to specialize in organized crime stories, a high-visibility beat. The mob was something she knew a thing or three about; half her friends back in South Philadelphia were connected. Her reporting won the newspaper an armful of state press awards and herself a succession of quick raises.

It was a happy time for Robbie: she was getting into the paper every other day—on page one, more often than not—she was young and healthy, she was making good money, and she was on her own for the first time in her life. She even met a nice young man and married him. His name was Thomas Lewis and he was a federal prosecutor assigned to the state's organized crime task force which, like Robbie, was trying to put New Jersey Mafia boss Anthony "Tony Pro" Provenzano in jail. They were married less than a year after Robbie arrived in Newark, and divorced three years later, when the *News* folded and she took a job with *Newsweek* magazine.

"Oh," was all he had said when she told him that she was taking the job and an apartment in Manhattan. "Does this mean you expect me to do the commuting?"

"Not really," she said. "Do you want to commute?"

"Not really," he said.

And that was that.

They had dated less than six weeks before being married in a quick civil ceremony, without anyone from either family in attendance, and, what with his busy schedule and her busy schedule, they never seemed to find time to get acquainted. Sometimes Robbie thought she only married Tommy to change her name. Lewis made a better by-line than D'Agostino, she joked to friends. Classier.

She spent the next three years in New York, working for the magazine's Nation section. The London assignment came up unexpectedly, after one of her stories led to the arrest and indictment of a *capo regime* in the Brooklyn family of Joseph Bonanno, also known as "Joe Bananas." Robbie was hustled out of town after her editors were tipped off by federal sources—specifically, a Mr. Thomas Lewis of the U.S. Department of Justice—that her name had been found on a list. A hit list.

Robbie, convinced that her ex-husband was deliberately trying to make things difficult for her out of spite, tried her best to pooh-pooh the report. She was enjoying New York and did not want to go to London, or anywhere else.

"The *goombas* don't zip civilians if they can possibly avoid it," she argued. "And they *never* clip reporters. Bad for business."

"Oh yeah?" her editors countered. "What about Don Bolles of the *Arizona Republic*?"

And that was that.

London had been a drab couple of years. She had traveled a bit on the Continent, but otherwise the job bored her to tears. Dreary economic stories mostly, the Common Market and the trade unions' negotiations with Harold Wilson's Labour government. The only excitement or drama came on her periodic forays into Northern Ireland, where she could report on real people with real problems, untethered from her desk in London.

But in spite of her discontent, Robbie did good work in London, good enough to be offered a bureau of her own. True, it was only a one-person bureau, and in Boston at that, but it was quite an honor nevertheless: there was only one other woman bureau chief in the entire system. She turned it down. While she had no use for London, she had grown to appreciate the lifestyle of the foreign correspondent, particularly the advantage of being several thousands of miles removed from the home office. Abroad, Robbie enjoyed a freedom that simply was not possible stateside, to say nothing of the perks that went along with any foreign posting, from the housing allowance to the tax break to the no-questions-asked expense account. So, she asked for Nairobi instead.

The Nairobi bureau was open, but her editors in New York balked. Black Africa was the toughest assignment on the masthead, they informed her in paternal tones, one that had broken more than one experienced male correspondent.

Robbie stuck to her guns. All she knew about Africa was what she had seen of it in the movies: Ava Gardner and Grace Kelly clawing it out over Clark Gable in *Mogambo*. But when it came to freedom, to doing the kinds of stories she wanted to do with a minimum of interference from New York, Robbie figured that Africa, where real people fought real battles against hunger and disease, was the place to be. The trouble with London was that the phones worked. It was easier for a Manhattan editor to ring up the U.K. than it was to dial the Bronx.

New York, not exactly swamped by requests for the Africa job from more senior correspondents, gave in, agreeing to let her have Nairobi on a trial basis. Three months later it was hers to keep. Africa was every bit as tough as they had said it would be, but by then she had shown them that she could be tough too.

Now, after a year and a half of it, she was not so sure anymore. Africa was wearing her down, draining her reservoir of energy, sucking her dry like a Mombasa mosquito, fluidram by fluidram. Robbie was afraid that one of these mornings she would wake to find only a shell, with nothing left inside, no heart, no soul.

But not this morning. This morning she had three Bloody Marys inside, warming her nicely. And she had nature's great variety show for her amusement. The wildebeests had the stage at the moment. Most of them grazed with dignity, looking like runtish bison, while a frisky few gamboled along the edges of the herd, running and cutting and kicking up their heels, all without apparent reason. They looked like four-legged clowns, she thought. God's court jesters.

Robbie checked her watch and saw that it was almost time to meet

Inspector Odongo. She had no idea where the last hour had gone. She drained the last of her breakfast, screwed the cap back on the thermos, turned off the cassette player, and started the car. A few more wildebeests, startled by the noise, took off on one of their zany, zig-zag runs.

Robbie laughed, backed slowly down the slope and drove away, singing a ditty as she went:

If you knew what the gnu knew . . .

Inspector Odongo was waiting for her outside the animal orphanage administration office. He shook hands with her and greeted her politely enough, but she noticed that he couldn't help glancing at his watch. She was fifteen minutes late.

"Had a flat at Sign Post 16 . . . Lion's Camp," Robbie said by way of apology "That spot really lives up to its name. A goddamn lion was camped twenty yards away while I changed the tire, just eyeballing me and licking its chops."

Odongo regarded her in silence for a moment, looking for a lie, then he saw the grease smudges on her hands and clothing, and grinned. "You were in no real danger, Miss Lewis," he said. "That very same lioness was there last evening, feeding on a wildebeest. She won't need to kill again for a day or two."

"Now you tell me," she said, grinning back. "Can't they wear a goddamn sign or something? It would have been nice to know."

He laughed and tapped his chest. "I myself didn't learn until quite recently that lions do not kill every day. I am slowly becoming knowledgeable about animals."

"I thought Africans were born knowing everything there is to know about animals."

"I am Luo," Odongo said. "I was born knowing everything there is to know about fish."

"How do you know the lion was there yesterday?"

"When I rang you last night to arrange this meeting I'd just come from the park," he said. "Come. I want to show you something."

Instead of leading the way into the admin building as she expected, Odongo took her around back, into the maze of game pens where sick or injured animals were kept until they were well enough to be released back into the wild. Orphaned young also were nurtured there until they were old enough to make it on their own. Robbie, ever the sucker for the little ones, had visited the orphanage several times.

They passed a wire pen that held a pair of cheetahs and a cage full of baboons, before stopping at a rail fence. On the other side was a large patch of brushy ground. Three rhinos, two adults and an infant, browsed in the bushes. The infant, nearly as big as a Volkswagen, turned to look at Robbie, its hooked beak full of leaves which jutted out from either side of its face like a false mustache.

"Oh, how cute!" Robbie bubbled, her hard-nosed demeanor melting instantly. "He's not hurt, is he?"

"He is a she," Inspector Odongo said, "and she's in fine health."

Robbie made faces at the baby, which continued to watch her inquisitively while it chewed. After another minute or so, the inspector said, "Come, Miss Lewis. I have something else to show you."

She waved goodbye to the little rhino and followed the inspector back to the admin building. He pointed to a white Suzuki with GK— Government of Kenya—plates, parked alongside her Peugeot. They got in and Odongo drove through the main gate and into the park proper, over the set of speed bumps and down into the plain.

At Sign Post 1, just past the warden's house, they left the tarmac and turned up the dirt road leading to Hyena Dam. After another mile, Odongo pulled off the track and stopped. He got out of the car, had a quick look around and signaled for Robbie to join him. Then, without waiting, he hooked the back panel of his bush jacket behind the pistol holstered on his hip and started across a field of high grass, making for the edge of a rocky ravine.

Robbie followed, almost trotting in an effort to catch up, watching out for dangerous animals and feeling like the last man in a British Army patrol in Belfast.

Odongo went over the lip of the ravine, disappearing as suddenly as if he'd been swallowed by the earth. By the time Robbie reached the spot, he was already at the bottom of the gully, standing in the middle of a small clearing, holding his nose with one hand and throwing stones with the other. A flock of large birds, a dozen or so vultures, were quickly moving out of harm's way with indignant cries and a furious flapping of feathers, although none of them had been intimidated enough to take to the air.

Robbie worked her way down the steep slope on all fours and, standing up and starting toward the inspector, walked into a pocket of stink as bad as anything she had ever experienced, including North Philly on a hot and humid August afternoon.

"Holy shit!" she cried, pinching her nostrils closed and casting an accusing look at the nearest bird, a jowly vulture with blood on its face.

She turned to Odongo to ask what was happening, but was stopped by the absurd picture the two of them made, standing there facing off with their hands fused to their noses. She began to laugh, and only stopped when she glanced beyond the inspector and saw the carcass.

"Holy shit!" she said again, whispering this time. She edged closer, fighting an urge to gag and squeezing her nose even tighter, knowing that if she let go she would lose her Bloody Mary breakfast.

The remains were so badly decomposed that Robbie could not even tell what kind of animal it had been, other than a large one. The skin, a sooty gray in color, was wrinkled and loose, covering the skeleton like a dingy blanket. The skull was fully exposed and both the bone and the teeth shone like new porcelain. The eye sockets were empty, picked clean.

"What is it?" Robbie asked through pursed lips, loath to let any of that foul air into her mouth. Filtered through her clamped nose, her voice sounded reedy and ridiculous.

"*Kifaru*," said Odongo. "A black rhinoceros. The mother of the young one you saw at the orphanage." The inspector's voice sounded just as silly.

"Who did it? The gang you're after?"

He shook his head. "No. Someone else did this. I brought you here to show you what a poached animal looks like. So you will know what we are dealing with, what is at stake. See how the horns are missing?"

Robbie nodded weakly. "Can we get away from this smell?" she asked. "If we don't, I'm going to be sick."

Odongo led her around the animal. When they were upwind a ways, he let go of his nose and gave an experimental sniff. He smiled and nodded.

Robbie released her nose. "Whew! That's better." Looking around, she shook her head. "I wouldn't think a poacher would have the balls to try something in this park, so close to the city and all."

"They don't, usually," Odongo said. "The fences keep them out and it's too long and exposed an approach to come in from the unfenced end. This time they cut through the fence. It is an indication of what we're up against these days, how brazen they have become."

"But how is that any different from the way it's always been?" Robbie asked. "There have always been poachers."

"Not like today," Odongo said. "Take a single species in a single park as an example: the elephant of Tsavo. Ten years ago Tsavo had an elephant population of forty thousand. Two years ago there were twenty-six thousand. Today there are only eight thousand four hundred. It is the same or worse for rhino. The professional poachers are now hunting elephant and rhino with machine guns. In one recent six-month period, poachers killed more than a thousand elephants, two hundred thirty-five rhinos and twenty leopards. Yes, there has always been poaching, Miss Lewis. But never like this."

The statistics sobered Robbie. She had known it was bad, but not that bad. "Why the big jump in numbers?" she asked.

"There are many theories, but who is to know which, if any, are correct," Odongo said, shrugging. "The hunting ban is blamed by some, especially the former hunters. They argue that once hunting became illegal, simple laws of supply and demand came into play. As the legal supply of game products dwindled, the illegal demand for them increased. They also say that the professional hunting camps served as a network of monitors in the bush. Where there were animals there were hunters, and the poachers had to think twice about invading any area where heavily armed white men were prowling about."

Odongo paused and glanced quickly at Robbie to see if she had heard a racial insult in his last comment. But she was not looking at him. She was staring at the mess on the ground.

"Poaching is always a problem in a country where meat is scarce and costly," Odongo went on. "There are two threats to wildlife in Kenya: loss of habitat, which will continue to be a problem as long as our birthrate stays around four percent, and poaching. And there are two kinds of poachers. Those who do it for meats and hides for self and family. And those who do it for money, the professionals. It's unlikely that we'll ever stop the first kind. But I've vowed to do everything in my power to put an end to the other."

Robbie, still looking at the carcass, nodded and said: "And I am going to help you. You kick ass, I'll take names. When do we start?"

Odongo laughed. "I am going to the Aberdares first thing tomorrow morning," he said. "If you want to come along, be at Jogoo House at seven o'clock."

"I'll be there."

They backed away from the dead rhinoceros and began the climb out of the ravine, Odongo aiding Robbie on the steepest sections. When she reached the top, Robbie took a deep breath of fresh, unpolluted air and looked down, and saw that Africa was, indeed, a place where little went to waste. The vultures were already back at their meal.

10

There was a feast that night in the Turkana encampment, a second wake of sorts for Damon, with Pythias and Adrian as guests of honor.

They ate roast goat, slaughtered just for the occasion, and drank milk laced with cow's blood, and *pombe,* homemade beer. They sat around a dung fire in the cool desert evening, watching dancers and listening to songs that extolled Damon's prowess as a hunter. That night, for the first time, Pythias met his brother's fiancée, a widow before she had a chance to be a wife. She wore a lip plug and a nose ornament fashioned from bits of bone and was, Adrian and Pythias both agreed, a very handsome young woman. She also was a very pregnant young woman, six or seven months along from the look of her.

Unfamiliar with Turkana society, Adrian wondered if that would be a problem. It would be one thing if the coming child were pure Turkana. But a half-breed? Would she now be damaged goods in the eyes of a prospective suitor? In the eyes of her family? He made a mental note to ask the clan's headman about it. If there was going to be a problem, he would have to make arrangements to see that the young woman and her baby were provided for. He owed that much to Damon.

The chief, a distinguished-looking man of about seventy who looked as if he would still be a ferocious adversary in a fight, was a genial and generous host. Damon had obviously been popular with the Turkana. Throughout the evening, both elders and warriors went out of their way to seek Pythias out, offering him their condolences and sharing their anecdotes of his brother. Most of their stories, all of them highly complimentary, had to do with Damon's brilliance as a tracker and hunter.

The clan's women weren't so bold as to approach Pythias directly, leaving male things to the men. But they displayed a certain sympathy by association by hovering around Damon's fiancée as if she were newly bereft, whispering into her ear and pressing their palms flat against her bulging bare belly.

Seeing the genuine concern and affection in their faces, Adrian had a feeling she was going to be all right.

He was not so sure about Pythias. The little Dorobo was understandably quiet and subdued during the festivities, but Adrian discerned an alarming tightness in his friend, as if some internal clockworks had been wound past the snapping point. Pythias ate and drank, but sparingly, barely enough to be polite. And while he was civil to everyone who approached him, he seemed distracted and sluggish, lost somewhere inside his pain. Something vital was missing, something besides the ever-ready grin. A light had gone out in those luminous eyes of his, those tracker's eyes which, normally, never missed a thing.

Pythias paid no attention to the stares he was getting. Either he simply didn't care, or else he was growing used to them, having been under a microscope from the moment he came into camp. In other circumstances, Adrian would have been the center of attention—the Turkana did not see all that many white men—but he had been largely ignored, while Pythias could not take more than two steps without drawing a gallery. The Turkana had their explanation of the remarkable likeness between the two Dorobo brothers, but it seemed that some of them still were not fully convinced. And they were taking no chances. It wasn't every day that one had the opportunity to see a ghost up close.

Damon's woman had collapsed when she had first seen the man who was to have been her brother-in-law, and even after she revived it was a while before she could be persuaded that her lover had not come back to her from beyond the grave. She still seemed to experience a swooning sensation whenever she looked at Pythias, but she couldn't seem to keep her eyes off him. Even now they sought him out from the other side of the fire.

Adrian's own reaction to Damon's death had been slowly gathering force as the day wore on. His initial concern, to help Pythias get through it, had gradually given way to an ache all his own. The brothers had been just as inseparable in his mind as they had been in the mind of his mother, she who had named them. To lose one of them was like losing both, like losing a member of his own family. For Damon and Pythias had been more than just his playmates. They had been his guardian angels, commissioned by his father to watch over him from the time he could walk. Pate had given him his first rifle, a .22, when he was seven, and he had started with rabbits and guinea fowl, gradually working up to bigger bores and bigger game, and always shadowed by the two African boys with their spears and bows. They were only a couple of years older than he was, but they seemed much more mature, passing from infancy into manhood with only the briefest of stops at childhood. Pate must have sensed it too; he hadn't hesitated to entrust them with the care and tutelage of his only son.

By the age of thirteen, Adrian, accompanied only by his double shadow, was going out into the bush for three or four days at a time. The boys would hunt all day and tell stories around the fire at night. He taught Damon and Pythias how to fire a rifle—secretly of course, since instructing natives in the use of firearms was discouraged by the local whites—while they helped him polish what they had already taught him of the spear and bow.

And it was they, more than Pate, who had taught Adrian the ancient art of tracking, one they had learned from their father, Pate's headman, although Adrian was firmly convinced that as Dorobos they had been born with the skill. They could track a pad-footed leopard over the stoniest ground, or a solitary honey bee through the densest forest. And while Adrian could never hope to match their accomplishments, he liked to think that he came as close as anyone who was not born Dorobo.

Adrian vividly remembered the day, two months before his fifteenth birthday, when all the things that the twins had taught him were put to the test. Pate had called him into the library, given him a .256 Mauser and six cartridges and said, "We need meat for the labor force. Bring me six kongoni."

Terrified at having no margin for error, he'd run to the African *boma* to fetch his friends, only to find they had gone to Sugota Marmar, near Rumuruti, to visit relatives. And so he'd gone out alone, with only a packhorse for company. He was away four days, most of them spent on his stomach, stalking to get close enough for point-blank shots.

He had come back with the six kongoni, unloading them in front of the house and turning them over to the *boma* cooks as Pate looked on from the veranda. And when he went to give the Mauser back to his father, Pate had given him a long look and said: "Keep it. It seems to suit you."

The look of love and pride in his father's face that day had been a gift from Damon, who helped teach him tracking, and Adrian would never forget him for it.

He was still thinking about his friend when the Turkana headman sat down beside him. He did not speak right away. He played with a finger-knife, flicking it idly, the firelight glinting off its curved blade. He glanced at Pythias, at Adrian, at the weapon in his hand.

Finally he put away the knife and said, "I am told that you came here to get your friend Damon and take him away with you. That you needed him for an important task."

"That's right."

"What is this task?"

"A dangerous one," Adrian said. "We are hunting a gang of bad men who have been killing animals in the government's reserves. They have killed a man as well."

The headman nodded solemnly. "The one you call Damon we called by a Turkana name that means He Who Smells Tracks," he said. "He was going to find these bad men for you by smelling their tracks?"

"Yes. Along with Pythias over there." Adrian pointed to Pythias with his chin.

"Pythias," the chief echoed. The name made no sense to him, in either Turkana or Swahili, the only tongues he knew. But then neither did the name Damon. He guessed it was clear enough in Kalenjin, the language of the Okiek, the Wandorobo.

"If Damon had helped you to find these bad men, would he have been called upon to fight them?"

Adrian shrugged. "I suppose so."

The chief fell quiet again, staring at the fire. Then he said: "The Turkana cannot smell tracks like Dorobo, but we are better fighters than the Dorobo. We are the best fighters in all the world, even better than the southern Masai who are famous for fighting. I can provide you with a replacement for your dead friend."

"A replacement?"

"Yes. You came here for a man. Leave here with a man."

Adrian smiled, amused, but also intrigued by the offer. "Do you have a particular man in mind?"

The chief shrugged. "All our young men are excellent fighters. Tell me what more you would require of him."

Adrian thought a moment, then said, "Physical endurance. I need someone with great stamina."

The chief grinned. "We will have a contest. I will send word in the morning to all the clans in the area. Any man who wants to fight the bad men for you will come here for a test the day after tomorrow. At midday, when the sun is hottest."

Adrian glanced at Pythias, who was listening. The Dorobo gave him a listless shrug.

Adrian hesitated, asking himself if he had time for such beer and skittles, if he could afford to wait another day. He had told Odongo that he would need a week to collect his team and his week was up. That first day, when he recruited Joseph and Tembo in the space of a few hours, seemed a month ago. It was his own fault, of course. He would be bang on schedule if he had not wasted a whole day on a self-indulgent pilgrimage to Bushbuck Farm.

On the other hand, it would take much more than a day to come up with someone else to fill Damon's spot. And he didn't want to offend his host. He made a decision and turned to the chief. "Thank you, *jumbe*. I accept your generous offer."

The chief clapped his hands once. "Good. It's settled."

Then, after a short pause, he said, "There is one other matter. . . ." He threw a quick look at Pythias, who was staring into the fire and paying him no mind. "The woman your friend Damon was going to marry is carrying a child."

"Yes," Adrian said. "I couldn't help but notice."

"She is a good woman, from a good family. A prosperous family with many cows, many camels." He stopped and watched Adrian expectantly, as if awaiting an answer.

But if there had been a question in his words, Adrian hadn't heard it. He nodded at the chief, encouraging him to continue.

The headman, who was waiting for Adrian's response, frowned. Then his face lit with understanding. "Ahh . . . perhaps there is a problem I'm not aware of," he said delicately, casting yet another quick look at Pythias. "It may be that your friend already has more wives than he can support."

Confused, Adrian shook his head. "Pythias? Pythias has no wives at all."

The Turkana chief clapped his hands again. "Good. It's settled."

"What's settled?"

The grinning headman held out his hands, palms up, as if presenting Adrian with a gift. "It was destined to be so," he said happily, always pleased when God's pattern was revealed. "The woman's name is Nimonia, which in Turkana means forest people. And what are the Dorobo if not a forest people?"

It was as if Adrian were back in the Masai kraal playing riddle games with Joseph. Only he didn't know the appropriate Turkana responses the way he did the Masai.

"That's all very interesting, *jumbe,* I'm sure," he said, "but I still don't know what you're talking about."

"But it's so simple! So perfect!"

With an exasperated sigh, Adrian glanced at Pythias for help and saw that the Dorobo was staring at the headman with bulging eyes, alert for the first time all evening. And when he turned back to the chief, he saw that the old Turkana was smiling fondly at Pythias.

"Bloody hell!" Adrian swore in English. Then, in Swahili: "You want Pythias to take Damon's place?"

"Of course! What did you think?" the chief said. "Leave him with us. With our sweet Nimonia. Take another man in his place. Take as many men as you wish."

"No one is taking my place."

Adrian and the headman swiveled their heads to stare at Pythias. For a moment they had forgotten all about him, that he had a say in the matter.

"I'm going hunting," Pythias said emphatically.

Without missing a beat the headman said, "Good! You are as brave as your brother. Go! Go hunt the bad men. Earn some money for the cows or camels you'll need for the bride price. Then return and live among us. Be a father to your brother's child and a husband to his woman. I've spoken with her about this, just a short while ago, and it is what she wants too."

"I'm going hunting," Pythias repeated, his voice weaker.

"You don't have to decide now," the chief said smoothly. "Spend tonight in her *akai,* in her night hut. Talk with her. Lie with her. Make up your mind in the morning."

Pythias did not answer. He watched the fire, hugging his knees to his chest, resting his chin on them. The chief stood and walked over to the goat roasting on its spit. He used his finger-knife to cut two large strips and, both hands dripping grease, offered one to Adrian and one to Pythias. Adrian took his, but Pythias declined with a shake of his head. The chief shrugged and began chewing lustily on it himself.

Damon's wake went on, growing louder and louder as the men consumed more and more beer. The warriors, most of them thoroughly pissed by now, joined the dancing, lining up on opposite sides of the fire, squaring off by generation-sets, with the *Nimur,* the Stones, on one side and the *Nerisa,* the Leopards, on the other. They jumped and jangled, their arm bracelets and leg ornaments reflecting the firelight, their hairdos rocking on top of their heads like big blue baskets. They brandished their spears at one another and made hideous, gap-toothed faces; like the Masai, Turkana men had their two bottom front teeth extracted, a custom which, in their case, replaced circumcision as a rite of passage into manhood.

The music came from a percussion orchestra of drums and gourds, played by elders. The rest of the clan sat around the fire in a series of circles, singing and clapping. The women, most of them bare to the waist, were as colorfully turned out as the preening warriors. They wore short leather skirts and even shorter haircuts, and armbands made from skinny brass rings, and heavy collars consisting of twenty or more beaded necklaces in descendingly larger sizes.

The younger women seemed to be having the best time of all. They were on their knees in the first ring of onlookers, shimmying to the incendiary beat of the drums, their breasts bobbing, their feverish eyes glued to the cavorting warriors. All but one. On the other side of the fire, just inside its nimbus of light, the one called Nimonia sat perfectly still, watching Pythias through the flames. And every now and then Pythias would turn his head ever so slightly and their eyes would lock.

They ate and drank and watched the dancers and listened to songs far into the night. At one point Adrian, his bladder bursting, staggered to his feet and went off into the desert to relieve himself. When he returned, Pythias was nowhere to be seen. The woman Nimonia also was gone.

*   *   *

Adrian slept that night in the headman's *awi,* a familial compound of sorts, consisting of several huts. He did not see Pythias again until the next morning. Adrian was back in front of the fire, now a smoky heap of ash and coals, breakfasting on cakes made by mixing crushed berries with blood, when Pythias squatted down beside him.

"So tell me, my brother . . ." Adrian said, not looking at him. "Is it true what *Bwana* Wilkinson says about body bumps?"

It is a myth that Africans cannot blush. The Dorobo's whole head seemed to swell with blood, making his face even darker than before, as black as a Turkana's.

Pythias did not say anything in response to the teasing, but Adrian could see that the light had returned to his eyes. Whatever had happened the night before, he decided, had done his friend a world of good.

They didn't see much of each other after that. Pythias, unable to keep his eyes open, spent the rest of the morning and much of the afternoon napping, trying to sleep Turkana style, just to see how it worked, with his neck propped on one of the short stools that the men used to protect their fragile hairdos. Adrian, with von Höhnel's journal of the Teleki Expedition in mind, made a day trip to the eastern shore of Lake Turkana, taking one of the warriors along as his guide.

In his journal, von Höhnel had described coming upon a vast pile of bones, the skeletons of two hundred camels, the result of a Turkana raid on the Rendille. Adrian wanted to see the spot, and his companion, who wanted a ride in the Land Rover, claimed to know exactly where it was.

There was only sand to be seen when they got there, of course, but Adrian's guide recounted the story with sweeping hand gestures and a voice throbbing with pride. First a band of Turkana warriors had stolen the camels in a well-executed, lightning-quick raid. Then, when the Rendille gave chase with an overwhelmingly superior force, the Turkana had speared the camels before making good their escape. It was a sad thing to have to kill the camels, Adrian's guide readily admitted, but there had been no real choice in the matter. Leaving them for the Rendille to reclaim was unthinkable.

Later, back in camp, Adrian watched the first contingent of warriors arrive, coming to take part in the next day's contest. They kept coming, scores of them, all through the afternoon and into the evening, and when he went to bed that night he fell asleep to the soft sound of hooves on sand, and the jingle of camel bells.

The next morning Adrian emerged from his *akai,* his night hut, and saw the smoke from a hundred or more breakfast fires darkening the sky. From what he could see, an army was camped in the surrounding desert.

The headman, sporting a huge smile, was waiting for him at the entrance to the *awi*. Pythias was at his side, watching Adrian's face and trying not to laugh.

"A good turnout, yes?" the chief said, obviously pleased with himself.

Adrian made a heroic effort to show a little enthusiasm. "Much better than I expected," he said. He cleared his throat and asked: "Just how many of them are there?"

Still beaming, the old man shrugged. "A thousand. Maybe more."

"Super," Adrian mumbled in English.

"How do you want to conduct the test?" the chief asked.

Adrian didn't know. The number of candidates overwhelmed him. "Gather them together in one place and then I'll let you know," he said, playing for time.

The headman rushed off to comply, appointing a number of warriors to pass the word among the new arrivals. The initial collection point he chose was a broad, sandy *lugga* only a few hundred yards away, but he quickly shifted them downwind when he saw that the dust they kicked up was blowing right through his camp.

By midmorning they were all gathered, sitting on their shields to keep the hot sand from scorching their backsides, or leaning on their spears. With their bright blue coiffures they resembled a mass migration of exotic birds.

They scrambled to their feet, jabbering with excitement when Adrian pulled up in the Land Rover, and it wasn't until he climbed up onto the roof of the cab and stood there for a minute or two that they began to quiet down.

When they were settled, Adrian raised a fist and shouted in Swahili: "Greetings, Turkana warriors!"

They answered him with a visceral roar and a rattling of spears.

Adrian surveyed them silently for a moment, then asked: "Why are you here?"

"To fight!" came the response, accompanied by two sharp, deafening noises—*WHAM! WHAM!*—the sound of spear shafts being slammed against hippopotamus–hide shields.

"Who among you is strong?" Adrian shouted.

"I am!" came the answer from a thousand throats.

"Who among you is the strongest?"

"I am!"

Adrian grinned and raised a fist again and they answered with another guttural roar. Then, using his finger to draw an imaginary circle around the Land Rover, he yelled in English, "All those who speak English, gather around me."

There were only about fifty of them. When they were all together, standing in a loose ring around the Land Rover and looking at him expectantly, Adrian said: "I'm sorry but I won't be able to use you. Thank you for coming."

Their smiles flaked, then crumbled as the words sank in. Confused, yammering in Turkana, they turned to their sponsor, the chief, for confirmation. He heard them out, then signaled for silence and looked up at Adrian, seeking a clarification. "You do *not* want those who can speak the English tongue?" he asked uncertainly, in Swahili.

"That's right, *jumbe*. No English." He didn't elaborate, but he wasn't interested in "a missionary boy." He needed a strong, simple bush boy. One whose native instincts had not gone to rust in a classroom.

When the disappointed English-speakers had started back to camp, Adrian asked the headman if he would tell those who did not speak Swahili to come forward. Delighted to have the chance to demonstrate his importance to warriors from other clans, the headman scrambled up onto the Land Rover to stand beside Adrian. He translated the order with dramatic flourish.

There weren't many who did not speak Swahili, fewer than two hundred, and when they too had been dismissed, Adrian had the men who were left, seven hundred or so, arrange themselves in ranks of fifty. He got down off the Land Rover and passed among them, weeding out those who were too old, or too young, and those he simply didn't like the look of. He was fairly ruthless about it, but when he finished there were still some five hundred warriors left.

He told them to relax awhile, then drove five miles out into the desert, using the odometer to gauge the distance. He left Pythias there with orders to plant a wooden stake in the ground, then drove back alone. When he returned to the group, he set out the rules of the contest.

The candidates were to follow the Land Rover's tracks to the wooden stake, at a brisk walk. They would wait behind the stake until Pythias gave the signal, and then run all the way back to the starting point. The first man to reach Adrian had himself a job.

Adrian waited another thirty minutes, until the sun was directly overhead, before launching them with a volley from Jock Wilkinson's shotgun.

To the cheers of the women they set off in one line abreast, chanting a Turkana war song and banging their spears and knobkerries against their hippo-hide shields. *WHAM! WHAM!* Their soaring hairdos, swaying in rhythm with their shuffling gait, reminded Glenton of the tides off Diani Beach, south of Mombasa. Even after the human phalanx was gone from view, the dust it raised hung on the horizon like a brown curtain.

Adrian didn't think to clock them, but it seemed no time at all before he heard the women cheer and glanced up to see the lead runner materializing like a chimera from out of the heat waves rising off the desert floor. No more than a small blue dot at first, which became a stickman without legs, who appeared to be bobbing along on a thin sheet of ground water. Far behind, another blue dot popped out of the haze, quickly followed by a dozen more.

The front runner maintained his lead and came in holding his spear high over his head, covering the last hundred yards without changing pace, running hard but not sprinting.

He stopped directly in front of Adrian, his chest rising and falling evenly. He had a splendid physique. He was almost as tall and as well muscled as Joseph. And if the look on his face was any indication, almost as arrogant.

A crowd of young girls flocked around the winner. Adrian saw one of them run her finger across his sweaty back and pop it into her mouth.

Adrian's friend, the chief, was nearly as demonstrative. He pushed through the throng of chittering women and embraced the young warrior, who, it happened, turned out to be his son. Adrian would have suspected foul play if the losers, who were now beginning to straggle in, had not rushed to the young man's side to congratulate him.

"What is your name?" Adrian asked him.

"Ekali."

"Can you tell time, Ekali? Englishman's time?"

"Yes."

"Good. You have thirty minutes to collect your things, say your farewells and be back here, ready to go."

The youth nodded and bashed his spear twice against his shield. *WHAM! WHAM!* Then he turned and started for camp, his father and the rest of his adoring fans trailing in his wake.

Adrian climbed into the Land Rover and sped away in the other direction, off to pick up Pythias. Without being aware of it he was grinning, and his grin got wider and wider with each turn of the wheels.

He had his team!

He let out a whoop and slammed the heel of his palm on the steering wheel. Twice. *WHAM! WHAM!*

||

They made Aberdare Ranch late the following afternoon, after spending the night at Maralal and cutting east across the southern edge of the Il Bonyeki Plains and intercepting A-2 just above Archer's Post. Glenton logged out of the NFD at the Isiolo checkpoint, using the same ledger in which he had signed in.

His first stop was at the main house to check in with Stephen Hone. Adrian expected to find him on the veranda with his sugar biscuits and his japes about showing up at tea time, but the houseman told him that the *efendi,* the master, had gone to visit the guest compound.

He remembered the way easily enough, and he found Hone all right, along with what seemed like everyone else in the world. There were people and vehicles everywhere. There was Hone's Land Cruiser, and a Suzuki with government tags, and an army lorry with the stencil markings of the 7th Battalion of the Kenya Rifles. A troop detail was ferrying crates from the truck to the nearest cottage. Inspector Odongo was there, ticking off the crates on a clipboard and chatting with Hone. Under a nearby mimosa tree, Joseph squatted, anointing the blade of his long spear with animal fat to prevent rust and talking to three men whose backs were to Adrian.

They stopped what they were doing and looked around when the Land Rover pulled up, and Adrian saw that one of the men with Joseph was Tembo, his Liangulu elephant *fundi,* and that another was Chege, his former tourist camp headman. He didn't know the third man.

"What's Chege doing here?" he wondered out loud. Ekali and Pythias, sitting together in back, already fast friends, looked at each other and shrugged; Pythias because he didn't know who Chege was, Ekali because he didn't know English.

Leaving the two Africans with the Land Rover, Adrian joined Hone and Odongo. "Good afternoon, gentlemen."

"Hullo, Adrian."

"*Jambo,* Mr. Glenton."

"So what's this?" Adrian asked. "Piccadilly Circus?"

"Your supplies have arrived," Odongo said.

"Super." Adrian shaded his eyes and peered into the back of the lorry.

"Not so super, I'm afraid," Odongo said, coming over to stand behind him.

"Oh? Why is that?"

The inspector reached in and pulled a long wooden crate onto the lowered tailgate, using the rope handle attached to the end of the box. He unbuckled a clasp and raised the lid. Inside were half a dozen Enfield rifles.

"Enfields?" Adrian croaked. *"Enfields?"*

The inspector nodded.

"But the poachers have automatic weapons!" Adrian said, almost shouting.

The inspector nodded.

"Then just what the bloody hell am I supposed to do with Enfields?"

"It is all that the Assistant Minister would authorize," Odongo said, his voice apologetic.

"Well then fuck the bloody fucking Assistant Minister!" Adrian said. He was shouting now. "He can take these bloody antiques and shove them up his bloody arse!"

Odongo reached back into the lorry and pulled forward a small, square box. He opened it. "We have some grenades," he said encouragingly.

"Oh, we have some grenades," Adrian mimicked. "How bloody fucking marvelous. Be certain to thank the Assistant Minister for me."

"Mr. Glenton. Please . . ."

Adrian had picked up one of the grenades and was shaking it in the inspector's face. "I'd like to pop the spoon on one of these and put *it* up the Assistant Minister's arse."

"Please . . ."

"Save your breath. You'll need it to tell that bastard of a bureaucrat to get someone else for the job. Because I'm out. And so are they." Adrian jabbed a finger at his African recruits, including Pythias and Ekali, who had drifted over to watch the pyrotechnics. "These men are my responsibility. More than that, they're my friends. And I will not send them out into the bloody bush with Enfields."

"But the Assistant Minister . . ."

"Now there's a leader for you," Adrian said with a snort of derision. "There's a man who'll make a damn fine nation of you. But it's us who'll die in the making. Well I say to hell with that. I'm not going to let that . . ."

"Kipling."

Adrian, interrupted in mid-tirade and thrown off stride, stuttered to a stop. "W-What?"

"That phrase. It is from Mr. Rudyard Kipling, from his story 'The Man Who Would Be King.' "

"You don't say."

Odongo nodded seriously. "I do say."

"And which phrase was that?"

"You mangled it a bit, I'm afraid," the inspector said. "The exact quotation goes: *I'll make a damned fine nation of you, or I'll die in the making.*"

Flummoxed, Glenton turned to Stephen Hone. "Well what do you make of that?" he asked. "An African quoting Kipling, the grand poobah of imperialist literature."

Hone, regarding them both with ill-concealed amusement, just shrugged, staying out of it.

"A secret vice," Odongo confessed. "But if you read his work carefully, between the lines, you will find that all of the folly of colonial rule is in there as well."

"You don't say."

"Yes, I do say." The inspector was smiling at him now.

Glenton, his rage defused, laughed and shook his head. He rolled his eyes skyward. "Jesus Christ Almighty. What am I doing here."

"The same thing I am," Odongo said. "Trying to serve your country."

"Some bloody country."

"It is the only one we have," Odongo said with a shrug.

And that was the sorry fact of it, Glenton had to agree. Here they were, two marginal men, a *mzungu* and a Luo, trying to serve their country. It was a country that did not always serve them well in return, but as the inspector said, it was the only one they had.

Adrian sighed and peered into the box of Enfields. They were clean at least, wrapped up in heavy waxed paper smeared with cosmoline.

"I'm assuming that you made your objections known to the Assistant Minister," he said.

"Vigorously."

"And that the Assistant Minister pleaded considerations of budget."

"Vigorously."

"So I take it there will be no airplane either."

"Correct," Odongo confirmed. "But I was just talking to Mr. Hone about that very thing when you drove up, and . . ."

"And you can use the ranch plane," Hone said. "I think I can talk Holger Jensen into piloting it for you."

"The Daring Dane? Is he still around?" Adrian asked. "I would have thought he'd have killed himself by now."

"Oh he's still trying right enough," Hone said, "but at the moment he hasn't an aeroplane to do it with. Pranged his Beech just last week. It's sitting on top of Kulal Mountain."

"Christ knows we could use a plane," Adrian said. "But I wouldn't want to put you in the dog box. What would your Yank say about it? It does belong to him, after all."

"He won't have to know, will he?"

Adrian stared at Hone without speaking for a moment, and then said, "Thank you again, Stephen."

Hone shrugged and looked away, uncomfortable in the face of such naked gratitude. Adrian turned on Odongo. "What about our other generous benefactor?" he asked bitterly. "What else has the Assistant Minister been kind enough to contribute?"

The policeman slipped a sheet of paper off his clipboard and handed it to him. "Here is a complete inventory."

The list was broken down by category: Weapons, Transport, Signals and Rations. Under the Weapons heading were the half dozen bolt-action Enfields he had already seen and two boxes of fragmentation grenades, a dozen to the box. Transport was a single Land Rover. For Signals, there was a mixture of the primitive and the modern: six whistles, six hand mirrors and seven radios. Six of the radios were VHF hand-held units with 20 watts of power and 30-foot omnidirectional antennas, and the other was a single-sideband, backpack base unit mounted with a dipole antenna. Rations included two weeks' worth of a daily ration of twelve ounces of maize meal, six ounces of tinned meat, one and a half ounces of vegetable ghee, two and a half ounces of sugar, three and a half ounces of dried beans, four ounces of fresh onion, seven ounces of dates, a half ounce of tea leaves, three quarters of an ounce of salt and two ounces of curry powder.

Listed under Miscellaneous were maps, folding camp beds, blankets, a set of handcuffs, a pair of 8 x 40 binoculars, an assortment of batteries for the radios and a battery charger.

"Special team, my arse," Adrian said in disgust, handing the inventory back to Odongo. "This is the standard issue for a Field Force ranger section."

"That is precisely what I told the Assistant Minister," Odongo said.

"And what did he say?"

"He said that the success or failure of the mission will depend on the men, not the matériel."

Adrian groaned. "Let us pray that it doesn't depend on his cooperation and leadership."

The inspector smiled, then issued an order in Swahili to the unloading detail. Three of the soldiers immediately broke away and trotted over to the Suzuki with GK plates. One came back cradling a bundle in his arms, something long and thin, wrapped up in a woolen blanket. The other two returned with a large wooden box, pulling it along the ground. Odongo opened the wooden box first.

"Good Christ!" Glenton exclaimed. There, stacked neatly in rows, were his guns, the ones he was forced to keep in the safe at the Firearms Bureau in Nairobi . . . his Weatherby .300; his Holland and

Holland .375 magnum; his 7-mm Remington magnum; his .470 Nitro Express; even his 12-gauge shotgun, an exquisitely engraved Holland and Holland over-and-under.

"How did you get these?" he asked, flabbergasted. "How did you even know about them?"

"Oh it's all computerized now," Odongo said blithely. "I put your name into the Central Station's computer to see what guns you owned and where they were stored. Then I confiscated them, citing official police business. It was simple enough."

The inspector squatted beside the second parcel, turned back the blanket, and said: "This, on the other hand, took a bit of doing."

There lay two automatic rifles, both Armalites, one an M-16 assault rifle, the other a shorter version of the same weapon, an AR-15.

"With the compliments of the Kenya Police," Odongo said, standing up so he could see Adrian's face.

Adrian, still looking stunned, bent down and snatched up the AR-15. It was bandbox new and it was the real thing, not some Israeli or South African copy. He brushed his fingertips over the Colt trademark, caressing the rifle.

Odongo put the soldiers back to work unloading rations. When he turned back around, he saw that Glenton was staring at him with new respect.

"What's your name, Inspector?" Adrian asked. "Your given name?"

"Peter."

"Do you mind if I use it?"

"Why, no, of course not. Please do."

"Well you're a right bloody wizard, Peter."

"Merely a matter of having the right friend in the right place in the right department," Odongo said with a shrug. But his attempt at nonchalance did not fool Adrian. The policeman was clearly pleased, reveling in his own surprise.

A few minutes later Odongo checked the last of the boxes off his list and excused himself, heading for the bungalow to see that the soldiers had stacked the supplies the way he had told them to.

Hone waited until he was out of earshot, then remarked: "Unusual chap."

"Isn't he though?" said Adrian.

The team members had been hovering on the fringe of the discussion, just far enough away not to intrude, waiting for Adrian to finish with the *bwanas*. He turned his attention to them, making a point of greeting Joseph first, to establish him as a leader in the minds of the others.

"*Keserian ingera? Keserian ingishu?*" he asked in Masai. How are the children? How are the cattle?

Joseph reported that they were fine. He was a bachelor, and officially childless, of course, but he had lain with so many young girls during his freewheeling years of living in the warrior's kraal that it was impossible to be certain.

"Who is first to eat meat when a cow is slaughtered?" Adrian asked, picking up their riddle game.

"The knife," said Joseph.

Adrian made a disgusted face. He couldn't remember the last time he had stumped the man.

"When did you get here?" he asked.

"Three days ago."

"What have you been doing with yourself?"

"Walking in the forest," Joseph said. "Trying to find its heartbeat."

"Did you find it?"

Joseph shrugged. "It is difficult to find anything in this forest. It is dark and close and at times a man can't see the tip of his spear."

"Don't worry, you'll get used to it," Adrian told him.

Tembo was patiently waiting his turn, twisting a filthy beret in both hands and grinning obsequiously, showing off a mouthful of rotten teeth. He cut an outlandish figure and it was all Adrian could do not to laugh. Both of the Liangulu's earlobes were elongated and shaped into loops, but loops of different sizes. In one he carried a packet of Rooster brand cigarettes. The other was just the right size to accommodate a plastic, throwaway lighter.

Adrian looked him over carefully, checking to see if he was sober. "*Jambo,* Tembo. I see you made it."

"*Jambo, bwana. Ndiyo, bwana. Asante sana, bwana.*" The old poacher kept smiling, ducking his head each time he spoke. If he'd had a forelock, Adrian thought, he would have tugged it.

"You can thank me by doing good work," Adrian said. "And by staying away from the *pombe.*"

"*Ndiyo, bwana.*"

Adrian looked at Chege. "What are you doing here, Chege? You were supposed to dry him out, clean him up, and ship him off to me in a *matatu,* not bring him yourself."

"I know, Adrian, but I wanted to work for you. I thought to myself: If he has a job for an old man, he will have a job for a young man like me, too."

"You already have a job. A good job."

"I've taken two weeks holiday so I can work for you."

"But there's no place for you," Adrian said. "You're a good man, Chege, and I enjoyed working with you, but I need a different sort of man here. These others are bush experts, skilled hunters or trackers or both."

Odongo had come back outside and was standing with Hone, listening. Adrian looked over Chege's shoulder and caught the inspector's eye. Odongo shook his head and turned out both of his front trousers pockets. Empty. If he took on another man, Odongo was telling him, it would be out of his own pocket.

Adrian said, "I'm sorry, Chege, but there's no money for you."

Chege shrugged. "Then I'll work for no money. Give me a camp bed and maybe a little food. That is all I need."

"But what would you do?"

"I can be camp headman, like always. You know I can cook and keep the camp clean. I can do laundry." Chege lowered his voice to a conspiratorial whisper. "I can watch Tembo for you to see that he stays away from strong drink."

Adrian gave in with a sigh. "Oh all right. Bed and board and a hundred shillings."

Chege beamed, grabbed Adrian's hand and pumped it. "You won't be sorry, *rafiki*. You'll see."

The remaining African, the one Adrian did not know, had gone over to stand next to the inspector. Ever since Adrian's arrival he had been hovering at the edge of things, there but not there. He was tall for a Kikuyu, considerably taller than Chege, although not as tall as either the Masai Joseph or the Turkana Ekali. He was wearing the forest green uniform of the Field Force ranger: a beret, shorts, a jersey with reinforced patches at the shoulders and elbows, and boots with leggings. His body was as thin as a whippet's, but his face was the face of a fat man, round and fleshy, and finished off with a thin mustache. It was an alert face, sly rather than intelligent.

Inspector Odongo made the introductions. "This is Ranger Corporal Charles Ndirangu, the Kikuyu you asked for. He comes from Mweiga and he was recommended highly by the park warden. Corporal, this is Mr. Glenton."

"How do you do, sir?" said the ranger, extending a hand. His English was excellent, virtually accentless.

"Hullo," Adrian said, shaking his hand. "Has Inspector Odongo briefed you on what your duties will be?"

"Yes, sir. I'm to go into the town and into the *shambas* to gather information."

Adrian nodded. "So you're from Mweiga. The town proper?"

"Yes. I know these townspeople well. They won't be able to hide anything from me."

Odongo cut in. "It was Corporal Ndirangu who helped us to identify the murder victim as one of the Mwangi brothers. He'd had them under surveillance for several weeks."

"Is that so?"

The ranger nodded. "I've done intelligence work for the park warden," he said. "I know who engages in minor poaching, who crosses into the forest to gather firewood, who uses park land to grow extra crops. We let the little fishes off with a warning, but when we find a big fish . . . we net him. So, as you can see, I have a system of informers already at work."

"Hmmmmm," was Adrian's only comment. He would have been more impressed if the corporal's informers had tipped him to the gang they were after. This ranger was too self-satisfied for his liking. A cheeky bugger, Pate would have called him.

He brought the men in closer and conducted them through a series of formal introductions, seeing to it that each man shook the hand of every other man. They made a motley bunch. Six men from five different tribes.

Mixing the tribes could be a risky business, Adrian well knew. It wasn't unlike the dilemma that so vexed the nation's elite—the whites, the Asians, the Wabenzis—when it came to putting together a domestic staff. Take your servants from different tribes and they bickered constantly, forcing you to spend your day refereeing their arguments or removing *thahus,* the spells they put on one another. Take them from one tribe and harmony ruled, but they banded together to rob you blind.

However apt the comparison, it made him feel silly, like one of those wives who congregate at dinner parties to talk, yet again, about "the servant problem." Besides, what choice had he? These men were the best he knew, regardless of tribe. They did not have to like one another as long as they worked well together. Except for the two unknown quantities—the Turkana warrior Ekali and the Kikuyu ranger Charles— each one of them was loyal to him personally, and he was counting on that loyalty to make it all work.

When the introductions were done, he addressed them in Swahili. "You've met Joseph. He will be my second-in-command. If he tells you to do something, do it without argument. You can come to me if you feel he's not treating you fairly, but only after you've carried out his order, not before. Our camp headman will be Chege. He'll serve as quartermaster and will disperse rations and ammunition. He's a good cook if you tire of tinned beef. If you have washing, give it to him. Pythias is our chief tracker. When you come across sign, consult him. Most of you are fine trackers in your own right, but believe me, he's the best. He will also be our man on leopard. Tembo will be our man on elephant. I will be our man on rhinoceros. Charles will deal with the local population. Ekali will serve as a message runner in case of radio failure. As for military tactics, ambushes, and the like, Joseph will be the man if I'm not available. Any questions so far?"

The men shook their heads, seeming satisfied with the assignments.

"Tonight we will meet in my cottage and go over the maps of the park. I have a set for each of you. When we're through I want you to study them on your own. I'll expect you to know all the roads and major trails, all the streams and glades."

He looked at Hone who was standing with Inspector Odongo at the rear of the pack. "Stephen, could you go over the maps with us tonight? You know the Aberdares as well as anyone."

"Be happy to," Hone said.

Glenton thanked him with a nod and resumed the briefing. "Tomorrow at first light we'll go out in the Land Rover for a recce, a familiarization run. Bring your maps and a pencil so you can mark all roads and major animal paths. Take notes on the effects of light and shadow at various times of day. Later in the day, we will come back here for a classroom session. I will check you out on the radios, and Joseph and Pythias will go over the weapons with you. If you've never used a firearm before, we'll give you a shooting lesson, free of charge. Any questions?"

The talk of firearms caused a stir, but there were no questions.

"As for housing assignments," Adrian said, "this nearest cottage will be the arsenal and storeroom. It will also serve as camp HQ. Joseph and I will sleep there. Charles, Chege and Tembo will take the cottage to the left of the swimming pool. Pythias and Ekali can share the remaining bungalow. Are there any objections to the sleeping arrangements?"

The ranger, Charles, spoke up. "I live only a short way from here. I have two wives. Can't I sleep at home?"

"I'm sorry, Charles. No one is to leave this camp until our mission is accomplished. For security reasons. No one on the outside is even to know we're here."

The Kikuyu opened his mouth to say something but Adrian raised a hand to stop him. "I know what you're going to say. That you will be working outside the compound anyway, in town and in the *shambas*. That's true, but I'll still want you here at night. I want an intelligence report from you each evening at six o'clock, and I'll need you close to hand because we will be operating at night. Once these poachers realize we're onto them, they'll be moving under cover of darkness. We will have to move as well."

Seeing the look of disappointment on the ranger's face, Adrian smiled and said, "I realize that a man with two wives has certain, um, obligations, but with all the time you'll be spending in Mweiga, I'm almost certain that you'll be able to squeeze in a visit home."

The ranger shrugged and said: "It's not that important. *Aka eri ni nyungu igiri cia urogi.*"

Those who understood Kikuyu—Adrian, Chege, and Stephen Hone—laughed.

Joseph nudged Adrian. "What did he say?"

"He said that two wives are two pots full of poison."

Joseph did not laugh. "He should speak so that everyone can understand," he said, speaking to Glenton but looking at Charles.

Before Adrian could say anything, the ranger answered for himself. In Kikuyu. *"Ciunagwo rukomo, kimenyi akamenya ikiunwo."*

"What did he say?" Joseph asked Adrian, not taking his eyes from the ranger's face.

"Oh for Christ's sake," Adrian said irritably. "You both speak English and Swahili. You don't need me in this."

"What did you say, Kikuyu?" Joseph's query went directly to Charles this time.

The ranger shrugged again and answered in English. "We speak by proverbs: he who is intelligent will understand."

Adrian saw the Masai's eyes change, a kind of pulsing of the pupils, a subtle, almost imperceptible movement. He would not have seen it at all if he hadn't been watching for it. It was the same thing that happened in a lion's eyes just before it charged.

"The Masai have proverbs as well," Joseph said in a flat voice. *"Menyanyuk enchikati enkutuk o eno siadi."*

"Which means?" Charles asked.

"The odor from the mouth is stronger than the odor from the anus."

Charles stared back unblinkingly, then nodded and said, "Yes, now I can smell it." He pretended to sniff the breeze. "It seems to be coming from upwind."

Joseph, standing upwind of Charles, went stiff. Anxious to head off the brewing trouble, Adrian muttered a warning in Masai, another proverb. "You, eye, observe; you, mouth, don't reply."

Joseph turned on him and fired one right back. "It is better to be laughed at by beasts than to be laughed at by men."

Adrian retaliated with still another: "Mountains do not meet, but people do."

None of the others understood Masai, but they followed the volley as if at the center court gallery at Wimbledon, their heads swiveling in unison to watch Joseph, then Adrian, then Joseph again. They gave out a soft collective sigh when they saw Joseph smile.

"How many more of these silly proverbs do you know?" he asked, still speaking Masai.

"Enough to make my point," Adrian replied.

Joseph nodded and, no longer smiling, said: "All right, Adrian. But keep that monkey-faced Kikuyu away from me or I shall have to kill him."

"Just remember that there is no man without gum plant in his hand," Adrian said. It was a proverb meaning that even an enemy may possess something which can help you.

The Masai shook his head and, imitating perfectly their last hunting client, a toy manufacturer from New York, said: "Gimme a fuckin' break."

Adrian laughed, more in relief than anything else. The dangerous moment had passed. "All right," he said in English, talking to the group, "don't just hang about like a dag on a sheep's bum. Chege, you can start handing out the bedding and the rest of it. You others queue up at the door and go in one at a time to draw your kit. You will have to sign for it. If you can't write, make your mark. You will be expected to turn everything back in when the operation is finished. Be warned, gentlemen: if you lose something, I will be forced to take it out of your wages."

The team dispersed, leaving Adrian alone with Hone and Odongo. "That ranger's rather a courageous chap," Hone said, watching them go.

"Foolish is more like it," Glenton said. "Joseph is not someone to fuck about with."

"That is what I meant," Hone said. "As they were having at it, I was remembering the day Joseph took the lion charge up at Elliots Camp. Couldn't you just see him waiting behind his shield, calm as can be, singing that blasted song as old *simba* bore down on him?" Hone stopped and both he and Adrian began chuckling.

Finally, when it became clear that Hone was not going to go on, Odongo asked: "What happened?"

Hone, lost in reverie, looked startled. "Hullo? Oh. Yes. Well. The client—a bloody Boche wasn't he, Adrian?—had emptied his magazine in the course of potting a rather small female when this male comes bounding across the bundu at us. Huge bloody brute he was, too. I had just handed my rifle to my gun boy, who immediately scarpered off with it. Adrian put up his rifle, but before he had a chance to shoot, Joseph ran into his line of sight. Joseph unslung his shield and kneeled behind it, planted his spear butt-first in the ground and was singing a song when he took the charge."

Hone stopped again, apparently done with his story. The inspector sighed and asked again, "What happened?"

"The lion impaled himself on the spear, of course. Right through the heart. But he landed on Joseph, burying him under the shield. Squashed him flat. It took four of us to haul the beast off him, and when we lifted the shield there was Joseph lying spread-eagled, all covered with *simba's* blood and still humming that silly song."

"All in a day's work for a Masai warrior," Glenton said. "Joseph had been doing lions that way ever since his manhood ceremony at age twelve."

"I noticed that you seem to know a great deal about the Masai," Odongo said.

"I know a great deal about Joseph," Adrian said. "He was my number one gun-bearer and my safari headman off and on for ten years. He's the bravest man I know."

"Why thank you," Hone said, pretending to be insulted.

Adrian shook his head and asked: "Did *you* ever cut off your own earlobe just to make a joke?" He was about to say more when a splashing noise caused him to glance toward the swimming pool. He could not quite believe what he saw there. Climbing out of the pool was a woman. A white woman. She placed both hands flat on the grassy bank and lifted herself out of the water in one smooth motion, then stood and shook herself like a wet dog, her short dark hair throwing off a fine spray that caught the light and sparkled round her head like a halo.

"Who in the bloody hell is that?" Adrian asked of no one in particular. He gave Hone a lascivious look. "You should be ashamed of yourself, you randy old goat. From here, she looks young enough to be your granddaughter."

"Thank you for the compliment, as backhanded as it was," Hone said dryly. "But she's not mine. She came with Inspector Odongo."

"Oh. Oh, I see." Adrian glanced at Odongo with surprise. Then he shrugged. *Harambee* and all that, he reminded himself. One Kenya, black and white, pulling together.

The inspector was watching him archly, aware of what he was thinking. "No, you do not see, Mr. Glenton," he said. He turned to face the pool, cupped his hands to his mouth, and called: "Miss Lewis!" When the woman looked up, he beckoned her over.

Glenton watched her walk toward them. She was a handsome piece. She had the kind of body he liked, lithe and hard, and most of it was on display. She wore a skimpy bathing costume, not quite a string bikini, but the kind they called a "French cut," two breast cups on a string and a bottom which left her flanks almost completely bare. Her stomach was as flat as the Chalbi and as muscled as an athlete's, with a convex navel.

The closer she came the better she looked. She had long, nicely turned legs and her breasts were small but beautifully shaped. Her nipples, responding to the cool air, had hardened and showed clearly through the wet fabric of her costume. But it was the way she moved which left the biggest impression on Adrian. She walked with a sinuous grace, springing lightly on the balls of her feet like a cat. It was a sensuous walk, one made all the more provocative by the fact that it was so obviously unconscious.

With her coloring, an alloy of copper and brass, Adrian decided that she was Greek or Italian, or perhaps Israeli; a Mediterranean type despite the English-sounding surname. No, not Israeli. The contours of her face, an oval-cut diamond, were a bit too softly defined for that. And not really Greek or Italian either; there was far too much going on behind her large brown eyes to reflect a convincing image of white-washed, sun-stunned villages.

Adrian realized that he'd been gawking when he suddenly saw that she had come to a stop and was standing in front of him, those lively dark eyes studying him with amusement. She was letting him have a good look, standing with her legs spread a little apart, her hands just above the slight swell of her hips, her long fingers almost touching as they circled her waist. She was still dripping wet and shivering slightly, and he could see goosebumps almost anywhere he cared to look.

Odongo's voice seemed to come out of another dimension. "Miss Lewis, may I present Adrian Glenton. Mr. Glenton, this is Roberta Lewis. She likes to be called Robbie."

"How do you do?" Adrian said, holding out his hand.

The woman shook it. Then she grinned, showing dazzling white teeth, and said: "Yo! Adrian."

Glenton looked at her blankly. "I beg your pardon?"

"I've been waiting almost two years for a chance to say that," she said, still smiling. "Ever since I saw *Rocky*."

Adrian shook his head, as if to clear it. The woman's accent identi-fied her as an American. Perhaps that was the problem. "I'm afraid I don't know what you mean," he said.

"*Rocky*. The movie. You must've seen it. Everyone's seen it. Hell, it's been playing in Nairobi for more than a year." She glanced at Odongo, who was smiling and nodding, and then back at Adrian, who was shaking his head.

She shrugged. "Oh well."

There was an awkward silence which Odongo finally broke by saying, "Robbie is the Africa correspondent for *Newsweek*, the American news magazine."

Adrian nodded and smiled, relieved that the inspector's words, at least, made sense, belonged to a language he knew. Then he stopped smiling and stared at Odongo. "A journalist?" he asked, a catch in his voice.

Odongo nodded.

"Inspector, may I see you alone for a moment?" Adrian's tone was calm, but there was an almost hysterical edge to it.

Before either of the men could move, the woman declared: "You don't want me here."

"What I want," Adrian said coldly, "is to see Inspector Odongo alone for a moment."

The woman looked at Odongo. "We have a deal, Inspector."

"Deal? What deal?" Adrian asked quickly.

Odongo sighed. "Um, well, you see . . . Robbie is preparing an article on endangered species," he said. "She went to see the Assistant Minister of Wildlife . . ."

"The Assistant Minister again!" Adrian erupted. "I might have known. Goddamn that man's eyes!"

". . . who told her all about our plans and sent her to see me," Odongo went on, as if there had been no interruption. "I impressed upon her the need for strict secrecy, and she agreed that if I gave her full access to the operation she would not print anything until our mission is completed."

"And you trust a journalist to honor a promise?" Adrian asked scornfully.

"Whoa! Hold it right there, buddy," the woman said. "Are you saying I'd go back on a deal?"

"I know journalists," Adrian said.

"You don't know shit, *paisan*. And you don't know a damn thing about me!"

"And I don't think I want to," Adrian said, taken aback by her language.

"I don't give a damn what you think," she said, calm now. "I have Inspector Odongo's promise, and I intend to hold him to it. Or don't you think a Kenya police officer can be trusted to honor a promise either?"

Adrian, a man who thought nothing of going into the bush after a wounded Cape buffalo, was rattled at suddenly finding himself arguing with a half-naked woman. He switched targets, turning on Odongo. "How much does she already know?"

"All that there is to know at this point," Odongo said. "The Assistant Minister was quite thorough."

"And if you cut me out now I will go straight into print with everything he told me," the woman said. "If I'm going to be punished, I might as well go ahead and commit the crime."

"I see that your ethics are somewhat elastic," Glenton said, managing to sound both droll and superior all at once.

The woman merely smiled and said, "Perhaps you could see more clearly if you took your eyes off my tits."

The men reacted in different ways. Hone, trying to choke back a laugh, nearly gagged. Odongo turned his twitching face away and stared into the park. Adrian flushed a deep rose and jerked his guilty eyes away from the woman's torso. He lashed out at Odongo. "Deal with her any bloody way you choose. Just keep her away from me. And off this ranch."

"Sorry, old man," Hone said, "but I've already told Miss Lewis that she can stay in the main residence. It wouldn't be very chivalrous of me to go back on my word."

"That's all right, Stephen," the woman said. "Sam Weller is holding a room for me at the Aberdare Country Club."

So it's *Stephen* is it? Adrian thought bitterly, feeling betrayed, the victim of a conspiracy.

"I told you that you could stay in the residence," Hone said, speaking to the woman, but giving Adrian a challenging look, "and you are most welcome to do so."

She shook her head. "Under the circumstances, I think I should stay at the club."

"As you wish, my dear," Hone said. "But please feel free to come visit. I take tea at half past four every afternoon."

"I'll pour," she said. "I learned the right way to do it when I lived in London." She turned big brown eyes on Adrian, batted her lashes like a silent-movie heroine, and said in a sultry, mock-sweet voice: "Perhaps Mr. Glenton could join us some time."

"Have your sport, Miss Lewis," Glenton said. "Just stay out of my way."

"With pleasure, Mr. Glenton."

Adrian glared at her balefully, careful not to let his eyes wander any lower than the point of her outthrust chin, until he gradually became aware of a high whining noise, the sound of a fast approaching vehicle. The car, a police van, pulled up in front of the cottage and the uniformed driver jumped out and presented Odongo with a salute.

"Constable Ngala, sir."

"God's holy trousers," Adrian muttered. "Does the entire bloody planet know we're here?"

Odongo ignored Adrian's grumbling and returned the man's salute. "What is it, Constable Ngala?"

"Your presence is urgently required in Nyeri, sir."

"Urgently required by whom?"

"By the district commissioner and the superintendent of police, sir."

"All right. Tell them I'll be along in about an hour."

"They say you must come right away. I have been ordered to bring you in myself."

Odongo sighed. "Very well then. Have you any idea what it's about?"

The constable bobbed his head and grinned. "Yes, sir. We have the missing Mwangi brother in custody."

12

The interrogation of Amos Mwangi, if one could properly call such a one-sided affair an interrogation, was conducted not at police headquarters as was customary but in a heavily guarded ward at the Nyeri district hospital.

He had been brought there immediately after being picked up near the Wananchi Saw Mill just above the aerodrome north of town. A routine police patrol had found him walking naked in the road, dazed and incoherent. At first they had thought he was drunk, but a closer examination revealed that he had been physically abused. And it wasn't over yet. The arresting officers had to club him unconscious to get him into the van. Only then did one of them recognize him as the missing Mwangi brother.

When Inspector Odongo, accompanied by Adrian Glenton and Robbie Lewis, arrived on the ward, he found it full of people and confusion. Mwangi was the only patient, but crowded around his bed was a mob of doctors, nurses, policemen, and district officials.

Technically, both the superintendent of police and the district commissioner outranked him, but Odongo quickly took charge. His first order was to clear the ward. He stationed two constables outside the entrance and shooed the rest, all except for the chief surgeon, one nurse, the superintendent, the DC, and Glenton and Robbie. No one thought to challenge him; he was from Nairobi, after all, and the emissary of an assistant cabinet minister.

Odongo stood over the bed, studying the patient. The man was asleep on his back, with his arms straight down along his sides. His wrists were secured to the bedframe by straps, and another strap was buckled across his chest. Plastic tubes fed into his nose, mouth, and both arms. His head was bandaged and his face was marked by a split lip, puffed bruises, and a rash of tiny bumps. His breathing was regular, but every once in a while his eyelids would flutter and his body would twitch.

"Why is he tied down?" Odongo asked. "Was he violent?"

"A wild man," said the surgeon, an Asian named Ramanujam who was adorned with the badges of his office: a long white coat, a parabolic disc mirror, a stethoscope. "I had to sedate him."

"When will I be able to talk to him?"

The doctor looked at his wristwatch and shrugged. "Nine or ten o'clock tonight."

Peter made an irritated face, then bent over the patient for a closer look. "What are those little welts on his face?"

"*Dudus*," said Dr. Ramanujam.

"Insects? You mean mosquito bites?"

"No. We think they are spider bites."

"Hmm, that's odd. He doesn't appear to have been bitten anywhere else."

"No," the doctor said. "Only his face."

Odongo studied Mwangi some more, then asked: "How badly is he hurt?"

The surgeon shrugged. "Physically, his condition is not too serious. He is weak from exhaustion and a lack of proper diet. I found minor cuts and abrasions over a wide body area, including the bottoms of his feet. He's been beaten, but not too badly. Most of the marks you see were probably caused by going through the forest barefooted and without clothes. His most serious injury is a mild concussion, and that was given him by your bullyboy policemen when they arrested him."

"Is that all that's wrong with him?" Peter asked coldly. He didn't like doctors, and he didn't like Asians.

Ramanujam nodded. "Except for the psychological trauma, of course. The man clearly has been terrorized."

"Oh? Did he say something before you sedated him?"

The doctor shrugged. "Nothing that made sense. But then I wasn't really listening. I was too busy trying to find and treat his wounds. The police were asking the questions."

"He was raving . . . off his head," said the superintendent, a dapper man almost as lean as the district commissioner was corpulent. He wore a crisp uniform, and a swagger stick was tucked under his left arm. "He kept calling for his brother, and babbling something about being attacked by an animal."

"What kind of animal, sir?" Peter asked politely.

"A hyena."

Odongo and Glenton exchanged a quick glance.

"Nonsense," Dr. Ramanujam said imperiously. "I found nothing in the way of wounds to substantiate such a claim."

"Perhaps not," the superintendent said, "but that does not change what the man said." The super didn't like Asians either.

No one said anything until Peter asked: "Was he carrying anything on him when you picked him up?"

"No," said the superintendent.

"Nothing in either hand? Or in his mouth?"

"His mouth?" The superintendent clearly considered the question odd. He shook his head. "No, nothing there either."

"And he was wearing no clothes?"

"Not a stitch."

"Then where was the tooth?" Odongo asked quietly.

The superintendent gaped at him, then said, "On a string around his neck. But how do you know about the tooth?" Odongo didn't answer and the superintendent made a gargling sound as he swallowed a reprimand. He did not appreciate being kept in the dark by a mere inspector. A Luo inspector at that. He added it to his list of bones to pick with Nairobi.

Robbie Lewis, wearing a hastily donned pair of designer overalls over her still damp swimsuit, stayed out of the way, artfully using her hip to shield the act of taking notes. She was only there at Odongo's sufferance, over the objections of Adrian Glenton, and she didn't want to be seen doing anything to cause the inspector to change his mind.

Robbie still didn't understand Glenton's rabid animosity toward her and she did not know what to make of it. She found him to be a thoroughly disagreeable man, totally without tact or charm. Which was too bad, because she also found him to be one of the sexiest men she had ever met.

She did not quite know what to make of that, either. It wasn't as if he fit the Hollywood profile of the Great White Hunter. He was no Clark Gable, nor even Stewart Granger; Ava Gardner wouldn't have given him a second glance. Rather than lean and weathered, he was blocky and weathered, with thick, powerful-looking wrists and forearms, and an embryo of a beer gut. Like the cinematic model, he was the strong, silent type—except when he was shouting at her, of course—but there the likeness began and ended. His eyes were green, not steely gray, and his facial features were rough, not chiseled. He had thin, straight, sandy hair, not thick, dark, and curly. And if what he had on was any guide, he was one of those men always in dishabille. His clothes were wrinkled and too big for him, obviously selected for comfort and freedom of movement rather than style. Not exactly the suave leading man of her girlhood fantasies.

Robbie glanced at Glenton and caught him staring at her. She winked. He flushed and looked away. She grinned and went back to her notes.

"I want a doctor or nurse to be with him at all times," Odongo was saying. "Summon me the instant he wakes. For the next hour or so I will be at the police barracks talking to the policemen who found him.

After that I'll be at supper." He looked at Adrian. "The White Rhino Hotel?"

"I'd prefer the Aberdare Country Club."

Odongo shook his head. "Too far away."

"The Outspan then."

"I'll be at the Outspan Hotel," Odongo told the surgeon. "Send one of the constables. Remember, as soon as he wakes."

"I quite understood you the first time," Dr. Ramanujam said archly, unaccustomed to being ordered about in his own hospital. And certainly not by an African.

The district commissioner coughed. "Um, Inspector, if I might have a word with you . . ."

"It will have to wait," Peter said brusquely. "I want to interview those constables before they tell and re-tell their tale so often that they forget what's true and what's not."

"I see," the DC muttered, stung at being dismissed by a policeman, but cowed by Peter's intimidating air of authority and decisiveness. He could not help thinking of the last time they had seen each other, the day on the mountain when he had been sick after seeing Adam Mwangi's corpse.

Odongo and Glenton left immediately for the Nyeri police barracks. Odongo invited Robbie to come along, but she begged off. She had them drop her at a service station which doubled as a car hire agency, where she rented a rusty old Citroen at an outlandish rate, then drove the twenty or so kilometers to the Aberdare Country Club to check in and deposit her things. She caught up with them at the Outspan Hotel. She checked the dining room and, not finding them there, went directly to the bar. "Finished supper so soon?" she said, taking a stool next to Odongo, putting the inspector between herself and Glenton.

"We're drinking supper," Odongo confessed. He was having a beer, a Tusker Export; Glenton sipped a whisky soda.

Robbie ordered a White Cap and pulled out her notebook. "So give me a fill," she said. "Did your cops have anything useful to add?"

The inspector gave her a rueful smile. "No. Which is why we are drinking our supper rather than eating it. The suspect was naked. When they saw him they thought he was drunk. When they approached him, he assaulted them. Blah, blah, blah. . . ." He shrugged.

Robbie sighed and put the notebook back in her tote bag. Her beer came and she downed half of it in one go, drinking right from the pint bottle. Then she ran her tongue over her top lip, skimming off a mustache of white foam. She looked up to find Odongo and Glenton staring at her. "Hey, I was thirsty, okay?" she said with a grin, no hint of embarrassment in her voice. "Besides, Kenya has good beer. Makes American beer taste like watered-down cat piss."

Odongo nodded gravely, trying not to giggle. There was a quality about this strange young woman, something he couldn't quite put a name to. All he knew was that he felt better when he was around her. She was a nuisance, of course, but she did liven things up. Suddenly, unexpectedly, he was glad that she had come along.

Glenton, however, was obviously of another mind. He had done little but complain about the woman's presence from the moment the two set eyes on each other. Peter hadn't expected him to be happy with the situation, of course, but his wrath seemed quite beyond reason. And when he questioned him on it, Glenton had answered with a query of his own. "Have you ever been on a hunting safari before, Inspector?" When Peter, who had been born into a tribe of fishers and farmers, said that he hadn't, Glenton said, "Well, I've yet to see a successful one that included a woman. Women and the bush don't mix. Try to remember that if you can. Women and the bush don't mix."

This last was a flat declaration, a bit of bombast which preempted all argument, delivered in a tone Peter remembered all too well from the time before *Uhuru*. He had heard it from English administrative officers, from Boer farmers, even from American priests. He hadn't liked it then and he didn't like it now. All he'd said was, "It depends on the woman, wouldn't you say?" But he had been disappointed. It was the first time Adrian Glenton had played the *bwana mkubwa* with him.

The woman in question had left the bar and was standing before a photograph of Lord Baden-Powell, founder of the Boy Scouts, who had lived out the final few years of his life in a *banda* on the hotel grounds. She was already at work on her second White Cap, sipping from the bottle while she wandered about the hotel, examining its display of memorabilia. Built in 1926 by Eric Sherbrooke-Walker, the Outspan had a colorful history that was preserved in the many clippings and photographs mounted on the walls. Many celebrities had stayed here, from American movie stars to European royalty, and at least one—Philadelphia's own Grace Kelly—who had managed to be both. Philadelphia's own Roberta D'Agostino was impressed.

These days, the hotel was known primarily as a luncheon stop and transit point for tourists on their way to overnight at Treetops, the world famous game-viewing lodge located just inside Aberdare Park, in that part now known as the "Treetops Salient." Sherbrooke-Walker had put up Treetops in 1932 as an adjunct to the Outspan. His idea, a shrewd one, was to bring the wildlife to the tourists rather than the other way round, so that overweight stockbrokers from The City could go home having seen the "Big Five"—lion, leopard, elephant, Cape buff and rhino—without having to work up an unsightly sweat. He put his new lodge on a water hole, put out salt, and put money in the bank. Treetops was already relatively well known in 1952, when it made world headlines: the young Elizabeth was a guest when her father, George the Sixth, died and made her Queen of England. And when the Mau Mau burned the place down two years later, Sherbrooke-Walker simply rebuilt it, bigger and better than ever.

Robbie was still examining the photographs when a young policeman, looking anxious and full of purpose, came rushing along the corridor. He went past her without a second glance and she called out after him. "Yo! You looking for Inspector Odongo?"

The constable stopped and spun around. "Yes I am, Miss. Do you know where I can find him?"

"Sure do. Follow me." Robbie led him into the bar.

Peter Odongo was watching the mirror behind the bar and saw them come in. He was on his feet and settling the drinks *cheti* before the constable even had time to salute and state his business.

"Amos Mwangi is awake," Peter announced.

"Uh, yessir," said the constable.

"What condition is he in? Did you get a look at him?"

"Uh, nossir. But the doctor said to tell you that he is calm and that he is talking sense now."

Moments later they were racing through the tunnel of gum trees that lined the approach to the hotel, on their way back to the hospital Peter rode with Robbie in her rented Citroen rather than in the Land Rover with Glenton; partly because it was the first vehicle he came to in the lot, but also because he wanted to make a point, to let Glenton know that, like it or not, Miss Lewis was part of the team now. He had given her his word, and the word of a Luo man was a thing done.

At the hospital they found Mwangi sitting up in his bed, buttressed by two pillows. The plastic tubes had been removed from his nose and mouth and his restraining straps were off. His face was still drawn but his eyes were clear and lively; they flitted to and fro, from the doctor to the new arrivals and back again. No one else was in the ward. Odongo had left discreet, but specific, instructions that the superintendent and district commissioner not be called.

"This man is Inspector Odongo of the Kenya Police," Dr. Ramanujam informed his patient in Swahili. "He will ask you some questions." Mwangi slowly turned his head on the pillow and looked at Peter with frightened, wary eyes.

Peter dug into his tunic pocket and brought out a small notebook and a stub of pencil. "*Jambo,* Amos," he said with a reassuring smile. "No need to be nervous. You're safe now."

"He is an uneducated man," Ramanujam said. "He does not know English."

Peter gave Robbie a little shrug of regret and repeated himself in Swahili. Mwangi nodded, but said nothing.

"How are you feeling?"

"Better, *bwana*."

"How did you get those bite marks on your face?"

Mwangi blinked once, twice, then said: "They put a sack over my head. A sack full of woods spiders."

"Mother of God!" Peter blurted in English. After a short pause, he said, "You know that your brother is dead," telling him, not asking.

Mwangi nodded.

"And you know who killed him."

Mwangi nodded again and, his voice a hoarse croak, said: *"Fisi."*

Peter smiled indulgently. "You mean a man named *Fisi*. Or perhaps a group of men who call themselves *Fisi*."

Mwangi shook his head. "No, *bwana*. Not a man. An animal. A hyena."

Peter stared at him for a moment, then turned and glared at Ramanujam. "I thought he was making sense now," he said in English. The surgeon shrugged.

Odongo turned back to Mwangi with another smile and said in a gentle voice, "Perhaps it would be better if we start at the beginning. You and your brother Adam were poaching in the park and you . . ."

Mwangi shook his head. "That is not so, *bwana*," he said quickly, his tone that of a grievously wronged man. "We were in the park, yes, but we weren't poaching. No, no, no, *bwana*. Our *shamba* is very close to the boundary. One of our pigs got loose from its pen and ran into the park. We were chasing it, that's all."

Peter did not believe a word of it. The Mwangi brothers' poaching activities were a matter of public record. They had been supplying illegal game meat to Mweiga butcher shops for years. Separately and together, they had been hauled in front of the magistrate on a dozen different occasions, and both of them had spent time in prison. Then there were the arrows and the quiver made out of bongo hide, covered with Adam Mwangi's prints. But Peter bit his tongue. He did not want to frighten the man into silence. He nodded and asked, "And what happened when you went into the park after your pig?"

"We were deep in the forest, following our pig along an animal path, when we ran into a large gathering of men. They were standing over a dead *kifaru* and one of them was cutting out its horns. They had guns. We tried to run away, but they chased us and caught us. They m-made us p-prisoners." Mwangi was becoming agitated. His voice cracked. His eyes teared up and his hands shook.

Peter jotted in his notebook, giving Mwangi a moment to compose himself. Then, anxious to keep the story flowing, he asked: "Did you recognize any of the men? Were they from this area?"

Mwangi shook his head. "Almost all of them were Somalis, except for the leader and one or two others, who were Kikuyu like me."

Peter wrote in his notebook, then looked up. "All right, now you and Adam are prisoners. Then what happened?"

"Then they . . . then they . . . then they murdered my brother." Mwangi shut his eyes and began to cry, softly at first, then harder and harder. Odongo glanced away quickly, and saw that Robbie Lewis looked as if she were about to cry as well. She hadn't understood a word of what Mwangi said, but she hadn't needed to. The sound of grief was the same in every language. Glenton, on the other hand, was regarding the sobbing Kikuyu with impatience, no trace of sympathy in his face. He looked at Peter and rolled his eyes.

It was a while before the man cried himself out. When he had, Peter resumed his questioning. "Can you tell us how many of these men there were? Did you have an opportunity to get a count?"

Mwangi's mouth still shook a little, and he was wracked by an occasional hiccuping sob, but he answered the question. "Ten of them there in the forest. Later, at their camp, I saw more. Maybe another ten. Maybe more. I'm not sure."

"But at least twenty?"

"Yes, *bwana*. At least twenty."

Peter glanced at Adrian, who was pursing his lips in a silent whistle, and entered the information in his notebook. Then he took a deep breath and asked in an apologetic voice: "Amos, did you see Adam die? Did you see who killed him?" It was a brutal question, but one he had to ask. He had to know if he would have an eyewitness when the case went to trial.

A shudder rippled through Mwangi's body. "They . . . made me watch," he said in a quivering voice. "They put him in a tree and shot him with arrows. They took turns and they made jokes about each other's marksmanship. But first their leader . . . the hyena . . . chewed off his face!" He buried his own tear-streaked face in his hands, unable to go on.

"What bloody nonsense!" Glenton muttered.

Robbie gave him a disgusted look. "Why don't you put a cork in it?" she said angrily, though she had not understood Mwangi's actual words. "Can't you see he's hurting?"

"He's a bloody poacher, no different from the ones we're after," Glenton said in an unforgiving voice. "If you want to play the game, you have to be ready to pay the price."

Odongo shushed them with a venomous glance, then turned back to Mwangi. "Chewed off his face? How do you mean, Amos? Did you see this man . . . this leader of theirs . . . do something bad to Adam?"

"How many times do I have to tell you?" Mwangi shouted, his grief momentarily displaced by anger at their refusal to face facts. "He's not a man! He is a hyena with the power to change himself into a man!"

Peter nodded, as if that made perfect sense. "I see," he said in a neutral voice. "And what does this . . . this *Fisi* look like?"

"Surely you know what a hyena looks like."

Odongo sighed. "Yes, I know what a hyena looks like. I meant after . . . after he has, um, changed himself into a man."

"Big and powerful, like this *mzungu* here," Mwangi said, pointing at Glenton. "But he has long hair, all twisted and tangled and hanging halfway down his back. Like Bob Marley."

"Bob Marley?" Glenton said in English. "Who the bloody hell is Bob Marley?"

"A reggae singer," Odongo said, entering the description in his notebook. "Now how do you know that he is a hyena?" he asked Mwangi, feeling ridiculous but keeping a straight face.

"He told me . . . that very first day in the forest," Mwangi said. "Oh, I didn't believe him at first, just like you don't believe me now. Not even after he dragged Adam into the bush and then brought him back with no face. . . ." He paused to take a breath. "I could hear the sound of a feeding animal coming from the bush, but even then I didn't believe him. But later, when I was in their camp, I would hear the same noises coming from his tent late at night. Slobbering noises . . . grunts . . . the sound of bones cracking. The next morning there would be one or two bones and a skull outside the entrance to his tent. A human skull!" Mwangi shuddered at the memory, then continued: "He would go out of the camp for an hour or two each evening. I would see him leave and then, a few minutes later, I would hear the hyena's laugh. One night, after he left the fire and walked into the forest, I heard a rustling noise coming from the bushes, and then I saw a pair of orange eyes shining out of the darkness, watching me from the trees."

Peter was nodding noncommittally. "I'm sure that there's a logical explanation for . . ."

"Wait, Mr. Policeman. I have more to tell," Mwangi said. "I was kept naked and chained to a stake in the center of the camp. In the mornings, they would untie me and let me go into the bush to relieve myself. I began to notice that all around the perimeter of our campsite, at the edges of the clearing, were these long white turds, as if an animal had gone around marking the boundaries of his territory. Do you know which of the Devil's beasts shits a long white turd?"

Odongo glanced at Glenton, seeking confirmation. Glenton shrugged, and nodded. "The hyena is the only animal with jaws strong enough to eat bones," he said, amusement and exasperation blending in his voice. "The feces turns white after a few hours due to the high mineral content in the undigestible parts of the bones. Calcium mostly."

Amos Mwangi closed his eyes, sank back into his pillows, and laughed a trilling, untethered laugh. When he opened his eyes again they were bright and merry, full of mischief. In an instant his mood had done a complete turnabout. Gone was the devastating grief of just a moment ago. Gone too was the debilitating fear that had leaked from him like a sour odor, almost tactile in its intensity. Peter, Adrian and Ramanujam exchanged looks of amazement.

Mwangi reached out and tapped Peter on the arm. "What's that word you policemen use to describe evidence like mine," he asked, still grinning insanely. "I should remember . . . the district magistrate once put me in jail because of it."

"Circumstantial evidence," Peter said.

"That's it!" Mwangi exclaimed cheerily. "Do the things I saw and heard sound like circumstantial evidence?"

Before Peter could answer, Adrian gave a snort and said in English, "It sounds like the raving of a bloody madman is what it sounds like." He turned to Odongo. "I know the man's had a shattering experience and all, but do we really have to listen to this shit?"

"What shit?" Robbie asked eagerly, anxious for a précis of Mwangi's story. "What's he said so far?"

Peter tapped his notebook with the pencil. "Yes, much of this is what you call shit," he said, talking to Adrian. "But there are jewels in this pile. We now know how many they are. We know that most of them are Somali. We know that the leader is a Kikuyu and we even have his description. And if you two could show a little patience, we might learn even more." His tone was patient and long-suffering, but tinged with sarcasm.

"Sorry," Robbie mumbled. Adrian sighed and said nothing.

Odongo turned his attention back to Mwangi. "I am sorry for the interruption. What were you saying?"

"I asked if the things I've told you about—the turds, the noises, the bones—sound like circumstantial evidence?"

"To be honest with you . . . yes."

Mwangi laughed again, an unhealthy sound, bordering on hysteria. "Then what do you make of this?" he said, his voice a hoarse whisper, his smile already fading. "I saw it! I saw the monster's face! The face of *Fisi!*"

"What are you talking about?" Peter snapped at him, his own patience beginning to wear thin. Glenton was grinning at him.

Mwangi leaned forward and, taking the lapels of Peter's bush jacket in both hands, pulled the policeman's face close to his. Odongo could smell his foul breath. "He tricked me!" the Kikuyu said urgently. "He told me he had a louse in his hair and asked me to pick it out for him. He turned around, and I parted his hair, and there it was! The face of

Fisi! Beneath his hair! He has the face of a hyena at the back of his head!"

Adrian laughed out loud. He looked at Robbie and said, "Write this down in that little book of yours: it seems the leader of the gang has a head with two faces. A man's on one side, a hyena's on the other." To his amazement, she wrote it down.

"For God's sake!" Adrian shook his head and turned to Odongo. "I've wasted all the time here I'm going to. I'll be at the ranch if you need me, going over the maps with the lads." He turned on his heel and walked off the ward.

Peter and Robbie watched him go. They heard him laughing to himself, and the last thing they heard, just as he reached the door, was his perfectly pitched imitation of the hyena's chilling night call. *"Whoo-oo-up! Whoo-oo-up!"* A godless howl that echoed around the ward until it was joined, then drowned out, by Amos Mwangi's screaming.

13

The fog made driving difficult. Adrian Glenton eased the Land Rover up the narrow path in four-wheel drive, ever aware of the steep drop-off on the right, only inches away from the wheels. He drove with his head sticking out the window, which allowed him to keep an eye on the right front tire, but which also gave him an unsettling glimpse down into the mist-filled void below.

Had the steering column been on the left, as in American cars, he wouldn't have tried it at all. The path was a morass of red, viscous mud. Water leaked from the mountain wall to their left, miniature waterfalls which trickled down the rock face and flooded the track before draining off the other side.

He was also grateful for the weight he was carrying: all six of his Africans, including Chege who had argued that even though he would be spending most of his time back at base, he should at least know what the inside of the park looked like. They all sat squeezed together with their maps on their laps, making notes only when Adrian told them to.

They were deep inside Aberdare National Park, well south of the Treetops Salient, about halfway up an unnamed mountain that lay midway between The Twelve Apostles and The Elephant. They had not seen a proper dirt road since leaving the Karimu Circuit below Fishing Lodge and taking out across the Mutubiu Track. There were no roads of any kind in this section of the park, only animal tracks of varying breadth. Stephen Hone had marked the better ones for them on a hand-drawn map.

"One of you—how about you, Ekali?—should watch the sky for cookfire smoke," Adrian called out over his shoulder, unwilling to take his eyes off the track long enough to do it himself. "It's about time for the midday meal."

A snort came from the back where Ekali was slouched down in the rear seat, jammed between Joseph and Tembo, the top of his warrior's coiffure scraping the roof of the cabin. "God's own fires are everywhere," he said. "Their smoke rises out of the very earth. How am I to distinguish one from the other?"

A valid point, Adrian had to admit. The mist was getting thicker as they climbed. He was just thinking that perhaps he should start looking for a place to turn around when Pythias shouted, "Stop!" Adrian hit the brake hard, which locked the wheels and nearly sent the Land Rover sliding over the edge. "Bloody hell, Pythias!" he yelled in a shaky voice. "Don't do that!"

"Go back a little ways," Pythias called calmly, his head sticking out of the window. Grumbling, Adrian backed up until Pythias again said, "Stop!" Pythias was peering intently down into the gorge below through a hole in the fog. Adrian looked too, but didn't see anything.

After another minute, Pythias said, "I see it. Take us down."

"See what?"

"I don't know. But something." He pointed. "Look. Do you see the reflection? Light is shining off something. Something white." Adrian dutifully looked again, and still couldn't see anything. But he knew better than to doubt his Dorobo friend. If Pythias said he'd seen something, then something was down there. The man had eyes like an osprey.

He went another quarter mile before finding a place wide enough to turn around, then he eased the Land Rover back down the mountain. At the bottom, he took directions from Pythias, jouncing over rocks and around stands of hygenia trees, until they came to the entrance of a wide and grassy canyon. By now the rest of the team members were jostling for a place at the windows, looking for . . . something. It was Tembo, the Liangulu, who found it. "There! Stop here, *bwana*!"

Adrian stopped and killed the engine. "What is it?" he asked, but Tembo was already out the door. The others piled out after him and Adrian joined them. Tembo was examining a set of animal tracks. He poked at a print, then walked over to squat beside a mound of elephant dung. There were a half dozen droppings in the string, each shaped like a big round ball and measuring between twelve and fifteen centimeters in diameter.

"Only one day old," Tembo declared. Using both hands, he broke open one of the dung balls and began sifting the pieces through his fingers. He sniffed at one piece, then touched it with the tip of his tongue. "An old bull. An outcast."

Chege pulled at Glenton's sleeve. "How does he know all that?" he asked, whispering so the others would not hear and laugh at his ignorance.

"It's a big male by the size of the print, and the depth of the depression," Adrian explained. "The fact that there is only the one set of tracks tells us it's a rogue, cast out of the herd."

"But how does he know it is an old one?" Chege asked.

"See how the dung is full of unchewed leaves and grass?" Adrian said. "Elephants have only four chewing teeth, two on top and two on the bottom. They go through several sets in a lifetime, but once into their sixties they are on their last set. When those are worn down they can't chew their food and eventually starve to death."

"Adrian!" Pythias was signaling frantically. He was on his knees a few yards away, in the center of a bald patch of ground. The circle of onlookers around Tembo and his pile of dung dissolved and reconstituted itself around Pythias.

"What have you got?" Adrian asked, shouldering his way through the ring of men.

"Footprints," Pythias said triumphantly. "Three men. One wearing sandals, one wearing boots, one barefooted. They went west." He had a stick in his hand and used it to point up the canyon.

"And so did the elephant," Tembo announced importantly, not yet ready to relinquish the limelight. He rearranged his beret at a more rakish angle and grinned, showing his rotten teeth.

"That's it then," said Adrian, his voice rising. "Those are the lads we want, all right. How fresh are those prints?"

"One day old," said the Dorobo. "But don't get excited, I see their tracks coming back as well, also a day old."

Adrian studied the footprints, which showed clearly in the damp dirt of the grassless patch. "I'm afraid I have to disagree, Pythias. As far as I can see, they only go in one direction. West."

Pythias shook his head. "No. They were very clever. When they returned to this bare spot they turned around and walked backwards across it," he said. He poked one of the footprints with his stick. "See how the heel mark is deeper than that of the ball of the foot? And look, see how the pace is shorter?" He stood and drew Adrian over to where the grass began again. He squatted to examine the ground for a moment, then beckoned to Adrian to look. "Yes. His boots left mud on the grass. And here. See how these blades point east? They were tramped down by someone traveling in that direction and have not had time to spring back."

There was no arguing with such expertise. Adrian sighed. "If *Bwana* Hone's map is correct, this canyon is closed off by a sheer wall of rock at the other end," he said wistfully. "I was rather hoping we had them boxed."

"There will be other days, other canyons," Pythias said philosophically.

"Do you think you can track these three back to wherever it was they started from?" Adrian asked him.

"Of course," the Dorobo said with a certainty that made Adrian feel better.

"The men may have returned this way," said Tembo, "but not *tembo*. There are no elephant tracks coming back."

"Then I suppose we had better go find him," Adrian said wearily. "It shouldn't take long; this canyon's a short one."

He checked to see that each man was armed with a weapon he knew how to operate, then started them out in an extended line abreast. As soon as they had picked up the trail again, he sorted them into single file. He put Pythias, the team's best tracker, up front. The two men right behind, Tembo and Joseph, watched for tracks breaking off to the side, one man checking the right and the other the left. Standard tracking technique.

It proved to be easy enough; elephants weren't the most light-footed or inconspicuous of God's creatures. There were no surprises. They found the elephant lying on its side, less than half a mile into the wide canyon. The ivory was missing, of course, and judging from the size of what remained of the carcass, the tusks had been big; a hundred pounds or more on each side.

"Aieeeee!" exclaimed the ranger Charles when he saw the leavings. "I know this elephant. It's Jamal."

"*The* Jamal?" Adrian asked with a quick sinking feeling. *The* Jamal was a wildlife celebrity, the second oldest known elephant in the country. Only Ahmed, the old bull living out his final years up in the thinly populated Northern Frontier District, was older. Ahmed's tusks were estimated at one hundred and fifty and one hundred and seventy pounds respectively, and Jamal's weren't much smaller.

"Yes, sir," Charles said, touching the carcass gingerly with the toe of his heavy boot. "All the rangers who work in this park know him. The Game Department moved him to this park from Tsavo about two months ago . . . to keep him away from poachers."

"The same poachers who killed him, I'll wager," Adrian said bitterly. "The poor bloody bastard."

Bloody indeed, Adrian thought. The once-proud pachyderm, dead only a day, had been torn apart by scavengers. The most tender flesh, the trunk, had probably been first to go. Then the hoofs; the soft meat there had been eaten away to expose the toes. The hide was streaked with vulture droppings which had run down the sides like white paint spills. An animal of some sort had bored into the chest and dragged out the heart, leaving a cavity the size of a four-gallon paraffin tin. They hadn't been able to reach the brain, tasty as it was, because that organ, about one foot long and shaped like a rugby ball, was tucked securely away in a recess well back in the massive head, and the head was a honeycomb of fibrous tissue so hard that it was practically bulletproof. But something had tried. The flesh covering the skull had been stripped away, exposing an expanse of white bone. It was this, or a reflection off it, that Pythias had spotted from high on the mountain.

The men were standing around in a loose bunch, fondling their weapons nervously and awaiting his orders, so Glenton issued one. "Get the tooth, Joseph. Inspector Odongo will be wanting it."

Adrian watched impassively as the Masai groped around in Jamal's bloodied mouth and found the hyena's tooth. He wasn't worried about fingerprints; Odongo had assured him that there wouldn't be any.

He had the men poke around in the carcass, just in case there was anything else to be discovered, then led them back to the dung heap at the entrance to the canyon.

Pythias had picked up the poachers' tracks again without difficulty, and Adrian had just established an order of march when, without warning, the sky opened up. Softly at first, then harder and harder still, it started to rain, until Adrian, the last man in the file, could no longer see the man ahead of him.

It was another hour before Pythias gave it up and halted the column to inform Adrian that their trail was gone, washed away by the driving rain. But by then, of course, Adrian knew that more than a few sets of footprints had been washed away. From now until the end of December it would rain for several hours every day, and when it wasn't raining the fog and mist would reduce visibility to near zero. There would be no plane now, no simple tracking, no quick resolution. He had lost his race with the weather. The short rains had begun.

Part Two

MBWA KALI

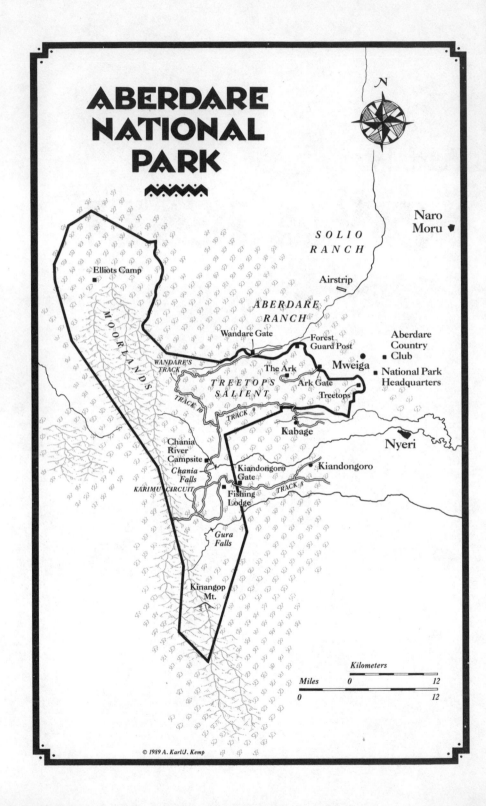

ABERDARE
NATIONAL
PARK

N

SOLIO
RANCH

Naro
Moru

Airstrip

ABERDARE
RANCH

Elliots Camp

Wandare Gate

Forest
Guard Post

Aberdare
Country
Club

MOORLANDS

WANDARE'S
TRACK

The Ark

Mweiga

National Park
Headquarters

TREETOPS
SALIENT

Ark Gate

Treetops

TRACK 10

TRACK 9

Chania
River
Campsite

Kabage

Nyeri

Chania
Falls

Kiandongoro
Gate

Kiandongoro

KARIMU CIRCUIT

Fishing
Lodge

TRACK 8

Gura
Falls

Kinangop
Mt.

Kilometers

Miles   0   12

0   12

© 1989 A. Karl/J. Kemp

14

The rains settled over the Kikuyu highlands in earnest, as punctual as nightfall along the Equator, as monotonous as a work chant. It rained every afternoon. On the *shambas,* all planted in maize or beans or bananas or sorghum or yams, the earth greedily drank its fill. On the larger estates, coffee trees and spike-leafed sisal plants were soaked clear to the roots. In the towns, termite mounds popped up on front lawns overnight, and their flying ants swarmed around street lamps and drummed against lighted windowpanes. Roads turned to mud. Thatch roofs leaked. Mildew grew on boots left at the back of closets.

In the thick rain forest of Aberdare National Park, the water holes and low-lying glades and lava-tube caves flooded. The park's tallest peaks, Satima and Kinangop, at 13,104 and 12,186 feet, respectively, were lost among dark thunderclouds. The midmorning fog limited visibility to thirty or forty yards, and even the 9,000-foot-high moorlands plateau, a dreamy world of undulating heathers and tussock grass, of quicksilver streams and shimmering tarns, took on the ghostly look of a neglected graveyard. There were hard frosts at night and the dawns were clear and brilliant and cold. Before the fog moved in to hide them, the heaths and heathers shone like burnished silver, and frosted spider-webs hung in the lobelias and giant groundsels like suspended snow-flakes. It was a very special time of year in a very special place. The Aberdares were spooky and lovely and a wide-awake nightmare for Adrian Glenton and his team of African trackers.

The rain made tracking virtually pointless, washing away footprints as soon as they were made. Aerial surveillance was ruled out by fog-filled valleys and hidden peaks; even if Stephen Hone had agreed to put the ranch's airplane at risk, which he did not, Adrian would not have found anyone reckless enough to fly it. Even Holger Jensen, the nerve-less pilot who lived on the neighboring ranch, turned him down flat. "Not in the rainy season, old friend," the Daring Dane told him. "Not in these fock-ing mountains."

Even the creatures they were trying to save refused to cooperate. Normally, Adrian would have had little difficulty in keeping a protective eye on the park animals; they had to go to water sooner or later, and he would simply have staked out the main water holes. But now there was water everywhere. It pooled up in the glades and ran free in roadside ditches. The animals could wander the park's two hundred and twenty-eight square miles at whim, no longer tethered to their usual water holes. It made things hard for Adrian's men, who were stalking a specific prey, and easy for the poachers, who were after targets of opportunity.

Of the poachers themselves there was no sign, merely the bloody evidence of their passing. Three more carcasses in the first week alone: two bull elephants and a leopard, all slain with automatic weapons, all found with a hyena's incisor left under the tongue.

Late one rainy afternoon, three days into their mission, they heard the sound of gunfire coming from the other side of the game ditch, just inside the Treetops Salient, and quickly converged on the noise only to find a skittish ranger banging away at shadows. As a result, Adrian asked the warden to keep his men out of the park. He also recommended that the park be closed to unescorted tourists—impassable roads would do as an excuse—and to admit only those who could be kept under tight supervision, those being bussed to game-viewing lodges like Treetops or The Ark. There weren't that many self-drive visitors during the rainy months anyway, Glenton argued, and it would keep the innocent out of harm's way and make things easier for the anti-poaching unit. What he wanted, in effect, was to turn Aberdare National Park into a free-fire zone. The warden was reluctant, but he was even less willing to be held accountable for tourist casualties. He agreed.

A daily routine was quickly established. Every morning, Glenton would split the team in two, leaving only Chege back to tend camp, and they would set out in the unit's twin Land Rovers, his own and the one donated by the Wildlife Ministry. Glenton drove one, Joseph the other. They tried to canvas the park section by section, mapping out a target area during the evening briefing and then going over it grid by grid the next day. In the park, the teams would converge upon a prearranged rendezvous point, stopping frequently along the way to send a man down this path or up that one, staying in touch by radio.

When that failed to produce results, Glenton was forced to switch tactics. Selecting the six most promising trails he could find in any given section, he assigned one man to each of them, taking one himself. They stayed out in the wet, cold bush for nights on end, hoping to catch the poachers at their trade. When they did, Adrian told his trackers, they were not to engage, but to radio for help.

The warning proved presumptuous, and a few days later he was forced to change tactics yet again. This time he assigned his men not to specific animal paths, but to specific animals themselves. Although their intensive scouting had yet to turn up any poachers, it had led them to several animals which any poacher would have been proud to bag. Whenever they came upon a rhino with an especially fine horn, or an elephant carrying respectable ivory, Adrian would put two men on it. They would follow the animal, hoping that the poachers might also find it, so that they in turn might find the poachers. It was purely a blindman's buff approach, Adrian readily admitted to Odongo on the night before the inspector went back to Nairobi to pursue his investigation into how the poachers were moving their contraband out of the country. But with no way to focus the hunt, he could not think of anything else to do.

But no matter what he tried, the results were always the same—nil— and with each new day, each fresh carcass, his temper shortened. He pushed the men mercilessly, keeping them out in the bush night after night, constantly on the radio to see that they weren't sleeping. And when he wasn't yelling at them, he was increasingly moody and withdrawn, often refusing to talk to anyone, not even Joseph or Pythias.

Joseph, who had accompanied Adrian on a hundred safaris, was both surprised and puzzled by his friend's behavior, but no more so than Adrian himself. Patience had always been his strong suit, a professional signature of sorts. His approach to a hunt had always been to put himself on level terms with the thing he hunted, to study its habits and idiosyncrasies and outwit it. And while he'd undeniably enjoyed the action associated with professional hunting—the close calls, the sense of constantly living on the edge—for him the appeal had always been largely cerebral. The animal left clues, the hunter interpreted them and acted accordingly. It was a game of tactics, human intellect against animal instinct, and the bushcraft involved was often more important than the trophy, an end in itself.

But this time it was different. This was no intellectual exercise, no game, and he was taking no joy in the bushcraft, which didn't seem to be working anyway. This time he was goal oriented. He wanted these bastards, wanted them more than he could remember ever wanting anything. Besides being murderers and torturers, they had committed an equally unpardonable sin as far as Adrian was concerned: they'd made a travesty of the special relationship that existed between the hunter and the hunted, a relationship governed by rules and protocols which, no matter how unspoken, or how quixotic they might appear to outsiders, were as unbending as the Ten Commandments. By all indications, these poachers did not give the animal anything resembling a sporting chance. They used automatic rifles and poisoned baits. They ambushed their prey at water holes. They shot pregnant females. They sometimes collected their bloody booty while the animal was still alive. They killed for cash and left good meat and skins to rot. They mocked and profaned a way of life. Adrian Glenton's way of life.

What was worse, in a way, was that they were forcing him to

compromise his personal code of conduct. He had always been unwilling to put the lives of the men who worked for him at risk. True, he usually used trackers when he worked with a client, but for the truly dangerous jobs, like going in after a man-killer, he always insisted on doing it himself. Many of those hunts involved days, often weeks, of stalking and being stalked, of sitting motionless in a tree for hours at a time, hungry and tired and chilled to the bone in rain-wet clothes. Exactly the sort of thing he was putting his men through now. In fact, his shortening temper could be traced to his growing sense of impotence, a feeling that on this particular hunt he was powerless to prevent his men—his friends—from getting hurt. And someone *was* going to get hurt, he was convinced. As outmanned and outgunned as they were, it was only a matter of time.

"What am I doing wrong, Joseph?"

There was no answer from the other side of the bedroom, no sound of any kind, but Adrian knew that Joseph was awake; his very stillness confirmed it.

There were two beds in the room, but only one was being used. Joseph, complaining that his was too soft, had taken to sleeping on the floor. Adrian supposed that except for Chege, and probably Charles, it was much the same story in the other two cottages. He knew that Ekali had tried sleeping outdoors those first few nights, equipped with only a blanket and the Turkana neck stool he used to keep his hairdo off the ground, only to be driven inside by the highlands cold, so different from the drier night chill of his native desert.

"If you've any ideas, I'm all ears," Adrian said.

"You know forest hunting better than I do," Joseph said at last, his voice echoing in the sparely furnished room.

"Perhaps," Adrian said, "but this is not a routine hunt. This is a war party, and you're the one with warrior's blood in his veins."

"*Aiya*," Joseph agreed. "But it's been a long time since we Masai last bloodied our spears." There was an unmistakable note of sadness and regret in his voice.

"Balls," Adrian said good-naturedly. "How about the raid in January when the *moran* crossed the border and killed those three renegade Tanzanian soldiers? That very nearly started a war. Nairobi and Dar still aren't speaking."

"They crossed the border first, to steal Masai cattle," Joseph said matter-of-factly. "Besides, I didn't go on that raid. I was a respectable man by then . . . an elder."

"And then there was that cock-up when the *moran* speared those two Kambas."

"They too tried to steal cows. And I had no part in that one either."

"Come on, Joseph. You must have some ideas I can use."

There was a lengthy silence broken only by the squawking call of a hyrax coming through the open window from somewhere on the other side of the game ditch, a ratcheting sound, like the winding of a giant clock in need of oiling.

"Such a large noise from such a small creature," Joseph said at last. Then, after another lengthy pause, he said, "A man is no more than a two-legged animal. You hunt one the way you would hunt the other."

"Cor! Why didn't I think of that?" Adrian said cuttingly. Then he sighed. "I'm trying to do it that way now, but it's not working. This Fisi fellow, or whatever his name is, is a bloody kink."

"Aiya." Joseph had spent enough years on safari to know that "kinks" were a professional hunter's nightmare, animals which deviated from the normal behavioral patterns bred into the species. There was no way to predict what they would do, and that made them doubly dangerous.

Joseph was silent a moment, then asked: "This Kikuyu you spoke to—the one who was captured by the poachers and then released—does he truly believe that the man who killed his brother is a hyena?"

"Oh yes. No question about it."

There was a snorting sound from Joseph's end of the room. "The Kikuyu are a foolish people."

"How odd . . . they say the very same thing about the Masai," Adrian said. "They say that anyone who would hunt a lion for sport is worse than foolish. He's crazy."

"At least in Maasailand a lion is a lion. It is not a man who only looks like a lion."

"The Kukes do fancy their magic," Adrian conceded with a low chuckle. "And one of their most pervasive beliefs is in a kind of lycanthropy."

"I don't know that word," Joseph said accusingly. "Is it Kikuyu?"

"English. It means when a man takes on the form of a wolf . . . a werewolf, if you will. The Kikuyu substitute *fisi,* the common hyena, for the wolf. They have many stories of hyena spirits dwelling within a man's body."

"Then it's as I said; the Kikuyu are a foolish people."

"Oh, I don't know."

"No? You believe in such nonsense?"

"Of course not, but one must keep an open mind," Adrian said, knowing that Joseph would have accepted the possibility readily enough had it been a Masai legend rather than Kikuyu. Joseph was one of the most interesting men Glenton knew, part primitive, part man of the world. A good many Africans tended to be schizophrenic these days, trapped in transition between tribal values and more modern, mostly European, ways. But in this, as in most everything else he did, Joseph stretched the limits. When he was primitive, he was profoundly so, capable of acts of utter savagery; once, he had disciplined a camp thief by cutting off the man's hand, Moslem style. Yet when he was modern he was, by Kenyan standards, practically avant-garde, more American than anything, an inevitable result of spending so much time with Yank clients. He knew the slang, especially the more vulgar expressions, and understood subtleties of the American mind and landscape far beyond the ken of the average white Kenyan . . . such as what an Okie from Muskogee was, or the differences between New Mexico and New Hampshire. Joseph was, as one of the clients once put it, "a real piece of work."

"Kikuyu foolishness," Joseph pronounced, his final word on the subject.

"Perhaps. Probably. But . . ." Glenton paused, then asked: "Do you recall me telling you about Bror Blixen? *Bwana* Bror?"

"You said he may have been the greatest of all the white hunters. You usually mentioned him when you were bullshitting the clients."

"That's right," Glenton said, laughing. "Well, he didn't think much of Kikuyu magic either. Then one day, on a safari, a party of Kikuyu elders from a nearby village came into his camp and asked him to go after and kill a hyena that had been bothering their livestock. He asked them why they didn't kill it themselves, and the elders told him that a sorcerer lived inside the beast and that they were afraid. So Blixen laughed and went after it, taking along a single gun-bearer, the only man he could persuade to accompany him. He put out a bait and waited and, right enough, the hyena came. Blixen could see it quite clearly in the moonlight. He fired and it dropped, but then it got up and limped away into a clump of bush. As they approached the bush, they saw it come out again. Blixen shot again, and this time it went down and stayed down. But when they reached it, they found not the carcass of a hyena, but the body of a man . . . with two bullets in him. And when *Bwana* Bror dug out the bullets, he discovered that they were his."

Joseph was silent a moment, then asked, "This is a true story, Adrian? No bullshit?"

"No bullshit. Blixen himself told it to my father, who passed it along to me. After that, when anyone asked Blixen if he believed in magic, he'd just shrug and say nothing."

Another hush fell over the room, longer and deeper than before. That was the genius of the poachers' methods, Adrian thought; the way Fisi capitalized on native fears. For Kikuyus, magic wasn't limited to the local witch doctor's bag of tricks. The tribe recognized nine different categories of magic, ranging from protective charms to destructive sorcery to a variety of fetishes and *thahus,* or curses. They believed that hyenas in human form roamed the land, and that such creatures could be summoned to carry out a specific deed, and that these beasts were detectable only by some sign such as the occurrence of a mouth in the back of the head, like the one that Amos Mwangi thought he'd seen.

The hyrax clacked again, and when Adrian rolled over on his pillow, turning to the sound, he saw that Joseph was standing at the window, wrapped in a blanket, staring out into the park. Adrian had neither seen nor heard him get up and cross the room. "There's a good moon tonight," Joseph said quietly. "We should be in the forest."

"We were in the bloody forest every night this week; the lads needed a break," Glenton said defensively. "There was a good moon those nights too, for all the good it did us."

Joseph did not speak for a long time, then he said: "If you chase a vulture off a kill without giving it a chance to disgorge the meat in its gullet, it will choke and fall dead out of the sky."

Adrian, lying with his hands behind his head, smiled up at the ceiling. When Pythias and he were boys, they had used that trick to collect feathers. They'd sold them to the other Dorobos to use as arrow vanes.

When Joseph remained silent, Adrian raised himself up on one elbow and said, "What's your point?"

Joseph came away from the window to stand at the foot of the bed. Adrian could not make out his face in the dark, only a silhouette. "They know that we are after them and that they will have to be mobile," Joseph said. "They can't be carrying things like elephant tusks around with them."

"No, I don't suppose they can. They'll have cached their goods somewhere in the forest. A cave, most likely."

Joseph shook his head. "I don't think so. The low-lying caves might flood, and the high caves do not have sufficient cover; they could not be sure we wouldn't find them. Besides, the high caves are too far away from the roads, and they will have to take their spoils out of the park sooner or later."

"You're right, I suppose. But what's any of this have to do with vultures falling out of the sky?"

"Let's not give them the chance to disgorge the meat in their gullets," Joseph said with a grin, a flash of teeth in the darkness.

"I'm not sure I know what you mean."

"Perhaps my English is too crude, too simple for a *Bwana Bongo,* for a big brain like yourself," Joseph said. "Perhaps you would prefer to speak in riddles?"

Adrian groaned. "No. No riddles if it's all the same to you."

"Proverbs then?"

Adrian laughed. "Christ! Please! No more proverbs."

"Then let us use the one true language, the language of Maa," Joseph said in Masai, a signal that it was time to get serious. "If they aren't keeping their spoils in the forest, or in a cave, then they must be moving them out of the park as they work, every few days or so."

Adrian sat up and groped on the bedside table for a book of matches. He lit a paraffin lamp, trimming back the wick so that he had just enough light to see Joseph's face. "And that would mean that they are meeting up with a lorry somewhere on the boundary of the park," he said musingly. "To disgorge the meat in their gullets."

"*Aiya.*"

"If we can't find the poachers themselves, then we watch for their middleman," Adrian said quickly, his voice becoming excited. "For whomever they're passing the goods off to. They will have to meet where there is a road, or at least a decent track, and we should have a bit more luck in trying to spot a lorry than we've had in looking for men on foot."

"*Uui!* Now he has it!" Joseph exclaimed, throwing up both hands and speaking to the ceiling. "He truly is *Bwana Bongo!*"

Adrian ignored Joseph's sarcasm. He was already out of bed and pulling on his trousers. "Someplace isolated . . . away from the *shambas,* but not too far from a road," he muttered, thinking out loud. "We'll have to use park rangers to cover all the possibilities . . . I'll pop in and see the warden first thing in the morning." He picked up the paraffin lamp—for all its amenities, the cottage was not wired for electricity—and padded, barefooted and shirtless, into the front room.

Joseph, still wearing only a blanket and a bemused look, followed. He lit another lamp while Adrian cleared off the dining table and laid out his maps and notebooks.

The two men labored over the maps straight through until dawn, marking every road and track that passed anywhere close to the park's boundaries. But even after they had eliminated the eight official entrances routinely manned by the warden's rangers, they still were left with nearly two dozen potential rendezvous points.

"Well, that's all we can do for the moment," Adrian said with a yawn as he pushed his chair away from the table. "I'll show these to *Bwana* Hone this afternoon, after I've spoken to the warden about getting some help. Hone will be able to tell us if we've missed anything."

"I have a better idea," Joseph said, trying to suppress a smile. "Let's show the maps to a Kikuyu witch doctor instead. With his magic, he can tell us right where to find this Fisi, this hyena that thinks it's a man." Then he gave up trying to keep a straight face, threw back his head, and laughed.

15

It was a coincidence, nothing more, that he arrived at Hone's just in time for tea. And that he had shaved and put on fresh khakis. The possibility that Robbie Lewis might be there had never occurred to him, Adrian told himself. If he had known, of course, he wouldn't have come. He stepped out of the Land Rover with his roll of maps tucked under an arm and pretended not to see her until he was almost halfway up the veranda steps.

"Hi there!" she called brightly, flashing a warm and welcoming smile.

"Oh. Uh, hullo." He paused uncertainly at the top of the stairs. "I didn't realize you had company, Stephen. Perhaps I should come back later."

"Don't be daft, old man. Join us." Hone held up a finger to the hovering house man. *"Tusker moja. Baridi sana."*

Stephen Hone and Robbie Lewis were sitting beside each other in chairs made from acacia branches, the glass-topped tea trolley between them. Adrian took a chair opposite, his back to the mountains, and set his load on the floor beside his feet. "I need help with the maps again, I'm afraid," he told Hone apologetically.

"As Robbie here would say: no sweat." Hone flashed her a flirtatious smile and turned back to Adrian. "But it can wait until we've had our tea, I trust?"

"No sweat," Adrian said dryly.

The three of them sat there, figures in aspic, sealed in a gelatinous silence that went on and on, until the house man brought Adrian's beer, poured it into a frosted mug, and went back to his station in the doorway.

Robbie Lewis spoke up first. "I've been meaning to drop by the command post, Mr. Glenton, just to see how things are going. But I wasn't sure I was welcome." She said it lightly, her eyes friendly above the rim of her teacup. She had on a pair of haunch-hugging jeans, a bush shirt unbuttoned down to her sternum, and open-toed sandals. Her toenails were painted a dark red color which matched her lip gloss and accented her complexion. She presented, Adrian had to admit, an altogether fetching picture.

"How frightfully perceptive you are," he said, giving it in his best upper-class English. "I would rather keep things as they are, actually." Then, dropping the accent, he said: "Get what you need from Odongo and leave me and my men alone." It came out sounding even harsher than he'd intended.

"Odongo, as you damn well know, is in Nairobi," Robbie snapped, her frustrations spilling over. She had worked the telephone until her finger was numb, but the little she had to show for it, and that was precious little, was second or third hand at best, wormed out of Stephen Hone or passed on by phone from Sammy Mbituru who in turn was getting it from his source in the Nyeri police headquarters. All the others—the police superintendent, the park warden, the district commissioner—had been no help at all. Either they simply weren't talking or they didn't know much themselves.

"I can't help that," Adrian said. "Your so-called deal is with Odongo, not me."

"I haven't been able to get a call through to him," she said.

"Then try your chatty friend, the Assistant Minister. He knows what's going on because I have to put in a radio report every evening. Odongo's orders."

"I haven't had much luck with him, either. I can't seem to get past that bimbo secretary of his."

Adrian shrugged. "As I say, your problem, not mine."

"Tell me something," she said quietly, in a tone softer than he would have expected. "Why are you always so angry?"

Adrian glared at her. "Angry? I don't know what you're talking about."

"I'm talking about your attitude," she said, pronouncing it the Philadelphia way—*addy-tood*. She didn't know what it was about the Brits, but whenever she was around them she had a tendency to lapse back into her old neighborhood accent, as if she felt compelled to confirm their abiding suspicion that all Americans were semiliterate hooligans, direct descendants of gangsters from Al Capone's Chicago. "I mean, is it just me you're mad at, or the whole world?"

To her surprise, Glenton's face grew pensive; he seemed to be giving her question real consideration. Then he smiled disarmingly and said, "The whole world, I suppose. It's been rather a trying year."

Stephen Hone was nodding. "It's the end of the hunting that's done it," he said with a sigh. "The end of romance."

"Romance?" Robbie asked.

Hone shrugged and grinned. "There were some who thought so,

what with champagne safaris and white hunters and titled clients and all that rubbish."

Goodbye Clark Gable and Stewart Granger, Robbie thought. She nodded sympathetically. "Must be hard to give it up."

"Oh, it hasn't been so terrible for me, because I'd more or less retired," Hone said. "But for young chaps like Adrian here . . ." He brushed some sugar grains from the corners of his mouth. "Well let's just say it's been a difficult adjustment. It always is when one era ends and another begins."

"Do I detect the voice of experience?" Robbie asked.

"I've been through it twice now," Hone said. "The first time was in 1947 when I was still a young subaltern in the Indian Army." He smiled, shaking his head. "I remember we were drunk as lords when midnight came round—they always seem to want to do these things at midnight, don't they?—and restricted to the regimental mess, under orders to keep off the streets so as not to provoke the natives. Second time was on December 12, 1963. I was in civvie street by then, of course, a hunter like Adrian here. I remember we all gathered in the square in Nanyuki to listen to the radio. A few minutes before midnight the lights were dimmed, and when they came on again the Union Jack was gone from the flagstaff, and the new black, red, and green ensign of Kenya"—he pronounced it in the old British way—"was in its place. Just like that."

Hone, his face gone suddenly red and splotchy, gave a feeble snap of his fingers and repeated in a barely audible whisper: "Just like that."

Robbie, embarrassed without really knowing why, quickly looked away. Fifteen years, and he still wasn't over it. She put down her cup, and tried to pick up her conversation with Adrian Glenton as though there had been no interruption. "So, this attitude of yours . . . it's nothing personal then?"

"No, nothing personal," Glenton said quickly, as if he, too, were embarrassed by Hone's outburst. "But that's not to say that I don't have reservations about your involvement in all this. Look at it from my point of view. I don't know you, or anything about you. All I know is your job is antithetical to mine. You want to reveal everything to the public. I want to do my job in secrecy, so that I don't jeopardize the lives of my men. So I can only regard you as a security problem. My first priority is the safety of the men in that compound over there. To you, they are little more than a bunch of nameless, faceless Africans. To me, they're my responsibility and, more important, most of them are my friends."

"I wouldn't do anything to endanger those men, or anyone else," she said. "Journalist is not necessarily a synonym for irresponsibility, you know."

"No, I don't know."

"Well then I'm telling you. It's not."

Adrian smiled. "And I'm to take your word for it?"

"Damn right."

He laughed, and nodded. "All right, then. I will."

"Good," Robbie said. "Does this mean I can drop by your command post?"

"No."

She sighed and slumped in her chair. "I don't understand you at all. Why not?"

"For starters, we're not at the command post most of the time," Adrian said. "We spend a great deal of our time in the bush."

"No sweat. I'll go into the bush with you."

"Absolutely not! It's dangerous."

Robbie laughed. "You gotta be kidding . . . right?"

When he shook his head, Robbie rolled her eyes. "Jesus. Is there a bigger chauvinist on the planet than your typical Kenyan male?"

Adrian grinned. "Certainly. Your typical South African male. Or your typical Australian male."

Robbie didn't find it the least bit amusing. "Look," she said earnestly. "This time last week I was in the Ogaden with Western Somali Liberation Front guerrillas, dodging Ethiopian jets. And this time next week I'll probably be patrolling the Vumba with the Rhodesian Light Infantry, hunting for Mugabe's boys. I can take care of myself, thanks very much."

Glenton was staring at her. "Do you really do that sort of thing?"

"Yeah, I really do that sort of thing."

"I'm impressed. But I'm afraid the answer is still no."

"Why not?" she wailed.

"Because I'd be responsible for your safety. I'd have to detach a man to watch over you, and I haven't enough manpower as it is."

Robbie opened her mouth to protest, but Adrian held up a hand to stop her. "Also, your presence would be a distraction to the men. They aren't used to being around *mzungu* women. My second-in-command, Joseph, says it's bad luck to take a woman into the bush. Any woman; white, black, or green. If I were to take you along, he'd be off home to Maasailand straight away, and I can't afford to lose him."

"Is that Joseph speaking . . . or *Bwana* Glenton?" she asked. "Women and the bush don't mix. Isn't that how it goes?"

Adrian groaned. "Christ. Is there nothing Odongo doesn't tell you?"

Robbie just shrugged. "So we're back where we started, is that it? Cobra and mongoose? Montague and Capulet? Tutsi and Hutu? Enemies unto death?"

"Not at all," he said smoothly. "I'll keep you informed as best I can. All I am saying is that I'd rather you didn't hang about the men."

There was a bristling silence, broken at last by Stephen Hone. "I've a suggestion. Why don't you two plan to meet here on a regular schedule; say once a week? You can take tea with me and have a nice long chat. It works out for everyone, even me; I wouldn't mind being kept informed, and I'm always glad for the company. What do you say?" His guests eyed each other suspiciously, until Robbie Lewis shrugged and said, "Okay by me." Adrian just nodded.

"Super! We're agreed!" Hone crowed. "Let's see . . . this is Monday. We'll meet again Monday next . . . at half past four. Now then, would anyone like this last scone?" Without waiting for a reply, he snatched up the pastry, dusted it with a spoonful of sugar, and began eating.

Robbie stood. "Excuse me. Tea goes through me like shit through a goose," she announced.

The men watched her walk to the house, their eyes on her switching bottom. "Oh what I wouldn't give to be thirty years younger," Hone said wistfully. "Or even twenty."

"Not your type, I shouldn't think," Adrian said. "As I recall, your taste ran to titles . . . Lady This and Lady That. That black book of yours read like Burke's bloody Peerage."

"Stuff and nonsense," Hone said. "When it comes to women I'm as democratic as the next man. Besides, there's something about that one. A raw sexuality . . . something."

It was Glenton's turn to sigh. "There is, isn't there?"

"I suspected as much," Hone said, chortling. "Your bad manners give you away every time." Adrian reddened but held his tongue. So Hone added: "I think she's on to you as well."

"Oh? What makes you say that?" Adrian asked quickly, a note of panic in his voice.

"It was just something she said."

"What?"

"Oh, nothing too terribly explicit, really," Hone said, drawing it out, thoroughly enjoying watching the younger man squirm. "It was just a question she asked me."

"For Christ's sake, Stephen! You're having your bloody fun, aren't you? What question?"

"I think her exact words were: 'Mr. Glenton doesn't know a whole hell of a lot about women, does he?' "

"Bloody hell! She said that?"

Hone nodded. "As you said, she is frightfully perceptive, isn't she?"

Adrian, preoccupied with trying to decide if he had time for a getaway before Robbie Lewis returned, didn't answer.

"She also asked if there was a woman in your life," Hone said.

"What did you tell her?"

"That there were none that I knew about. No white women, anyway.

I did say there'd been some talk about you having an African mistress tucked away somewhere. A Somali girl, rumor has it."

"You didn't!"

Hone grinned. "No. No, I didn't. But it's perfectly true that I've heard talk."

"Balls. That was years ago."

Hone laughed outright this time. Then, suddenly serious, he asked, "Why haven't you ever married?"

Adrian shrugged. "Who's had time to look for a wife? I've spent the last ten years in the bush."

"And women and the bush don't mix?" Hone said, taunting him.

"That's right," Adrian replied in a neutral tone, hoping they could drop the subject.

It was all true enough, he reminded himself. Most of the women he'd met were the wives of clients or the air hostesses who hung out in the bar at the Norfolk or the New Stanley, none of them very good adverts for the species. He had sampled his fair share of the air hostesses, but he'd made it a point of honor to stay away from his clients' women. You didn't pot their trophies for them and you didn't roger their wives. Rules to live by.

He had come close to succumbing to a number of female tourists during the past year, but he always backed out at the last moment. They were too much like the women he remembered from his hunting years. He had been forced to take all sorts on safari, from the merely silly, like the American girl who tried to feed a banana to an elephant, to the truly vicious, like the English woman who, inspired no doubt by Hemingway's Mrs. Macomber, tried to shoot her husband. They slipped into his tent and under his mosquito netting in the dead of night. They joined him in the camp shower. They had even surprised him in the thunder box with his trousers around his ankles.

He could only attribute their preoccupation with sex to the phenomenon he and his fellow professionals called "safari heat," an irrational passion on the part of certain women for their white hunter. Whatever the cause, it only went to prove his point: women and the bush did not mix. As to local girls, it seemed to Adrian that all the good ones were packed off to boarding school in England and never came back, while the ones who stayed were a bit wild for his liking—Kenya Cowgirls, they were often called, interested only in riding, drinking, and fucking. There was certainly nothing wrong with that. The Kenya Cowgirls constituted a class of women you might take to bed, but whom you certainly didn't marry.

He looked at Stephen who remained silent, and for reasons he didn't completely understand, found himself saying, rather defensively, "Besides, I'm quite content with my life just as it is."

"Of course you are," Hone said soothingly. "Your sunny disposition is proof enough of that."

"Mind your own business you bloody old busybody," Adrian said, laughing. Hone laughed right along with him.

"What's so funny?" Robbie Lewis was back, carrying two bottles of beer. She handed one to Adrian and sat down. She took a long pull from her bottle and looked at Hone. Then at Adrian. "Well? Did I miss a joke or something?"

"No," both men chimed in unison.

"Must have been really dirty," she said, giving Adrian a broad wink. "You're blushing."

"I am not. I don't blush," Glenton blustered, going even redder as Robbie and Hone began to laugh. He was still lamely trying to defend himself when he was interrupted by a muffled but distinct booming sound.

Robbie Lewis looked at the sky, shading her eyes with a hand. "Sonic boom."

"The bungalows," Glenton said quietly, carefully setting his beer on the tea cart. Hone, just as deliberately, put his cup down next to it. "That's just what it is, I'm afraid," he said calmly. Then both men were on their feet and running for the Land Rover.

Hone began to curse when they saw the smoke. It billowed blackly, a roiling plume in the distance. The forest was much too wet to burn like that. It had to be the cottages.

"Oh, my Yank . . . what's my bloody Yank going to say?" Hone muttered. "I'll get the sack for sure."

Adrian didn't hear him; he was engaged in a soliloquy of his own: "If they hurt any of my boys I'll see every last one of them in hell," he said, gripping the wheel so tightly that his knuckles showed white. "I swear. I swear to goddamn God." He glanced at the rear mirror and saw Robbie Lewis's Citroen in the Land Rover's dusty wake, still trying to catch up.

Their fears were confirmed when they finally reached the compound. All three cottages were burning. Adrian's bungalow, where the grenades had been stored, had all but vanished. The ministry's Land Rover also was on fire. Its petrol tanks had blown and the explosion had flipped the vehicle over onto its back. A fine white ash and the acrid stench of burning rubber were in the air. Debris clogged the swimming pool, most of it bits and pieces of Glenton's command cottage.

Joseph, dressed in high-top basketball shoes and a blue sweatshirt with "University of Arizona Wildcats" emblazoned across the chest, was standing in the road, an AR-15 cradled in the crook of his arm. In his other hand was a burlap sack. Standing under the mimosa tree, near the charred patch where the front bungalow used to be, were Tembo, Ekali, and Pythias. Glenton almost wept with relief when he saw them, especially Pythias. He pulled the Land Rover to a sliding stop in front of Joseph and jumped out with a shotgun in his hand, leaving the engine idling. "Joseph! Thank Christ!" He glanced around quickly. "How bad is it? Was anyone hurt?"

"It could have been worse," Joseph said. "We were in the big clearing on the hill when they attacked the *kraal* . . . I was giving a shooting lesson. We still have our guns, but the grenades are gone. And the radios."

"That isn't important," Adrian said. It was a stroke of luck that the team had been away from the compound, but the sense of relief he should have felt wasn't there. There was something evasive in the Masai's manner. Joseph, normally so direct, was watching the fires burn, avoiding Adrian's eyes. "Was anyone hurt?" Adrian asked again.

Joseph turned and faced him, but still wouldn't look at him directly. He looked first at Hone, then at Robbie Lewis, both of whom had come up to stand behind Glenton. Finally he looked at Adrian, but still didn't speak.

"Shit," Adrian said softly. Some of the air seemed to go out of him. "Who?"

"The Kikuyu."

"Charles?" Adrian was too full of dread to try to hide, or even to be ashamed of, the note of unabashed hope in his voice. If it were Charles, then it wouldn't be Chege. In the back of his mind he knew that Charles was perfectly safe and sound, on the job in Mweiga, yet he grabbed at the fact that the Kikuyu ranger was nowhere in sight.

But Joseph was already shaking his head. "Not Charles. The little one. The good one."

Glenton closed his eyes for a few thudding heartbeats, then asked: "How bad is he?"

"He's dead."

Adrian just stared, so Joseph went on: "He was in your hut, cleaning your boots. They threw dynamite in the window. I'm sorry, Adrian. I know he was your friend."

Adrian shook his head. "It isn't fair," he said finally, inanely, as if life were ever fair. "It wasn't his fight. He wasn't even supposed to be here."

No one said anything for a moment. It was utterly still except for the pop of burning timbers and a thin, scratching noise. Adrian turned his head, looking for the source of the sound, and saw Robbie Lewis jotting notes. "Put that fucking thing away," he said in a quiet, deadly voice.

She started to say something sassy, then saw the twisted look on his face and quickly put the pad and pencil back into her tote bag.

It was another long moment until Hone cleared his throat and asked: "Where is he, Joseph? Where's Chege?"

"He's gone, *bwana*."

"Yes. Yes, I know," Hone said patiently. "I meant where is his body?"

"I know what you meant, *bwana*," Joseph said evenly. "And my answer is the same. He's gone." He slung his rifle to free up his hands, then turned over the burlap sack he was holding and shook out its contents, a fat L-shaped object about eight inches long. It landed in the dirt at his feet.

It took a moment for the three *mzungus* to recognize the object for what it was. A chukka boot. Chege's chukka boot. With his foot, ankle, and a short length of shin still inside.

"It was all we could find," Joseph said apologetically.

16

"Jamal! You let them get to Jamal? You imbecile! Do you know what this means? That fucking elephant was the symbol of our preservation policy. The international wildlife community will be up in arms when it finds out. They'll crucify me . . . if there's anything left of me when State House is finished. No! No excuses! Get out of my office! Now! Before I summon a *real* policeman and have you dragged out!"

The Assistant Minister's spittle-flecked shouts rang in Peter Odongo's ears long after he left the corner office. He had never seen anyone so angry, or so frightened. Even while he was screaming at Peter, the Assistant Minister's eyes had been on the big color portrait mounted on the side wall. And it did seem, even to Odongo, as if Mzee were scowling.

By the time Peter got back to his own office deep in the bowels of Jogoo House, the telephone was ringing. It would be the Assistant Minister's secretary, calling to order him back upstairs because her master had thought of some new names to call him. Odongo let it ring. He buckled on a hip holster and went out again, heading for the car park, anxious to be away before the Assistant Minister remembered that the Suzuki was ministry property and decided to confiscate the keys.

He went west on Kenyatta Avenue, going through Uhuru Park where preparations were already under way for the Independence Day celebration, still nine weeks away. An army of carpenters was raising the grandstand from which Mzee would speak to the nation, and primary school children in uniforms were arranged in untidy formation on the lawn, rehearsing a patriotic song. In another part of the park, tribal dancers from the renowned Bomas of Kenya troupe were choreographing a routine of their own. Banners were strung everywhere, proclaiming "15 Years of Freedom! Uhuru! Dec. 12, 1963 to Dec. 12, 1978," and sporting the national slogan, "*Harambee*"—all pull together.

He continued up the hill, passing the turn-off to State House, then angled off onto Ngong Road from the roundabout at the city mortuary. He tried not to look at the building as he went by. What was left of Adam Mwangi was still in there, the bits and pieces still being examined by the pathologists. He had a sudden vision of that pink body dangling upside down in the tree, staring at him through empty, vein-crossed sockets. He rolled down the window and took a deep breath.

It was turning into a pleasant day. Although the name Nairobi came from the Masai *n'erobi*, "place of cool waters," the rains had yet to arrive in the capital; in the weather, if in nothing else, Nairobi always lagged behind the highlands. It was still bone-dry on the encircling plain, but dark clouds and an expectant air hung over the city. Even so, it was a popular season with residents and tourists alike. Days were mild, the nights were cool, and there was a perfume in the air, the beguiling aroma of bougainvillea and frangipani and distant rain. It was cool enough for a fire in the evenings, and the homey hearth-smell of woodsmoke mingled with the fragrance of flowers to create a spicy scent that clung to everything.

Peter drove past the Jamhuri housing estate—the site of his cheerless, two-room flat—and turned into the Ngong Racecourse. He parked under a flowering mimosa tree and went looking for Martin Karume, better known to his cronies in the Nairobi underworld as Boney M, so called because of his thin, almost skeletal build, and because of his fanatical devotion to the disco band of the same name. He was the same race tout and smuggler Peter had questioned earlier.

Odongo found his man in the paddock, talking to one of the jockeys. Karume tried to hide his face when he saw Peter approaching, but it was too late. "Hey, Inspector! Hey dude! Here you be at last, mon," Karume said, speaking an English of sorts, a mixture of Afro-American jive and Rastafarian rap he had picked up from reggae records and karate films. He put emphasis on the "Inspector," a warning to the jockey. "I been hoping you be by, bro. I got something for you."

When Odongo just looked at him without saying anything, Karume pushed on, talking fast. "Money, mon! I got money for you. You won Sunday! Voi's Pride in the third . . . just like I said. Didn't I tell you it was a sure thing?"

Peter nodded. "You told me. Now tell your friend here to go away. I want to talk to you."

"What you want . . . baby you got it," Karume sang breezily, paraphrasing an Aretha Franklin song. "You know me," he said. "Anything I can do for my brothers in the Kenya Police." The jockey was already backing away.

Peter cocked a thumb at the departing jockey. "Fiddling this Sunday's race too, Boney?"

"Hey, mon! Boney M don't have to cheat," Karume said, trying his best to seem insulted. "A man don't gotta cheat when he know horses. I know horses."

"And I know thieves," Odongo said. "You've been holding out on me, Boney."

Karume unslung his purse, a Gucci shoulder bag, and dug into it. "No way, bro. I got your winnings right here. Voi's Pride paid four to one. That come to two hundred and forty shillings, and that what I got for you."

"That's not what I'm talking about," Odongo said, taking the wad of money and pocketing it.

"Then I don't know what . . . aggghh!" Whatever Boney M was going to say was cut short. Odongo had the little man by the throat and was pinning him against the paddock wall, several inches off the ground.

Peter had seen one or two American films himself. "Don't fuck with me, boy," he said in a tone as flat and as menacing as he could make it. "I'm not someone to fuck about with." He was not conscious of it, but they were the same words Glenton had used to describe the tough-looking Masai, Joseph.

Boney M's feral face was sending out distress signals, so Peter released him and took a step backward. Gasping, Karume slid down the paddock wall, winding up with both legs splayed out in front of him, sitting in a patch of hoof-churned dirt, loose straw, and horse manure. He massaged his throat, sucking for air. Odongo stood over him impassively, his arms crossed, waiting.

When Karume got his voice back, he croaked: "Why you do that, bro? I ain't done nothing. Look, if it's that poaching thing you asked me about before, I already said I don't know nothing about it."

Odongo shrugged. "Then you'll know someone who does know something about it," he said matter-of-factly. "It's too big, too well provisioned to be a free-lance operation. There has to be a broker—a Nairobi connection. And that means there's been talk on the street. There always is. Tell me what you've heard."

"Nothing. I heard nothing. I swear it."

Peter squatted, putting him eye to eye with Karume. "How about Room Six?" he asked quietly. "Have you heard of that?"

Karume didn't reply, so Peter went on in a soft, lulling voice: "Room Six is where we policemen get the answers to all our questions, isn't it, Boney? Room Six is where we bring people who have the answers but don't want to share them. And we both know where Room Six is, don't we, Boney?"

Odongo paused, but Boney M just stared back at him. "Ah, I can see it in your eyes," Peter said, smiling. "You *do* know where it is, don't you, Boney? It's at the mortuary isn't it? And do you know *why* it's at the mortuary?" When Karume closed his eyes without replying, Peter laughed and answered his own question. "For convenience."

There was a lengthy silence, then Peter said: "Let's try again, shall we? What have you heard?"

Karume's eyes were open, and full of defeat. "Not much," he said, his jive accent forgotten. "Only that there's a new smuggling ring working the wildlife trade, and that it's big. Much too big for someone like me to be invited in. But—" He stopped.

"But you know someone who was."

"Yes."

"Who?"

"A man I used to work with, a long time ago. I still see him now and then in the nightclubs, at the Starlight, or the New Florida. I know that he's involved, but I don't know how. I don't think he has a very important role in the operation."

"What's his name?"

Instead of answering Peter's question, Karume asked one of his own. "Tell me something . . . is there really a Room Six? I mean, I've heard all the stories and all, but I never know whether to believe them."

Odongo didn't answer.

"What really goes on in there?" Karume asked.

Odongo didn't answer.

Karume sighed. "Gichinga. James Gichinga."

Peter pulled his notebook from his pocket and wrote down the name. "Where does he live?"

"I don't know exactly. Somewhere in Mathare Valley."

Odongo glanced up from his notes. "He's big enough to be included in a major smuggling operation and you're telling me he lives in Mathare Valley?"

"I know, I know," Karume said. "But he told me once that he actually likes living there."

Peter lowered the notebook and shook his head. "This is worthless," he said, the coldness coming back into his voice. "There are a hundred thousand people, maybe more, living in Mathare . . . if you want to call that living. There aren't any house numbers. There aren't any proper streets. Just shanties and alleyways. How am I supposed to find anyone in a shit hole like that?"

"Simple . . . just ask," Karume said. "Everyone in Mathare knows James Gichinga. He's a big man there, a *bwana mkubwa*. He's involved in all sorts of things."

"Like what?"

"Like prostitution. Like smuggling. Like robbery." Boney M shrugged. "You name it, he does it."

Peter made a note to check the Central Police Station to see if James Gichinga had a charge-sheet, and a more specific address. "All right. What else can you tell me?"

"Nothing else. That's all I know. I swear it."

"If you're keeping anything from me, Boney, you'll find out soon enough whether there's a Room Six."

"I swear it, Inspector. On my mother's grave."

"Your mother isn't dead," Odongo said. "In fact, she's the one who usually tells us where we can find you."

"I know," Karume said with a grin. "Wishful thinking."

Peter laughed and stood up. "All right, Boney. But don't leave the city without checking with me first. If I need you, I want to be able to find you."

"You can find me right here, Inspector . . . at the office," Boney M said, getting to his feet and brushing himself off.

Odongo was putting away his notebook, ready to leave, when he caught a furtive movement out of the corner of his eye. It was Karume's jockey friend, watching from the dappled shadows under the grandstand. It reminded him of something. "One last question, Boney . . ."

Karume's face sagged. "What?" he asked wearily.

"Who do you like in the feature this Sunday?"

Odongo took his time on the return drive to Jogoo House, going by way of the western suburbs, taking St. Austin's Road through Lavington and picking up Waiyaki Way for the run into center city. He wanted time to himself to think about what he was going to do with the name Boney M had given him. Besides, he was in no rush to see the Assistant Minister again so soon after their last encounter.

But his route also led him through the roundabout at the International Casino, and the sight of the sprawling gambling complex on the hill, half-hidden behind its flowering gardens and privet, started him thinking instead about how he had become involved with a wildlife case in the first place.

The International Casino murder case had started out as a routine homicide investigation. On a cool late July night, a young Luo prostitute named Alice Ogwella left the roulette table shortly after midnight in the company of six young men, all well-dressed Africans of obvious means. The next morning, her body was found by a gardener in the shrubbery lining the casino parking lot. She had been used sexually, by more than one man, and her throat had been cut. The medical examiner's original report concluded that one of her sexual liaisons had occurred after death.

It came as no surprise to anyone in the Central Station when the case was given to Peter Odongo, the division's hottest homicide investigator, who was already riding a wave of eighteen straight cases solved, a new station record. And since there was nothing outwardly complicated about this one, there was no reason to think his streak wouldn't be extended to nineteen in a row. The constable who held number eighteen in the station pool on where Odongo's amazing run would stop was not optimistic about his chances of winning and, indeed, there was some argument later over whether or not he should be awarded the money. For as it happened, Odongo wrapped up the case in less than forty-eight hours, and still saw his streak end at eighteen.

It was a seemingly straightforward and simple case: any number of people at the casino that evening either knew or recognized the six youths involved. Separately and together, they all were in the habit of spending three or four nights a week at the casino, and they all were the sons of important men. One was the son of a deputy director of the national bank. One was the son of an Air Force general. Three more had fathers in parliament. And one was the only child of a cabinet minister, one of Mzee's closest confidants.

The croupiers on the wheel that night reported that the girl and her companions had left the casino in high spirits, drunk and full of loud laughter, and that they seemed to be having a good time. All except for one of the young men, the cabinet minister's son, who'd lost a very large sum of money in a very short period of time. He was surly and belligerent and had tried to instigate a fight with some other young men at the table, a party of Asians. But his friends had managed to quiet him down and persuade him to call it a night. They all left a few minutes later, taking Alice Ogwella with them.

Armed with the names and descriptions of the six youths, Odongo went to see them, starting with the general's son. He interviewed the boy alone at the general's imposing house at Eastleigh Air Force Base and, in a matter of minutes, had the young man doubled over in his chair with his face buried in his hands, sobbing out the story of Alice Ogwella's last few hours on earth.

The six friends had picked her up at a blackjack table early on in the evening and let her tag along with them while they gambled, buying her drinks and giving her some chips to play with. Their plan was to gamble until they'd had enough, then retire to the home of the minister's son, whose name was Tony and whose family was away at Kilifi, on the coast. There the pretty young whore would service them all. And that was just what they did. When they got to Karen, the suburb where Tony lived, they dismissed the household servants, put some music on the phonograph and started their party. They continued to drink heavily while awaiting their turns in the bedroom.

Alice Ogwella finally emerged from the bedroom sometime around four A.M., fully dressed and ready to go home. When Tony, the minister's son, informed her that he and his friends had decided to take another turn with her, the girl balked. "I'm tired and I'm sore down there," she said wearily. "Just give me my money and drive me home." But when Tony said that they would pay her double the agreed price, she sighed. "Oh, all right then. But not you. I'll go again with the others, but not with you."

"What do you mean not me?" Tony asked. "Why not me?"

The girl made a lewd pumping motion with her hips, and said contemptuously: "Because you have no power."

The others burst into sniggering laughter. Tony, already ill-tempered over his losses at the casino and now humiliated before his friends, went berserk. He punched the girl so hard in the face that he knocked her unconscious. Then, continuing to pound her with his free fist, he dragged her back into the bedroom by her hair, screaming all the while: "You bitch! You smelly cunt! You want power? I'll show you power!"

The general's son said he and the others still couldn't believe what happened next. Tony dumped the unconscious girl onto the bed, strode into the adjoining bathroom and emerged with a straight razor. Before anyone could stop him, he slit Alice Ogwella's throat. Then, laughing and crying at the same time, he climbed onto the blood-soaked bed, flipped the dead girl over onto her stomach and mounted her from the rear. He held his friends at bay with the razor until he had finished.

As shocked as they were, Tony's friends tried their best to cover up the crime. One of the youths went to work on Tony himself, hustling him into a cold shower, trying to sober him up. Another did what he could to clean up the mess, scrubbing the blood-spattered wall and floor and burning the bed sheets in the living room fireplace. The remaining three boys rolled Alice Ogwella up in a comforter, stuffed her into the boot of Tony's Mercedes, and sped back to the casino to dump the body in the shrubbery. By sunrise, all six were back in their own homes, asleep in their own beds.

When the general's son finished his tale, Peter rang the Central Station to summon a stenographer and had the boy tell it again for the record. He waited until he had a typewritten transcript before going to see the next name on his list, the banker's son. One confession led to the next, and by the time he confronted Tony himself, the lad had no choice but to make a clean breast of it. That interview took place in a room off the departure lounge at Embakasi International Airport, where Tony had been prevented by alerted immigration officials from boarding a Kenya Airways flight to Lusaka.

The physical evidence matched up perfectly. With Tony's help, Odongo recovered the murder weapon, and the crime scene technicians found several samples of Alice Ogwella's blood on the carpets in the bedroom, and in the boot of Tony's car. It was a tidy package, all neatly bagged and labeled and tied up with a bow when Odongo handed it to his senior superintendent less than two full working days after the killing. So it came as something of a shock when the medical examiner, with the full concurrence of Inspector Odongo's superiors in the Kenya Police, ruled Alice Ogwella's death a suicide.

"But what about the confessions?" the dumbfounded Odongo had asked.

"What confessions?" came the response from on high.

Naturally, when Odongo checked the files, the signed confessions he had obtained were not there. The station's stenographer denied ever having taken them. Furthermore, the medical examiner's report had been doctored to eliminate any reference to necrophilia, and the M.E.'s original report had mysteriously disappeared. All the physical evidence connected with the case—the straight razor, the blood samples found in the house and in the Mercedes, even the car itself—had been purged from the police inventory as well.

"What did you expect?" one of Odongo's more sympathetic colleagues told him. "Did you really think they were going to let the reputations and careers of six powerful men be ruined because of one Luo whore?"

"Would they have done the same if she had been a Kikuyu whore?" Odongo had retorted bitterly.

"Of course they would," his friend had said with a shake of his head. "Why do you always try to make a tribal issue of everything? A whore is a whore."

"And murder is murder," Odongo declared hotly. "I'll go to the Police Commissioner himself. There will be an inquiry. He can't ignore a blatant cover-up."

But he could, and he did. There was no evidence left to support the charge, and the six young men were now telling a tale that differed markedly from the one Odongo was claiming for them. In their new, amazingly uniform, version of events, they had said *kwaheri* to Alice Ogwella in the casino parking lot and never saw her again. They not only denied having had anything more to do with poor Miss Ogwella after leaving the casino, but could not recall ever meeting a policeman named Odongo, let alone confessing murder to him. If further proof of innocence were needed, the fathers of all six boys signed statements saying their sons had been home and in bed by one o'clock on the night of the murder. What was the Commissioner to do? Call six of the biggest men in the country liars?

The day after his audience with the Police Commissioner, Inspector Odongo was abruptly relieved of his homicide duties and ordered to report to Jogoo House, the Ministry of Tourism and Wildlife, for a special assignment.

*   *   *

The New Florida was in a flying saucer–shaped satellite perched on top of a slender stem next to a petrol station in Koinange Street. From the street, the building looked like a mushroom cloud from an atomic explosion. The din coming from the nightclub reinforced the impression.

Odongo paid the cover charge, climbed the steep stairway, and stepped into Bedlam's hothouse. The nightclub's ceiling and walls, even the windows, were covered with aluminum foil, which reflected the noise and the pulsing colored lights and the smoke and the clammy heat generated by a hundred or more sweating bodies. The tiny, round metal tables were packed so closely together that the red-jacketed waiters could barely squeeze between them, and the small dance floor was an altar to anarchy. The dancers, so tightly bunched that they seemed to share a single body, writhed like some wounded beast, its Hydra-like head jerking in time to a driving disco beat being played by a Congolese band with its amplifiers turned as high as they would go. Peter, fresh from a similarly chaotic scene at the Starlight Club, chose not to repeat his error there by tackling the New Florida's crush directly. He secured a place against the crinkly, foil-covered wall, just inside the door, and began checking faces.

It was a motley, international crowd, a mixture of local people and venturesome tourists, mostly middle-aged European and Japanese businessmen in ties. Rather typical for Nairobi on a Friday night. The French smoked their smelly cigarettes and looked bored. The Germans guzzled prodigious quantities of beer while they waited for the floor show to begin, their red faces aglow with erotic expectation. The Japanese sat all together, as if there really were safety in numbers, cleaning their spectacles and giggling for no discernible reason; some of them had even brought along flash cameras. The locals were represented by Asian men wearing expensive shirts open to the navel, their chests strung with gold chains, and by the Kenya Cowboys and Cowgirls, young whites in rumpled safari clothes who spoke only to one another, their faces superior and smug and slightly stunned by drink. Each group in the room seemed intent on confirming its own stereotype, its own cliché.

But mostly it was an African crowd. Prelates and pimps, politicians and pickpockets, there to get drunk, or laid, or rich, there to hustle and be hustled. A younger Peter Odongo, the young Constable Odongo, would have been outraged by what he saw, and galvanized into action. An illegal transaction of one kind or other seemed to be taking place anywhere he dared to look. Confidence men worked the tables, zeroing in on the tourists, the *msafiris*. Some used the old money-change trick, offering an irresistible exchange rate, then pulling a switch whereby a few genuine notes were wrapped around a fat roll of worthless paper. Others went table to table flogging elephant-hair bracelets, and while it was true that the possession and sale of animal products was now illegal, the only crime being committed was simple fraud: the bracelets were made of cheap plastic. Still others were urging the tourists to sample some *bhang,* the local variety of hashish, and the smell of burning hemp wafted through the club.

There were a few legitimate girlfriends in the room, but most of the women—the majority of them Bantu, along with a few light-skinned, fine-featured Somalis—were prostitutes. They buzzed like flies around the unaccompanied men, Africans and foreigners alike, nibbling on ears, grabbing for genitals through trousers, and grinding their squirmy bottoms into any vacant lap they could find. Odongo knew some of them by name.

He took another peek at the picture he'd taken from the files— James Gichinga, it turned out, had a charge-sheet as long as a giraffe's tongue—then slipped it into his tunic pocket. If Gichinga were here, he'd have no trouble spotting him. The man had a face like no other, a sad and surprisingly sympathetic face which might have been endearing were it not for the scar that ran from the corner of his left eye to the curve of his jawbone.

Peter found his man ten minutes later, just as the floor show was getting started. The dancers on stage, a man wearing a sequined groin pouch and a bare-chested woman, were doing a limbo when Odongo idly turned his head and saw James Gichinga standing in the doorway. Gichinga paused there a moment, less than six feet away, scanning the crowd. Before Peter could do or say anything, Gichinga waved to someone on the far side of the room and began to push his way through the hand-clapping, cheering throng.

Odongo followed, slowly gaining ground as Gichinga broke the trail for him. He was only a few paces away, and thinking about reaching out and tapping Gichinga on the shoulder, when a young woman in a miniskirt, stiletto heels, and corn-rowed braids suddenly stepped between them. "Where are you going in such a big hurry, handsome man?" she asked, shouting to be heard over the noise. Then, grinning salaciously, she brought up a hand and cupped Odongo's genitals.

Odongo slapped her hand away. "Out of my way, girl."

"Hey, if you don't be nice, we won't be having no party tonight," she said, pouting. "Don't you want to have a party with me?" She flashed him another lewd smile, hooked a finger in her bodice and pulled, giving him a quick flash of nipple.

"No. Now move." Over her bare shoulder he saw that James Gichinga had joined a large group of people sitting along one end of the dance floor. He allowed himself to relax a little; his man wasn't going anywhere. He looked at the girl in front of him, smiled tolerantly, and said: "You have the wrong man, sister. I'm a police officer."

The young whore shot an annoyed look at the stage, where the musicians from Kinshasa were going wild, taking the limbo dancers into a rousing finale. She cupped a hand over her ear and yelled: "What?"

"I'm a police officer," Peter repeated, more loudly.

The girl shook her head and tapped her ear.

"I'M A POLICE OFFICER."

At precisely that moment the limbo ended and the band came to a full stop. It was that nanosecond of pure silence at the end of a performance when the audience gathers itself to applaud. Odongo's shouted announcement filled the vacuum. His words caromed off the foil-wrapped walls and ceiling like so many ricocheting bullets, whizzing through the room. There was another second of pure quiet, then . . . pandemonium. Shouts, and screams, and the crashing sound of chairs going over and beer bottles breaking. The hustlers and the whores, thinking that it was a police raid, clawed at one another as they battled their way to the exit, and their panic infected the innocent tourists as well.

Odongo, caught in a stampede of his own making, slipped in a pool of spilled beer and went down, hitting his head on the floor and almost blacking out. He rolled himself up into a tight ball and stayed where he was, tucking his knees into his chin and protecting his head with his arms, praying that he wouldn't be trampled to death. By the time he was able to get to his feet, there were only a handful of people left in the New Florida, walking wounded like himself. James Gichinga was not one of them.

17

It was only a matter of a few weeks since Peter Odongo had last ventured into the Mathare Valley, but one look was enough to remind him that every time was the first time. No matter how often a man experienced Nairobi's worst slum, he never really got used to it.

He parked on the berm of Juja Road, along the short rise overlooking the shantytown, and was immediately surrounded by begging urchins. They jostled one another and clamored at him until he shushed them by asking if they knew James Gichinga.

"Me, *bwana*! I do!" cried a little boy at the back of the pack, jumping up and down and waving his arms. He was dressed in cast-off clothing and his head had been shaved and smeared with ointment, a telltale sign of lice infestation.

"He's lying, *bwana*," one of the child's companions said hurriedly. "He is just saying that so you'll give him money." This boy, a twelve- or thirteen-year-old with the street-hard eyes of a grown man, gave the first boy a threatening look.

"He is right, *bwana*," the first boy amended quickly. "I don't really know him. I was only saying that so you'll give me money."

Peter gave the bigger boy a sour look, then shrugged and hired the lot of them, for ten bob, to guard the Suzuki. When the children began to trade sly, knowing grins, Peter laughed and showed them his police credentials. Then, before they had time to react or run, he grabbed one of his new helpmates and handcuffed him to the steering wheel. The others might strip the vehicle clean, but at least they would not be making off with it altogether.

The Mathare Valley was a massive excavation rather than a proper, natural valley. It would have resembled a sanitary landfill were it not for the fact that, while certainly full, it was conspicuously less than sanitary. From the road, Peter looked out over what seemed to be an endless expanse of garbage-strewn alleys and tin roofs. On the far side of the ravine, directly opposite his vantage point, was another bluff, this one lined with trees and a chain link fence. Beyond the fence, no more than a mile on the other side of it, was Muthaiga, Nairobi's loveliest and wealthiest neighborhood.

That irony wasn't lost on Peter as he made his way down the slope and approached the first line of shacks. In Muthaiga, where the *mzungus* and the Asians lived, there were emerald lawns. In Mathare, there were alleys that turned into rivers of dust in the dry season, rivers of mud in the wet. In Muthaiga, where the Wabenzi lived, there were lily ponds and swimming pools. In Mathare, there were oozing open public toilets and stagnant puddles. In Muthaiga, there were bougainvillea and hybrid roses. In Mathare, nothing grew except bacteria and nothing flowered except disease. Muthaiga was a place of charming homes and imposing embassies. Mathare was a place of lean-tos made out of mud or plank or cardboard boxes. Muthaiga had roofs of Spanish tiles. Mathare had roofs of tin or plastic sheeting, anchored with rocks. Muthaiga had peacocks on the lawn and lilac-breasted rollers in the trees. Mathare had no trees, and the only birds to be found were the vultures that circled overhead and picked in the refuse piles alongside hungry children.

This was a Nairobi the tourists seldom saw. Neither did the more privileged locals—the whites, Asians and Wabenzis. Visitors often went away thinking of Nairobi as a small city. In fact, close to a million people lived in the capital, most of them hidden away in slums like Mathare.

With its poverty and disease and crime, Mathare Valley was a national disgrace, a by-product of Kenya's scandalous birthrate, which, at four percent and rising, was the highest in the world. As an educated man, a rational man, Peter knew that in a land as ecologically fragile as Kenya, such growth was suicidal. There simply weren't enough jobs to occupy all the idle hands, or enough food to fill all the empty bellies. Simply put: Kenya had a people problem. They were filling up the last of the empty places in their quest for living space. They were denuding woodlands as a result of their hunger for fuel. They were putting an intolerable pressure on the land, gobbling up habitat and crowding out the animals which lured the tourists who brought in the money. As an educated man, a rational man, Peter knew all the arguments. But underneath it all he was still a Luo man, and a Catholic man of sorts, and while birth control was something he believed *in,* it was not anything he believed.

Neither, it seemed, did anyone else. Old ways died hard. There wasn't a tribe in Kenya, or the rest of Africa for that matter, that did not put a premium on progeny. That there was strength in numbers was a deeply ingrained, nearly irradicable, conviction. How was a tribe to gain influence without being larger than the next? How was a man to gain his small pittance of immortality without sons to spread his seed and his name? How was a simple man to gain wealth without daughters to marry off for the dowry of cattle and goats?

As an educated man, a rational man, Peter knew that such old-fashioned practices bore a high price tag. And the people of Mathare were paying it. Every sizable town in Kenya had a Mathare Valley, and the slums would continue to proliferate as long as people flocked into the cities in search of work that wasn't there. When the harsh reality of the situation finally sank in, some of these pilgrims went back to the *shambas* from which they had come; if they had to starve, they said, better to do it among friends and relatives. But the others, seduced by the flash and excitement of urban life, stayed on in spite of everything, hoping things would change, while the daily scramble for survival took its toll on their lives. Husbands deserted their families and took to crime. Wives turned to prostitution. Children often were left to fend for themselves.

Peter was getting a close-in view of their sorry lives as he methodically moved from shack to shack, busting in without knocking to ask startled occupants about James Gichinga, the man with the sorrowful face and disfiguring scar. He bullied and cursed and shoved and, in general, behaved the way these people expected a policeman to behave. It was not his normal way, but fellow policemen who knew Mathare best had told him it was the most effective way. Also, something always seemed to come over Peter whenever he worked the Mathare Valley. He became uncharacteristically cruel. Perhaps it was his way of denying such mean lives, and the disturbing idea that there but for the grace of God went he. Literally by the grace of God. If he had not been singled out in primary school by the Consolata Fathers as a boy with possibilities. If he had not won that scholarship to university. How easily he could have ended in Mathare. How easily any of them could.

Besides, if the people of Mathare were expecting it, he did not want to disappoint them.

But no one in Mathare seemed to know James Gichinga, the man "everyone" in Mathare was supposed to know. Either Karume had been lying then, or the good people of Mathare were lying now. Either way, Peter was stymied. Without help, the odds of finding his man were low, and dropping by the minute. He was vaguely aware of being watched as he worked his way along the filthy alleys, and he suspected that it wasn't because he was better groomed and better dressed than the people around him. The people in the last few shacks he'd visited had not seemed terribly surprised to see him. Word of his presence, and his purpose, was preceding him.

He was standing in front of a sagging hut, ankle-deep in dust and wondering if it was worth the trouble to go in, when he heard someone hissing at him from a passageway between the two neighboring lean-tos. "Psst! *Bwana!* Psst!" It was the boy with the cast-off clothing and the shaved head, motioning for him to come over.

"*Jambo, toto,*" Peter said as he approached.

The child put a finger to his lips and peered nervously up and down the alley. He was no more than nine or ten years old. In addition to his lice problem, he had a nasty-looking skin rash, and his distended stomach suggested malnutrition. He also stank to high heaven, giving off an acrid odor which Peter could detect even over Mathare's pervasive aroma of paraffin and raw sewage.

The boy grabbed Odongo's hand and pulled him deeper into the passageway. "I know the man you are looking for," he said breathlessly.

"Yes, I know you do," Peter said. "But do you know where he is?"

The boy nodded.

"Show me."

"How much money will you give me?"

"Show me and I'll give you a pound. Twenty shillings."

"Three pounds," said the boy.

"Two pounds."

"Three pounds."

Sixty shillings was a small fortune in Mathare. Odongo shrugged. It was the Assistant Minister's money, after all; recoverable on expenses. "All right. Three pounds it is."

"Give it to me now."

"No. When I'm satisfied."

The boy thought it over, watching Peter's face closely, looking for clues to his trustworthiness. "Okay. Follow me." He turned and led the way up the narrow passage.

"When's the last time you had a bath?" Peter asked, his eyes stinging, caught in the child's foul wake.

The boy shrugged and called over his shoulder: "Who can afford a bath? A bucket of clean water costs five shillings."

At the other end of the long passageway, the boy stopped and poked his head out to scan the adjoining alley. He pulled back and faced Odongo. "Now you must pretend not to know me," he said gravely. "I'll go out first and you can follow. When you see me stop and raise my hand to my mouth to cough, that will be the house he's in."

Odongo nodded, stifling a smile. The child took another look at the alley then sauntered out nonchalantly, his hands jammed into the torn pockets of his torn trousers, his dirty bare feet churning up dust.

Peter waited until enough passersby were between himself and the child, then stepped into the alley and followed. They went through a maze of twisting lanes and passages, deep into the heart of the shantytown, before Peter saw his young guide stop suddenly and put his hand to his mouth. The boy doubled over and faked a massive, desperate coughing fit, overacting outrageously. Then, just as suddenly, he straightened up and moved on.

Peter paused in front of the house, a shack like the rest, cobbled together from several shipping crates. There was a door, but no windows to give him a view of what might be waiting for him inside. He did not much like the idea of going in cold, but there was nothing to be done about it. He slipped his revolver from the holster on his hip, took a few deep breaths, and kicked in the door.

The door came completely off its crude hinges and landed on the dirt floor with a clatter. Odongo came in at a running crouch, both arms fully extended, holding the pistol with two hands. He steadied the sight on the first thing that moved, a reclining figure on a pallet against the wall. The shanty was filled with a blue haze, and it was a second or two before he saw that it was a woman, a naked woman, and that he was alone with her.

"Where is he?" he yelled, quickly swinging the barrel of the revolver up so that it was pointed at the ceiling. "Where did he go?"

The woman did not answer. She had a plastic container in the bed with her, a rag stuffed in its mouth, and she brought it up to her nose and inhaled. The room smelled of petrol and dried sweat and a lingering scent of smoked *bhang*.

"I'm the police!" Odongo shouted, leveling the revolver at her once more. "I'm not going to ask you again. Where did he go?"

The woman stopped sniffing at the petrol-soaked rag long enough to nod at the hut's back wall. Peter had to look twice before he saw that there was a back door. Cursing, he fumbled at the latch and threw it open. The rear of the shanty looked out onto another alley lined with more shacks. There wasn't a soul in sight.

"Shit!" Odongo wheeled about and faced the woman on the pallet. "Was it Gichinga? Was James Gichinga here?"

She smiled wanly, and when she answered her voice had a dream-like quality to it, the result of a head full of petrol fumes. "Sure. He visits me two or three times a week. He says I'm the best fuck in Kenya." She sat up and carefully set the petrol jar on the floor next to the bed, then used both hands to lift her big breasts and jiggle them. "And it's only going to cost you five shillings to find out that he's right."

"Didn't you hear me, woman? I'm a police officer," Peter said, holstering the pistol.

"Sure, I heard you. Why do you think you're getting it for five? It's ten without the police discount."

Peter shook his head at her audacity. "I thought the price of love in Mathare was only two shillings," he said.

The woman, who might even have been pretty under all the dirt, laughed. "For the best fuck in Kenya, it's ten."

Peter, knowing he was overmatched, elected not to banter with her. "Where did he go?" he asked.

"You never know with that one. He moves a lot."

"Where does he live?"

"Here. There. Everywhere." She made a sweeping motion with her arm. "He usually passes the night with one of his women."

"How many does he have?"

"Ten . . . maybe twenty," she said with a shrug. "It's that sad face of his. It's the kind of face that makes women want to take care of him. Besides, in Mathare only a very foolish woman would try to work on her own."

"And you're satisfied with such an arrangement?" Odongo asked.

The woman shrugged again. "He brings the customers. And he treats me good. He never beats me and he never takes more than half the money for himself."

The woman seemed only marginally disappointed when Peter declined her bargain rate. When he left, she was curled up on the pallet with her face to the wall, back to her petrol jar, hugging it to her bosom as if it were a favored child.

Outside, Peter went around back to see if he could pick up a clue as to which direction James Gichinga had taken. He was just giving it up as a waste of time when the little boy materialized at his side. "Give me my three pounds," the child demanded.

"He wasn't there," Peter said.

"That doesn't matter," the boy announced. "You asked me to show you where he was and I showed you. It's not my fault you got there too late."

"I said I would pay when satisfied. I'm not satisfied."

The look on the child's face was one of disappointment rather than anger. "My friends were right," he said. "It is stupid to believe anything a policeman says." He lifted his chin and added defiantly, "Now I suppose you'll beat me for saying that."

"No, *toto*. I'm not going to beat you." Odongo dug into his pocket, peeled three twenty-shilling notes from the roll Boney M had given him, and held them out. The child snatched the money away and stuffed it down the front of his trousers without so much as a simple *asante*.

"Have you any other ideas about where I might find him?" Peter asked.

"No, *bwana*." The boy's tone had softened; he had yet to say thank you, but he was back to addressing Odongo in terms of respect.

"Do you know the whore?" Odongo asked, pointing at the shanty with his chin. "The woman who lives here?"

"Yes, *bwana*, I know her. Her name is Mary Kyuna."

"She works for Gichinga, yet she tells me she doesn't know where he lives. What do you think? Is she lying? Does she know more than she's saying?"

"No, *bwana*," the boy said. "She is telling you all she knows. She doesn't know where he lives."

"How can you be so sure?"

"I'm sure," the boy said. "She's my mother."

Odongo stopped by the Central Police Station in Harry Thuku Road on his way back to the Ministry of Wildlife. He was at the Xerox machine, running off copies of Gichinga's file picture, when the superintendent spotted him and came over.

"Well, that was quick, I must say," the superintendent said.

"Good afternoon, sir. It's a pleasure to see you again," Odongo said, meaning it. Superintendent Jaynes was one of the few *mzungus* still with the Kenya Police, and while Odongo was not inordinately fond of whites as a rule, the superintendent was also one of his few champions in the department. The only trouble he'd ever had with the super was in understanding him at times. "*What* was quick?"

"Your getting over here, of course. I left that message for you at Jogoo House not more than ten minutes ago. But you needn't have come round for it in person. I could have given it to you over the telephone easily enough."

"I haven't received any messages, sir. I haven't been at Jogoo House since early this morning."

"Oh. Then what brings you here?"

Odongo held up a copy of James Gichinga's photograph. "I wanted to circulate this. I'm going to need some help finding this man."

"Well then, I'll prod the lads and see that they give it a top priority. It's the least I can do for the best homicide investigator this station's ever had." Jaynes coughed to mask his embarrassment before adding: "We miss you here, Inspector Odongo."

Peter smiled. "I appreciate your saying so, sir. But I don't think the senior superintendent misses me much."

"Oh bugger the senior superintendent; the man's a bloody fool," Jaynes said. Then his face went a rose red. "Oh, dear. I probably shouldn't have said that in front of you."

Peter smiled. "Quite all right, sir. It's not exactly a state secret."

"Yes. Well then. How's your poaching case coming along?"

Peter shrugged. "You've seen the reports. No real leads. No one in custody."

The superintendent shook his head sympathetically, then he smiled and clapped Odongo on the back. "Well, don't worry. Just carry on. You'll get them. You always do."

There was a moment of awkward silence, then Peter said, "You said something about a message?"

"Two messages, actually. When I tried to ring you, I was told that Jogoo House is also looking for you. There seems to be a spot of bother over something or other. In any case, you are to get on to the Assistant Minister straight away."

"Thank you, sir, I will," Odongo said. "And what was it you wanted with me?"

The superintendent went into his breast pocket, took out a slip of paper, and glanced at it. "Chap named Ansentus rang up from Dunga, looking for you. Said he was your brother."

"Yes. My older brother," Odongo said. It was a momentous thing for Ansentus to venture into Dunga to use the call box; it could only mean trouble at home. "Did he happen to say why he was ringing?"

"No. I gave him your number at Jogoo House and suggested that he try there. When he failed to reach you, he telephoned here again. I asked him if he wanted to leave a return number but he said no."

Peter shook his head. "He was probably using a call box in town. There aren't any telephones in my village."

"Perhaps he left a message for you at Jogoo House."

"Perhaps. Well, thank you, sir. I should probably go and see about it."

The superintendent took the photo from Odongo's hand and said: "You go along. I'll see to it that the lads all get one of these. We'll find this chap for you."

Odongo thanked Jaynes and headed for the exit, waving to colleagues as he made his way across the room. When he passed by the senior superintendent's glassed-in office and saw that the man was watching him, he forced himself to smile and wave at him too. The senior superintendent, a scowl on his coarse Kikuyu face, did not wave back.

Odongo's brother had, indeed, left a message for him at Jogoo House. The Assistant Minister's secretary delivered it when he presented himself at her desk. The message was terse and to the point, like Ansentus himself: "Father sick. Come home."

There wasn't time to speculate about how sick his father might be. The Assistant Minister was waiting. The secretary, her nose buried in a magazine, a year-old copy of *Elle* this time, showed him in.

Judging from the look on the Assistant Minister's face, he had calmed down considerably since their last meeting. It wasn't a particularly happy face, but neither was it full of murderous rage. He did not rise to greet Peter, just pointed to a chair and said without preamble: "Bad news, I'm afraid."

Peter, still holding his brother's message, nodded. "Yes it is. But I can't say that I'm all that surprised. I've been expecting something like this. He's almost eighty, and his health hasn't been good for some time now."

The Assistant Minister was staring, his face as blank as an owl's. "Whatever are you talking about?" he asked finally.

"My father, of course," Peter said. "Isn't that what you were talking about?"

"Why should I be talking about your father?"

Peter leaned across the desk and handed him the message. The Assistant Minister scanned it quickly and handed it back. "I didn't know about this," he said. "I'm terribly sorry, of course. But it's not why I wanted to see you. There's been a disaster in the Aberdares."

"What kind of disaster?" Peter asked, neatly folding the slip of paper and putting it in his breast pocket.

"There's been an attack on your team headquarters," the Assistant Minister said. "A man's been killed."

"Who was it?" Peter asked quickly.

The Assistant Minister consulted a file. "A fellow named Chege. His surname wasn't included in the report."

Instinctively, unaware that he was doing it, Peter made a sign of the cross. "I don't know Chege's full name either," he said quietly. "What a terrible thing to have to confess."

"And that's not the worst of it," the Assistant Minister said. Before Peter could ask what might be worse than a man's death, the minister added: "It seems your Mr. Glenton and the others have gone missing."

"Gone missing? Gone missing how?"

"They've closed up the headquarters and vanished. I can only assume that they went into the park after the poachers."

Peter nodded thoughtfully. "That's what I would do, too. That was the problem with the Field Force rangers in Meru and Tsavo; they insisted upon maintaining a fixed base camp. Fisi knew where to find them whenever he felt like springing an ambush."

"Fisi?" The minister's moon face knotted. "Who is Fisi?"

"That is the name the gang's leader has given himself," Peter said, smiling wanly. "Amos Mwangi, the only person who has actually met the man and lived to tell about it, says he has the power to change himself into a hyena."

The Assistant Minister snorted. "What rot!"

"Yes, sir. But a belief in such magic is common enough among the Kikuyu."

"I'm Kikuyu, and I tell you it's utter rot," the minister said coolly.

What Odongo thought was: "*Utter rot*? You may be Kikuyu, but you are sounding more and more like one of your colonial predecessors every day." What he said was: "Yes, sir."

"Your Mr. Glenton failed to send his daily radio report last evening," the Assistant Minister said. "And the evening before that as well. So I rang the park warden this morning and asked him to send a ranger to look into it. If I hadn't, we still wouldn't know what happened."

"I am sure he'll contact us when he can, or when he has something important to report," said Odongo, who was growing tired of hearing the minister tack the personal pronoun *your* onto every reference to Adrian Glenton. Odongo knew what the man was doing: he was distancing himself from responsibility for Glenton in the event of failure. The Assistant Minister had not become a Wabenzi by forgetting to watch his back.

"That isn't good enough," the minister said. "I have to know what kind of mischief he's up to. Get yourself up there and find him."

"Yes, sir. But I would like to visit my father first. My brother is not an excitable man. If he says to come home, the situation is serious."

"You have my sympathy, Inspector, but the situation in the Aberdares is also serious," the minister said. "And the well-being of our nation is more important than that of any individual."

"My father may be dying," Odongo said stonily. "Are you telling me that I cannot go to him?"

The Assistant Minister held up both hands. "I don't mean to sound heartless, but it's a matter of priorities, of being where you can do the most good, is it not?" he said. "If your father is dying, your being there or not being there will not change anything. Whereas your presence in Kikuyuland may mean the difference between the success or failure of an operation which is vitally important to our country." He shook his head sadly. "It would be an act of treason for either of us to let personal feelings dictate our actions."

Peter stared at the minister without speaking for a long moment. Then, quietly but succinctly, he said: "You bastard."

The minister's face did not change. He merely nodded and said: "Being a bastard is part of the job sometimes. I cannot shirk my duty. But I can, and will, forget what you just said to me." When Odongo didn't respond, he went on: "I understand your distress, but you must understand me, too. I want you in the central highlands by nightfall. I'll be working late this evening. Ring me from Nyeri the minute you get there. That'll be all, Inspector Odongo."

Peter saluted stiffly and left the Assistant Minister's office without a word. He went directly to the car park, got the Suzuki and was clear of Nairobi in ten minutes. He drove north. Not northeast to Nyeri and the highlands, but northwest toward Kisumu and the Winam Gulf. If he pushed it, he calculated, he could be in Dunga in time for supper.

18

A drifting cloud passed, the moon popped free and there they were, suddenly and full-blown, like graveyard spooks on All Hallows Eve, crossing the game ditch one by one, using a plank for a makeshift footbridge. An instant later they were gone again, lost in shadow.

Charles, the Kikuyu ranger, was waiting for them on the other side of the ditch. He did not recognize Glenton, whose face was camouflaged with a light coat of mud, until Glenton spoke: "Good evening, Charles. You're on schedule, I am happy to see. How did you come?"

"By motorcycle," Charles said. "I parked on the road, by the *shamba* gate."

"Was that wise? Motorcycles are noisy brutes."

"No one heard me. I walked it the last mile."

Adrian nodded approvingly. "Then it seems we're all set. If you would be good enough to lead the way."

The *shamba* was a modest affair, a one-acre plot with two round, mud-and-wattle huts and a night pen for the cattle and goats. The property was fenced, more to prevent the livestock from falling into the game ditch and injuring themselves than to keep out the park's wild beasts. The fence proved to be no trouble at all. Glenton and his men were through the wire and into the huts before any of the slumbering farm animals could announce their presence.

The team dispersed according to instructions. Tembo and Pythias, the smallest and least warlike members of the unit, went directly to the larger of the huts, the one reserved for wives and *totos,* under orders to keep the women and children quiet and out of the way. Charles, whose intelligence report had led them to this particular *shamba,* remained outside and out of sight; if he were to go on working undercover in town, he had to guard his identity. The rest of the team—Adrian, Joseph, and Ekali—slipped into the smaller hut, where they found the Kikuyu farmer stretched out on a sisal mat with the newest and youngest of his four wives. Joseph held a flashlight on the sleeping couple while Adrian struck a match and fired the Coleman lantern he found on a table in the center of the hut, the only piece of furniture in the room.

The farmer and his wife came awake slowly, blinking and raising their arms to shield their eyes, utterly disoriented. Then the lantern's mantle caught and flared, filling the hut with a hiss and a harsh white light, and they both shrieked. The three Gorgons who stood over them would have turned even the stoutest of hearts to stone: a fierce-looking Masai with half of an ear missing, his skin painted with ocher in the traditional manner of the warrior but dressed in basketball shoes and a Princeton University sweatshirt; a Turkana with a towering stack of bright blue hair; and a tall *mzungu* with mud smeared over his pink face. All three of them were armed. Not one of them was smiling.

The farmer, stark naked and terrified to find strangers in his home, leaped to his feet. "W-Who are you? What do you w-want?" he stammered. His young wife, also naked, pulled the bedcovers up over her head and began to scream.

"Shut your mouth, woman!" Joseph bellowed. Something in his tone tripped the appropriate switch. The screams stopped, tailing away to a muted whimpering, but she did not come out from under the blanket.

"Get her out of here, Ekali," Glenton ordered. "Put her in with the others." The Turkana slung his hippo-hide shield and stuck his spear, point first, into the earth floor. Joseph quickly pulled it free and began brushing the dirt off the tip, amazed and disgusted that any warrior, even a Turkana, would insult his weapon in such a way. Ekali didn't notice. He bundled the woman up in the bedding, threw her over his shoulder, and carried her out. She had started screaming again, but the coarse blanket muffled the noise.

The master of the house made no move to stop his wife's abduction. He cowered against the wall, trying to cover his nakedness with his hands. "P-Please! Take whatever you want! But don't hurt me! Take everything! Just don't hurt me!"

Glenton stepped close and raised a fist. When the farmer put up his hands to protect his head, Adrian reached down and grabbed hold of his testicles. "I'll take these," he snarled, squeezing gently. "I'll roast them on a spit and feed them to you for breakfast if you don't tell me all you know about the poachers in the park."

The Kikuyu went limp and started to slide down the wall. Adrian straightened him up with another squeeze, harder than the first. "The poachers in the park," he prompted, speaking Swahili rather than Kikuyu, so Joseph could follow.

"Please, *bwana*!" The man was sobbing now. "I don't know any poachers."

Glenton squeezed again.

"*Aiyeee!* Please! I don't know what you want me to say."

Without relaxing his grip, Glenton slipped a knife from the sheath on his belt. It was an American-made knife, a W. D. Randall, a gift from a grateful client. Its fat blade, honed to a razor's sharpness, gleamed in the lamplight. The Kikuyu made a gagging sound when he saw it, and when Adrian brought it up between his legs and put the ice-hot flat of the blade against his scrotum, his eyes rolled up into his head and he fainted dead away. If Glenton had not let go and jumped back, the man would have gelded himself going down.

"Shit," Adrian muttered, staring down at the farmer's lax form, then looking helplessly at Joseph.

The Masai was laughing. "Have you ever seen anyone that frightened before?" he asked. "His shit was loose, for sure." Glenton, recognizing the bizarre idiom of yet another of his Yank hunting clients, a world champion surfer, found nothing funny in the situation. He was in no mood for jokes. Not now. Not with Chege so freshly buried.

He found a water bucket just inside the door and poured a gourd-full over the Kikuyu's face. It took two more before the man came around, spewing and sitting up groggily, trying to get his bearings. When he had them, he let out a wail and began to scramble away on all fours, moving clockwise around the room and hugging the wall, trying to get as far from the crazy *mzungu* as he could get.

Joseph went to give chase, but Glenton stopped him with a look. When the farmer was on his feet, his back against the hut wall, cupping his genitals protectively, Adrian moved the knife so that it reflected the lantern's light into the man's eyes. The Kikuyu froze like a bushbuck caught in a spotlight. Adrian approached him slowly, cooing as he came. "We will go away and leave you alone as soon as you tell us what we want to know. No one will hurt you if you talk to us."

"I'm talking, *bwana*. See? I'm talking. Just tell me what you want."

"I want you to answer my questions," Glenton said as he put the Randall back into its sheath. The farmer, watching raptly, nodded encouragingly and murmured: "Yes. That's good, *bwana*. Very good."

"It is going to sleep for a while," Adrian said, patting the sheathed knife. "Don't make me wake it. Because it always wakes up hungry. Do you understand what I'm saying?"

"Yes, *bwana*."

"Good. Now. Who are you? What is your name?"

"I am Mungai Njonjo. I am a simple man. I am a peaceable man. I never give anyone trouble. I . . ."

Glenton put a finger to his lips. "A simple man answers questions simply," he said chidingly. The Kikuyu clamped his mouth shut and nodded. Glenton smiled. "That's much better," he said. "Now then, have you ever gone into the park without authorization from the rangers?"

Njonjo fidgeted. "That would be against the law, *bwana*."

"That is not what the *bwana* asked you, Kikuyu," Joseph said sharply. "He asked if you ever went into the park."

The farmer's panicky eyes flitted between the Masai and the *mzungu*.

The white man was obviously crazy, and that huge knife of his looked as if it could disembowel a man with one quick swipe. But the Masai was an even scarier prospect. The farmer was a Kikuyu, after all, and his fear of the Masai was inbred; he could no more conquer or control it than a baboon could conquer or control its fear of the leopard. He hung his head. "Yes, I have been in the park, *bwana*," he said, talking to Joseph. "But only twice."

"What did you do there?" Adrian asked.

"Once I took some wood to build a pen for my cattle. The other time was to gather berries." He shrugged helplessly and added, "My new wife is fond of them."

"Did you bother the animals?"

"No, never," the farmer said emphatically.

"Never?" Adrian asked, his skepticism plain.

"Never," Njonjo repeated.

"Then what is your business with the poachers?"

The farmer seemed stunned by the question. "I-I have no business with them, *bwana*," he stammered. "I've never spoken to them. I've never even seen them."

"Seen whom? Spoken to whom?" Adrian asked. "First you've never even heard of any poachers in the park and now you know them, but not personally. Make up your mind. You know exactly who I'm talking about, don't you? You know they're in there."

"Everyone knows they're in there."

"How do you know?"

"I hear gossip in Mweiga. In the market. It's all anyone ever talks about these days."

"What do you hear?"

"That there is a large gang in the forest, and that they are bad men. They kill people as well as animals. They killed Adam Mwangi."

"Did you know Adam Mwangi?" Adrian asked.

"Yes, of course. He was born in this district, just as I was. Everyone here knew him and his brother Amos."

"Did you ever do business with the Mwangis?"

"What do you mean, *bwana*? What kind of business?"

"The Mwangi brothers were poachers, were they not?"

"They were local people, not like this other bunch."

"But poachers nonetheless," Glenton said. "Poachers who sold illegal meat to the butchers in Mweiga."

The farmer hesitated, then muttered under his breath, as if he were talking to himself, "What harm can it do them now? Yes, they were poachers."

"You didn't answer my question," Adrian said. "Did you do business with them? Did you buy meat from them directly?"

Njonjo didn't answer right away, not until Adrian patted the Randall again and said in a resigned voice: "Shall I wake my friend now?"

"No need for that!" the farmer said quickly. "I bought from them a few times. I'm not a rich man. I have wives and children to feed. I have to save money where I can. Besides, what harm was there in it? The animals were already dead."

"You had no part in the poaching itself?"

"No, *bwana*. I swear it. I'm a farmer, not a hunter."

Adrian looked at him without speaking for a long moment, then said, "Don't move." He went to the water bucket to get a drink, giving the Kikuyu a moment to gather his wits. When he returned, he asked: "Do you know how Adam Mwangi was killed?"

The farmer nodded weakly.

"How do you know?"

"I . . . I heard about it in the market in Mweiga. Everyone was talking about it."

"Well I don't shop in the market in Mweiga. So why don't you tell me."

The farmer looked at Joseph and then back at Adrian. He swallowed, took a deep breath, and said: "The hyena ate him."

Adrian frowned and shook his head. "No. He was shot full of arrows."

"Yes," the farmer said. "But first the hyena ate him."

"What hyena?"

The farmer hesitated, glancing at Joseph again, as if to ask for help; Joseph might be a Masai, but at least he was an African, someone who might understand. Joseph just stared back at him stonily. The farmer sighed and, in a voice barely audible, said: "Fisi. The hyena who is a man."

Glenton pretended to be confused. "A man? I thought you said it was an animal, a hyena."

"Yes," the Kikuyu said wearily, knowing that he would be misunderstood, and probably punished, but even more afraid to lie. "But a hyena that is also a man. A spirit."

Joseph, who was still holding Ekali's spear in one hand and his own in the other, suddenly clanged the tips together, making the farmer and Glenton both jump. "He's lying through his ass," he declared flatly. "Let your knife have its sleep, my friend. I'll cut off his tiny *toto's* balls with my spear."

The Kikuyu, feeling faint again, closed his eyes for a moment, and missed the broad wink the Masai gave the *mzungu*. Following Joseph's lead, Adrian waited until the man opened his eyes, then held up a staying hand and said, "You can do what you want with him in a minute. But let me try one more time to get him to tell us something of value."

The farmer fell to his knees, crawled the short distance separating them, and wrapped both of his arms around Adrian's leg. "Don't let him cut me!" he cried. "I don't know any more than what I've told you! It's the truth! Please!"

Adrian looked down at the farmer, then up at Joseph. The Masai gave him a disgusted look back and said in English: "He don't know squat." Adrian had to agree. The farmer's fear was too real to be doubted for a moment. "Then what in the bloody hell are we doing here?" he asked.

"Maybe you should ask that other Kikuyu dipshit," Joseph suggested. "The one who speaks in proverbs."

Adrian shook the sobbing farmer off his leg. "Go back to bed, *mzee*," he said. "In the morning you'll find that none of this really happened. It was all a bad dream."

Outside, Glenton sent Joseph off to collect the rest of the team, then went looking for Charles. He found the ranger by the cattle kraal, puffing on a cigarette. "Put that thing out," he said. "You can see the glow for a thousand yards on a night like this." Charles took one more deep, defiant drag before dropping the dog end in the dirt and grinding it out with a boot.

"Why did you bring us here, Charles?"

"Why do you ask that? Was there a problem? Couldn't you get anything out of him?" The corporal's tone was accusatory, as if to say he'd done his job, why couldn't the *bwana mkubwa* do his.

"There was nothing in him to get out," Adrian said.

"That's not what my sources say."

"Just who were your sources for this particular jewel of intelligence?"

Instead of answering the question directly, Charles said: "They are reliable enough for you to know that this man deals in poached meat."

"All he's done is buy a bit of pot meat from the Mwangi brothers," Adrian said.

"Then my information was accurate," said Charles.

Adrian sighed. "We aren't after the Mwangi brothers," he said. "We already know where they are. One is in the hospital and the other is in the morgue."

"But it's all connected, isn't it?" Charles asked. When Glenton did not respond, he laughed. "You don't believe that wild story of Mwangi's, do you . . . about human hyenas and all?"

"I believe he believes it," Glenton said. "You don't, I take it."

"No, of course not. He made it up to protect himself. He was a member of the gang. Him and his brother both. There was a disagreement of some kind and they killed his brother. Amos Mwangi told you about the gang to get his revenge, but he did it in such a way as to make him appear the innocent victim."

"Have it all figured out, do you, Charles?"

Charles shrugged. "It's obvious."

Adrian let a moment go by before saying: "What's obvious is that you weren't there to see Amos Mwangi's face as he was telling his story and I was. I have no doubt that he believes it happened just as he said it did. But that isn't the point, is it, Charles? The point is that it's not your job to assess the information you gather, only to gather it. And if tonight is an example of your work . . . well, let's just say you'll have to do better. We haven't time for wild goose chases. So let's not go off at half cock again, shall we?"

Even in the darkness Charles's grin was plainly visible. "You're the *bwana, bwana,*" he said, twisting the word enough to make it clear that no respect was intended. Adrian let it go. Joseph and the others were standing in a group, just out of earshot, awaiting orders. He gave a signal and they slung their weapons and started for the ditch. "Go back to Mweiga," he told Charles. "Spend the night with your wives . . . your two pots of poison. I'll meet you tomorrow evening, at the usual time and place."

"*Ndiyo, bwana.* I'll be there."

"Try and have something for me," Adrian said. "Something useful this time."

"*Ndiyo, bwana.*"

"Good night, Charles." Adrian turned and followed after his team, trotting to catch up.

They weren't a hundred meters into the forest when they ran into the ambush.

Tembo and Pythias were together at the front of the file when it happened, walking side by side and talking about that evening's escapade, both of them as at home in a dark wood as a leopard.

They were in almost perfect concert. Each was paying the other only half a mind, preoccupied with thoughts of his own. Pythias was thinking about the Turkana woman, Nimonia. Tembo was thinking about how long it had been since he had last had a jar of *pombe.* They stepped into the loop together—Tembo with his right foot, Pythias with his left—and were jerked clear of the ground together, like some single, four-legged animal. They dangled there helplessly in the air, clinging to each other in terror and confusion as the forest, normally an ally, blew up in their faces.

Glenton, the last man in the file, had never experienced combat, much less close-quarters combat, but his reaction was instinctive, born of a thousand hunts, as if the hostile fire were a charging Cape buffalo.

He threw up his 12-bore Holland and Holland and loosed both barrels into the dense curtain of underbrush flanking the trail, at the spot from which most of the firing seemed to be coming. Joseph was already in action. Adrian saw him release the spoon on the single grenade they'd managed to salvage from the raid on the bungalows, and lob it into the same patch of bush. Then both men leapt off the path and threw themselves to the ground.

Adrian was on his back, reloading, when the grenade went off. The detonation was like a thunderclap in his ear, but it did not prevent him from being aware of other noises as well: the popping of Joseph's M-16; the crash of his own shotgun as he rolled over and pumped another two barrels of double-aught buck into the foliage; the hysterical screeching of the Sykes and Colobus monkeys in the treetops. It also occurred to him that he and Joseph were the only ones shooting back.

He was reloading a second time when he heard Joseph come to the end of a clip. There was a sharp snicking sound as the Masai slapped in a fresh one, then . . . silence. The sudden hush was unnerving, Adrian closed his own weapon with the flick of a wrist and fired both barrels into bush. There was no return fire, only more eerie silence.

Adrian reloaded, but did not resume firing. The silence, even more unsettling somehow than the deafening chaos of just a moment ago, enveloped him like a shroud. After another full minute of it, he called in English: "Joseph! You all right?"

"*Aiya.*" Joseph's voice was utterly calm, his tone almost conversational.

"Do you think they've buggered off?"

"*Aiya.*"

"Are you certain?"

"*Aiya.* I heard them go." The Masai stood up and showed himself. Then, rifle in one hand and spear in the other, he sauntered over to where the ambushers had been and began poking about in the bushes with the tip of his spear.

Adrian got to his feet but kept the shotgun trained on the bushes. "How about the rest of you?" he called, raising his voice and switching to Swahili. "Pythias? Ekali? Tembo? Sing out, boys!"

"I'm here, *bwana.*" It was Ekali.

"Where?" Adrian shouted.

"Here. I'll switch on my light for you." Glenton saw the beam a second later, ahead on the trail. The Turkana, who had never seen, or even heard of a flashlight before joining the team, now rarely went out after dark without one. Forests were unfamiliar territory to him, and he did not want to step on a snake or bump into a wild beast.

Adrian called again. "Pythias? Tembo?"

"They are here too, *bwana,*" Ekali answered. "But you had better come quickly."

Glenton started up the path, homing on the torch's beam. "What's wrong?" he yelled, his voice full of dread. "Are they all right?"

"Oh yes, I believe so," the Turkana said with a laugh. "But my cousin Nimonia would be very jealous if she were to see this."

Pythias and Tembo lay curled up on the ground, caught in the tiny circle of light from the Turkana's torch, their arms wrapped around each other like lovers. They were still joined at the ankle by the sisal rope, and still much too frightened to realize or appreciate how lucky they'd been. They had been yanked out of harm's way when they stepped into the trap, the ambush's first fusilade passing harmlessly below them as they dangled in the tree. The ambushers, alerted by their screams, somehow missed again on their second effort, overcompensating this time, firing too high and clipping the rope instead. The two trackers had fallen from the tree like overripe coconuts, unhurt but thoroughly shaken.

Both men had voided their bladders, Adrian couldn't help noticing; their laps were stained with big dark rings. Adrian grinned, more in relief than amusement, and cut away the rope binding their feet. "You're all right," he said reassuringly, helping them up. "Nothing damaged but your dignity."

"Adrian!" It was Joseph, calling from the bushes. "Come and see what I've found."

Adrian pushed his way back down the path, Ekali hard on his heels. Tembo and Pythias lagged behind. The two trackers, still a bit shaky and more than a little embarrassed, stared at the ground, avoiding each other's eyes.

Joseph had cleared away some brush along the edge of the path. When the Masai stepped aside, Glenton saw the body of a man, pinned to a tree trunk by a spear through the throat. An eight-foot-long, leaf-bladed spear.

Adrian worked the spear loose, allowing the body to slip to the ground, and handed it to Ekali. "Jolly good throw," he said dryly. The Turkana grinned with pride and very carefully began licking the blood from the blade.

Goddamn heathen, Adrian thought, averting his eyes. "Find anyone else?" he asked Joseph.

"Just him."

Adrian sighed and said in English: "We use up half our bloody ammunition shooting up the bloody woods and the only one who hits anything is using a weapon straight out of the bloody Stone Age."

Joseph shrugged.

"Judging from the volume of fire we were getting, this poor sod wasn't working alone," Adrian said. "He had help."

"He had lots of help," Joseph said, going into a pocket of his sweatpants and producing a handful of brass cartridge casings. "I found these on the ground," he said, handing them to Adrian.

"Any weapons to go with them?" Adrian asked.

"No. Just those."

Adrian borrowed Ekali's torch for a better look. "Two of these are from an AK-47, looks like, and the rest are standard NATO issue 7.62-mm long rounds," he said. "They may have been using FN's, or those German G-3's we've heard so much about."

He put the casings in his pocket and began looking about for himself, studying the man-made burrow the way he would an animal's lair, paying particular attention to the surrounding foliage. A great deal of it had been shredded by gunfire, and he found pellets from his Holland and Holland imbedded in the tree bark, a good two feet higher than the top of the average man's head. One tended to shoot high from the prone position, he reminded himself. He also knew that he would not have made that mistake on an animal of similar size. There undoubtedly were other differences between shooting at animals and shooting at humans, he told himself. Much as Odongo might wish to believe otherwise, he was a hunter, not a soldier . . . and being a *fundi* at one didn't necessarily make you an expert at the other.

Only after he'd inspected the burrow did Adrian turn his attention to the body itself. The dead man was a Somali, with all of the delicately refined features of his people. Even in death he was strikingly handsome, almost as pretty as a young woman with his thin nose and lips and his high cheekbones and dark, sloe eyes. The rest of the team pressed round, grinning in anticipation as Adrian rolled the corpse onto its back and began going through its clothes.

The Somali was dressed in a dirty suit jacket ripped in the armpits, and khaki trousers cinched with a rope belt. He had plenty of pockets, but they were empty. All Adrian found was an amulet round his neck: the incisor tooth of a spotted hyena, strung on a thong.

19

The view from the grassy terrace of the Aberdare Country Club was impressive, even on a gray and dreary afternoon. To the north was the rhinoceros sanctuary of Aberdare Ranch and, looking west across a green valley, the mountains themselves, dark and secretive under a canopy of cloud. To the east, much farther off and barely discernible through the mist, were the foothills of fog-bound Mount Kenya. Separating the two ranges was another wide valley, this one tawny-colored and seeming endless, reaching all the way to the horizon and beyond, into the Northern Frontier District.

Robbie Lewis sat at one of the outside tables, enjoying the view and idly pitching breadcrumbs to a pair of strolling peacocks, a proud-plumed male and his dowdy hen. She had just finished a long and pleasant curry lunch with Sam Weller, the club's owner, and was still waiting for Stephen Hone, who was supposed to have joined them. While she was curious about why Hone had failed to keep the appointment—it wasn't like him to stand up a lady—she wasn't particularly upset about it. The last of the lunch crowd, tourists booked into The Ark for an overnight stay in the park, had been put aboard the combis by company guides and whisked away, leaving the club deserted except for Weller, his staff, and Robbie, the only registered guest. She rather enjoyed having the place all to herself; it made her feel like a proper *memsaab,* the pampered mistress of some grand country manor. Snyder Avenue and the Melrose Diner seemed a million miles, a million years, away.

She had just ordered a lime squash from the barman when Hone hove into view, bustling across the lawn and scattering the peacocks. "Sorry to be so late," he said breathlessly. "I was unavoidably delayed at Nyeri police headquarters. Are you through here?"

"I just ordered something to drink," Robbie said. "Sam's curry is burning a goddamn hole in my chest."

"Cancel the drink or bring it along. Inspector Odongo's waiting for us."

"Odongo? He's back? Why? Is something up?"

"Only Nairobi's *dander,* as you Yanks would say."

"Has he located the Great White Hunter?"

Hone shrugged. "I couldn't say. Too many people hanging about headquarters for a proper chat. I sent him on ahead to the house and dashed off to collect you straight away."

"Thanks, Stephen. I appreciate it."

"Then hop to it. I'm rather curious myself, you know."

They went through the bar on the way out to the car park and Robbie signed for the drink she had ordered. They arrived at Aberdare Ranch fifteen minutes later. Inspector Odongo was waiting on the veranda. He rose to greet them. "How very nice to see you again, Miss Lewis."

"Hello, Inspector. What brings you back to us?"

"Trouble. Policemen always go where the trouble is."

"You're talking about Doctor Glenton, I presume?"

Recognizing the play on the old Livingstone joke, Odongo sighed and nodded.

"Have you found him?" she asked.

"In a manner of speaking," Odongo said. "He's been seen several times in the past few days. The most recent sighting was reported only this morning." He looked at Hone. "That is why I was at police headquarters."

"Seen by whom?" Hone asked.

"Any number of unfortunate farmers whose *shambas* border the park. It seems that *Mbwa Kali* bullies his way into their homes in the dead of night, questions them—rather roughly at times—and then disappears back into the forest."

"*Mbwa Kali?*" Hone asked with a puzzled look. "Who is it we're talking about here, Inspector?"

"Mr. Glenton, of course," Peter said. "He's the talk of the Mweiga market. The townspeople have given him a name."

"Vicious dog?" Robbie didn't know much Swahili, but she knew what *mbwa kali* meant. It was written on signs posted on half the front gates in Muthaiga, including her own.

Odongo shrugged. "As I say, the interrogations have been rough."

"How rough's rough?" Robbie asked with a half smile. "No one has died, have they?"

"As a matter of fact, yes, someone has."

There was a shocked silence. Then Hone said: "Rubbish! I don't believe it. I know he was upset about that poor chappie of his—Chege, was it?—but I've known Adrian Glenton for donkey's years. He couldn't do a thing like that."

"Stephen's right," Robbie said emphatically. "He can be a sour sonofabitch at times, but he's no killer."

"Oh?" Odongo said, somewhat surprised by the vehemence of their defense. "It was my understanding that killing was his profession."

"There's a difference between killing animals and killing human beings," Robbie said. "Even in Africa."

"Yes," Odongo said drolly. "Even in Africa."

Robbie sighed. "Look, I don't mean . . ."

"I know what you mean," Odongo interrupted. "I know that to you and Mr. Hone, Africa seems like a savage and primitive place. The Dark Continent and all that."

"You needn't go explaining Africa to me," Hone said with a flare. "This is my home."

Odongo gave Hone a thin smile. "Of course. How forgetful of me." After an awkward silence, he added: "You are probably right about Glenton. There's reason to think the dead man was one of the poachers. And I don't think Glenton killed him."

"This is all rather confusing," Hone said. "Perhaps you should start again and tell us what you're talking about."

"All right," Peter said. "Four days ago, sometime before dawn, a body was dumped outside the Nyeri police headquarters compound. The dead man was a Somali. He was naked and carried no identification. There was a hyena's tooth on a thong around his neck and a note pinned to his ear with a sewing needle. The note read: 'For Inspector Peter Odongo and all the lads in Pathology. Do not open until Christmas.' It was signed, 'Happy holidays, A. Glenton.' The cause of death was a spear wound in the throat, which makes me think it was one of his Africans who actually did the deed."

"Ah, a poacher," said Hone, sounding both relieved and vindicated. "Now that's another pair of boots altogether, isn't it? That is why you hired him, after all. To rid us of these bloody poachers."

"I did not hire him to terrorize innocent farmers."

Hone shrugged. "Desperate situations call for desperate measures," he said firmly. "That's what I always say."

"I know you do," Odongo said. "You are still remembered here in Central Province for your desperate measures."

Robbie, unaware of Hone's controversial role during the Emergency, wondered what was going on between these two. She could feel the tension, but couldn't explain it.

Hone, the scourge of the Mau Mau, merely grinned. "Yes, I shouldn't be surprised that they remember me." When Odongo did not respond, he added, "People should remember something else. My measures worked."

"Yes, they worked."

"I was merely carrying out the mission entrusted to me by the government of the day," Hone said. "Just as Adrian's doing now."

"Yet you seem to feel the need to justify yourself. Even after all these years."

"Rubbish," Hone said flatly. "It was dirty work then and it's dirty work now, but it's work that must be done. The Mau Mau were a bunch of murdering jackals and so are these bloody poachers. They have to be hunted down and dispatched, same as any other animal that's had a taste of human blood."

"I don't disagree with that," Odongo said. "So long as the hunter is careful to dispatch only the guilty animal."

"You yourself said that this Somali chap is undoubtedly guilty. I don't understand what's bothering you, Inspector."

Odongo paused, then asked: "Didn't you find Glenton's note rather odd?"

Hone thought about it, then shrugged. "Should I have?"

"I thought there was something disquieting about it. It sounded as if he were enjoying all this."

Hone waved a hand, brushing the idea away. "I shouldn't worry if I were you, Inspector. Our Mr. Glenton has a rather bizarre sense of humor."

With a straight face, Robbie cracked: "I never noticed that our Mr. Glenton had a sense of humor at all."

Odongo did not smile. "I also cannot help thinking that if you are close enough to kill a man with a spear, then you might be close enough to take him alive," he said. "If the Somali was one of the poachers, he would have been a good deal more valuable to us alive than dead."

"Don't you suppose Adrian was aware of that?" Hone said. "One of his boys probably slotted the poor sod before anyone could prevent it. Those chappies of his are good in the bush, but they aren't the most sophisticated people on the planet."

"Unlike yourself, Mr. Hone. You seem to have an answer to every question." Odongo's voice was calm, but he was seething inside. He found it interesting that *mzungus* invariably found a way to blame everything on African incompetence.

It was then, as if guided by some instinctive, socially sensitive radar, that Hone's houseman materialized with the tea trolley. He put the sugar bowl where Hone could reach it without moving, and, assisted by Robbie Lewis, proceeded to serve, setting out the biscuits and scones while she poured.

Peter Odongo leaned back in his chair and lit a Rooster cigarette, using the interruption to calm down.

It wasn't fair of him to have baited Hone like that, he decided. When it came to *mzungus,* Stephen Hone was no worse, and probably better, than most. Just because Hone had hunted down and killed Africans during the Mau Mau uprising did not necessarily mean he was a racist. Christian Africans, a group which included most of Odongo's own family, had been the chief victims of Mau Mau. Of the more than thirteen thousand people killed during the state of emergency which had existed between 1952 and 1960, barely more than a hundred had been Europeans. The rest were Africans, either Mau Maus killed by the whites and the native police, or Christian Africans murdered by Mau Maus. No, it was not Hone's fault, Odongo told himself again. It was his own ill temper at work. What with Glenton and the Assistant Minister and his own family all giving him trouble at the same time, it had been a difficult couple of days.

His immediate problem was Glenton. The man was an errant missile; there was no telling where he would strike, or what kind of damage he might do. Odongo did not mind that Glenton had abandoned the Aberdare Ranch base camp—he'd have done the same—but he did not understand why he would also give up sending in his daily situation report. Even more than the insubordination inherent in such an act, it was the lack of communication, the not knowing what was going on, that upset the Assistant Minister. And what upset the Assistant Minister tended, almost by definition, also to upset Inspector Odongo.

The Assistant Minister was upset enough already. Peter's unauthorized safari to Dunga—a fool's errand, as it turned out—had delayed his arrival in the highlands by a full day. The minister had gone into a sputtering rage when he rang the Nyeri police headquarters and found that Inspector Odongo had not arrived. Peter hadn't spoken to the man since calling him a bastard to his face, and he was doing what he could to keep it that way. He had telephoned Jogoo House that morning, timing the call to beat the Assistant Minister to the office, and left word with the Kikuyu secretary that he was, finally, on seat in Nyeri. He doubted somehow that the news would be enough to placate their common master.

Then there was his family. His problem there was neither new nor pressing but it worried him more than anything having to do with Glenton or the minister. Peter did not know why it should; that scab should have grown over long ago. Perhaps it was because he couldn't stop picking at it.

Odongo's visit home had begun auspiciously enough. The first thing he looked for as he approached the *pacho,* the family compound, was his father's house, to see if the *kisusi* was still attached to the roof; the wooden cross was a signal to the world that the head of the family was still living. He exhaled with relief when he saw it there.

The next thing he saw was his brother sitting beside the road just outside the *pacho* gate, waiting for him, expecting him, confident that Fate had taken a hand and that Peter had somehow gotten his message and had set out for home at once. Peter had a feeling that if it had taken him a week he still would have found Ansentus waiting.

"Tell me, how is our father?" Peter had asked anxiously, first thing, as his brother climbed aboard the Suzuki to ride into the compound with him.

"Well," Ansentus said without expression or elaboration. Ansentus, who was five years older than Peter, was a big man, with the hard muscles and rough hands of a fisherman. He was easily the most taciturn man that Peter, a quiet man himself, had ever known. A conversation with his brother was always an awkward and painful experience. But Ansentus's was a sociable silence, unthreatening and inoffensive, unlike Peter's, which always seemed to rub everyone in the family the wrong way. It always amazed people that the two of them, so different in so many ways, could share the same natural mother.

"You mean as well as can be expected," Peter said.

"No. I mean well."

"Fully recovered?"

"Yes."

"But how?"

"He ate a bad piece of fish without our knowing about it. We thought he was dying." For Ansentus, it was the equivalent of a speech.

"That's wonderful!" Peter exclaimed, his relief pushing aside the nagging thought that he had just placed his career in jeopardy for nothing. Ansentus merely nodded. He provided no further details of their father's illness, issued no warm words of welcome, offered no apology for having pulled Peter away from his job. All Peter got from his brother was one of his famous silences.

In spite of the good news concerning his father, Peter's stay, as brief as it was, hadn't gone well after that. It had been some months since he had last been home—twenty, to be precise—and within an hour of being back he remembered why he did not come more often. These people had become strangers to him—and he, no doubt, to them. Apart from a few physical characteristics, they seemed to have nothing in common. Peter may as well have been in the southern Sudan, among the Dinka.

They had even greeted him as they would a stranger, with an exquisite, excruciating politeness. He found them waiting when he drove into the *pacho*. The children swarmed around the Suzuki, jostling for a turn behind the wheel. The rest of the family—brothers and sisters, aunts and uncles, cousins too numerous to count—gathered to shake his hand with a great formality, welcoming him to the land itself, as if he weren't familiar with it, holding the grip for a long time, as Luo do when trying to make an outsider feel at home. And when he was led inside it wasn't into the main hut, his father's hut, but the guest hut, reserved for distinguished visitors. There was tea, and bread and margarine and talk—slow, courteous talk, with the chairs placed in a circle so everyone could join in. How was his health? His job? His love life? . . . this last query put by his ever-hopeful mother, the third of his father's six wives. It was all very respectful, all very proper, but there was no gay laughter, no nostalgic weeping, none of the normal noises of homecoming and reunion. It was as if Peter were no less, but nothing more, than an important *bwana* from Nairobi.

It was regrettable, of course, and rather sad, but Peter could not really blame them for feeling the way they did. The brilliant and promising boy who had captured the fancy of his missionary school teachers, who had dazzled his professors at University, who had once been the source of so much pride and expectation, was something of a disappointment as a man.

It was not simply a matter of his having left the *pacho;* it wasn't unusual for a bright young Luo to go on and make a name for himself in the larger world outside Nyanza Province. It was more that his leaving had been so total. Unlike others who left, Peter seemed to have taken nothing of the *dhoot,* of the clan's ways, with him. Here he was thirty-four years old and still unmarried. At an age when some men were already grandfathers, he had sired no children, had acquired no cows or goats, had done nothing to increase the size or strength of his father's *pacho.*

In his family's eyes, Peter was no longer a true Luo. He didn't act like one; he didn't think like one. And it was all because of the meddlesome *mzungu* priests who had betrayed the trust the clan had shown in turning Peter over to them. In fact, most of Peter's family were Catholic—or at least they professed loyalty to what passed for Catholicism in Luoland, a practical stew of Christianity, animism and traditional Luo folklore—except for Uncle Akuku, who constantly criticized the missionaries, and who was fond of quoting Jomo Kenyatta's wry observation: "When the missionaries arrived, the Africans had the land and the missionaries had the Bible. They taught us to pray with our eyes shut. When we opened them, they had the land and we had the Bible." The family would eventually come to see things Uncle Akuku's way: the *mzungu* priests had kidnapped their Peter body and soul. They had praised him and pampered him and lured him to Nairobi with their promise of a charmed future. At University, and later, at the Kenya Police academy, his head had been filled with queer ideas, and when the family saw him again he was a different person. Gone was the sunny-souled, laughter-loving boy they remembered. In his place was a man. A serious, unsmiling man. A man in uniform.

For his part, Peter had not known quite what to make of them either. He loved them, but he was no longer comfortable with them. When he visited, which he did far more frequently during those early years, he always felt as though they were constantly watching him, judging him, looking for the change in him, looking for something they could admire, but finding, he feared, only cause for criticism.

Looking at it from the family's point of view, Peter had to admit that their complaints were largely valid. Their list of grievances with him, both real and imagined, was a lengthy one, reaching all the way back to the day he first struck out for Nairobi to claim his scholarship.

While young Peter had loved his family, he hadn't missed them. Not at first anyway. The world beyond the *pacho* was too new and exciting for the traditional bout of homesickness. In fact, he had been more than a little contemptuous of those he had left behind, unable to mask a feeling of smug superiority toward them. He was being introduced to things they could not even imagine, let alone understand. While they were spreading nets on the Gulf, he was immersing himself in the politics of a postcolonial Africa. While they were tending goats, he was debating the merits of various economic models for developing nations. While they spawned like lungfish, he was in bed with a book, with the literature of Africa—Lessing and Lumumba, Naipaul and Nyerere, Conrad and Kenyatta.

The trouble had begun almost immediately. The family had expected Peter to come home on weekends, but he had preferred to spend them in the university library. In fact, if he could have spent a weekend with the Luo of his choice, it would not have been with anyone in his family . . . it would have been with the ghost of the dead politician Tom Mboya, the most original and charismatic Luo of his generation.

They had no way of knowing that, of course, but as time went on they found other things to complain about. He placed first in his class at the police academy, but he did not use the leverage the honor gave him to ask for a posting to Kisumu District where he would be close to home. He had a steady job, but he did not take a wife, some sturdy Luo girl with whom he could start a family. He had a strong back, but he did not use it to build a house in his father's *pacho* and take his rightful place in the family hierarchy. He did not, in fact, do any of the things expected of him.

Worse still, Peter had not made the most of his special gifts. He had not become a school teacher, or trade unionist, or politician. He had not taken any of the traditional roads to success for an ambitious Luo. No, he had to go and become a policeman, a praetorian guard of the same Kikuyu-dominated regime that had turned against the Luo tribe without warning in 1969, after first murdering Tom Mboya.

The family's disenchantment with Peter seemed to begin in earnest after Mboya's death, about the same time that the Luo tribe as a whole began to become disillusioned with the Kenya Police. It may have been coincidence, but Peter did not think so. His clansmen were not over-joyed when he elected to become a policeman, but neither were they ashamed. In fact, they had been quite proud of him in the beginning. They were flattered that the Wabenzis recognized their Peter as some-body special. They were honored when he finished at the top of his class at both the University and the police school. Besides, he looked quite dashing in his new constable's uniform.

That all changed with Mboya. The police work—indeed, justice itself—had been swift enough in the Mboya case. A KANU party zealot, a young Kikuyu, had been tried, convicted, and sent to the gallows within four months of the crime. But few Luos believed, then or ever, that he had acted alone. At the time of his death, Tom Mboya was the Minister of Economic Affairs, and a State House favorite who, despite their tribal difference, shared an almost father-son relationship with the President. But Mzee's love wasn't enough to save him. Indeed, it may have hastened his end. The KANU leadership could live with Mboya's provocative and controversial public statements, with his intellectual arrogance, even with the idea that his popularity had begun to rival that of Mzee himself. But they could not live with the possibility that this ambitious young Luo—he was only thirty-five years old when he died—might someday succeed Mzee as president. And so they had killed him.

Whether Kenyatta himself knew of the plot beforehand was the subject of heated debate throughout Luoland. All that the Luo knew for sure was that the tribe had lost half its leadership overnight (the other major Luo political figure was the aging socialist Oginga Odinga, who had been the nation's first vice president and who'd been in and out of favor, mostly out, for years). Mboya, the chief architect of Kenya's tilt toward the West, had been their best and brightest hope. Without him the Luo, Kenya's second largest tribe with some fifteen percent of the population compared to the Kikuyus' twenty percent, had almost no chance of ever claiming a fair share of the political spoils.

A majority of Luos were convinced that the establishment had rushed to judgment in the Mboya case, that the police had taken the bait of the trigger man and ended its investigation prematurely, letting those who commissioned him get away with murder. And the killing of J. M. Kariuki six years later only served to confirm their suspicions. Like Mboya, Kariuki was a politician, a backbencher in Parliament. Unlike Mboya, he was a Kikuyu. But he was no typical KANU party hack. He had never displayed any of the tribal prejudices common among the other Kikuyu politicians, and he wasn't shy about pointing a finger at his own people when he thought them guilty of impropriety. While careful not to include Mzee himself in his accusations, he had used the floor of Parliament as a pulpit from which to charge State House with corruption, claiming that some of the people in Mzee's extended family were amassing great personal fortunes by questionable means. He ignored repeated warnings to stop from KANU party leaders. His mutilated body was found in the Ngong Hills by a Masai herdsman.

Peter had idolized Tom Mboya, and he had greatly admired J. M. Kariuki. He had sung their praises to his clansmen long before they had become martyrs to party politics. But Peter's personal position hadn't impressed his friends and relatives. The Kenya Police helped to preserve the status quo. Peter was a policeman. Ergo, he was guilty by association.

Peter was under no illusions that he could simply change his ways, apologize to all concerned, and blithely rejoin the family fold. It was too late; the damage was done. He was not sure he would if he could. He was too worldly to happily revert to the simple life of the *pacho*. What would he do there? Fish alongside Ansentus?

Limbo was not a place of Peter's own choosing. He missed his family, missed the comfort and security of knowing he was a part of something larger than himself. The years he'd spent away from the *pacho*—at University, in the police barracks, in his grim bachelor's flat in Jamhuri Estate—had left him feeling like an orphan, lonely and unconnected. The police, a tribe in its own right, had seemed enough for him at first, a substitute family of brothers-in-arms and father figures; but as time went on, he'd come to see that few of his colleagues, and none of his superiors, had ever honestly cared about him. They had praised him when they had to, and used him when they could, but none of them had offered true friendship. Even the other Luo kept their distance, from him and from one another. They did not want to leave themselves open to Kikuyu charges of belonging to a Luo tribal clique. Besides, they were much too busy kissing Kikuyu backsides.

Peter's brief visit home had only reinforced his feeling of isolation, of not belonging anywhere. Here in this village by the Lake were the people he loved most in the world, those he was closest to, and yet they were little more than amiable strangers. Seeing how easy they were with one another as they joked and bantered, how uncomfortably correct and polite they were with him, Peter's sense of loneliness crested and broke, a wave of melancholia that threatened to wash him away.

But his relatives' reserve toward him did not mean that they had suddenly forgotten their manners. There was a feast in his honor the evening of his arrival. His father, looking remarkably fit considering his brush with death and shouting orders to his wives to fetch him beer, invited clansmen from throughout the Dunga area. As a *dhoot* elder, the old man had donned festival dress for the affair: a traditional headdress of hippo tusks and ostrich feathers, the tusks arranged in a sunburst round his head and the feathers swaying like coastal palms above. The others wore their everyday clothes, colorful enough in their own right; it wasn't for nothing that the Luo were called "the Pharaohs of Kenya."

Throughout the long evening Peter's mother had ushered a parade of women past him, her intentions as subtle as an arrow through the heart, her eyes pleading with him to be nice to them, to like them. They were all of a kind for the most part, invariably too young or too old, unmarried girls and recent widows. Peter, who had not been with a woman who wasn't a prostitute since his student days, was perfectly polite but distant. With a determination born of desperation, his mother would not give up, and by the time Peter staggered off to the guest hut, drunk and milked of small talk, he was convinced he had been introduced to every husbandless hag in Luoland.

Early the next morning, hoping to walk off his hangover and avoid his mother, he had wandered down to the water. The day was windy and clear and he had an excellent view of Homa Mountain on the other side of the strait. He was too late to see Ansentus and the other fishermen set out for the tilapia beds, and too early to watch them come back; they would have caught the outgoing breeze at dawn and wouldn't return until midday when a convection wind would veer about and blow them home. The bulk of the village fleet was far out on the Gulf, down over the horizon, but a few boats were working close to shore and Peter sat on a rock and watched them rise and fall among the whitecaps.

A Luo lake boat was little more than an oversize wooden canoe with a sail. It had a long swing-mast and a triangular, raked sail. The keel was a solid piece of wood, with planks fixed to each side to form three washstrakes. Because of its large sail and shallow keel, and because steering was done with a stern paddle rather than a rudder, managing such a vessel single-handedly took enormous physical strength, a fact which helped explain Ansentus's powerful arms and upper body. Raw strength, along with stamina and a certain level of expertise, also figured in the fishing process itself. A Luo fisherman sailed off alone each morning at dawn, watching on the way out for his "marks" on the surrounding hills to help him locate the end of his net, which was indicated only by a bamboo stake sticking a few feet up out of the water. Finding a slender reed miles offshore was quite a trick, but one that any Luo fisherman worth the name could pull off in his sleep. When he found it, he dropped the sail and paddled the entire length of the net, a mile or more in some cases, taking it up hand over hand. It was backbreaking work, and the catch was often small, but it was a way of life for the clan's menfolk, and had been for more than two hundred years, ever since the ancestors migrated to Nyanza from Uganda across

Lake Victoria and turned from stock raising and farming to fishing. For all the clan's menfolk except Peter.

Peter vaguely remembered going out on the Gulf with his father as a boy, before his other "fathers," the ones in the white collars, realized his potential and talked his parents into turning him over to them, before he began spending more time in the missionary school than in the *pacho*. He had told Roberta Lewis that he had been born knowing everything there was to know about fish, but that had been a lie. Here he was, a grown Luo man, and he didn't know how to maneuver a fishing canoe or mend a gill net. He wasn't sure he could even find a fish in so vast a body of water, let alone catch one. Fishing was the foundation of *pacho* life, and Peter's lack of prowess, to say nothing of his apparent lack of interest, was just one more barrier between him and the rest of the family, one more thing making reconciliation unlikely, if not impossible. Just thinking about it made him heartsick.

In the end, he decided not to wait for Ansentus and the others to return from their morning's fishing. Hurrying back to the *pacho*, he thanked his father for the fine feast, kissed his mother goodbye, and drove away before anyone felt obliged to insist, halfheartedly but ever so politely, that he stay for the midday meal.

Hone was just dusting the last of the scones with sugar when he abruptly put down the spoon and shaded his eyes with his free hand. "Now who can that be?"

Robbie and Peter turned their heads, following his gaze, and saw a vehicle approaching at top speed, barely outracing its own tail of dust. When it got closer, Robbie Lewis said, "Speak of the devil."

The Land Rover stopped in front of the house and Adrian Glenton got out and slapped his wide-brimmed hat against his thigh, beating out the dust.

"Why, if it isn't the Great White Hunter, the last of a vanishing breed," Hone said drily, "and I do mean vanishing."

"Hullo, all," Glenton said, coming up the veranda steps.

"How good of you to call," Hone said. "What a marvelous surprise."

"Why? Weren't you expecting me?" Adrian asked. He looked at his wristwatch. "It's Monday and it's tea time, and unless I'm mistaken, I have an appointment with Miss Lewis."

"Damn right you do," Robbie said, grinning. "But try not to be tardy next time. The tea's all gone and Stephen ate the last crumpet."

"That's disappointing news," Adrian said, "but I suppose I could make do with a beer instead."

"Perhaps we should all have one," Hone said, looking for his houseman and not finding him. "Where is that damn chappie when you need him?" he muttered.

Robbie saw that Glenton was not paying the slightest bit of attention to Hone; he was still watching her. She suddenly wished that she had washed her hair that morning, or at least put on lipstick. "I can get it," she said quickly, hopping up and starting toward the house. She turned and wagged a finger at Adrian. "Don't say anything important until I get back."

Inspector Odongo had yet to say a word. He had taken out a small black notebook and a pencil and was staring at Adrian Glenton without expression. Glenton watched Robbie Lewis walk all the way into the house before finally turning to face the policeman. "*Jambo,* Inspector. *Habari?*"

"*Mzuri sana,* Mr. Glenton," the inspector said. "And how are you?"

"Oh, I'm fine, just fine."

"I'm very happy to hear it."

Adrian paused, then said somewhat sheepishly, "I suppose you're wondering where I've been this past week?"

"No not at all," Peter said. "I know all too well where you've been. You've been in the *shambas* terrorizing innocent farmers."

Glenton shrugged. "We can't be certain they are innocent until after we've terrorized them, now can we?"

"It's no joking matter, Mr. Glenton," the inspector said quietly. "There have been ten formal complaints filed against you and your team already, and God only knows how many others there are who are afraid to report you. The superintendent of police and district commissioner both have expressed concern. They are upset with me and I am upset with you."

"I'm only doing what I have to do, Inspector," Glenton said. "Do you want me to catch these damn poachers or don't you?"

"Yes, Mr. Glenton, I want you to catch them. But you are going to have to catch them while staying within the rules of civilized behavior."

"Civilization ends at the game ditch, Inspector Odongo."

"The Kikuyu *shambas* are on this side of the game ditch, Mr. Glenton."

Stephen Hone, who had been listening to the two of them partly with concern and partly in amusement, laughed. "Tough gaffer, isn't he?" he said to Adrian.

"Bloody minded is more like it," Glenton said, but he said it with a rueful grin.

It was a moment which should have eased the tension, but did not. Inspector Odongo was having none of it. "Do you know what the people in the district have started calling you?" he asked Adrian.

Glenton nodded and gave the policeman another half grin. "Yes, Charles has told me. *Mbwa Kali.*"

"Why are you smiling? Does it please you to be called a vicious dog?"

Glenton shrugged. "If a dog is vicious enough, he might just be able to bring down a hyena."

"It doesn't bother you then?"

"They can call me any bloody fucking thing they please," Adrian said with a flare. "If I can make them more afraid of me than they are of this hyena character, perhaps I'll start getting something useful out of them."

Odongo just stared at him for a moment. Then he asked: "Who killed the Somali man you left at police headquarters?"

"Ekali, my Turkana. Nailed him to a tree with his spear. Marvelous throw, really. Which reminds me . . ." Adrian reached into the pocket of his dirty safari jacket and handed Odongo a fistful of cartridge casings. "I didn't know you'd be here, but I was going to give them to Stephen to give to you."

Odongo began holding them up one by one, examining the markings. "Where did you get them?" he asked.

"Found them lying about the park. At the ambush site."

"Ambush?" Hone said quickly. "You were ambushed?"

"On the other side of the ditch, just inside the park," Adrian told him. He turned back to Odongo. "Did one of your complaints about the team come from a farmer named Njonjo?"

"Yes, I believe so."

"Well, it happened right after we left his place."

"Was anyone hurt?"

"No, we were fortunate. But it's as I said, Inspector, civilization ends at the game ditch."

"How do you suppose they knew where to find you?" Hone asked. He was sitting up straight, on the edge of his chair, and his round, doughy face seemed to have shed its softness. It was sharp and alert, the face of a big game hunter, or a once-and-infamous Mau Mau hunter.

"It's an interesting question, isn't it? Luck, perhaps. Then again, perhaps not."

"What do you mean by that?" Inspector Odongo asked.

Glenton stared at him a moment before saying, "I think they were waiting for us."

Odongo stared back unblinkingly. "Who knew you would be visiting that particular *shamba*?" he asked.

Adrian shrugged, looking away. "Only my team members, as far as I know. And only from about six o'clock when I briefed them on the operation."

"Do you think that the farmer, this Njonjo, might know something about it?"

"I shouldn't think so. But perhaps I should have another little chat with him."

"I don't think that would be a good idea," Odongo said quickly. "Another one of your little chats might kill him." He jotted something down in his notebook. "I'll have a word with him."

Glenton shrugged again. "Please yourself."

Robbie Lewis returned with the houseman in tow. The man was carrying a tray laden with four bottles of beer and four pewter mugs. Two of the mugs had obviously been put into the cold-box for a minute or two and had a thin coating of frost on them. "Have I missed anything?" Robbie asked.

"Nothing terribly important," said Glenton.

"Except for the ambush, of course," Hone amended.

"Ambush! There was an ambush?"

"We'll tell you about it later," Hone said.

Robbie gave Glenton a disgusted look and began clearing the tea trolley to make space for the beer tray. When Hone's houseman set it down, she put one of the frosted mugs at her own place and set the other one down in front of Adrian. She had to lean across him to do it, and her hip brushed against his chest. Adrian nearly tipped his chair over trying to get out of her way. "Have you told your Yank about the bungalows yet, Stephen?" he asked quickly.

"Yes. I telephoned all the way to Salt Lake City, Utah. I didn't tell him what happened, of course, just that it was a fire of unexplained origin."

"What did he say?"

"First he asked if any of our rhinos had been injured. I told him no. Then he asked whether the bungalows were covered by the insurance. I told him yes and that Lloyd's had already been notified. Then he told me to have a nice day."

Everyone smiled, even Odongo, but the policeman quickly grew serious again. "The Assistant Minister was worried when he didn't hear from you, Mr. Glenton. Is there a good reason why you've stopped sending in a daily situation report?"

"Yes there is. I don't have any bloody radios, remember? They went up with the cottages."

Odongo consulted his notebook. "You've two radios. One was here with you, in your vehicle, when the bungalows were attacked. And your man Joseph had one with him."

"They're hand-sets. They won't reach Nairobi. Our base unit was destroyed."

Odongo wrote in his notebook. "I'll see to it that you get a new one at once. . . . I can commandeer one from the police headquarters. But you've been well within radio range of the Nyeri station, and closer still to the park warden's HQ right here in Mweiga. Couldn't you have relayed your report through one of them?"

"I suppose so," Adrian said. "But the key to the success of our mission is secrecy, and I'm not about to send anything sensitive to the bloody bureaucracy. For God's sake, you should know about that—you deal with it every day. There's no telling who would get their hands on it. I wasn't terribly keen about sending it to Jogoo House either. There is no way of knowing what happens to it."

"It's strictly controlled, I assure you," Odongo said. "The only people who have access to your reports are myself and the Assistant Minister."

"And the chap in the message center. And the girl in the minister's office. And the bloody charwoman. And Christ knows who else."

Odongo sighed, then said: "There has to be a way for us to communicate, a way that will satisfy everyone. We have to know what you are doing at all times. The Assistant Minister insists on it."

"I'd like to keep it strictly between us," Glenton said.

Peter shook his head. "That's not practical, I'm afraid. I'm in Nairobi half the time."

"All right, I have a solution," Adrian said. "What if we were to use Stephen here as a relay?"

Both Odongo's and Hone's eyebrows shot up. "How?" Odongo asked.

"Quite simple really. When you get your hands on the new base unit, set it up here. My radios can reach the house from anywhere in the park. I'll speak with Stephen and he'll track you down by telephone in Nairobi, or wherever, and pass along my report. What do you think?"

Peter took a moment, pursing his lips and tapping on the notebook with his pencil. Finally he nodded. "All right."

Adrian looked at Hone. "I suppose I really should have asked you first, Stephen," he said apologetically. "We seem to be drawing you deeper and deeper into this mess. First we arrange for your guest quarters to be burned out, and now we ask you to work without wages."

Hone smiled. "You must be joking. I'm having the time of my life. Brings back my days in the Indian Army."

Robbie Lewis was smiling as well. The arrangement suited her perfectly. If Stephen Hone had full access then she would have full access; Hone seemed unable to deny her anything she wanted.

"When can you have the radio installed?" Glenton asked.

"Sometime this evening," Odongo said. He looked at Hone. "I'll send a police technician out to set it up and show you how to operate it."

"Super," Hone said, grinning broadly. "Now shouldn't we discuss frequencies or something?"

"We'll do it before I leave," Adrian said with a smile, amused by Hone's schoolboy enthusiasm.

"That resolves the signals problem," Odongo said. "But if all your rations were indeed destroyed in the fire, what have you been doing for food? Would you like me to see if I can get some more for you?"

"Don't bother," Glenton said. "We couldn't carry rations boxes about with us anyway."

"You haven't answered my question. How have you managed for food?"

"We've been living off the land."

"That's what I was afraid of," Odongo said primly, using his official voice. "What you mean is poaching, don't you?"

"No, that is not what I mean," Adrian said. "Some guinea fowl and francolin, and a hyrax or two. That's all."

"That doesn't sound like enough to feed your team."

"Well if you must know, we've had elephant steak quite a lot," Adrian said bitterly. "There's been no shortage of dead elephants in the park."

There was a lengthy silence, then Odongo stood abruptly. "Well, if I'm going to steal you a radio I should be off for Nyeri." He slipped his notebook into his jacket pocket and a momentary look of recognition crossed his face. When he took his hand out of his pocket there was a piece of paper in it. "I nearly forgot, I have some information for you," he said. "It's a few days old, but I had no way to reach you. So you see, Mr. Glenton, communication with the bloody bureaucracy can be a two-way road."

"What is it?"

"The district police have had a report from a farmer who owns a *shamba* near the park. He claims to have seen headlamps late at night near the boundary, and he has heard noises that sound like a vehicle."

"Our middleman," Adrian muttered. "Helping the vulture to disgorge the meat in its gullet."

"I beg your pardon?"

"Nothing, nothing at all. That's excellent information, Inspector."

Odongo smiled with satisfaction and handed Glenton the paper. "Here is the man's name, and I've drawn a map to his *shamba*. He says it's always a Tuesday or a Saturday, a little after midnight."

"Tuesday is tomorrow. Good. It gives me time to question this fellow and make a plan."

"Just be careful how you question him," Odongo said. "I trust we have seen the last of *Mbwa Kali*." With that, Odongo thanked Hone for his hospitality, said goodbye to Robbie, and walked to his Suzuki.

"I can't make up my mind about that chappie," Hone said as they watched the inspector drive away. "He's smart enough, that's for certain, but he doesn't seem to like *mzungus* much, does he?"

Adrian shrugged. "That's his problem, not ours."

"Well, I think he's nice," Robbie said, "even if he is a bit of a tight-ass."

"A tight-ass?" Hone said with a chuckle. "Good heavens! I won't even ask what that means."

"Tell me about the ambush," Robbie said, pulling a notepad out of her purse. Adrian told her. When he finished, she asked a few more questions about team operations, and seemed satisfied with his response: a sad story full of frustration and failure. When Robbie closed her notebook, she gave him a suspicious look and said: "You're being unusually cooperative today. What's the catch?"

"Catch? I don't understand."

"You want something. What is it?"

Adrian's face turned bright pink. "Bloody hell," he muttered. "I've never known anyone so . . . um, well, actually there is something."

Hone let out a loud guffaw. "This one's got your number all right," he chortled. "You might as well be made entirely of glass."

Glenton ignored him. "Um, will you be going to Nairobi anytime soon?" he asked Robbie.

"Maybe," she said. "Why?"

"I'd like you to do something for me."

"What?"

"There are some things at my house that I need. If you could pop in and get them for me, it would be a great help."

Robbie shrugged. "Sounds easy enough. Sure, no sweat."

"If you're certain it's no bother."

"I was planning to drive down tomorrow or the day after anyway. I have to check in with New York, and I need to pick up some camera gear. I'm going to take your picture. You and your team, all lined up like a class portrait."

"Oh, I see, well, yes, I suppose it would be all right," Adrian said, fidgeting. "Ah, there is one more thing you can do for me. . . ."

"I knew it," Robbie said. "What?"

"I'd like you to investigate Inspector Odongo for me."

After a long silence, she said, "How do you mean?"

"I want everything you can find on him. Who is he? Where does he come from? What is his reputation in the police? What cases has he handled before this and was there anything crooked about them? You're a journalist; this sort of thing should be just your cuppa."

"In other words, you want to know if he's straight."

"Yes, I suppose so."

"He's straight," Robbie said.

"How would you know?"

"My father was a policeman for twenty years. I can tell a bent cop just by looking at his eyes."

"Balls."

"Okay, okay, I'll check him out for you. But I'm telling you right now. He's as straight as they come."

"All I know is that Fisi's boys were waiting for us that evening," Adrian said. "Either they got lucky or it was a setup. I'd like to know which."

"Did Inspector Odongo know where your team would be that night?" Hone asked.

"The only ones who knew were my boys."

"There you are then," Hone said.

"I've known most of those boys for years. I hand-picked them for this job. All except one. That Kuke ranger, Charles. Odongo found that one."

No one said anything for a moment, until Glenton pulled a ring of keys from his trousers pocket and slipped one free. "Here's the key to my place," he told Robbie. "I'll jot down the address for you and make out a list of the things I need and where you'll find them."

"Do you live alone?" Robbie asked.

"Yes."

"Figures," she mumbled.

"What about you? Do you live alone?" Adrian's face began to color as soon as the words were out of his mouth. He could not quite believe he had asked her that question.

"Yes, I do," she said, giving him a peculiar look.

The next word that popped from Adrian's mouth, seemingly of its own volition, amazed him even more.

"Good," he said.

20

The farmer's name was Winston Ngweno and his *shamba* was directly on the park, a few miles north of Kabage village and not far from the Ruhuruini Gate. It was a neat and apparently prosperous farm, growing potatoes, *nduma,* and other tubers.

The *shamba* was atypically large for the district, thirty acres or better, with several kraals and huts; Winston Ngweno was an elderly man, about eighty, who had many wives and children and grandchildren to shelter. He was an impressive man with a dignified bearing and a full head of nappy white hair, and he walked with the help of an ornately carved cane. He saw to it that his three guests—Adrian, Joseph, and Charles—had a comfortable place to sit and hot tea to drink before settling down to business.

"It is as I told the police," he said. "Every Tuesday and Saturday night for a month now. They will come tonight."

"And you say it's always a few minutes after midnight?" Adrian asked.

"Yes. Never before midnight, never later than half past the hour."

"Lights and engine noises?"

"Yes, that's right."

"On your property?"

"Yes. There is no fence there because of the road that goes into the park. It is an old army road and the district officer won't let me put a fence across it."

"Have you ever gone to investigate the place, *mzee?*"

"Once I did. The next morning. But there was nothing to be seen except some tire tracks."

"But you have never gone to investigate when the lights were there?"

The old man shook his head. "I figured it was government business or illegal business. Either way, I wanted no part of it. I haven't lived this long by being a fool. I've heard the stories about what's going on in there."

"You mean Fisi, the hyena?"

"Yes."

"Do you believe the stories you've heard, that this Fisi is part man and part beast?"

"Certainly. And you'd better believe it too if you want to live as long as me," the Kikuyu said in a lecturing tone. He didn't seem at all intimidated by his visitors. Not by the nasty-looking Masai, not even by this Kikuyu-speaking *mzungu,* about whom he had also heard stories.

"If you believe the stories, then it was brave of you to go to the police," Glenton said.

"It was no more than my duty as a citizen," the old man said simply, but he was clearly pleased by Glenton's comment.

"Could you show us the place?"

Ngweno rapped his left leg with his cane. "It's hard for me to get about these days. But my grandson, Henry, will show you." He threw his head back and bellowed: *"Henry!"* A moment later, a man of about forty stepped through the doorway. "Henry, take these *bwanas* to the spot where we found the tire marks," the old man instructed. "And when they have finished looking, bring them back here for something to eat."

"Asante sana, mzee," Adrian said.

They followed the grandson out into the compound where the rest of Glenton's team lounged in the shade of the Land Rover. Pythias and Tembo were playing *bao,* using a borrowed wooden board, and seeds for draughts, while Ekali looked on. A large crowd, mostly children, ringed the players, some of them watching the game but most of them staring goggle-eyed at Ekali and his helmet of blue hair. The clay had begun to flake and come off during the course of the past week, but the Turkana's hairdo was still a spectacle to these Kikuyu.

Joseph studied the *bao* board for a moment—the Masai variation of the game was called *engehei*—and told Tembo: "You're in deep shit, my friend."

"Hate to disturb your game, Pythias," Adrian said, "but I need you to read sign for me."

The Dorobo got to his feet reluctantly. "I've memorized the board," he warned Tembo. "If you cheat, I will know it."

Tembo grinned, showing yellow-black teeth, and said, "I don't need to cheat to beat you." Pythias answered by drawing Ekali aside, testing the point of the Turkana's spear with a fingertip, and whispering loudly enough for the old Liangulu to hear: "Watch him for me, Ekali. If he tries anything, kill him."

Henry led them to the *shamba* boundary, then turned west. They walked for nearly a kilometer, following the game ditch. Adrian tried to question their guide as they went, but Henry proved to be less talkative than his grandfather.

"How long do you see the lights? How long do they stay?"

"Not long."

"How long is not long?"

Henry shrugged. "Ten minutes. Sometimes less."

"Does this old military road cross the ditch and go into the park itself?"

"Yes."

"Is there a gate across the road?"

"Yes."

"Do they ever cross over into the park?"

"No."

"Is the gate locked?"

"Yes."

"Nice chatting with you, Henry." Adrian dropped back a few paces and fell into step beside Joseph. "Why would they risk making the transfer on private property where they can be seen?" Adrian wondered out loud.

"Because of the road," Joseph said "Besides, it's quite a distance to the *manyattas*. Perhaps they do not realize they can be seen."

"But their meeting place is only two or three miles from Ruhuruini Gate, where there are rangers."

"Rangers who never leave the comfort and safety of their kiosks," Joseph said scornfully.

"Why not just drive on into the park then?"

"They would have to use boltcutters on the lock," Joseph said. "A broken lock would arouse suspicion."

"You know everything this morning," Glenton said with a smile. "So why aren't you in charge of this balls-up instead of me?"

"I have asked myself the same thing," Joseph said.

Adrian laughed. "If you've got all the answers, try this one: what object can never be overtaken?"

"One's shadow."

"Damn!"

Joseph smiled, pleased with himself. Not because he had known the answer to the riddle, but because it was the first time he'd seen Adrian laugh since Chege was killed.

When they reached the road, Pythias went immediately to work, getting down on hands and knees like an animal, almost sniffing the ground. The others, with the exception of Henry, stood in the road where it crossed the ditch, staying out of his way.

For the first time, Henry demonstrated some interest in the proceedings. He followed Pythias about, asking questions, listening avidly. It was a natural role for both of them. The Dorobo, of whom there was a large group in the Aberdares in and around Kanali, had been teaching bushcraft to the Kikuyu for hundreds of years. The Kikuyu had always been superior students, as the Mau Mau proved during their long hold-out in these mountains during the Emergency. The Dorobo were thought by many anthropologists to be the descendants of Kenya's true aborigi-nes, an ancient people known as the Gumba, pygmy-sized bushmen who were in the Aberdares when the Kikuyu first came. The Gumba had hidden in the woods and lived in pits to escape the stronger and more belligerent Kikuyu. The Kikuyu came to regard them, and later the Dorobo, almost as materialized leprechauns, who understood the language of wild animals. In some Aberdare villages the Kikuyu holy men placed their most potent symbol of witchcraft, an elephant verte-bra called the *Getharki*, into Dorobo hands for safekeeping, to hide in some dread spot deep inside the forest.

"Look, do you see these tire prints?" Pythias was saying to Henry. "How old would you say they were?"

Henry shrugged.

"They're between three and four days old," Pythias said, enjoying the role of teacher, well aware that the others were listening. "Now, how do I know that?"

Henry shrugged again.

"The ant line," Pythias said patiently. "Ants like even the slightest of depressions. See how they have built a home in this one? They would have begun to build twenty or thirty minutes after the track was left. You can tell how fresh the tracks are by how much progress the ants have made."

The lesson went on for another half hour before Pythias was ready to give Adrian a report. He called the rest of the group over and announced: "They used a single lorry, a small van, like a *matatu*. They backed it up to the gate and passed the cargo across by hand; I found some animal hairs and some drops of dried blood on the gatepost."

"How many men?" Adrian asked.

"The ground is churned up so it is hard to tell, but I'd say between seven and ten men," Pythias said. "There was only one man with the van. I found where he got in and out. And he had on city shoes, street shoes. The others wore plimsolls or army boots."

"Good show, Pythias. You're the best."

"Yes, I know," the Dorobo said matter-of-factly.

Joseph laughed and said, "You are also arrogant, little man," but Glenton could tell that the Masai was impressed.

"When it comes to arrogance, who knows better than you?" Adrian said.

"You would insult me, your circumcision brother?" Joseph asked indignantly, pretending to be hurt. "Just for that, I'm not going to give you any advice on how to go about ambushing these people."

"Oh yes you will," Adrian said. "I've never known you to pass up a chance to show off."

"Well, perhaps I'll help you this once. But only because if I don't, you'll fuck it up."

"Meishaa elukunya nabo engeno," Adrian said in Masai. One head cannot hold all wisdom.

"Oh ho, proverbs again, is it?" Joseph exclaimed with a grin, his eyes lighting up. *"Meibor ngeno lukunya."* Wisdom is not always white-headed.

"All right, I surrender," Adrian said quickly.

"Ore pee einosa oldia inkik mme ololiki etala," Joseph said. The reason the dog ate its own shit was not because it lacked an adviser.

"I said I surrender."

"You started it," Joseph said. "Fuck with the bull and you get the horn."

"That's not a Masai proverb," Adrian said.

"No. It's a Texas proverb. From the Cowboy tribe."

Adrian rolled his eyes and sighed. "So what do you have in mind?" he asked.

Joseph quickly outlined his plan. It was simple, as the best plans invariably were. The team would get into position early, just after dark, in case Fisi thought to send someone ahead to scout the transfer point. The team was fortunate in that there would be no shortage of available cover; moderate to heavy bush grew along both sides of the road, with only a small cleared patch where the road crossed the animal ditch. One man, Pythias or Tembo, would find a hiding place on this side of the ditch, the *shamba* side, and take care of the van driver. Two men would climb down into the game ditch, one on each side, in case anyone tried to use it as an escape route. Adrian and Joseph would position themselves on the park side of the ditch and deal with the main body of men, which figured to be heavily armed and dangerous. They would call to the poachers to give up. If they refused, the fireworks could begin. Once the shooting started the man assigned to the van would ignore the driver and concentrate his fire on the vehicle itself, to disable it. It was important to take the driver alive; he was a direct connection to whomever was behind the ring. It would also be nice if they could take one of the poachers alive, to lead them to the rest. It was unlikely that Fisi himself would turn up, but if all went according to plan, the team would be on its way to finding him.

When he was finished, Joseph gave Adrian a haughty grin and asked: "Did I forget anything, O Hairy One?"

Adrian grinned back at him, shrugged his shoulders, and said: *"Pooki olaiguenani olojo enilimu."* The best adviser is the one who says what you would say.

They spent nearly another hour picking out hiding places which offered both good concealment and clear fields of fire, then made the long trek back to the compound. A meal had been readied during their absence, and while Adrian was anxious to brief Ekali and Tembo on the plan, and then conduct a weapons check, he knew it would be an unforgivable insult to Winston Ngweno to turn it down; the old man's wives and daughters and granddaughters had gone to considerable trouble to prepare it.

Charles, who had come to the farm directly from Mweiga, was strolling toward his motorcycle when Adrian stopped him. "*Pole, pole,* Charles. Where do you think you're going?"

"Back to town," the ranger said. "Back to work."

"I'm afraid not."

"But I have a lot to do in town. Sources to see."

"You'll have to see them tomorrow," Adrian said. "You're going with us tonight."

Charles's eyes widened and he poked himself in the chest with a forefinger. "Me?"

"Yes, you," Glenton said. "I'll need every man I've got tonight. Besides, it's time you began pulling your weight on this team. You've had all the comforts of home while the rest of the lads have been crawling through the mud and muck."

"But I'm an information *fundi,* not a policeman. Inspector Odongo didn't say anything about fighting when he asked me to take this job."

"You are a corporal in the Field Force rangers," Glenton said coldly. "You are trained to deal with armed poachers and that's precisely what I need from you tonight."

Charles hesitated, wondering how far he could, or should push Glenton. Then he shrugged and said, "Whatever you say. I will be back in a couple of hours then."

"Whatever it is you have to do in town will just have to wait. I don't want you out of my sight until this business is finished. Do you understand?"

"But—"

"Do you understand?"

"Yes, *bwana.*"

"That's more like it," Adrian said. "And now we're going to eat a nice lunch with our gracious host. We will smile and be pleasant and show these people that *Mbwa Kali* isn't really so awfully *kali* after all."

Glenton walked Charles back to the Land Rover where the rest of the team was gathered. Pythias was returning the *bao* board to its rightful owner, one of the *shamba* children, and Adrian asked idly: "Who won?"

"We never finished the game," Pythias said with a shrug. "I can't find Tembo."

"Ekali, you were with him," Adrian said. "Where is he?"

Ekali shifted uneasily and did not answer.

"Do you know where he is?" Adrian asked, more sharply.

"Yes, *bwana,* I know."

"Go and fetch him then. It's almost time to eat."

"I do not think he will be eating with us, *bwana.*"

"Why not?"

The Turkana paused, then said, "Come see for yourself." He led Glenton to a nearby hut, stopping at the entrance to let him go first. The others, sensing high drama in the air, followed close behind, almost stepping on Glenton's heels.

The hut was a single room, completely unfurnished. Tembo lay on his back on the dirt floor, his long earlobes splayed to make his head look like Mercury's winged helmet, his face covered with flies. Lying beside the body was a plastic pail and a *kihuri,* the calabash which the Kikuyu used for a ladle. Glenton nearly gagged on the stench in the hut, airless room, a bitter and slightly yeasty smell, of vomit and home-brewed African beer . . . *pombe.*

Lying quietly in the bush with a gun in his hands wasn't exactly an unfamiliar experience, Adrian Glenton kept telling himself. Whether the prey was animal or human, it was all the same. The same constant shifting about so your legs would not go to sleep. The same straining to pick up any unusual sounds or movement. It was a skill, a science, perhaps even an art, and he had been one of the best in the world at it.

Had been. Perhaps that was the reason he was feeling so tense and anxious tonight. It was seventeen months since the hunting ban had gone into effect, even longer since his last safari, and he knew all too well that a hunter's skills were the same as any other professional's. Use them or lose them. He wondered how much edge he had lost through inactivity. He would find out soon enough.

Everyone was in place and had been for two hours. Pythias was hiding in the bushes near where the van would park. Ekali and Charles were down in the animal ditch, one on each side of the road bridge and about a hundred feet down the line, to prevent the poachers from using the ditch as an escape route. Joseph was just inside the park with Adrian, across the road from him and slightly off to one side so they wouldn't be in each other's line of fire. Tembo was at the *shamba,* sleeping off his drunk.

That afternoon, after their lunch, they had dug two pit traps, one on either side of the road. Adrian was hoping the poachers would react by jumping off the road, into the traps. Whatever happened, the team was ready. All that was left was the waiting, the hardest part of any hunt.

Glenton checked the luminous dial of his watch. An hour to go until midnight. As if Fisi himself were marking the time with him, a hyena's night call came from deeper inside the forest. *Whoo-oo-up! Whoo-oo-up!* It was echoed by the call of another, and another and another, until their demented howling filled the night.

A cold hand seemed to reach out of the darkness to touch him, an icy palm laid flat against the base of his spine, and he was suddenly sorry that he had frightened Amos Mwangi with that hyena's call in the hospital. Hell-hounds. That was what they sounded like. He shivered and tried to pretend that this was just another hunt, no different from the thousand or more he'd been on in the past. It was a reassuring thought. He had been one of the best. He was still one of the best.

What had Hone called him? Great White Hunter? Something he had gotten from Robbie no doubt. Stephen would never have used the term on his own; not after making such an effort to unlearn it fifteen years ago, at independence, when the word *white* was quickly replaced by *professional* on the letterhead of the East African White Hunters Association. A sign of the changing times.

The ban had been another such sign. The pressure to end hunting had come from several outside agencies, ranging from the World Bank to international wildlife groups, but Glenton, along with a majority of his former colleagues, never understood why Mzee caved in to it. Big game hunting was big business, bringing the government four million dollars a year in trophy and license fees alone, not to mention the vast amount of money it generated for the private sector. The restaurants and hotels. The Asian tailor shops on Biashara Street, where a man could be fully outfitted with safari togs in less than a week. Rowland Ward's, where a client could get his trophies mounted and shipped home. Mzee knew, even if well-intentioned outsiders didn't, that it was the professional hunter who did the most to protect wildlife, by careful culling, by being in the bush to watch for poaching. Two months after the ban took effect, in the spring of 1977, Glenton began hearing rumors about a massive elephant kill in Tsavo. He talked a friend in the Game Department into letting him go along on the aerial survey, and what he'd seen had frozen his soul: mile after mile of decomposing carcasses left by poachers. The stench had made their pilot sick to his stomach and they had turned back before they could complete a rough count that was already well into the thousands.

Adrian had always been puzzled by the animosity of most wildlife preservationists toward the professional hunter, by their persistence in misinterpreting his motives and methods. He and his colleagues had been governed by a licensing system dating back to 1905. Prior to independence, any would-be hunter had first to serve a long apprenticeship to a licensed professional. He had to drive the lorry, clean rifles, put up tents, pack the chop box, draw bath water. Adrian Glenton had served as dog's body for two excellent hunters—Eric Rundgren and David Glenton—just as Pate had served his mentors, Bror Blixen and Maj. C. L. "Muguu" Anderson. Jonathan Glenton, Adrian's grandfather, had served as an apprentice to Walter Dalrymple Maitland Bell, the legendary "Karamojo" Bell.

The professional hunter of Kenya was not, as so many wildlife conservationists seemed to think, a troglodyte with a rifle. His bloodline was too pure and his family tree too impressive for that. Each of them, through an intertwining lacework of venerable teachers, was a direct descendant of one or more of hunting's monarchs, a line as noble as any to be found in a European house of royalty.

It was the Hunters Association that had helped to draft the Kenya game laws, and those laws were the strictest of any nation that permitted hunting. No night shooting. No shooting from a vehicle or from less than two hundred yards away from any vehicle. No shooting at, or near, a water hole. No shooting the female of a species in most cases. The professional did not fire at an animal unless he could clearly see his quarry, and he shot only at vital organs so that he could kill the animal instantly and cleanly. That was the code of the professional white hunters of Kenya. Adrian Glenton had been proud to live by it.

He had also made a decent enough living at it once he'd completed his apprenticeship and taken over Bushbuck Safaris, Ltd. from a dispirited David Glenton. Bushbuck Safaris built a reputation for catering to the serious, no-nonsense hunter, the kind of client who couldn't have cared less that Adrian did not provide all the amenities of a European spa. What he offered them was the chance to fill their license. He guaranteed a clear shot at a worthy specimen of every animal for which they held paper. He couldn't and wouldn't shoot it for them, but he'd find it for them.

It took careful culling to find his kind of client. He rejected a dozen for every one he accepted, and a dozen more rejected him when he told them in no uncertain terms that he was a foot hunter who would walk them until they dropped. "I wear out a dozen pairs of Clark's in the average season," he would tell them, "and I expect that you'll go through a pair or two yourself."

Adrian had made a point of interviewing all prospective clients, for the benefit of both parties. They needed to know exactly what they would be getting for their money and Adrian needed to know exactly what he was letting himself in for, because one of the first things he discovered about the safari business was the truth in something Pate once told him: "The most dangerous animal in the bush is your client." Over time, he had become quite the expert at taking the measure of a man, or woman, in the course of a brief interview. He had his rules, and stuck to them. He did not take on the braggarts or the bloodthirsty. He did not take on heavy drinkers. And he would not take on bad sports. Even the rich ones. Especially the rich ones.

Kenya safari lore was thickly populated with rich boors, men who thought their money could buy them exemption from the rules, and it was largely because of them that the rules were eventually tightened. Men like the American millionaire Paul Rainey, who had come to Kenya with a large pack of coon dogs and bagged more than a hundred lions in two months at little risk to himself, although admittedly several of his dogs had been killed. And Winston Guest, another Yank millionaire who used his string of polo ponies to ride down Cape buffalo. And the Maharajah of Datia, who killed eighteen lions in a single night while shooting from the safety of an enclosure over a zebra bait.

Because of such excesses, the number of lions on a game license had been reduced to four, then two, then zero unless one had a special permit. Before that, "hitting the century," killing a hundred or more lions on a single safari, had been commonplace. The new rules had put an end to the worst of the abuses, but as recently as two years ago Adrian had heard about a party of Arabs who had, with the complicity of a well-placed government official, set up camp in the Masai Mara and killed scores of lions and other animals with submachine guns.

The majority of white hunters, Adrian Glenton included, had been honorable men. There were exceptions, of course, but in his opinion, the worst thing ever to happen to hunting in Kenya was *Uhuru*; it was the one thing regarding independence that Adrian Glenton and David Glenton were able to agree on. With *Uhuru*, and the eventual reversion of Game Department control to the African government, came new ways of doing things. The apprenticeship system for prospective new hunters was scrapped altogether. A man could buy himself a professional guide license if he knew whom to give the money to. He could be a licensed professional hunter without being a member of the Association, and without being bound by the Association's laws. By the spring of 1977, when the hunting ban suddenly made the issue moot, there were about seventy men accredited to the East African Professional Hunters Association, but twice that number held licenses and called themselves professionals.

And what a sorry lot they were. Incompetents who let the client gut-shoot an animal because they didn't have the skill to get him close enough for a clean shot, and who then didn't have the courage to go in and finish it off. They took lions with bait instead of stalking. They used Land Rovers instead of tracking, driving clients right up to the animal and firing away.

You couldn't miss them, these "Hollywood Hunters." They were the ones who were belly-up to the bar at the Norfolk, or lounging under the Thorn Tree at the New Stanley, in their form-fitting safari suits and elephant-hair bracelets, letting clients or prospective clients shout the drinks while they regaled them with stories about the night they got pissed with Ernest Hemingway, or how they knew of this special place in the NFD where no white man had ever been and how they were saving it just for them.

Adrian supposed that when it came to white hunters, the men matched the times. The proof, if any were needed, could be seen in the decline in standards over the years.

Until the turn of the century, there were only a handful of professional guides, and the only people making a living by hunting were ivory hunters. It was Theodore Roosevelt who put the white hunter's trade on the map, with his safari of 1909. The party was guided by Leslie Tarlton and R. J. Cunninghame, Nairobi's first white hunters, and included the man Roosevelt considered to be the world's best hunter, Frederick Courtenay Selous. Selous, who had fought the Matabele wars in southern Africa and who was to die in 1917 at age sixty-five while leading an infantry charge against the Germans, had authored the first adult book the young Adrian Glenton ever read from beginning to end, *A Hunter's Wanderings in Africa*.

Roosevelt's own safari book, *African Game Trails*, was a best-seller that sparked intense interest in big game hunting among the rich, and sent a wave of clients flooding into East Africa. To meet the demand, new firms popped up like anthills after a rain: Newland, Tarlton & Co.; Smith, Mackenzie & Co.; The Boma Outfitting Co.; Chas. A. Heyer & Co.

The early professionals were, like Pate and many of his contemporaries a generation later, farmers first and hunters second, men who thought of safari hunting as a part-time job. The best of them were well-known, and colony officials would call on them from time to time to take on visiting royals, a group that seemed to be inordinately fond of killing things.

It wasn't too long before the merely wealthy began to ape the leisure activities of the nobility, as the merely wealthy invariably do, and ushered in the so-called "champagne safari" era of the 1920s and 1930s, when every imaginable convenience was loaded aboard a lorry or lashed to a porter's back and carted deep into the bush, including, in one instance, a full-sized, claw-footed bathtub.

And as the merely wealthy imitated the nobility, so did the middle classes copy the rich, albeit on a less lavish scale. By the 1950s and 1960s, safaris were being pitched to businessmen as a status symbol. With the advent of air travel and short hunts, an ordinary man could now have the same experiences as kings and princes and film stars and captains of industry. The number of white hunters, naturally, expanded to accommodate the market.

After a few delicious safari scandals, which invariably featured a hunter-client-wife love triangle and all too often included gunplay, and a few Hollywood treatments, it wasn't long before the Great White Hunter entered popular folklore. Everyone knew him; he was the tall, tough, handsome, sunbronzed God of the African plains. The American Cowboy with a leopard-skin hatband.

The reality was different. Most of the truly top guides, the farmer-hunters, had left the trade, too old or disgusted to continue. Some of the new men were good, some weren't. The good ones broke new ground. The bad ones kept to the same old trails, to such an extent that it became unwritten law that a man had to bury every empty tin and bottle before leaving the campsite so that the hunter behind him, no doubt feeding his client a line about how they were pushing into virgin bush, wouldn't be made a liar by the debris of an earlier safari.

But whenever Glenton trotted out his theory that the men matched the times, his friend and former partner Stephen Hone would argue that it was more a matter of the men matching the clientele. "What worthless, wingeing wankers they were," Hone once said when speaking of their clients. Glenton, noting the alliteration, had just shrugged and responded in kind: "Blame the bloody Book."

That was Adrian's other pet theory, that hunting had been ruined by "The Book," *Rowland Ward's Records of Big Game,* the Bible of trophy seekers. He could remember a time when it had been enough to track an animal, skillfully stalk it, and down it with a perfect shot. Then along came The Book and everyone wanted his name in it. "Tape measure hunting," Adrian called it scornfully.

Still, in spite of the "wingeing wankers" and "Hollywood Hunters," Adrian Glenton's safari years had for the most part been good years. He was just thinking how much he missed them when he suddenly became aware of a noise, the rapid, guttural call of Scaly's redleg francolin: *"Kew-koo-wah! Kew-koo-wah!"* It was their old signal, his and Joseph's, the one they used to use when they stalked game in the high country.

An instant later, Adrian saw it too: headlights stabbing through the darkness, their light dancing eerily in the tops of the trees. Then he could hear the high-pitched whine of a vehicle as it labored up a grade.

He checked to see that the safety catch on his shotgun was in the off position. Then he said a silent prayer: that his boys would be ready, and that none of them would be hurt.

The vehicle, plainly visible in the moonlight, came to a stop right in front of where Pythias was hiding in his bower and turned around in a fitful, gear-grinding series of starts and backings. It was a *matatu,* with Nairobi plates and one of those clever names: "Another One Bites The Dust." When the lorry's nose was pointed back in the direction from which it had come, the driver backed up to within two or three feet of the gate and switched off the lights and the motor.

The driver jumped out, walked to the rear of the *matatu* and opened the back doors. He spent the next several minutes fooling about with the van, making quite a racket, seeming unconcerned with noise discipline. Then, leaning against the gate, he pointed an electric torch into the park and flashed a signal: two short, one long, two short. He waited a moment, peering intently up the road into the darkness, then lowered the torch and lit a cigarette. The smell of burning tobacco reached Adrian Glenton's nose a moment later, triggering in him an instant, almost unbearable craving for a smoke.

The driver waited five minutes and then went through the entire routine again, aiming his flashlight into the park, sending his message, waiting, even lighting another cigarette. On the fourth try, his efforts were rewarded with an answering flash from inside the park, some one hundred yards up the road: two long, one short, two long. The very next instant, the silence was shattered by a single gunshot.

There was a second or two of utter calm before the forest seemed to swell up and explode around Glenton. Muzzle flashes were like pinholes of light in the night's black curtain and a solid wave of noise shook the bush he was hiding in. He saw the *matatu* driver sag against the gate, using it for a crutch to hold himself up for a moment, and then slide slowly to the ground. Directly behind the man, the vehicle itself was being methodically disassembled by Pythias, firing from point-blank range. A shower of metal and glass rained down on him.

Glenton screamed—"CEASE FIRING! CEASE FIRING!"—but his voice was lost in the uproar. As far as he could tell, he and Joseph were the only ones not shooting. Charles certainly was; Glenton saw muzzle flashes winking from the ditch ahead. So was Ekali, in the ditch directly behind Adrian; the rounds from the Turkana's rifle made a crisp, snapping sound as they whipped past Adrian's ear.

Glenton kept his head down and waited until they emptied their magazines before trying again: "CEASE FIRE! CEASE FIRE, GODDAMN YOU!"

This time they heard him. A deep and wonderful silence fell over the forest, spoiled only by the urgent hissing of the steam escaping from the van's shattered radiator.

Armed with his shotgun and a torch, Adrian jumped to his feet and began sprinting up the road, toward where the lights had been. After a hundred yards or so, he stopped to look and listen, foolishly switching on the torch to probe the bushes. But there was nothing to see except forest and shadows, and nothing to hear except his own ragged breathing and the wild pounding of his heart. He walked back to the game ditch. The rest of the team had gathered on the *shamba* side. They stood in a loose circle, cradling their rifles and staring down at the body of the *matatu* driver.

"Is everyone all right?" Adrian asked as he approached the gate.

They nodded or mumbled, "Yes, *bwana,*" in subdued voices. Pythias, his legs visibly shaking, was holding onto the gate post for support.

Adrian handed his shotgun and torch across to Joseph and climbed over the fence, careful not to step on the body lying on the other side. The driver was on his belly in a spreading pool of blood, shot through the head just above the left eye. Adrian kneeled beside him, rolled him onto his back and began going through his pockets. The man was not carrying a wallet, or even a driver's license, but there was a packet inside his blood-soaked shirt, the size of a paperback book, wrapped up in butcher's paper and tied with a string. Adrian tore off a corner of the paper and saw that it was a bundle of currency, hundred-shilling notes. He thumbed the corner of the package, riffing quickly through the notes, and guessed that there was close to fifty thousand shillings there.

He tucked the bundle inside his own shirt, then stood up and asked in an arctic voice: "Now then, just what the bloody fucking hell were you people shooting at?"

No one said anything.

"Which one of you fired the first shot?"

No one said anything.

"Was it you, Pythias?"

"No, Adrian."

"Was it you, Ekali?"

"*Hapana, bwana.*"

"Was it you, Charles."

"No."

"Then it must have been a fucking forest spirit, because I know it wasn't Joseph, and it certainly wasn't me," Glenton said, his voice barely under control. "I don't suppose any of you saw or heard where the shot came from either?"

No one said anything. They merely looked at one another, shrugging and shaking their heads.

Adrian glared at them for a moment, then knelt back down beside the body, unsheathed his Randall, and began digging in the *matatu* driver's skull. It was messy work, and by the time he recovered the slug his hands were spackled with bone chips set in a sticky glue of blood and gore.

He cleaned the blade of his knife and his hands as best he could, splashing them with water from his canteen and wiping them on the grass, then rose and held up the misshapen pellet for them all to see. "I'm quite certain that Inspector Odongo's people in the police laboratory will be able to tell us easily enough which gun this came from," he said as he put it into his pocket; actually, he doubted it, but there was no reason why they should. Most Africans, the unlettered as well as the Westernized, had an inflated opinion of technology. He studied their faces carefully, but found no signs of panic in any of them, merely a vague curiosity.

He deliberately turned his back on them and went to the *matatu,* or what was left of it. Pythias, using the M-16, had done quite the job on it. It was a miracle he hadn't touched off the petrol tanks. The van was listing to one side, where Pythias had shot up the tires. The Dorobo had come up behind Adrian, beaming with pride as his friend and leader examined his work. Still furious about the blown ambush, Glenton gave him a withering look and snapped, "I told you to disable the goddamned thing, not vaporize it." The African's smile froze.

When Adrian glanced into the back of the *matatu,* he saw why the driver had made so much noise; he had been preparing the vehicle to receive its illicit cargo. At the far back of the bed were several large burlap sacks filled with charcoal. They were open on one end, and an oversize sewing needle was stuck into the first bag in the stack.

"The perfect place to conceal rhinoceros horn," Joseph said, peering in. "Push it into the middle of the bag, then sew up the ends."

"And this is how they transport the ivory," said Adrian, pointing to the left side of the lorry bed where there was an open hole. "A false floor."

"Let's have a look at the petrol tank," Joseph suggested. "It's the same idea." They found a small ax in the tool box beneath the driver's seat and used it to hack open the petrol tank. Joseph was right; it was partitioned.

It was Pythias who solved the puzzle of the tires. Adrian and Joseph found three spare tires in the back of the *matatu,* all of them apparently useless, nearly bald and missing their inner-tubes. They couldn't think what they might be for until Pythias, still smarting from Glenton's criticisms and anxious to make amends, asked if he might have a look. He borrowed a torch and peered inside one of the tires. "Ahh . . . they roll up leopard skins and put them in the tires," he announced with a triumphant grin. "The inside of this one is covered with tiny hairs."

There was nothing more to be discovered. Glenton led the team back to Winston Ngweno's *shamba,* where they were staying the night. He made sure they had cleaned their weapons before retiring, and asked Joseph and Pythias to remain up with him. He had Pythias tie the SSB radio's dipole antenna between two trees, ten feet off the ground, and got on to Stephen Hone to tell him to let Odongo know where he could pick up the body. It was his first call to Hone's newly installed base unit. Hone, not at all cranky about being awakened in the dead of night, tried to press him for details, but Adrian put him off: "I'm too tired to go into it tonight, Stephen. Let us just say it was a bloody cock-up."

When Pythias had taken down the antenna, Adrian sent him to bed. Then he offered Joseph an Embassy, lit it for him and said, "Let's take a walk."

They moved across the compound and past the last kraal, heading for the game ditch. Neither man spoke until they were on the edge of the ditch, looking into the park. Then Glenton asked: "Do you know who fired that shot?"

"Sure. The Kikuyu. Charles."

"He prevents the driver from falling into our hands and warns his mates in the park at the same time. Clever bugger."

"*Aiya.*"

"I don't know whether to give him to the police now, or play him along and see where he leads us," Adrian said.

"I don't think we should do either one," Joseph said. "I think we should kill him."

"Don't talk nonsense. That would be murder."

"Killing a Kikuyu isn't murder," Joseph said. Then he laughed and added, "It's only rock and roll."

Adrian knew that to Joseph the assassination of Charles Ndirangu wouldn't be murder. To the Masai, it was only murder when the victim was another Masai.

"Charles was too clever by half, because he confirmed my suspicions," Adrian said. "Still, it's a shame we had to miss a good opportunity like that."

"There will be other opportunities," Joseph said.

"I wish I could be certain of that," Adrian said with a sigh. "The truth is we're losing this little war."

"The war will be won by our side or theirs," Joseph said in Masai, quoting one of the tribe's more stoical aphorisms.

When Adrian didn't respond, Joseph asked, "Do you recall that war song we used to sing in the *moran* feasting camp?" He hummed a bit of the tune, then clapped Adrian on the back and said, "Come, sing it with me."

"Don't be bloody ridiculous."

"Come on, O Hairy One. The way we used to."

"For Christ's sake!" Adrian muttered. But he suddenly laughed, threw one arm around Joseph's shoulders and began to sing in Masai. The two of them stood there on the edge of the ditch, facing into the park with their arms over each other's shoulders, warbling the words together:

> *God, bird of prey,*
> *come with me on this raid,*
> *because if I do not get killed, I will kill,*
> *and you will always have one of us to feed upon.*

21

The young man from the East African Wildlife Society was a fellow American, from Atlanta. When Robbie Lewis called, he agreed to see her on short notice but said that he had a full calendar and could only grant her thirty minutes. Once he had a look at her, he quickly volunteered that if she needed more time they could finish the interview later that evening, over dinner at Bobbe's Bistro. He then proceeded to make sure that she would need more time.

When she left the Society's office in the Hilton arcade, Robbie went into a coffee shop in Government Road and changed enough money with the Sikh owner, Mr. Singh—her one and only connection with the black market—to pay the servants for the month. Her stay in the Aberdares had made her late with their wages and she knew how badly both Alphonse and William needed the money. She also knew that they didn't really mind it when she was late because she always gave them a guilt bonus.

When she completed her business with Mr. Singh, she drove home to Muthaiga to settle accounts with the servants and make some telephone calls.

She had checked the wires the afternoon before, as soon as she had gotten back to the city, and had been relieved to find that there wasn't much in the way of hard news going on. Black Africa was still sleeping; fitfully perhaps, but asleep nonetheless. She had also telephoned New York to make certain that the magazine's plans had not changed in the week she had been away, that her wildlife cover was still on. She had told her editor just enough about the developments in the Aberdares to keep his interest stoked—hyping it a bit, but not much—and had gone to bed thinking of Adrian Glenton.

Today was going to be busy. There were Glenton's errands to run and she had a lot of reporting to catch up on. She had wanted to touch base with the Assistant Minister of Wildlife, but his secretary said he was out of the city, and so she had settled for the Wildlife Society, thinking that at least they could provide her with the statistics she needed. The man she had seen this morning, whose name was John Markson, had given her some of what she wanted, and she had reluctantly agreed to meet him for dinner to get the rest. She realized, of course, that it was blackmail, but she didn't really mind; he wasn't at all bad looking, and Bobbe's had the best menu in Nairobi.

After she had paid off Alphonse and William, she changed into a *kanga,* took the telephone with the extra long cord out to the veranda and went to work. Her first call was to Samwel Mbituru.

"Sammy! What's new?"

"Oh, hello, Roberta. Nothing's new. The official line is that the inquiry into the murder of Adam Mwangi is continuing and I haven't been able to dig up much beyond that. My source in the Nyeri head-quarters did tell me about the dead man they found on the doorstep. Did you know about that?"

"Yeah. The gang tried to jump the anti-poaching unit and one of the ambushers was killed. A Somali."

"That's all I know too," he said. "You've been up there. You tell me."

She briefed him on the happenings in the highlands, then asked: "Sammy, how good are your Kenya Police sources here in Nairobi?"

"I thought they were excellent, until this poacher story came along. Why?"

"The cop heading the investigation is an inspector named Odongo," she said. "Could you check on him for me? I need his background . . . and what his fellow cops think of him."

"Hold on, let me get a pencil and paper." He was back on line a moment later. "All right. Odongo, did you say?"

"Yes. Peter Odongo. I think he's attached to the Central Police Station."

"How soon do you need it?"

"Noon tomorrow. I'm going back to the Aberdares early in the afternoon."

"I'll do what I can."

"Thanks, Sammy. I owe you one."

Samwel's effeminate giggle trilled down the line. "What do you mean *one*? This makes about fifty."

She spent the next couple of hours on the veranda, going through her clips file, searching for wildlife statistics she could crib from stories others had done. She was alone in the house, having given both Alphonse and William the rest of the day off so that they could get a head start on spending their salaries.

Robbie was still out on her porch when she became aware of a commotion next door. The security men had abandoned the perpetual card game and were dashing to and fro, cocking the bolts of their weapons and jabbering urgently into hand-held radios. The *askari* at the end of the driveway was out of his guard shed and opening the front gate. And the dogs, aroused by the excitement, were barking. Robbie had witnessed it all before: Dada was on her way.

Robbie raced upstairs to the top floor for a better view of the neighboring compound, getting to a bedroom window just in time to see a small convoy pull into the compound, a black Mercedes limousine sandwiched between two Lincoln sedans loaded with State House security men. The security men hopped out first, scanning the garden and taking up positions around the Mercedes. Satisfied that everything was as it should be, one of their number rapped three times on the limousine's smoked window, then opened the left rear door and helped Dada out.

The "Sister of the Nation" was a handsome, perhaps even pretty, woman by the traditional African standards of beauty. In her late forties or early fifties, she had a thick waist, breasts like plumped-up pillows, and an enormous derriere that swayed behind her like the caboose of a train. Although she usually favored simple dresses fashioned out of *kangas,* she had on a European ensemble today, a clingy design which made her look like an overstuffed cocktail sausage. Even from her upstairs observation post, Robbie could see the fiery flash of Dada's diamond rings as she greeted members of her family with hugs and went into the house.

Her curiosity satisfied, Robbie was just about to turn away from the window when another Mercedes, a sedan, pulled into the compound and came up the driveway. Three Asian men got out and went into the house. Seconds later, yet another Mercedes arrived and out stepped the Assistant Minister for Wildlife. Robbie made a face and muttered, "Out of town, my ass."

She returned to the veranda to complete her chores, then went back upstairs to take a bath and dress, selecting one of the floral print dresses she'd bought at Liberty's in London. When she finally left the house a few minutes before six, the meeting next door at Dada's was still going on.

Glenton's house was off Peponi Road, between Parklands and Spring Valley. He had neglected to inform Robbie that it was merely the caretaker's cottage on someone else's estate. The *askari* on the gate was a Kamba who spoke no English, and each time Robbie invoked Glenton's name, the Kamba shook his head stubbornly and said, *"Bwana hapana iko."* He's not here. When it became clear that Robbie wasn't going to go away, he motioned for her to wait and scampered off to the main house to fetch the *memsaab.*

The mistress of the house was a pretty young woman about Robbie's own age, and easily recognizable as a native Kenyan. She had the healthy outdoors look common to the species, with an ingrained tan that hadn't come from a holiday on the Costa del Sol and a fine mane of sun-streaked hair. She was wearing jodhpurs and knee-high riding boots and she gave Robbie Lewis a cool look of appraisal that was almost predatory.

A little unsettled by the discovery that Adrian Glenton didn't quite live alone after all, Robbie introduced herself and stated her business, producing Glenton's house key as if it were a passport. The woman gave Robbie a flinty smile and said, "Certainly, dear. I'm Philippa Lindsay-Bellville. Let me show you the way."

They chatted as they trekked through a landscaped garden and around the main residence, a sprawling stone house with a peaked thatch roof. More accurately, Philippa Lindsay-Bellville chatted while Robbie Lewis listened. Philippa Lindsay-Bellville and her husband Michael had known Adrian Glenton "for donkey's years." Michael Lindsay-Bellville and Adrian had been at school together at Pembroke until Michael left for Cambridge. Philippa Lindsay-Bellville, nee Philippa Carlton-Browne, had grown up on a farm outside Nakuru not far from Bushbuck Farm, the Glenton place. She and Adrian had had a "rather serious romance" some years ago, but she'd tired of waiting for him to do something about it and had eventually married Michael, stealing him away from Jocelyn Whitney during a bash at the Muthaiga Club given to announce Michael and Jocelyn's betrothal . . . quite an accomplishment considering that Jocelyn's family had "bags of money." Philippa and Michael, "rather well-fixed ourselves, you know," had owned two hotels, one on Lake Naivasha and another near Mt. Elgon, before they had been forced to sell out to an African syndicate secretly backed by Dada. Just recently they had purchased a Peugeot dealership in partnership with Harry Balfour, another one of Adrian's classmates at Gilgil, and were getting on "quite nicely." They'd all tried to talk Adrian into managing the showroom for them after the hunting ban put him out of business, but he had taken that "horrible little job" with the tour company instead. Oh well, at least he'd accepted their offer of the caretaker's cottage. It was going to waste anyway and someone might as well get a bit of use out of it. . . .

Robbie, almost regretting that she hadn't given her name as Roberta D'Agostino-Lewis, listened to this outpouring with a stunned smile, a symptom of advanced hyphenitis. She felt a vague disappointment that Adrian Glenton could ever have been romantically involved with such a brainless twit.

"How long have you known our Adrian?" the woman asked, making the pronoun sound very personal indeed.

"Not long," Robbie said. "Barely more than a week."

"Really? That's rather quick, I must say. He's never let a woman into his rooms the entire time he's been with us. You must have hit the poor boy like a lightning bolt."

"I'm just running an errand," Robbie said with a forced pleasantness.

"Yes, of course you are," Philippa Lindsay-Bellville said. "Well, here we are then. If you think you might need help, I could come in with you."

"Thanks, but I think I can manage," Robbie said quickly. "I'll just get what I came for and be on my way."

"Oh no, you mustn't!" Philippa Lindsay-Bellville exclaimed. "Pop in at the house when you're through here. We can have a gin and chat some more." Before Robbie could say a thing, the woman turned and cantered away briskly.

Robbie was relieved when the key fit the door. For some reason she had been fearful that it might not, that Glenton had taken the wrong one off the ring. Perhaps it was because of his competence in the bush that she was ready to think of him as something of a clown in more civilized settings; fish out of water and all that.

What she found inside confused her even further. It was a modest cottage—one bedroom, a small kitchen, and a large common room that comprised both living and dining room—but the place was actually homey. There were rugs on the polished hardwood floor. The makings of a fire, a neat pile of logs and kindling, were laid out in a walk-in fireplace, which had a mantel of whitewashed stone. There was plenty of furniture, sturdy country things mainly, and pieces of African art were scattered about. But it was the collection of personal items that most surprised her. Not so much the animal heads on the walls, or the huge elephant tusks framing the fireplace like ivory parentheses, but rather the books and the old maps and the dozens of photographs. Especially the photographs.

They were everywhere: on the mantel, the credenza, even grouped on the dining table. Most of them were pictures of a grown Adrian Glenton and most of these were on-safari photos. The safari snapshots were divided into two categories. There were the dead-animal shots: Adrian Glenton with a vanquished impala with impossibly long, curlicue horns; standing on the neck of a spraddled elephant like some circus performer; with the biggest lion Robbie had ever seen; with the Masai Joseph, both of them smiling obscenely and covered with blood as they peered coyly out at the camera from inside the stomach cavity of a dead elephant. Then there were the celebrity shots, the Great White Hunter with his famous clients. Robbie recognized several American sports heroes, two or three politicians, and a handful of film stars, including one libidinous actress who was famous for being something of a hunter in her own right. This particular photograph was inscribed:

"For Adrian, who gave me Africa . . . and the best two weeks of my life. With love."

But it was the earlier photographs which most interested her. There was one of a teenaged Adrian Glenton, already tall and hard-bodied, yet improbably young, with freckled face and a cowlick and an infectious grin, his arms wrapped around the shoulders of two much shorter African boys, the mirror images of each other. All three were wearing nothing more than baggy shorts, and their bare chests were decorated with what looked like warpaint. Scrawled across the bottom of the picture was: "The Three Musketeers. Bushbuck Farm. May 1959."

In another snapshot, an even younger Adrian was sitting on the veranda steps of a charming old farmhouse, sandwiched between a man and woman Robbie assumed were his parents. The man looked weathered and friendly, with crinkly lines around laughing eyes and a short bushy mustache. The woman had the loveliest face Robbie had ever seen. It was a beatific face, like that of a saint, full of quiet joy and compassion and a kind of innocent wisdom. Adrian Glenton sat cocooned between the two grown-ups, looking directly into the camera, a happy and enormously contented grin on his freckled face. The face of the boy showed none of the misanthropy which was to later cloud the face of the man.

With Glenton's list to guide her, Robbie quickly located the items he wanted—a compass, a pair of plimsolls, a rain mac, and an antique, illustrated, two-volume edition of H. M. Stanley's *Through The Dark Continent*—then switched off the electric lights and left, locking the door behind her. It was fully dark out now, and Robbie had no trouble sneaking across the garden and out the front gate without being seen from the main house.

Bobbe's Bistro was on Koinange Street, in the passageway leading to Caltex House. Alan Bobbe himself unlocked the door for Robbie—the door was always kept locked to stop beggars from wandering in—and informed her that her dinner partner was already at an upstairs table. "Is it business or pleasure this evening?" Bobbe asked, cocking a conspiratorial eyebrow, ever on the alert for gossip.

"Strictly business," Robbie said.

"Hmmm," Bobbe murmured. "He's quite handsome."

"Stop it, Alan. Look. See. I even brought my notebook."

The owner escorted her to the foot of the stairway and turned her over to the head waiter with a promise to stop by the table later.

John Markson, wearing a coat and tie, rose to greet her. "Evening,

Miss Lewis," he said, outmaneuvering the waiter to pull out her chair. "I hope you like this restaurant."

"It's the best in town," she said. "And about the most expensive. Couldn't the Wildlife Society save a rhino or something with what this dinner is going to cost?"

"The Wildlife Society isn't taking you to dinner, Miss Lewis. I am."

"In that case, I'll eat small."

She could have used something stronger, but Markson had a *Fumé blanc* chilling in the ice bucket, so she made do with a glass of that.

"I, um, this is my first time here really," he admitted, sheepishly. "Do you recommend anything special?"

"If you like caviar, try the Parrot's Eye as a starter. After that, everything is good."

Markson was, indeed, quite handsome and Robbie liked the soft lilt of his Georgia accent, but he was far too young for her, no more than twenty-four or twenty-five, and he was acting as if this were a real date. She pulled out her notepad and pointedly put it on the table. The young man quickly hit her with a barrage of personal queries, the what's-your-sign and where-are-you-from variety, trying to postpone the inevitable, but the moment he stopped to draw breath, Robbie flipped open the notebook and asked brusquely: "Where were we?"

He sighed and said: "I was telling you about how CITES, the Convention on International Trade in Endangered Species of Wild Flora and Fauna, was supposed to end the worldwide trade in animal products."

"Yeah, that's it," Robbie said. "But it didn't."

"No. It put an end to officially sanctioned hunting in the signatory countries, but very few of them have had much luck in stopping poaching."

"Why not? Aren't the penalties stiff enough?"

"They're very stiff in most places," Markson said. "But there is a lot of money to be made in poaching. The bad guys have been willing to take the risk."

"What kind of money are we talking about?"

"Big money, and getting bigger all the time. Let's take rhinoceros horn for an example. The black rhino's front horn can weigh as much as ten pounds, and the back horn about six. Either whole or ground into powder form, it brings about $30 an ounce in the Far East and the Gulf region, specifically Yemen. That makes a single rhino worth something in the neighborhood of $7,500. A native farmer can triple his annual income by killing just one rhino and selling the horn. Then there's elephant. Ivory prices were fairly stable throughout the 1960s, around $5.50 per kilo. In 1970 it went up a couple of bucks, to $7.50 per kilo. Now, just eight years later, it's almost $75 per kilo. That's enough of a return on investment to tempt someone like a game warden. An average pair of tusks—say between twenty-five and thirty pounds on each side—is worth more than what he earns in five years."

Robbie wrote down the numbers and said, "I know a couple of ex-hunters who think the ban is to blame, that the reduced availability of animal products is what's driving up prices."

Markson smiled indulgently. "I'm not surprised that they see it in personal terms," he said, "but I'm afraid it's more complicated than that. The seventies have been highly inflationary, and ivory is a nice hedge against inflation. It's also been a decade of strife in our area— especially in the Horn—and one result has been an increase in the availability of modern weapons. It's no great surprise that many of the professional poachers these days are Somali. Whenever the Ethiopians mount a new offensive in the Ogaden, Somali fighters cross over the border into Kenya with their automatic weapons. While they're here, they kill animals to eat. Most go back when things cool down, but some stay on to become full-time poachers. My point here is that there are more factors involved than the hunting ban. You have to look at the big picture, at what's happening in the international market."

The waiter came to take their dinner order. Markson, on Robbie's recommendation, decided to try Beef Neptune, a slab of filet stuffed with oysters, and she went for the calamari *piri piri*. They both ordered a Parrot's Eye to start. Trying to use the interruption to move the conversation back onto a personal footing, Markson asked Robbie why she had gone into journalism, but she simply parried by pretending not to hear the question and asking one of her own: "These international markets you mentioned. Why the demand? I mean, what does the Far East and Yemen want with so much rhino horn? There can't be *that* many horny Arabs and Chinese."

Markson laughed and said, "It's a myth that rhinoceros horn is an aphrodisiac."

"Then what is it used for?"

"First off, the horn isn't horn at all, of course; it's a mass of tightly compressed hair. The Orientals grind it into a powder and put it into their traditional medicines, for everything from headaches and nose bleeds to lumbago. In South Korea, for instance, it's used to make *chung sin hwan,* a remedy for high blood pressure. It's rolled into balls, wrapped in gold leaf and swallowed whole."

"Then where does the aphrodisiac idea come from?"

"Probably from the phallic shape of the horn," Markson said. "That and the fact that lovemaking between two rhinos can be a powerful and somewhat shattering thing to witness. Male rhinos can copulate for half an hour or more without a pause."

"Do they have phone numbers?" she said before she could stop herself.

Markson blushed slightly and rushed ahead: "Um, in Yemen the horns are used to make handles for the *Djambia,* the ornamental dagger worn by the men. Before the recent oil boom only the rich could afford one, but now that so many men have found work in the Gulf oil fields, nearly everyone has money. The demand for rhinoceros horn has gone up accordingly."

"What about the ivory?" Robbie asked.

"Most of it ends up in Hong Kong or Japan where it goes into jewelry, piano keys, things like that. The Japanese use 300 metric tons a year, half of which goes into making *hanko,* the seals the Japanese use instead of signatures. The demand from Hong Kong translates into 2,500 dead elephants a month."

Their food came and the interview was abandoned for the time being. As they ate Markson tried again to get Robbie to talk about herself, but she would not cooperate. Finally, he blurted: "Are you married, Miss Lewis?"

Robbie, a fork full of calamari *piri piri* in her mouth, shook her head.

"Do you have a beau?"

Robbie swallowed, then laughed. "A *beau*? You really are from Atlanta. Weren't you a character in *Gone With the Wind*?"

"You know what I mean. A boyfriend."

"Do I have a beau?" Robbie said musingly, still smiling. And then she stopped smiling and, sounding rather surprised, said: "You know something? I think I do."

22

Winston Ngweno was asleep when they came for him. He was dreaming that he had just found a large *thatu* crawling across the floor of his hut, a bad omen. Killing the big caterpillar would have been courting even more bad luck, of course, so he was smearing it with fat to appease the spirits, almost ready to take it outdoors and send it on its way unharmed, when the men burst through the door.

At first he thought that the men, strangers all, were a part of his dream, that they had come to help him remove the *thatu*. Then he felt a sharp pain in his scalp and he woke to find that he was in bed, and that the *thatu* was gone but the strange men were not. One of them was lifting him out of bed by the hair.

He cried out to his number one wife for help, forgetting for a moment that she had stormed off to sleep in her own hut because of his snoring. He made a grab for his cane which was propped against the wall next to his bed, but a powerful hand came out of the gloom and slapped him hard across the face, a stunning blow which loosened what few teeth he had left. Then the other hand, the hand in his hair, yanked him clear out of the bed and dumped him onto the floor with a thump.

One of the men stood by the door with a torch of burning faggots while the others—four or five, he couldn't be sure in the wobbly light—picked him up roughly and began to hit him. They hit him with short, punishing blows, delivered with labored grunts, working the body: belly, ribs, kidneys. Their sweaty faces shone cruelly in the torch light, like the faces on statues of angry gods. The old man tried to speak to them, to beg them to stop, but each time he opened his mouth he was struck in the face. As for the intruders, they had yet to say a word.

He was barely conscious when three more men came in with his grandson Henry and stood him against a wall. They were just going to work on Henry when the man with the torch whistled softly and stepped away from the door. The other men stopped what they were doing and faced the doorway. There was a long moment of stillness, of sinister expectancy, then the door swung slowly open and there it was. The Hyena.

The creature was up on its hind legs, as tall as a tall man and covered from neck to toe with a cape of dirty yellow fur marked by irregular dark spots. But it was the head that commanded attention: bared fangs, reddish-orange eyes, and a dark muzzle streaked with blood. The thing took two or three steps into the room, lifted its snout toward the ceiling and issued a string of low, snuffling grunts.

Henry Ngweno screamed, but the sound was cut short when one of the men holding him hit him with a cowhide sap and put him out cold.

The old man didn't see his grandson slump to the floor. He was mesmerized, watching the beast with morbid curiosity, not in fear so much as resignation, knowing that he would be dead soon and almost thankful for it. If he had lived to see this, he had lived too long. Slowly, circuit by circuit, his brain shut itself down. His shoulders slumped, his mouth fell open and his eyes glazed over. For all practical purposes, he was dead even before The Hyena stepped up to him and blew its foul breath into his face.

The hut was a mess. There was blood everywhere, even on the thatch ceiling. "Christ Almighty!" Glenton said. Then he announced, "I'm going to chunder," and stumbled outside to be sick. The district commissioner, one hand clamped over his own mouth, was right behind him.

The forensic team from Nyeri carried on without comment, working rapidly. There was no reason to think that anyone had tampered with the evidence. Winston Ngweno's grandson had run screaming from the hut the instant he regained consciousness, and the rest of the family had no intention of going anywhere near the place. They huddled outside, keeping their distance, some of them weeping, others still mute with shock. When they saw the *mzungu* and the DC being sick, the weepers sobbed even louder, their worst imaginings confirmed.

A witch doctor, hastily summoned from the nearby village of Kabage, sat cross-legged out in front of the hut entrance, chanting and drawing designs in the dust, doing what he could to cast a counter-spell to palliate the unspeakable evil that had invaded the *shamba* of Winston Ngweno. But he had gotten a peek inside the house, and he had doubts that his magic would be enough.

Glenton wiped his mouth with a sleeve, took several deep breaths and went back inside. He found a place beside Joseph, just inside the door and out of the way of the constables who were gathering up what was left of Winston Ngweno.

Working under the critical eye of Dr. Ramanujam, who had been called in by the police commissioner, the constables put the smaller pieces into cellophane bags filled with ice. Like Adam Mwangi, the old man had been skinned—alive, Ramanujam ventured to say—and his eyes, ears, nose, tongue, and teeth had all been removed and strewn about the room. Unlike Adam Mwangi, he had not been shot full of arrows and spared a lingering death.

"Where is the uncircumcised fish-eater?" Joseph asked out of the blue. "Shouldn't he be here?"

"What?" Glenton asked with a start, still watching the collection process in horrified fascination. The constables had just found Fisi's calling card, a hyena's incisor tooth, in one of Winston Ngweno's empty eye sockets. "Who?"

"The Luo policeman."

"Oh. Odongo. I don't know where he is. Still in Nairobi, I suppose."

"I thought he was the one who let you know about this."

"No," Adrian said. "*Bwana* Hone told me. He was mucking about with his new radio and intercepted the police traffic. I don't know if Inspector Odongo even knows yet."

Joseph was looking at the body in the center of the hut, a glistening red, white, and pink mass of exposed tendons and muscles and fat. "He was a Kikuyu, but he was helpful to us," the Masai said. "He was a friend to us."

"Yes, he was a friend to us," Adrian said bitterly. "And this is his reward. Like Chege."

The Masai was quiet for a long moment, then: "May I ask a favor of you, Adrian?"

"Of course. What?"

"It is a very large favor, and if you refuse me I will understand."

"You're my circumcision brother . . . how can I say no? What is it?"

"When we find this Fisi, I'd like the honor of killing him."

Glenton nodded slowly and said, "You're right. It is a very large favor."

Part Three

23

Fisi was short. Fisi was tall. He was big and burly; he was thin and ascetic. He was a former Mau Mau general, which explained his familiarity with the Aberdares; he was a former officer in Idi Amin's notorious State Research Bureau, which explained his talent for torture and murder. He was a Kikuyu witch doctor, an escaped convict, a deserter from the South African Defense Force, a bastard son of Prince Philip. He was a Somali, an Asian, a renegade *mzungu*, a Zulu prince. He was all of these things; he was none of them. It depended on who you asked.

Adrian Glenton asked a great many people. Spurred by the murder of Winston Ngweno, he intensified the team's nocturnal forays into the *shambas* abutting Aberdare Park, often hitting three in a single night. He returned to the same farms again and again, giving Joseph a little more leash with each visit, until the Kikuyu farmers were reluctant to go to bed at night for fear that *Mbwa Kali* and that pet Masai of his would appear like ogres in a nightmare.

But the *wananchi*, the people, had their own reaction to Winston Ngweno's murder. News of the incident spread through the district like cholera, accumulating horrible details with every telling and re telling, and when all was said, sensible folks decided to fear Fisi more than *Mbwa Kali*. No matter how rough the questioning became, they were the proverbial three monkeys: they heard nothing, saw nothing, said nothing. They were certain now, if they weren't before, that Fisi was, in fact, a devil. The Masai might knock them about a bit, but he wouldn't peel them like a ripe banana. The *mzungu wazimu*, the crazy white man, might hurt them, perhaps even kill them, but Fisi would do worse: he would devour their souls. Their minds made up, they could not be moved. Even when *Mbwa Kali* brought out that huge knife of his, all they would, or could, give him was common marketplace gossip, this theory or that as to who Fisi might be when he wasn't being The Hyena.

The Anti-Poaching Unit—minus Charles, who resumed his work in Mweiga—fared no better in the bush. The rains that week were particularly bad, no more constant but heavier than normal, making effective tracking all but impossible. Pythias would pick up a promising trail in the morning only to see it washed out by the afternoon downpour.

Glenton could only hope that Fisi was having as difficult a time of it. He would have sold his soul for use of the airplane moored so tantalizingly nearby, at Aberdare Ranch.

But despite their lack of success, Glenton and his team were beginning to get a clearer picture of their adversaries. For one thing, they were growing bolder. The APU found a set of footprints in the Treetops Salient, less than a mile from The Ark, one of the park's two lodges. Until now, Adrian had largely ignored the Salient—a peninsula-shaped finger of parkland poking out from the main body—to concentrate his patrols in the deepest, most remote sections, working on the assumption that the poachers would steer clear of the lodges because the tour operators were still running clients in and out on a daily basis.

Tembo was the one who discovered the footprints. It was purely a matter of chance, of course, but it was a coup that got him out of Glenton's dog box, where he'd languished ever since his drunk. Glenton had sent him to The Ark in the Land Rover to pick up some fresh vegetables to augment their game diet. Tembo had had a puncture on the way and saw the prints when he got out to change the tire.

The prints were quite clear and the APU could see where the poachers had crossed the road. It wasn't like Fisi to be so careless, but that was the one afternoon it hadn't rained, and Adrian surmised that the poachers had mistakenly assumed that their tracks would be washed away in a couple of hours.

It was a rare lapse on Fisi's part, and the novelty only served to point up another thing that Adrian and his men were learning about their enemies: the poachers were quite good in the bush. "These men really know what they're doing," Pythias reluctantly conceded after more than three hours of following the footprints that Tembo had discovered for them. The Dorobo was able to keep up with them, but it required every last bit of skill that he possessed.

When they realized that it might not rain after all, the poachers had become more careful, complicating Pythias's task considerably. At each road or animal path they came to, they jumped over it if they could, or dragged brush behind them to erase the prints, or turned and walked across backwards. When they came to bridges, they crossed by swinging hand over hand along the underside. They waded into rain-fattened rivers and emerged far upstream or down. Using animal paths was the only way to get through the heavier forest (the alternative was to cut through with a *panga,* which made slow going, as well as a clear track and a lot of noise), but they used vertical paths when they could, climbing up and down the mountainsides.

There didn't seem to be any way for the poachers to know that they were being trailed, that Tembo had discovered their footprints, but Glenton worried about walking into an ambush nonetheless; Fisi had a habit of knowing things he shouldn't. To ease Glenton's mind, Pythias employed an ancient scouting technique: he scampered up a tree and took a look before the team went round a bend. The little Dorobo was in his element and having a wonderful time, showing off for the others.

Ekali, for one, was duly impressed. The Turkana, desert born and raised, was having trouble with the terrain. Thorns turned his tunic into a useless rag, and his elevated hairdo kept snagging on low vines and branches. When they went down on hands and knees to crawl through brushy tunnels, he might as well have been blind, unable to lift his head high enough to see the way ahead.

Joseph too was impressed, although he would never admit it. He had always thought of himself as an excellent tracker, but that was in the savanna of Maasailand; he had never seen anything like this rain forest. He walked with Adrian at the front of the file, directly behind Pythias, ostensibly there to give covering fire in the event they were ambushed but in reality trying to absorb the Dorobo's methods, eavesdropping as Pythias gave Adrian a refresher course in forest tracking, just as he and his brother had done when they were boys.

"All right, Adrian," Pythias said as they came to a fork in the trail. "Which one do we take?" They were on a two-foot-wide path, made by a herd of Cape buffalo.

"Don't you know?"

"Of course I know," Pythias said patiently. "I'm trying to find out if you do."

Adrian stood in the crotch of the Y where the path's two forks split off, studying one, then the other, with a frown of concentration. Finally he said, "The left one."

"That's right," Pythias said. "Why?"

"The broken spiderweb."

Pythias nodded. "Good."

"And someone has stepped on that log recently," Adrian said, pointing to a rotting log lying on the left-hand path. "You can see where a bit of the bark has been scraped away; the wood is lighter underneath."

"Very good," Pythias said. "So you really were listening all those times when Damon and I thought you were dreaming of *Bwana* Carlton-Browne's skinny daughter."

Joseph, listening carefully, learned a great deal about forest tracking. He learned that leaves, when wet, show up a darker color when disturbed. He learned that dead leaves and twigs, being brittle, crack and break when a man walks on them. He learned that where the undergrowth is particularly thick, any green leaves that have been pushed aside will show their underside, which is lighter in color than the top side, and that to spot such sign the tracker must look *through* the forest instead of directly at it.

When they came to the Muringato River—a small stream during the dry season; now swollen by the short rains—the footprints vanished. Glenton split the unit in half, sending Joseph and Tembo upstream and Pythias and Ekali down, giving each team one of the two radios. He would stay where he was.

"One man on each bank," he instructed. "Look for prints along the banks, and in the shallow water on the edge of the river. Look for discolored water, and for mud on the foliage along the banks. Watch for water on the ground away from the river. That could be the exit point." Pythias just listened, nodding his approval, proud of his pupil.

It was Joseph who picked up the trail again, more than a thousand yards upstream. He found a single heel print, filled with brown water, three feet in from the bank. He radioed the other search team and they came running, collecting Adrian on the way.

It was Joseph who found the cave as well. He remembered seeing it from the path, quite a way back, its mouth no more than a dark shadow on a solid wall of vegetation, a third of the way up a thickly forested mountainside. He hadn't thought anything of it at the time and hadn't mentioned it to anyone. That he had even seen it at all didn't fully register in his consciousness until the scent turned cold again, and Pythias announced that it looked as if the poachers had doubled back on their own trail.

"I think I know where they may have gone," Joseph said. "Follow me." He led them back to where he had seen the cave, pointed out the entrance and received a pat on the back from Pythias when the Dorobo found a narrow, well-disguised trail snaking up the mountain.

Still fearing an ambush, Glenton had Ekali stay there on the trail to watch their backs, choosing him because he would be the most worthless in heavy bush. Then he led the others up the hillside, using the faint track, but proceeding slowly and carefully, watching out for pits and traps.

It took the better part of an hour to reach the cave. It was a lava tube, left empty millions of years ago when molten lava ran out of the volcano under a shelf of cooled rock, and if it were indeed being used by the poachers, they had chosen it for security reasons. It was in the mountain's last strand of rain forest, just below where the bamboo forest started up, and there was no way for anyone to approach the cavern from above without first hacking noisily through the almost impenetrable bamboo.

When they were fifty yards from the cave, Adrian halted the team and called Joseph up. "What do we do now?" he asked, whispering so the others wouldn't hear. "If it was a buffalo lying up in there I'd know, but this isn't exactly my cuppa."

"Send the Dorobo ahead to scout," Joseph advised. "He is the most at home in this kind of bush."

"That's true," Adrian said, looking skeptical, "but he's not terribly brave."

Joseph thought about it a moment, tugging absentmindedly on what was left of his right ear, then said, "He's confident when he is in the forest. He'll be fine. Go on and ask him."

Adrian called Pythias over and asked him. "We can't just walk into someone's house unannounced, now can we?" he added, trying to keep it light. "It simply isn't done, old man."

"What do you want to know?" Pythias asked tentatively.

"I have to know if there are sentries, and where they're posted," Glenton said, serious now. "It would also help if we knew how many men we're up against."

Pythias glanced at Joseph, then back at Glenton. "Okay," he said, "I'll be right back." And with that he was gone.

"Well, you were right," Adrian said to Joseph, sounding surprised. "That was certainly simple enough."

Joseph nodded. "A man is usually more courageous when he is in familiar surroundings."

Pythias was back within fifteen minutes. "There aren't any sentries," he said. "I couldn't see into the cave, but I think it's empty. Do you want me to go back and look inside?"

"I'll do it," Joseph volunteered.

"We'll all do it," Adrian said. "We'll approach from the side so we can't be seen from inside. Joseph, you and Pythias go in from the left. Tembo and I will take the right flank."

It took half an hour to get into position—two men on each side of the entrance—and they burst into the cave on a signal from Adrian, crouched low and ready to shoot, aware that with the light behind them they were in full silhouette. The cave was empty.

The cavern was large for a lava tube—just high enough for Adrian to stand erect, seven or eight feet wide and about forty feet deep. Adrian left Tembo to guard the door, telling him to lie down on the ground just inside the entrance, while he and the others explored the interior. They found the cache at the far rear of the cavern, a pile covered over with brush and leaves and bat guano: four elephant tusks, two rhinoceros horns, and a rolled-up leopard pelt.

Glenton picked up one of the horns, used a fingernail to chip a flake of dried blood from a scrap of flesh attached to its base, and said: "A day old. Two at most." He showed it to Pythias who examined it briefly and handed it back with a nod of agreement.

Joseph, too vain to resist the impulse to flaunt his own expertise, unrolled the leopard pelt and announced: "This one is at least four or five days old." He could tell because the skin had been carefully and professionally prepared, and he'd done up enough trophy hides for Adrian's clients to know what that entailed. The skin had to be removed immediately so that the hairs wouldn't slip. Then every bit of fat and tissue had to be removed and the hide rubbed thoroughly with salt to dry it out. The areas under the lips, and inside the nose and eye sockets, had to be turned out to salt them properly. Then the skin had to be dipped in an arsenic insecticide for a full twenty-four hours before it could be put up to dry. It took time to do it right, and this poor leopard with the beautiful coat had been done right.

They were still at the pile, hefting elephant tusks and trying to guess the weights, when Tembo's call echoed in the cave: "*Bwana*! Someone is coming!"

They rushed to the front of the cave and sprawled in the dirt alongside Tembo, their weapons pointing down the path. A moment later Ekali burst through the bush wall and stopped in the small clearing at the mouth of the cave. He looked about, then put up a hand to shield his eyes, trying to see into the cave. "Psst! *Bwana*! Are you there?"

Glenton stood and stepped out into the light. "I'm here, Ekali. What is it?"

"Someone is coming. Behind me on the trail."

"How far behind you?" Adrian asked.

"Ten minutes, maybe fifteen."

"How many men?" Joseph asked.

"I saw only one man on the trail below, but there may be others," the Turkana said. He wasn't even breathing hard, but his once-proud coiffure had been ruined, finally and utterly, by his mad dash through the bush; the main edifice was canted precariously to one side, like the leaning tower of Pisa, and stray tendrils of dark hair hung down his back and around his face.

"Did he see you?" Adrian asked.

"No."

"Are you certain, Ekali? It's important."

"He did not see me, *bwana*. I'm sure."

Glenton shot Joseph a questioning look and suggested in Masai: "*Entomito ilmoran tooengejek?*" It was the traditional, if rarely used, Masai call for retreat: Save the warriors by their feet.

"Fuck that," Joseph said, in English, disappointed that Adrian would even consider such an idea. "We've been hunting these assholes for too long to run away like women the first time we find them."

"They may outnumber us," Adrian said.

"In battle, one Masai is equal to one hundred non-Masai. Or have you forgotten that?"

"Lovely for you," Glenton said dryly. "But I'm merely an honorary Masai. I'm only the equal of fifty."

"It's not something you joke about," Joseph said, deadly serious.

Adrian sighed. "All right, listen," he said, switching to Swahili, speaking to the group. "We'll take up positions in the forest—two men on this flank, the other three over there. Keep quiet and wait for my orders. Do nothing unless I give the order. Is that absolutely clear?" He waited for each man to acknowledge that he understood. "Good. We need them to go into the cave. It's vital, especially if we are outmanned. Five of us should be able to cover the cave entrance without any trouble, and they'll be boxed. If it's just the one man, the man Ekali saw, let him go into the cave. Then we'll call him out. If he doesn't want to come, I'll go in and get him. Is that agreeable to everyone?" They all nodded.

Glenton spent the next couple of minutes positioning his men where he wanted them. A few minutes after that there was a rustling noise and a man walked out of the forest and into the clearing. He was a Somali, light-skinned and lean, with his long hair done up in braids, Rastafarian style. He wore an open, dirty greatcoat over an old Robert Hall sport jacket, trousers with the knees out, and military boots. He was carrying a pair of elephant tusks over one shoulder, and a Belgian FN rifle was slung over the other. He started for the cave, then suddenly veered off and walked to the edge of the clearing, coming to a stop no more than three feet from where Tembo was crouched in the bushes. He set down the ivory, unslung the rifle and propped it against a tree, then unbuttoned his trousers, dug out his penis and urinated into the bush.

When the Somali finished, he gathered up his things and walked back to the cave, disappearing inside. Glenton waited five minutes to see if anyone else would follow, then gave a hand signal. Joseph, Tembo, and Ekali stepped from the bush. Glenton held up two fingers and pointed to the cave entrance, then held up one finger and pointed to the trail. Ekali went back into the forest and started to work his way back to the track, to watch it. Joseph and Tembo inched their way slowly toward the cave. Adrian and Pythias left their hiding places and approached the cavern's entrance from the opposite side. They could hear the Somali inside, singing softly to himself, "Ooo, ooo, ooo, ooo, stayin' alive, stayin' alive."

Glenton, intent on "stayin' alive" himself, still wasn't quite certain what he was going to do. While it was true that the poacher wouldn't be able to leave the cavern, it was also true that he did not relish the thought of going in after the man. A Belgian FN was no toy. He was mulling his options when he saw Joseph signaling to him from the opposite side of the opening. The Masai pointed to himself, then to the outcrop of rock above the cave's mouth. He used his fingers to pantomime a man climbing up to the ledge and jumping down onto a victim below. Adrian shrugged, then nodded.

Joseph backed away from the doorway and disappeared into the forest, rematerializing a few minutes later on the slope above the cave's entrance. He squatted there motionless for a moment, waiting to see if the man inside had heard him on the roof, then gave Glenton a grin when they heard another chorus of, "Ooo, ooo, ooo, ooo, stayin' alive, stayin' alive."

Joseph held up a rock, made a tossing motion, and pointed into the woods. Adrian shrugged again, then nodded. The Masai flashed him another big grin, stood up, and threw the rock as far as he could down the path. It landed with a loud rattling of leaves.

The singing from inside ended abruptly. There was a long silence and then they could hear the Somali come to the front of the cavern, still just inside the doorway and out of view. He stood there for a few seconds more, obviously scanning the bush, then gave a signal, the monotonous "tink . . . tink . . . tink" of the golden-rumped tinkerbird. When there was no answer, he stepped cautiously from the cave, his rifle raised.

Joseph nearly waited too long. The Somali saw Adrian out of the corner of his eye and reacted with startling speed. He already had his rifle up and around when Joseph landed on him with both feet. There was a burst of gunfire. Adrian took the muzzle blast full in the face. He stumbled backward, clawing at both eyes and screaming: "I'm shot! I'm shot!" Or at least that's what he thought he screamed. Deafened by the blast, he was unable to hear himself.

It was several seconds before his sight returned. When it did, he saw Joseph and Tembo laughing at him. Pythias and Ekali had the poacher by the legs and were dragging him back into the cave. The man was out cold.

Adrian ran his fingers over his face, checking to see if all the parts were there. When he was reasonably certain that they were, he raged at Joseph: "Fucking hell, Joseph! I could have been killed! What were you waiting for?"

Still grinning, Joseph said, "A favorable wind."

"Bloody jokes!" Glenton sputtered. "That bastard almost got me!"

"Well, he did get me," Tembo said, sniffing at his shirt sleeve. "He pissed on me."

"I'm going to send Ekali back down the mountain to stand guard," Joseph said, getting back to business. "If the others are in the area, they'll be coming to investigate." He turned and went into the cavern. Adrian, still muttering to himself, followed him in.

Giving Glenton time to collect himself, Joseph issued a flurry of instructions, sending Ekali back down the mountain to monitor the main track, and ordering Pythias and Tembo to go outside and keep watch. Then he went over to check on the poacher, prodding him with a toe. The man moaned but did not wake up. Joseph then walked to the end of the cave and began rooting about in the trophy pile. He came back with a length of sisal rope and used it to tie the prisoner's hands behind his back. Then he sat down with his back against the wall of the cave, said, "Wake me when the dipshit wakes," and closed his eyes. He was sound asleep in ten seconds.

The Somali tried first what every Somali caught poaching in Kenya tries first: he pretended ignorance of all languages except Somali.

"That's quite all right," Adrian told him pleasantly. "I know Somali." He spoke it passably rather than well, but that was no reflection on the skill of his teacher, Fatima Hassan, the seventeen-year-old Somali girl he'd kept for more than two years after he had left Pembroke.

"Kiss my ass, you white piece of pig's shit," the Somali replied lanquidly, in perfect Swahili. "I don't care how many languages you know. I won't be telling you anything in any of them."

Glenton smiled, impressed by the man's belligerence. He admired the Somalis. He had heard them called many different things—from "The Jews of Africa" to "Africa's mercenaries"—but the one thing he knew for a fact was that the Somalis were just about the toughest people on the continent, if not the planet. Their only competition was the Masai.

Joseph, aware of the Somali reputation for toughness and of their contempt for other Africans, was apparently thinking along the same lines. There was an unholy gleam in his eye as he watched the poacher.

"Where are Fisi and the rest of your companions?" Adrian asked the man.

"Off fucking your mother."

"My mother is deceased," Glenton said in a quiet voice, no longer amused.

"They know that," the Somali said. "They went to Nakuru and dug her up. They're fucking her skeleton. In the mouth."

Adrian slapped him hard in the face. The Somali wiggled his jaw, testing it, then looked up and grinned.

"Let me have him," Joseph said. "A few minutes. That is all I need."

Adrian did not acknowledge him. He was staring oddly at the poacher. "You mentioned Nakuru," he said, calm now. "How do you know about Nakuru?"

The Somali laughed. "We know all there is to know about you," he said smugly. "Fisi knows all there is to know about everyone. He's a spirit."

"He's a murdering bastard," Glenton said, "and I want to know where he is."

The Somali said, "You can't always get what you want."

"Mick Jagger," said Joseph, mumbling to himself.

Adrian asked the same question again and again, but the Somali, as if bored with the exercise, just stared up at the roof of the cave. He did not seem to be very concerned about his predicament.

Finally Joseph could stand no more of it. "Enough," he said in Masai. "Get out of here, Adrian. Go. Wait outside. I will take care of this."

Glenton shook his head slowly. "I don't think that is a good idea."

"What would be a good idea?"

"If he won't talk to us, I'll give him to the police and let them have a go."

The Masai snorted derisively. "Those fools?" He switched into English, or, more accurately, American: "Gimme a fuckin' break."

"Whatever that means," Adrian said.

"It means that he won't talk to the police any more than he'll talk to you. But he will talk to me."

"I would curse Allah first," the Somali said, his first words in several minutes.

"So, you speak English, too," Glenton said. The man just looked away.

Adrian felt a rush of anger surge through him. He turned to Joseph and said, in Masai: "He's all yours. But I want him alive when you're done with him."

"Leave me your knife," Joseph said.

"I mean it, Joseph. You can't kill him."

"I'm not going to kill him. I just want to frighten him a little . . . and that knife of yours is very frightening."

Glenton hesitated, then took the Randall from its sheath and handed it over. As he walked out of the cave he heard the Somali say to Joseph, in English: "What happened to your ear, you black monkey? Did your monkey girlfriend bite it off?"

Pythias was waiting outside. "What's going on in there?" he asked. Adrian started to tell him, but he was interrupted by a high-pitched scream from inside the cave. He winced and muttered, "Goddamn!" There was a minute of total silence, then another shriek. Glenton put his hands over his ears but it didn't seem to help. He heard the next scream as clearly as the others.

"That's quite enough of that!" Adrian said, starting for the entrance.

Pythias reached out and grabbed his arm. "Let Joseph do it his way," he said quietly.

"It's inhuman!" Adrian snapped, shaking off the Dorobo's hand.

"Is it any more inhuman than what they did to the *mzee,* the old man?"

"Joseph might kill him."

"You mean like they killed Chege?"

Adrian hesitated, then shook his head. "No. If we do the same things they do, what's the bloody point? I've got to put a stop to it." He strode purposefully toward the mouth of the cave, then stopped when Joseph emerged.

"Christ, you've killed him!" Adrian said as Joseph held out the Randall, trying to return it. There was blood on the blade.

"No. I . . ."

Glenton didn't let him finish. He brushed by him and ran into the cave. The Somali was lying on his back on the ground with his hands still tied behind him. He was not moving. When Glenton rolled him over and reached for a wrist, intending to check his pulse, he saw with a shock that the thumb and first two fingers of the man's right hand were missing. Two of the severed digits were there in the dirt. One of the fingers had stuck to the back of the Somali's shirt.

"He's fainted, that's all," said Joseph, coming up and standing behind Adrian.

"That's all, is it?" Adrian asked bitterly, glancing up at Joseph with cold eyes. "Christ! Look at this bloody mess."

Joseph looked, and shrugged.

"Was it worth it? Was it, Joseph? Did he tell you where Fisi and the others are?"

"No, he was very strong," Joseph admitted. "But he did have some interesting things to say."

"Christ!" Adrian said again, looking back to the Somali. All the color had drained from the man's face, but he was breathing easily enough. Adrian reached a hand out to Joseph and snapped his fingers, asking for the Randall. When Joseph handed it to him, he cut the poacher's bonds and laid him out straight, trying to make him as comfortable as possible under the circumstances. He pulled out the man's shirttail, cut off a long strip, and used it to bandage the maimed hand. When he had finished, he looked up at Joseph and asked quietly: "What sort of interesting things?"

"This is just a storage cave, not one of their camps."

"Is that it? You crippled him for that?"

"He told us to give up the hunt," Joseph said. "He said that Fisi won't be punished even if we do catch him. He said that Fisi is protected."

"Protected? Protected by whom?"

"Nairobi. Important people in Nairobi."

"Which people?"

Joseph shrugged. "He gave no names. He just said it was rather funny that we were working for the Wildlife Ministry, because so was he."

"He said that?"

Joseph nodded. "And he said not to expect too much help from the police either."

"I'll be buggered," Adrian said. He was silent a moment, then he looked at Joseph and said, "It still does not excuse what you did. It's bloody savagery is what it is."

Joseph shook his head and said, "No, it's only rock and roll. But I like it."

"Aberdare Base, this is Tea Time . . . over."

"Aberdare Base, this is Tea Time . . . come in please."

Hone answered on the fifth try. "Hullo, Tea Time. Sorry. I was in the bath."

"Stephen, how secure is this frequency?"

"Quite secure. The signals *wallah* from Nyeri gave us a special band or frequency or something. He explained it, but that technical jargon is double Dutch to me."

"Super. Listen, I need you to do two things for me."

"Righty-o. What are they?"

"First, get on to the police at Nyeri and tell them they can pick up a prisoner at The Ark. Tell them to bring along a medical officer. He's been damaged."

"One of Fisi's chappies?"

"Yes."

"Hmm, The Ark's staff won't appreciate that," Hone said. "Mustn't upset the tourists, you know."

"Sod the bloody tourists."

"And the second item?"

"Find Inspector Odongo in Nairobi and inform him that the team will be overnighting at the Chania River campsite tomorrow . . . beside the bridge."

"Tomorrow night?"

"That's right."

"I'll do that straight away. Anything else?"

"That does it. Just be certain that when you talk to the police, you don't tell them where we will be camping tomorrow night. Don't tell anyone. Only Odongo."

"Right-o. Oh, by the way, Robbie's back with the things you asked for. She says to tell you Philippa Lindsay-Bellville sends her love."

The camp looked perfectly normal in the weak moonlight; five men wrapped in blankets, sleeping around the remains of a fire, its coals still hot and glowing. The supper pots had been scrubbed out with sand and put into buckets of water so that the odor of grease would not attract the pride of lions which sometimes frequented the site. The Chania, a riffle of white water as it flowed beneath the bridge, sang a burbling lullaby, and the sound of Chania Falls, a hundred yards downstream, was muted by the surrounding foliage. A peaceful, idyllic scene.

"They'll be suspicious when they see that there are no sentries posted," Adrian whispered.

"They'll just think we're careless, or stupid, or both," Joseph whispered back. "They'll be too relieved and grateful to be suspicious."

The two men were in a large, bushy tree on the opposite side of the river, wedged in crutches formed by two adjacent branches coming off the bole, only a few feet from the crown. It was just the opposite of hunting leopard, Glenton thought. With a leopard, an animal virtually unhuntable by fair means, the hunter stayed on the ground and put the bait in the tree. In this case, the bait was on the ground, arranged by the campfire across the river. The sleeping figures were dummies made of rocks and brush. The rest of the team was miles away, in the real night camp.

It was not until two hours later, a little after two A.M., that either man spoke again. "I don't think anyone's coming," Joseph said.

"Then you think wrong," Adrian whispered back. "Because they're here."

Shadows were moving, materializing from the thick brush where the river made an abrupt S-turn on the far side of the road bridge. Then more figures emerged from under the bridge itself, wading in the river's shallow but fast-moving riffle.

The assault was direct, and over almost as quickly as it began. Four of the dozen or so attackers lobbed fragmentation grenades into the camp, sighting on the fire. The instant the grenades exploded, the other men charged the ring and sprayed the sleeping forms with automatic rifle fire. A reverberating silence came next, quickly followed by a string of curses.

"Where are they?" one man shouted in Somali, his voice tinged with panic. "Where the fuck are they?"

"It's a trap!" shouted another. "Let's get out of here!"

They formed a ragged skirmish line and backed away from the blast-scattered campfire, weapons trained on the surrounding trees. When they were free of the clearing, they broke ranks, turned and ran.

Adrian and Joseph waited another half hour before coming down out of the tree. They waded the river and examined their ruined blankets. "These are *kwisha,* finished," the Masai said regretfully, poking a finger through one of the bullet holes.

"It's fair exchange," Adrian said grimly. "We've learned what we needed to know."

24

Peter had just sat down at his desk when Superintendent Jaynes phoned from the Central Police Station. "I've located your chap for you," Jaynes said, sounding obscenely cheerful for seven o'clock in the morning.

"Which, um, chap is that, sir?"

"Gichinga, of course. The chap you were looking for."

"Wonderful!" Peter said. "Do you have him in custody?"

"You didn't say anything about taking him into custody, only that you wanted him found," Jaynes said. "Actually, he *is* in custody after a fashion."

"How do you mean, sir?"

"He's in hospital."

"Is he ill?"

"Mathari Mental Hospital, man. In Thika Road. Just along from the Muthaiga Police Station."

"Oh, yes. Er, how did he come to be there?"

"I'm not sure, actually," Jaynes said. "I wouldn't have known he was there at all if the name hadn't leapt out at me while I was looking over the teletype log. Seems the Mathari Depot had a complaint last week of a Mathare Valley chap who was acting a bit crackers. Mathari dispatched two constables to look into it and they took him to hospital straight away."

"Last week?" Odongo asked incredulously.

"That's right. Tuesday, I think it was. Dreadfully sorry about the delay, but as I said, I didn't learn about it until yesterday evening. I rang your flat but there was no answer."

"Thank you, sir. I didn't mean to sound ungrateful."

"You never did say who this Gichinga chap is," the super said. "Does he have to do with your poaching case?"

"Yessir. I don't mean to be rude, Superintendent, but I must ring off now. I want to interview him as soon as possible."

"Of course. I'll telephone the physician in charge and tell him you're coming. *Kwaheri,* Inspector."

"Goodbye, sir." Peter left Jogoo House as if it were the start of the annual Safari Rally, pulling out of the car park with a squeal of tires just as the Assistant Minister arrived in his big Mercedes, barely avoiding a collision. He used his siren and flasher, and made the hospital in six minutes flat.

There was no one in the administrative offices, not even a clerk, so Odongo wandered the corridors, peeking into rooms until he found someone who could tell him where they kept the patients. Following directions, he went through two more dilapidated, one-story buildings and came at last to the ward he wanted. He was about to push through the door when a voice behind him said: "Where do you think you are going? You can't go in there."

He turned and saw a woman in a nurse's uniform standing with her hands on her hips. She was quite pretty and she was a Luo.

"Police business," Peter said in his best official tone, the bored voice of authority. He fished out his identity card and flashed it at her. He was putting it back into his pocket when she said, "Let me see that."

He sighed and handed it to her. She took an inordinately long time to look it over, then handed it back and said, "You are better looking in your photograph than in person."

"Hasn't anyone ever told you that it is usually wiser to flatter a policeman?"

"Only if you've broken the law, or are trying to avoid a beating," she said.

"This must be your lucky day then, because I've decided not to beat you," Odongo said, smiling. "Now that you know I am a policeman, may I go inside?"

"I already knew that you were a policeman. I didn't have to see your papers for that."

"Oh, really? And how did you know?" Peter asked warily, anticipating some derogatory remark, something to the effect that he had the look of a bully.

Instead she said, "Because I know exactly who you are. I was a guest in your family's *pacho* only last week, at a feast in your honor. My mother is a friend of your mother."

"Oh," Odongo said lamely, thrown off balance. "I, um, I didn't see you there. I would have remembered."

"We weren't introduced," the nurse said.

"Then you must be married," Peter said with a smile. "My mother made sure I met all the unmarried women."

"Well, you didn't meet me," she said matter-of-factly. She put out a hand and said, "I'm Millicent Ogara. Everyone calls me Millie."

Caught by surprise, Odongo shook her hand. He could not recall the last time he'd shaken hands with an African woman.

Seeing the look on his face, Millicent Ogara laughed and said, "I'm a modern girl." She had a wonderful laugh, full of perfect white teeth and lively brown eyes, and it transformed her from a merely pretty woman into a truly beautiful one.

Dazzled, Peter smiled back at her and said, "Yes, I can see that."

"What is this police business you mentioned?" she asked.

"I'm looking for a man. Gichinga. James Gichinga."

The nursed frowned. "You can't go worrying my patients."

"I just want to talk to him," Peter said.

She shrugged. "It doesn't matter anyway. There is no one here by that name."

"I was told that he was here."

"Well, he's not."

"Could you check, please?"

"I don't have to check. I run these wards."

"Perhaps he was admitted under another name. May I go in and look?"

"What would you do if I said no?"

"I'd go in anyway," Peter said.

The nurse hesitated, then said, "Okay. But I'll have to go in with you."

Peter started to push open the door, then stopped when Millicent Ogara said, "That is a women's ward." She pointed across the corridor. "The men are over here."

The ward was equipped with forty beds, but there looked to be one hundred fifty or more patients in the room. Many of the beds had two, and in some cases three men in them. More patients were stretched out on blankets on the floor. The majority of them displayed no interest in Odongo. Others, their faces stunned and blank, approached him timidly, reaching out to touch him, ready to jump back at the first sign of hostility.

The ward was surprisingly quiet. Peter was about to mention it when Millicent Ogara, as if she had read his mind, said, "We keep them sedated."

Peter walked up one side of the ward and down the other without finding Gichinga, then made a second circuit just to be certain. "He's not here," he said at last.

"I told you he wasn't," the nurse said.

"He must be somewhere. Are there more wards?"

"Quite a few more, but there's no James Gichinga in any of them," Millicent Ogara said. "When was he supposed to have been admitted?"

"Last week."

"Last week!" she exclaimed. "Well, why didn't you say so in the first place? He'd still be in the cage."

"The cage? What is that?"

"A receiving area of sorts," she said. "It's where they put new people until the doctors can look at them and decide what to do with them. It is also where the untreatable cases are kept . . . the criminally insane."

"So Gichinga's in this, um, cage?"

"It's possible. I certainly wouldn't have him on my list of patients if he's only been here a week."

"Let's go see," Peter said, making for the ward door, so anxious that he grabbed the nurse's hand and pulled her after him. When they were out in the corridor, she slipped her hand free and said, "It's outside the building. Through that door at the end of the hallway."

"Aren't you coming?" Peter asked.

She shook her head. "Only doctors and orderlies can go out there. They say it's too dangerous for the nurses."

Peter just stood there. As much as he anticipated coming face to face with the slippery James Gichinga at last, he was strangely reluctant to leave this young woman. In the end, it was she who left him. "You wait here," she said. "I'll go get a doctor to escort you." Peter watched her go, his eyes fixed on her pistonlike buttocks under the starched white uniform.

He waited until she turned the corner, then made for the door at the end of the hallway. He threw it open, stepped out into a large outdoor courtyard and was instantly struck dumb, paralyzed, his senses overwhelmed by the noise and by a stink worse than anything he had ever experienced. "Mother of God," he blurted.

The cage literally was a cage, like a pen at a zoo, only larger, the size of a basketball court. It was fully enclosed by an eight-foot-high fence, and there was additional fencing across the top so that none of the inmates could get out that way. The pen was open to the elements except for a small area protected by a narrow overhang. The cement floor was littered with banana peels, milk cartons, and piles of human excrement.

The pen was big enough to hold a thousand patients, but there looked to be twice that many inside. Another five hundred or so people, visiting relatives most likely, were pressed against the fence, talking with those inside and passing cigarettes through the links. Together, they made enough noise to raise the dead, an indescribable cacophony of shouting and wailing, of uncontrolled laughter and hysterical weeping.

Unlike the indoor wards, male and female had been mixed together in the cage, all of them naked. Odongo saw a number of rapes in progress, and several of the men were openly and joyfully masturbating.

He saw one man who had beaten himself raw; blood oozed from between his frantically flying fingers. Another was shooting his semen
into the matted hair of a man lying unconscious on the cement floor. It
was, Peter decided when his mind was functioning again, the last circle
of Hell.

No white-coated hospital staff were in evidence. Odongo, despairing
of finding his man in the chaos, began walking the fence's perimeter,
pushing through the visiting relatives and shouting in an effort to make
himself heard above the tumult: "Gichinga! James Gichinga!"

He was about halfway round the enclosure when he became aware
that someone inside the cage was following him. He spun about suddenly and found himself looking into a sad face with a long, puckered
scar running from the corner of the left eye to the curve of the jawbone.

"Hello, James."

"Get me out of here," James Gichinga said. He was naked and Peter
could see why he was so popular with the ladies of the Mathare Valley;
his flaccid penis reached halfway to his kneecaps.

"I'm Inspector Odongo of the Kenya Police," Peter said.

"The one who's been looking for me," Gichinga said with a nod.

"How do you know that?" Odongo asked.

"The boy told me about you," James Gichinga said. "Well, here I
am. Arrest me. I'll confess to anything you want. Just get me out of
here."

"I want to ask you about the poaching operation."

"Fine. Get me out of here and I'll tell you anything you want to
know."

"Why are you in here?" Peter asked.

"They said I was crazy."

"Who said?"

"The policemen who took me away."

"*Are* you crazy?"

"Not yet. But I will be if I have to stay another day in this place."

"What did the constables say when they took you?"

"Nothing. They just grabbed me. When they got me outside there
was another man waiting. He was Police too, an officer. One of the
policemen asked, 'Is this him?' and the officer said, 'Yeah, that's him,'
and then they brought me here."

"Had you ever seen the officer before?"

"No."

"How did they know where to find you?" Peter asked. "It was more
than I was able to manage."

"I don't know," Gichinga said. "Hey, we can talk about all this later,
okay? After you get me out of here."

"Tell me about the poaching operation."

"Not until you get me out. I tell you now, you'll leave me here."

"I'll leave you here if you don't," Peter said.

"*Bwana,* please! You can't do that! They keep you in the cage until a doctor comes and examines you. There are people in here who have been waiting eight years!"

Peter was horrified, but he tried not to show it. "Then talk to me," he said quietly.

"No way," Gichinga insisted, adamant. "Not until you get me the fuck out of here."

"Have it your way," Odongo said with a shrug. "*Kwaheri,* James." He turned and walked away.

"*Wait!*" Odongo paused and turned. Gichinga was motioning frantically for him to come back. "All right, I'll tell you," Gichinga yelled, looking as if he were about to cry, his face sadder and more forlorn than ever.

It was the oddest interview Odongo had ever conducted in his nearly twelve years with the Kenya Police: talking with a petty criminal through chicken wire while a madman was having a bowel movement on the floor a few yards away, and all under the watchful gaze of another madman who was dangling from the side of the cage like a monkey, holding on for dear life with one hand while he masturbated with the other.

James Gichinga didn't know as much as Peter had hoped he would. He didn't know much about The Hyena, for example. He'd never laid eyes on the man. All he knew was that Fisi was said to be a brilliant leader, and that he'd been hand-picked for the task by the top person in the operation, whoever that might be. Fisi was Kikuyu, but he mostly used Somalis because they were less merciful than his own tribesmen.

Gichinga's own role in the operation was a fairly minor one. Twice a week he was given an attaché case full of money to pay off a *matatu* driver who moved the goods from Aberdare Park to Nairobi. He then arranged for the goods to be crated and delivered to the person who had given him the cash, a Customs official at Embakasi International Airport.

Gichinga's personal involvement ended there, but he knew what happened to the goods. The rhinoceros horn, destined for markets in the Near and Far East, was loaded on board a Kenya Airways flight to Mombasa and smuggled out of the country by sea, on everything from freighters to dhows. Crates of ivory were labeled as innocuous cargo—farm machinery was always a favorite, in spite of the fact that Kenya usually imported farm machinery rather than exported it—then given a false export permit and bill of lading, and shipped on a major air carrier to Antwerp, for transshipment to Dubai in the Persian Gulf. From there the crates were shuttled from country to country, picking up documents along the route so that the ivory's origins were obscured even as the consignment became legitimatized. Even if the goods were seized somewhere along the way, there was always a chance they would simply be returned to sender.

Whoever had devised the game had wisely limited contact among the players. Gichinga, for instance, knew only two men by name and sight: the *matatu* operator from whom he received the goods, and the Customs officer to whom he gave them. The *matatu* driver had failed to show up for his last appointment, and Gichinga had heard that he'd died in an ambush. The name of the Customs official was Ambrose Nyeusi.

Odongo, his little black notebook almost full, asked a few more questions, but Gichinga had been squeezed dry.

"So, are you going to get me out?" James Gichinga asked quietly as Peter put away the notebook. His tone was filled with doubt.

"I said I would, and I will."

"What will the police do to me?"

"Nothing, because I'm going to release you," Peter said. "You're going back to work for your friends . . . only this time you'll be working for me as well."

"Whatever you say," Gichinga said, nodding quickly.

Odongo gave him a quizzical look. "I know you've been a petty criminal all your life, James, but do you ever stop to think about the consequences of your actions?"

"Hey, I just do what I have to do to survive," Gichinga said. "I'm not a Wabenzi like you."

Odongo almost laughed to hear himself called a Wabenzi. "I don't suppose you gave a moment's thought to your country, to how killing animals hurts the tourist trade, and how much tourism means to us?"

Gichinga made a snorting sound. "What does tourism mean to the *wananchi*, to folks like me? Tourists might make money for the government, but they don't put a damn thing in my pocket unless I decide to rob one."

Odongo was trying to think of a rebuttal when he felt a tap on his shoulder. When he turned, he saw a man in a white smock. "Inspector Odongo? I am Dr. Gituru."

"Good! Just the fellow I wanted to see," Odongo said. "I want you to release this man into my custody at once."

"I thought Nurse Ogara asked you to wait for an escort," the doctor said petulantly.

"Shut up and do what I tell you. Let this man out. Now."

"Who do you think you are, talking to me like that?" the doctor said, bristling. "I'm a doctor."

"You're no doctor," Odongo said disdainfully. "You're a fucking zoo keeper." He looked around him and shook his head in sorrow. "What kind of nation is it that treats its people this way? Shame, Doctor. Shame on you. Shame on *us*."

At Embakasi, Odongo learned that Ambrose Nyeusi was the second ranking Customs official assigned to the airport, and that he was away on business. He had taken the morning Kenya Airways flight to Mombasa.

Odongo returned to Jogoo House, took the lift to the top floor, and asked if he could see the Assistant Minister for a minute.

"What is it about?" the Kikuyu girl in the outer office asked in a bored tone. She was applying purple polish to her nails and scarcely looked up.

"A private matter," Odongo said.

"He will just make me come back and ask you," she said. "I'd like to save myself the trouble."

Odongo sighed. "I have to go to Mombasa for my inquiry," he said. "I need his authorization for my air ticket."

The girl blew on her fingernails, rose and went into the minister's office. She was back in less than fifteen seconds. "He says to take the overnight train. Third class. He says if you decide to go any other way, it comes out of your pocket."

There was no time to argue. He had to rush to get to his flat in Jamhuri, toss some things into an overnight case, and make it to the railway station in time.

The coast train left from the Nairobi Railway Station at the end of Government Road at six-thirty in the evening and arrived at Mombasa at eight the following morning. It was the slowest way to get to the Kenya coast, but it was also the most pleasant, and the discerning traveler who had the time preferred it to going by air or by road. The sleeping compartments were small but cozy, and the dining car food was surprisingly tasty. The evening meal was served in two sittings, with wine, and linen tablecloths, and fine silver which still bore the logo of the old East African Railways.

But that was first class. In the third-class cars, there were only hard benches to sit on, and the only food to be had was what you brought on board yourself, or a stale mystery-meat sandwich purchased from the vendors who sold their wares through open windows. Odongo, shoehorned between a stout Digo woman and a Bajun girl with a squalling baby, was up half the night. Several times during the long night, the train stopped without apparent reason, dead on the tracks out in the middle of nowhere, probably so that it wouldn't arrive in Mombasa at an inconveniently early hour.

The track ran through Tsavo National Park and Peter saw giraffes silhouetted against a platinum moon. Once, during a long stop, he heard a lion's coughing roar. When the railway engineers were laying this stretch of track in 1898–99, they lost close to thirty men—Asians and Africans mostly—to the notorious man-eating lions of Tsavo. The first six people to be buried in Nairobi cemetery were laborers killed by lions.

Odongo stepped off the train stiff-limbed and tired. He was hungry, his clothes were rumpled and he smelled bad. The railway station was roughly in the center of Mombasa Island, at the head of Haile Selassie Road and only a short distance from Mombasa police headquarters, but Peter did not check in with his coastal colleagues. He ate a breakfast of bread and fruit at an Arab coffee shop in Old Town, then went directly to the Customs and Excise office in Old Port.

He had to ask four different Customs officials before finding one who knew Ambrose Nyeusi, only to be told that the man he was looking for was on the shipping docks at Kilindini Harbor, on the other side of the island. Odongo took a *matatu* to the docks and found a Customs man on duty at the baggage shed. Fortunately, the man was a Luo, from Kadimu Bay, and he was more than happy to talk to a fellow tribesman from Nyanza Province.

"Sure, I know Ambrose," said the Customs man, whose name was Ayodo. "He comes to Mombasa maybe twice a month. He stays from one to three days, then goes back to Nairobi. He is here now, in fact."

"Where?" Peter asked. He looked about but could not see anyone wearing a Customs uniform. They were just outside the baggage shed, next to a storage area stacked high with boxes. Nearby, a giant crane was loading Sea-Land containers onto a rusting ship of Liberian registry.

"Not right here, right now," Ayodo said. "I only meant that he is in Mombasa now. But he's not on the docks today."

"Why not?" Peter asked, hopping up to sit on one of the wooden crates.

Ayodo shrugged. "All I know is that when I spoke to him yesterday afternoon he said he wouldn't be in today."

"Do you know where he is spending the day?" Peter asked. "Or where he stays when he's here?"

The man shook his head. "I think he stays with a friend in Nyali Beach, but I don't know who it is." He paused, then added, "But I think I know where he will be tonight."

"Where?"

"He usually goes to the clubs. Wherever the whores are is where you will find Ambrose."

Odongo shrugged, a gesture of helplessness. "I'm afraid I don't know Mombasa very well, and I don't know what Nyeusi looks like," he said. Then, hesitantly, he asked: "Could you take me to these clubs and point him out to me?"

Ayodo gave the policeman a long look. "He doesn't look like a bad man," he said finally. "What has he done?"

"I just want to ask him a few questions relating to an inquiry I'm working on," Peter said offhandedly, trying to make it sound as if it weren't all that important. From the skeptical look on the Customs man's face, it wasn't selling.

"What I really want to know is whether he's dangerous."

"Oh no, I shouldn't think so," Odongo said reassuringly.

Ayodo let a few more seconds pass, then asked: "Will you be buying the drinks?"

Peter nodded quickly and tried to smile, saying goodbye to the money he'd saved by buying a third-class train ticket.

"Okay," Ayodo said. "We should plan to start about nine o'clock."

"Excellent! Shall we meet here?"

"No. The Castle Hotel bar, at the end of Kilindini Road. He sometimes goes there, and it's near most of the others."

"There is one thing that puzzles me," Peter said. "What brings a Customs man posted to Nairobi airport to Mombasa?"

"Money, of course," Ayodo said. "The salaries in Customs aren't so high that a little extra isn't always welcome."

"Don't tell me about civil service pay," Peter said with a rueful laugh, playing the fellow sufferer, which in fact he was. "But how does Nyeusi earn this extra money?"

"He provides special cargo handling for Nairobi bigshots who are willing to pay extra to have somebody in Customs keep an eye on their important shipments for them. That is what he told me, anyway. It makes sense. Things have a way of getting lost on these docks."

"I see," Odongo said. "Are any of these special cargoes here now?"

Ayodo grinned. "You're sitting on one."

Odongo hopped off the box as if it were a hot stove. He circled the crate slowly, looking for a clue to its contents, but all he could find was a destination address stenciled on the side. The crate was going to an import-export company in Kuala Lumpur.

"Where is the paperwork for this box?" Peter asked.

"Ambrose has it," Ayodo said.

"Have you looked inside?" Peter asked.

"No, of course not," Ayodo said. "The shipment is being handled by a fellow Customs officer."

"Let's have a look," Odongo said. "Do you have a pry bar I can use?"

Ayodo looked uncomfortable. "I know you're a brother Luo and everything," he said hesitantly, "but this is really most irregular."

"I am not asking you as a brother Luo, I am telling you as an officer of the law," Peter said coldly. "Now go get me a fucking pry bar."

"Yessir. Right away, sir." Ayodo ducked into the baggage shed and was back with the tool a minute later. Peter had the top off the box in less time than that.

They hadn't even bothered to hide the contraband beneath something legitimate. The crate was packed top to bottom with whole rhinoceros horns.

"How many more containers in the shipment?" Peter asked.

"Those there," Ayodo said, pointing to four more wooden crates, stacked in twos.

"Let's get them open," Peter said. The Customs man went back to the shed for another tool and, working together, the two of them soon had the boxes open and unpacked.

Odongo estimated that each of the five crates contained about two hundred pounds of horn, for a total of one thousand pounds. Market value would be close to half a million dollars, which was nearly four million Kenya shillings, which was more than twice what Peter could expect to earn over the course of his career with the Kenya Police—assuming, of course, that he lasted long enough to collect his pension.

He was just laying the last of the horns back in its box when he glanced up to see a handful of dock workers strolling over to see what the activity was about. "Keep those men away from here," he told Ayodo. "Then ring police headquarters and have them send someone to collect this stuff."

"Yes, sir," Ayodo said submissively. Embarrassed that a fellow Customs officer was involved in a criminal enterprise, he hadn't said a word during the unpacking of the crates. He trotted off to intercept the dockers, even more anxious than Odongo that they not learn what was going on.

When Ayodo returned from making his phone call, Peter asked him: "Does your friend Nyeusi have any more of these so-called special cargoes here?"

"Not that I know of."

Odongo gave him a baleful look, then sat on one of the boxes and chain-smoked Rooster cigarettes while he waited for the police to come.

The Castle Hotel was in the center of town, not far from one of Mombasa's landmarks, the four hollow, sheet-metal tusks which arched over Kilindini Road. The hotel bar was a popular meeting place and was so crowded that it took Peter and Ayodo a while to find each other. To make things worse, an aircraft carrier from the United States' Seventh Fleet had docked that morning and the place was full of sailors. They had one drink while Ayodo scanned the room for Ambrose Nyeusi, then left to begin their rounds of the city's night spots.

They tried the Star Bar, and the Cave, and the Sunshine Day and Night Club, and the Casablanca. All four places, and the entire town it seemed, were filled to the bursting point with American sailors. And where there were American sailors there was the inevitable school of pilot fish feeding on the leavings, the whores and pimps and *bhang* dealers. The whores came from all over East Africa to greet the Fleet, some from as far off as Rwanda and Burundi and Zaire in Central Africa.

It was the same at the New Florida—did every city in Kenya have a New Florida Club? Odongo wondered—where they found Ambrose Nyeusi.

The New Florida Club was at the southern end of Mombasa Island, on an esplanade lined with baobob trees, overlooking the Likoni Channel. Except for its spectacular setting and a lack of foil on the walls, it wasn't much different from its Nairobi namesake. The clientele was the same mix of tourists and locals. On this particular evening, most of the tourists were crewmen off the American carrier and most of the locals were prostitutes.

Ayodo spotted Nyeusi as soon as they walked through the club's door. "There he is," Ayodo said. "See. Over there. At the corner table. Sitting with three girls."

"Yes, I see him," Peter said. "Introduce me. But only as Peter Odongo."

Ambrose Nyeusi was a slight, middle-aged man with a neat beard and horn-rimmed spectacles. "Ah, Ayodo . . . just in time!" he cried when he saw the two men approach his table. "You and your friend must join us," he said with a grin, coming to his feet. "What luck, eh? I was just sitting here thinking that I was going to have to disappoint two of these beautiful ladies and it was breaking my heart. But now you're here, and with a friend no less. You have saved my life!"

"*Jambo,* Ambrose," Ayodo said. "I would like you to meet Insp . . . Peter Odongo."

When Nyeusi offered his hand, Odongo took his own hands out from behind his back and slapped on the cuffs. There was a gasp from one of the whores. It was a second or two before Nyeusi reacted. He glanced down at his right hand, which was now manacled to Peter's left hand, then up at his friend and fellow Customs officer, Ayodo. "A joke, yes?" he said, still smiling uncertainly.

"A joke, no," Odongo said, producing his police card and thrusting it in the man's face. "Ambrose Nyeusi. You are under arrest."

"Arrest! On what charge?"

"You mean charges, don't you?" Peter asked, emphasizing the plural. "Let's see now. Smuggling. Conspiracy. Violation of the animal conservation laws. Who knows, we might even be able to stick you with accessory to murder. Not to worry. We can sort it all out at headquarters."

Nyeusi looked as if he were going to be sick. "But there must be some m-mistake. I don't know what . . ."

Peter didn't give him a chance to finish. He had already turned and was pulling his prisoner toward the door.

25

Odongo returned to Nairobi the same way he had left, on the overnight train—but in a first-class compartment this time. The Mombasa police made the arrangements and it didn't cost Peter, or the Wildlife ministry, a thing. It would have been a delightful safari if he had not been traveling alone, without Ambrose Nyeusi.

When the train pulled into Nairobi that morning, he was still upset about losing his suspect, but he was really more confused than angry. The whole episode stank like a net full of dead fish.

Considering how shaken he had been when Peter slipped on the handcuffs, Nyeusi had been remarkably composed during his questioning at Mombasa headquarters. As a government official he was shown every courtesy, of course. He was allowed to use the station telephone—to summon a solicitor, presumably—and when he rang off, he seemed to have been infused with new courage. He turned as immutable as Mount Kenya. His statement consisted of nothing more than a flat profession of innocence and a declaration of ignorance regarding the contraband found on the Kilindini dock.

His story was a simple one. He had been privately hired in Nairobi by a *mzungu* named Smith to usher a consignment of goods through the Customs process. When he had looked inside the crates in Nairobi, as per standard Customs procedure, he had found them to contain nothing more than an assortment of handwoven baskets and some small wooden animals carved into napkin holders—simple, innocuous, Kenya crafts. He had no idea where the rhino horn had come from. The boxes must have been switched somewhere along the line.

Who was Mr. Smith? Nyeusi did not know. The man had come to Embakasi Airport looking for someone who could do a two- or three-day job for him. Nyeusi, who had holiday time coming to him, had been available.

Where were the consignment's papers, the export license, and the like? At the house where Nyeusi was staying.

Where was the house? In Nyali Beach.

Whose house was it? Nyeusi didn't know. It was a vacant house. Mr. Smith had arranged for him to stay there.

Had Nyeusi ever done special jobs for Mr. Smith before? No. Had he ever met Mr. Smith before? No. Had he ever done a special job for anyone before? Yes. It was a common practice in the Customs service. Who? Big companies, highly respected companies. Which companies, exactly? Nyeusi couldn't seem to recall offhand.

Odongo had known that Nyeusi was lying of course, and he briefly considered having the man beaten until he changed his story—every police station in Kenya had men who were quite expert at that sort of thing, men who loved their work—but he had the feeling it wouldn't have done any good. Nyeusi was relaxed and confident, cloaked in an aura of invulnerability.

No solicitor turned up, which made Peter wonder just who it was that Nyeusi had telephoned, and the prisoner had spent the night in one of the police station's holding cells. Peter spent the night, what was left of it, at the nearby Excellent Hotel. He was up and out early, enroute for Nyali Bridge in a taxi, wanting to go through the beach house before collecting Nyeusi in time to catch the Nairobi train.

The house was a large private residence overlooking the beach and surrounded by palm trees. Odongo had the taxi wait and went through a trellis covered with bougainvillea to get to the house. He knocked on an ornately carved door imported from Lamu. When no one came, he used the key he'd taken from Nyeusi, and discovered that the door was already unlocked.

Like most beach villas, the house had been only sparsely furnished, but the few pieces had been accumulated by someone with a keen eye; antiques mostly, culled from up and down the Swahili Coast: finely worked wood-and-brass chests from Lamu, chairs from Madagascar, tables from Zanzibar. Odongo had gone directly to the desk by the window and rifled through the top drawer. The shipping papers weren't there. Ambrose Nyeusi had lied yet again, or else someone had been there before him and had removed them. Could that explain the unlocked door? Peter would have given a month's wages to know just who it was that Nyeusi had telephoned from police headquarters.

After a cursory search of the rest of the house, Odongo had returned to the desk and gone through it more thoroughly. All he could find of potential interest was a blank sheet of letterhead with *The Old Delhi Trading Company (Ltd.)* printed across the top, and a desk-top appointment calendar with that day's page torn out of it. When he held the datebook up to the light he saw the merest suggestion of script writing, an indentation left by an entry on the missing page. He took his stub of pencil from his pocket, shaded in the impression, and was able to make out part of the entry: "Telephone Mr. P at noon. NBO 763–2 . . ." The rest of the number was illegible.

But if there were no shocking discoveries to be made at the house, the one waiting for Odongo at police headquarters that afternoon more than made up for it. When he went to get Nyeusi to take him to the train, he was told by the sergeant on seat that the Customs officer had been released.

"The superintendent rang and told me to turn him loose," the sergeant explained to the flabbergasted Odongo. "He said he'd spoken to Nairobi and that Nairobi did not think we had enough on him to prosecute successfully. They said unless we had evidence directly linking the accused to the contents of the boxes, there is no case."

"*They*? Who is *they*?" Odongo had screamed. "Who did your superintendent talk to in Nairobi?"

"I don't know, sir," the duty sergeant said. "It is not my place to ask such questions of a superintendent."

"When did all this happen?"

"About four o'clock this morning, sir."

"In the middle of the night? What is going on here?"

"I don't know, sir," the sergeant said.

"Did your superintendent say anything else?"

"No, sir. Only that the criminal in this instance is the shipper Mr. Smith, not Mr. Nyeusi."

"There is no fucking Mr. Smith!" Odongo yelled.

"Yes, sir. I mean no, sir. I mean I don't know, sir."

"Where is your super?"

"He hasn't come in yet, sir. I suppose he's at home."

"Get him on the telephone for me."

"But sir—"

"*Now, goddamn you!*"

But the superintendent merely repeated what the sergeant said, and when Peter asked him who he'd talked to in Nairobi, he wouldn't say. "I was specifically told not to divulge that information," the superintendent said. "All I can tell you is that the person who telephoned ranks a police superintendent, the same way a superintendent ranks an inspector."

Back in Nairobi empty-handed, Odongo went directly from the railway station to Jogoo House. It was only a little past seven and the Assistant Minister's Kikuyu guard dog wasn't at her desk yet, but the minister's door was closed, a sign that he was in. Peter knocked, then went in when he heard, "Come!"

The Assistant Minister was behind his desk, going over a thick sheaf of reports. "Ah, you're back," he said. "Just the fellow I wanted to see." Peter, listening for sarcasm, didn't hear any.

"Good morning, Minister. May I smoke, sir?"

"Please, have one of mine," the Assistant Minister said hurriedly, offering Peter one of his Benson and Hedges. "You look tired, and rather discouraged. Didn't things go well on the coast?"

Odongo told him about finding the rhino horn, and about Nyeusi's arrest and release. When he finished, the Assistant Minister said, "I'm no barrister, of course, and they may be right about the case against this Nyeusi not holding up in a court of law, but I see your point too. The police certainly could have held onto him a bit longer. The longer we had our hands on him the more likely we'd be to get some information out of him, eh?"

"Yes, sir. That is what I thought too."

"Well then, let's just pick him up again," the Assistant Minister said.

Odongo's face brightened. "Are you authorizing me to do that, sir?"

"Sure, why not?" the Assistant Minister said breezily. "Go ahead and arrest him again. And if anyone gives you any trouble about it, have them talk to me."

"Thank you, sir," Peter said. Then he frowned and added, "If I can find him. I have a feeling he'll be going to ground for a while."

"Don't be so bloody pessimistic, Odongo," the Assistant Minister said with a laugh. "You Luo are such a sour lot."

"I would still like to know who from Nairobi authorized his release," Odongo said, ignoring the tribal slur.

"Why don't you let me try to find out for you," said the minister. "I'm not entirely without influence, you know."

"That would be wonderful, sir. I appreciate it."

The minister gave him a benign smile. "It is the least I can do after all of your fine detective work in tracking down this fellow."

The two men smiled at each other, aware that the meeting was the most cordial of their brief, but bumpy, acquaintance. Then Peter said, "When I came in you said that I was just the one you wanted to see. Why is that, sir?"

The Assistant Minister put on a sour face of his own and said, "You aren't going to like what I have to say."

"What is it, sir?"

Instead of answering directly, the minister pointed to the pile of papers on his desk and asked, "Do you know what those are?"

"No, sir."

"Complaints. Complaints from citizens of Nyeri District, Central Province, about being harrassed in their homes by Mr. Glenton and his men."

"Um, yes, sir. I've seen them."

"Not these you haven't," said the minister. "These are new complaints, all filed in the last three days. *Mbwa Kali* is at it again."

"Oh, no," Peter moaned.

"Oh, yes."

"How serious are they?" Peter asked.

The Assistant Minister pulled a sheet of paper from the stack on his desk and began to read: "We feel like blades of grass beneath the feet of two fighting elephants." He picked up another one. "You must help us. We are caught between two devils, a Hyena and a Mad Dog. They are pulling us apart. The people are suffering. The people are afraid. Help us."

"Sometimes you must fight fire with fire," Odongo said. The argument was thin and unconvincing even to his own ears.

"Your *mzungu* is out of control," the Assistant Minister declared flatly. "He hasn't stopped the poachers. All he has done is alienate the *wananchi*. Do I have to remind you that Central Province is the party's power base? If the situation is allowed to get any worse it could mean political troubles for the government. That mustn't happen. Call him in, Odongo. Your mission is *kwisha*. Finished."

"But Minister! We're getting so close. Another week or two—"

"Not another week . . . not another day. You are going back to the Central Police Station. And your Mr. Glenton is going back to wherever he came from. Call him in."

"And give the park to The Hyena?" Peter said hotly.

"I will put my Field Force rangers into the park," the minister said. "It is what I should have done to begin with."

"But, sir—"

"This discussion is also *kwisha*, Inspector. Call him in. Today."

"Yes, sir." Peter got up to leave.

"You tried, Odongo, and I appreciate your effort," the minister said, his tone softening. "It just didn't work out."

"No, sir."

"I'll make a good report for your superintendent. There will be no damage done to your career."

"Yes, sir."

"I would like one final report from you before you leave the ministry; a complete summation of everything your inquiry has uncovered to date. I'm certain it will be a great help to the rangers."

"I'll have it for you by the end of the week."

For once, the trek from the Assistant Minister's office back to his own tiny bolt-hole went faster than Odongo would have liked. The lift was like a rocket ship falling to earth. He was dreading what he had to do.

The Jogoo House operator put the call through to Mweiga for him, and Stephen Hone picked up on the second ring.

"*Jambo*, Mr. Hone. Odongo here. *Habari*?"

"*Mzuri*, Inspector. What can I do for you?"

"Will you be speaking with Mr. Glenton today?"

"I expect so. Why? Have you a message for him?"

"Yes. Tell him that his mission is over. He and his team are to leave the park immediately. I'll be up tomorrow to pay them what they are owed."

"Hullo? What the devil's going on, Inspector?"

"We have been relieved."

"Relieved? Relieved by whom?"

"The Assistant Minister for Wildlife."

"I see. Adrian won't like it. He won't like it at all."

"I don't like it either, Mr. Hone, but I don't have a say in the matter, and neither does Glenton."

"Where are you?" Hone asked. "In your office?"

"Yes."

"Stay there. I'll get on to Adrian." Hone rang off without waiting for a reply and was back on the line in less than five minutes. "Peter," he said, using the African's given name for the first time. "Bad news, I'm afraid. He won't come out."

"What do you mean he won't come out?"

"He says he's not leaving the park without Fisi."

"He can't do this to me!" Peter wailed.

"It seems he just did. Does it really surprise you?"

After a short pause, Peter said, "No. I don't suppose it does." Then, after another short pause, Peter asked, "Can you talk some sense into him?"

"I doubt it," Hone said. "Besides, are you sure you want me to?"

"Yes," Peter said emphatically. Then, in a weaker voice, "No." And finally, "I don't know."

"Look, I don't want to see the lad get himself into any trouble," Hone said. "I'll have another go at him. If he has a change of heart, I'll let you know straight away."

Peter sat perfectly still for several minutes after Hone rang off, trying to summon up the courage to go back upstairs and face the Assistant Minister. When he finally did move, it was to pick up the telephone again and dial Mathari Hospital.

He asked for Millicent Ogara and was told by the girl on the administration desk that it was Nurse Ogara's day off. He asked if Miss Ogara had a telephone in her home, and was told that she had, but that it was against hospital policy to give out home phone numbers. Odongo identified himself as a police inspector, demanded the number and got it. He could have been anyone, of course, but he used his policeman's voice, and the cowed receptionist had heard in it an authority that couldn't be faked.

He waited another minute before dialing the number with a trembling finger. It was ringing when it suddenly occurred to him that for all he knew, Millicent Ogara was married and had ten children. Perhaps that was the reason his mother had not bothered to introduce them. He was still trying to think of something to say if a man should answer, when he heard her voice on the line. "Hello?"

"Um, Miss Ogara?"

"Yes, this is Millie. Who is this, please?"

"Um, Miss Ogara . . ."

"Yes, I just told you it was. Who is this?" She sounded impatient.

"Inspector Odongo. Um, Peter Odongo. I don't know if you remember me, but . . ."

"How could I possibly forget you," she said with a soft laugh. "I'm still in trouble with Dr. Gituru because of you."

"I'm sorry about that," Peter said.

There was a long silence, until she prodded: "Was there something you wanted to speak to me about?"

He was embarrassed and he might have stopped there under normal circumstances, but he knew that he was going to need a friend tonight, and while he barely knew her, Millicent Ogara was from home. He took a deep breath and plunged ahead, "It's forward of me, I know, but would you have dinner with me this evening?"

"You want to take me to a restaurant?"

"Yes."

"No," she said, and Peter's heart sank.

"Come to my house and I'll cook for you," she said, and Peter's heart soared.

"That isn't necessary," Peter said. "I wouldn't want to make work for you."

"Cooking for a man is not work," she said.

"Your house it is then," Peter said, and all at once the thought of going back upstairs to tell the Assistant Minister about Glenton didn't seem half as daunting as it had a moment before.

"I live in the Jamhuri housing estate," Millicent Ogara said.

"I know where Jamhuri Estate is," Peter said excitedly. "I live there too."

"Yes," she said, laughing. "I know you do."

Although it had officially ended, Odongo's investigation had a life of its own. Before the next morning was out, three lines of inquiry, opened while he was still in Mombasa, were beginning to show results.

First, the telecommunications people sent over a list of all Nairobi telephone numbers starting with 763–2; a Muthaiga prefix as it turned out. Then came a call from the coast; the Nyali Beach house was owned by the Old Delhi Trading Company. Finally, a commerce official called to say that the Old Delhi Trading Company (Ltd.) was registered to three Asian brothers named Patel. When Odongo checked the name against the list of phone numbers, he found nine Patels, one of them a Mr. Chandu Patel, one of the Old Delhi Trading partners. Peter knew that a policeman should never assume anything. He also knew he had found "Mr. P."

Under orders from an outraged Assistant Minister to "get that fucking *mzungu* out of Aberdare Park—arrest him if you have to," Odongo had fully intended to drive to the Aberdares to deal with the problem of Adrian Glenton. Instead, he spent the day on the phone with various business sources, trying to find out more about the Patel brothers.

What he learned was enlightening but a bit daunting. The family patriarch, Motilal Patel, had come to East Africa from Delhi in 1898, hoping to find work on the Kenya railway. When the track was finished and the labor force let go, he decided to stay on. He sent to India for his young bride, his widowed mother, and his bride's widowed mother, and used what was left of his savings to open a *duka* in Nairobi. The one shop became two, then three, then half a dozen. Soon there was a hotel in Dagoretti and a restaurant in Tom Mboya Street—or Victoria Street as it was called then—and an import-export company, Old Delhi Trading, specializing in the ivory trade. He was a clever and industrious young man, and he prospered along with the growing colony. His personal life was equally blessed and his family grew almost as rapidly as his financial interests. When he died in 1948, he had five married daughters and three grown sons, each an excellent businessman in his own right.

In the thirty years since the old man's death, his three sons—Chandu, Pranay, and Sujay—had parlayed the family's already considerable holdings into an entrepreneurial empire. They owned a number of businesses in Nairobi, from a Mercedes dealership to a bush airline, and had extensive land holdings throughout Kenya, including a hotel-casino on the south coast and tea and coffee estates in the highlands.

Odongo's sources also passed on the considerable gossip attending the Patels, those things that "everyone" knows but no one can substantiate. In addition to their Kenya holdings, the Patels, like many Asians, were heavily invested abroad, a hedge against an uncertain future. The Asians of East Africa, who made up the bulk of the merchant class, periodically came under attack from African politicians looking for a scapegoat for their own economic mismanagement, and most Asians liked to keep a number of resources outside the country, a practice which only caused more African resentment since it seemed to corroborate the suspicion that the Asians were exploiting the Kenya economy. The Patel brothers, for instance, were said to own several office buildings in Toronto and a block of luxury flats in Miami Beach. It was also widely rumored that the Old Delhi Trading Company sometimes served as a front for no less a silent partner than Dada herself, the "Nation's Sister." It made Odongo nervous; he had to have his facts in order before confronting such powerful men.

Nervous or not, the Patels were all he had. He looked up the Old Delhi Trading Company in the phone book and dialed. A moment later, he was speaking to Chandu Patel himself, asking if he might meet with him.

"May I ask what about?" Patel's accent was more British than Indian, with none of the usual subcontinental singsong.

"I would prefer to wait until we can talk face to face, sir."

"But I was just about to leave the office," Chandu Patel said with a sigh that could be heard down the line. "Oh, very well. Come to my house in one hour." He told Peter how to get there and rang off.

Driving to Muthaiga, Peter was gripped by an odd feeling of excitement, of euphoria. He didn't know whether it was because of the Patels, the new development in his investigation, or a lingering afterglow of his evening with Millie Ogara, the new development in his life. All he knew was that in spite of his being taken off the case he felt fine, rejuvenated, as though things were beginning to go his way at last.

In layout and furnishings, Millicent Ogara's tiny studio flat in Jamhuri Estate had been a duplicate of Peter Odongo's tiny studio flat in Jamhuri Estate, but it couldn't have been more different if it had been State House. Where his apartment was cold and uninviting, hers was warm and welcoming. His contained no sign of human habitation; no pictures on the walls, no drapes on the windows, no plants in pots. Even his cupboard held but one plate, one drinking glass, and one set of flatware; Peter ate out most nights, and never had company. Millicent Ogara's place was, if anything, overly decorated. The walls were hung with the work of a Kisumu artist much admired in Luoland, and hand-sewn curtains covered the windows. Potted plants and Luo crafts were in every corner and covered every flat surface. It was a home, not merely a lair, and it had a comfortable, lived-in look and feel about it.

She had given him an excellent dinner—the main course was freshly baked fish, of course—and there was a bottle of Johnnie Walker Black Label from the airport duty-free shop to help ease the conversation before and after the meal.

They had talked about their families and friends back in Nyanza Province and about their work. Millie had been a nurse for eight years. She had attended Kenyatta University College for one year and then nursing school. When she was a girl she had dreamed of becoming a doctor some day, but that was still out of reach for most of the women of her generation. Perhaps it would be easier when a daughter of hers came of age.

Unlike Peter, Millie went home to the family *pacho* every weekend. She made an effort to keep up her ties to the *dhoot,* the lineage, the way of the clan, but she admitted that there were times when she felt isolated and cut off. If Peter thought he was under pressure to get married, she said with a rueful laugh, think what it was like for her.

They had enjoyed each other's company, and Peter, who had limited experience with women who weren't whores—he seldom met any other kind—had found Millie to be remarkably easy to talk to. He behaved like a gentleman, in spite of a sexual attraction that was stronger than anything he had experienced since the rutting frenzy of his university days. It was after midnight when he got up to go, and they'd agreed to see each other again when he returned from the Aberdares. She thought that Peter should try to patch things up with his family and suggested that he go home with her the following weekend. To his surprise, he agreed, and that was how they had left it.

Patel's house was in Tchui Road, not far from the Muthaiga Club. Like many Asians, the Patels lived together in a family compound which included the houses of all three brothers. The grounds were extensive, nearly five acres, but the homes were positioned so closely together they were almost touching. All three houses looked alike: multistoried and angular, painted in garish colors, bright blues, egg-yolk yellows, and salmony pinks. Most of the shade trees had been cut down but the lawn and garden were meticulously maintained.

The compound had only one gate, and the *askari* on duty, a Kamba wearing the uniform of a private security firm owned by the Patels, was unimpressed by Peter's police credentials. He left Odongo standing in the road while he went to confirm the appointment. When he returned, he opened the gate and pointed Peter toward the nearest of the three houses.

Walking to the house, Peter noticed that the compound's car park was full: two Range Rovers, a Jaguar, an Alfa-Romeo roadster, and two black Mercedes sedans with Government tags. Two pairs of peacocks, two cocks and two hens, announced his approach. They flitted across the lawn, issuing their clarion calls. Using peacocks instead of dogs was the latest fancy of the wealthy; the neurotic birds were the most efficient alarm system money could buy.

Peter was let into the house by a Kikuyu manservant and ushered into a sitting room decorated in typical Asian style, a riot of colors, tassles and bric-a-brac. He was left to wait for half an hour before a dark-complexioned man in a business suit came in and introduced himself as Chandu Patel.

Patel did not shake Odongo's hand. He did not offer him a cup of tea or coffee. He did not even ask Peter to sit and remained standing himself, making it clear that he wanted to conclude this business as quickly as possible. "Now, how can I help you, Inspector?" he asked.

Odongo explained that he was conducting an inquiry, but did not go into specifics. He asked Patel if his company had shipped any goods from the port of Mombasa recently.

"We ship from Mombasa every day," Patel said patiently. "We have an export business. That is what export businesses do. They export things."

Odongo ignored the man's patronizing tone. "Have you had any consignments bound for Malaysia? Kuala Lumpur?"

Patel's face creased in thought, then he shook his head. "No. Nothing recent."

"Do you know a European named Smith?" Peter asked.

Patel sighed. "I know a dozen Europeans named Smith."

"Have you done business with any of them recently?"

"No," Patel said, glancing pointedly at his wristwatch, a gold, wafer-thin Patek Philippe.

"Do you happen to know a Customs official named Nyeusi? Ambrose Nyeusi?"

"Nyeusi . . . Nyeusi . . . no, I don't believe so."

"Do you own a house in Nyali Beach?"

Patel nodded and said, "Yes, I do. Although technically speaking, it is owned by one of our companies. The Old Delhi Trading Company."

"Have you let anyone use it recently?"

"No."

"No? Well, it was certainly being used two days ago. By Ambrose Nyeusi."

Patel shrugged. "My family uses the house one month out of the year. The rest of the time it is managed by an estate agent in Mombasa. They rent it out to people on holiday. You will have to talk with the estate agent about it." He took a gold-plated Cross pen from his breast pocket, wrote down the name of the realtor and handed the paper to Odongo. "If there's anything else I can help you with, Inspector, please don't hesitate to call." With that, he turned and walked out of the room. A moment later the Kikuyu manservant reappeared, ready to show Odongo out.

Odongo went meekly, but he was stung at being dismissed so cavalierly. Walking back to the street, he discovered that the final indignity was that there was no *final* indignity. He was halfway through the garden when he felt something land on the back of his shoulder. He brushed it off, thinking that it was a leaf or an insect, and when he pulled back his hand his fingers were covered with a wet, white treacle.

He glanced up and saw that he was standing underneath a flame tree and that roosting in its branches was one of the Patel peacocks.

Chandu Patel stood at the window, peering through bright orange drapes. He waited until the policeman cleared the gate before he turned and called in a loud voice: "You may come in now." The French doors at the end of the room swung open, and three men came in and sat down.

Chandu Patel, pacing the room, gave them a brief summary of his interview with Odongo and then turned to the Assistant Minister for Wildlife and said, "I thought you pulled him off the investigation."

The Assistant Minister sighed. "I thought I had too," he said mournfully, shaking his head. "All the dogs seem to have slipped their leashes. Odongo can't control Glenton . . . I can't control Odongo . . . you can't control Fisi."

"If you weren't such a bloody fool there wouldn't be any need to control Fisi," Sujay Patel said from his chair beside the window. He was the youngest of the Patel brothers and the carbon copy of Chandu—dark and thin and sleek. Pranay, the middle one, was lighter-skinned and stouter than his siblings but just as immaculately groomed. He sat on the divan next to the Assistant Minister.

"Let's not indulge in name-calling and let's not panic," Chandu Patel said. "None of us are entirely without blame in this affair. What we must do now is decide what we are going to do about it. It's time for us to begin snipping off loose strings so we can get back to making money."

"Yes, making money," Sujay Patel muttered. "That is the important thing."

"We've all made our share of mistakes," Chandu went on. He turned to the Assistant Minister. "You should never have given Odongo approval to form a special unit, and I—"

"What choice did I have?" the Assistant Minister asked plaintively. "He threatened to make a scandal, to go to the newspapers. And besides, I thought that the publicity would force Fisi out of the park."

" . . . and I should have insisted Fisi leave the Aberdares and set up elsewhere the minute Glenton entered the picture," Chandu Patel continued, as if there had been no interruption.

"We tried to get him to move," Pranay Patel reminded his brother. "He won't listen. He doesn't listen to anyone except that woman. I think he enjoys matching wits with this Glenton chap. Fisi is a strange one, no doubt about that."

"Just who is Fisi anyway?" the Assistant Minister asked. He had been told that Fisi was Kikuyu, but nothing more.

"We wish we knew," Sujay Patel said. "His identity is known only to our senior partner, and she refuses to tell us anything about him. All we know for a fact is that he has great influence over her. With all that nonsense about hyena spirits, perhaps he's her witch doctor. Or perhaps he's fucking the bitch. She can be reckless at times."

"So can you," Chandu Patel said. "That kind of talk can get you killed. The point is, if Fisi won't go, then we must get rid of Glenton. Immediately. The Assistant Minister here says that *Mbwa Kali* is making the park warden nervous."

"He's afraid that Glenton will catch The Hyena," said the Assistant Minister, "and he's worried about his own neck."

"Aren't we all?" Pranay Patel cracked. Everyone laughed except for Chandu Patel, who said, "The ones who should worry are that Luo policeman and his crazy white hunter."

"What are we going to do about them?" Sujay Patel asked.

"I'll deal with Odongo," said the minister, "but I must confess that I don't know what to do about Glenton."

"I will take care of Glenton," said Chandu Patel.

"Yes?" the Assistant Minister said skeptically. "How?"

"I will speak with our senior partner."

"What can she do?"

"She can arrange to have the GSU inserted into Aberdare Park." Mention of the General Service Unit elicited a murmur of approval from the others. Glenton and his ragtag band of trackers would be no match for Kenya's toughest, most feared military unit.

"But won't there be talk?" asked the Assistant Minister.

Chandu Patel shrugged. "They can always say it's routine maneuvers, mountain training or something. It will give us an excuse for closing Treetops and The Ark for a few days."

"Is closing the lodges absolutely necessary?" asked the Assistant Minister. "We've already closed the park to casual traffic. Isn't that enough?"

"We can't have witnesses," Chandu Patel said.

"But what can the tourists see?" the Assistant Minister asked. "They are brought in by coach and taken out by coach. In between times, they are restricted to their lodge."

"Once he knows the GSU is after him, Glenton may decide to take refuge in one of the lodges," Chandu Patel said.

"If you close those game lodges, my counterpart at Jogoo House, the Assistant Minister for Tourism, is going to demand an explanation."

"And State House will be happy to give him one," Chandu Patel said with a faint smile. "National security."

"Who can argue with that?" Sujay Patel said with a grin.

"I suppose so," the Assistant Minister said, still not entirely convinced.

"Three, four days maximum," Chandu Patel reassured him. "The GSU won't need more than that. We can arrange it so that the tourists who are inconvenienced by the change in schedule can visit the lodge free of charge. That should eliminate any complaints." The Assistant Minister shrugged and nodded.

"Good, then we're agreed," Chandu Patel said with a wide smile. He stepped on a button set into the floor and, seconds later, a servant came in with a tray bearing a bottle of whisky and a soda dispenser. When the servant had fixed each of them a drink and left the room, they raised their tumblers in a silent toast.

26

The troops, a platoon of them, were loading into trucks when Robbie pulled up to the front gate of park headquarters in Mweiga shortly before eight on a cold and drizzly morning. Assuming they were Field Force rangers, she probably wouldn't have paid them any mind if the gate ranger hadn't aroused her curiosity by barring her from the compound.

Park headquarters was just up the road from the Aberdare Country Club where she was staying, and she usually popped in first thing every morning to see if she could grab the warden for an update on how the Great Hyena Hunt was going. He never had much to tell her, and she might have skipped this morning if she hadn't had a specific question for her: Sam Weller had told her at breakfast that his Ark bookings for the next four days had been cancelled on orders of the Ministry of Defense. A quick call to the Outspan Hotel in Nyeri had revealed that the park's other game lodge, Treetops, also had been closed. Robbie was hoping that the warden could tell her the reason.

The gate ranger was one she had come to know fairly well over the past few weeks, a Kikuyu who liked to flirt. "What's happening, Harry?" she asked him through the open car window. "Why can't I come in?"

"The warden, he say not to let anyone in until those men have gone," the ranger said, hooking a thumb in the direction of the trucks.

The headquarters buildings were nearly a hundred yards from the front gate. Robbie poked her head out the window and shielded her eyes with a hand, trying to see through the mist and soft rain. "Those aren't rangers, are they Harry?"

"No, missy."

"And they don't look like Kenya Rifles either."

"No, missy. They are GSU."

The activities of the General Service Unit were sheathed in secrecy, and it was rare for anyone actually to get a look at them. "What are they doing here, Harry?"

"Don't know, missy."

"They are being put into the park to hunt the poachers, right?"

"Don't know, missy."

She gave him an exasperated look. "Remember that tape I was playing when I drove in the other day? The one you liked so much? The Four Tops?"

Robbie leaned across the car seat, got the tape from the glove box and handed it to him. "They're going after the poachers, right?"

Harry looked around furtively, then slipped the cassette inside his shirt, both to protect it from the rain and to get it out of sight. He shook his head. "Not poachers. They go to look for the European . . . *Mbwa Kali*. They go to arrest him."

"Arrest him! What for?"

"Don't know, missy."

She rummaged in the glove compartment, found an old Otis Redding tape and passed it over.

The ranger slipped the second tape into his shirt and repeated, "Don't know, missy."

"*Stronzo*," she said, swearing at him in Italian. "C'mon, Harry. You must have heard something. And don't go looking at the goddamn glove compartment. I don't have any more tapes."

He shrugged. "I think maybe because *Mbwa Kali* frightens the people, but I don't know. I tried to talk to the GSU men, but they think they're too important to speak to me." He gave her a sheepish look and asked, "Do you want your tapes back?"

"Nah, keep 'em. Be seeing you, Harry." Robbie turned the car around and found a place to park across the road, a short distance from the gate. Using binoculars, she watched the GSU troops complete their loading. Their officer stood off to one side, deep in conversation with the park warden and a man who Robbie recognized as a member of Adrian Glenton's team—the ranger Charles. Then the officer shook hands with Charles and the warden and got into the cab of the first truck in line. A few moments later, she saw Harry snap to attention and salute as the convoy rumbled through his checkpoint.

The trucks, six in all, turned in her direction and went roaring by with a whoosh of diesel fumes and spray, the tires throwing up water from the road. Robbie waited a moment, then started up the engine and pulled in behind. She followed them until they passed through the Treetops Gate and into Aberdare National Park.

"Where is he, Stephen?"

"In the park."

"No shit, Sherlock. I know he's in the park. But *where* in the park?"

"Haven't the foggiest."

"Sure you do. He radios you his position every evening. Come on, Stephen. Where is he? Look. Here's a map. Show me."

"I can't do that, my dear."

They were seated at the table in Stephen Hone's dining room where Robbie had found him at his breakfast, eating in this morning because of the weather. He was having buttered toast and fried bananas, all sprinkled liberally with sugar. "Why do you want to know?" he asked.

"I want to see him."

"That is quite evident. But you still haven't said why."

"I've got some vital information for him. If he doesn't get it, he could be in trouble. Big trouble."

"Tell me and I'll relay it," Hone said.

"No."

"Very well, then," Hone said. "I'll get him on the radio and you can tell him yourself."

"No, Stephen. I'll tell him in person or not at all."

Hone put down his fork and grinned at her. "Do you mean to say you'd let the General Service Unit snatch him without even warning him?"

Robbie stared at him a moment, then blurted, "How do you know about that?"

"I've lived twenty-five years in this district," Hone said, "and while it's unlikely I'll ever be put up for Parliament, I do have *some* friends. One happens to work at park headquarters."

Robbie slumped in her chair, her ace trumped, her only bit of leverage gone. "Have you told Adrian yet?" she asked in a dispirited voice.

"Three hours ago," Hone said, talking around a bite of fried bananas. "He was in a foul mood. I think I woke him."

"What did he say?"

"He said thank you."

"That's all?"

"Just to be fair, he polled his chappies. They voted to stay in the park until they caught The Hyena."

"But that's crazy!" Robbie exclaimed, jumping up to pace the room. "The GSU doesn't screw around. I got a good look at those guys this morning. They were loaded for bear."

"I told him it was daft," Hone said, in full agreement with her, "but he wasn't having it. All I can do is collect what information I can and radio it to him."

"I still want to see him, Stephen."

"Then you're as dotty as he is."

"Here's the map. Show me where he is."

"No!" Hone said. "And for God's sake, sit down!"

She stopped pacing and sat down abruptly. "Where is he, Stephen? I have to see him."

"Why?" Hone wailed.

"So I can persuade him to haul that cute little butt of his out of the park before those storm troopers blow it off."

"Ahh, I see," he said, giving her an understanding look. "You care for him."

"Well . . . sure," Robbie said defensively. "Don't you?"

"Yes. And he cares for me. But he wouldn't listen to me. What makes you think he'll listen to you?"

"It's an entirely different situation and you know it," she said hotly. "He likes you. He *loves* me."

"Really?" Hone's eyes widened with surprise. He put down his knife and fork and leaned back in his seat, smiling at her. "Has he told you so?"

"You must be kidding. He's so thick he doesn't even know it yet."

"Don't be so sure," Hone said. "Adrian isn't thick; he's just slow."

"V-e-r-y slow," Robbie said.

Hone chuckled. "Well, I'm certainly happy to know that you don't suffer the same myopia," he said. "I was beginning to think that you two would never figure it out. You've been snuffling round each other like a pair of rhinos, and taking almost as bloody long about it too, I must say. Did you know that it takes rhinos between three and four years finally to get round to mating?" He chuckled again when he saw her face go pink. She was usually the outrageous one. It felt good to catch her out for once.

"There's something else I have to discuss with him," she said quickly, to change the subject. "I don't think I can sit on the story any longer."

"No? Why not?"

"Gosh, I don't know," she said breathlessly, in a young girl's voice, a Nancy Drew voice. "Call it woman's intuition or something, but I think I'm on to something." She reverted to her own voice, her South Philadelphia voice. "I got bodies all over the sidewalk. I got a game of hide-and-seek going on between some guy who thinks he's a goddamn hyena and our guy, who thinks he's Jungle Jim. Two of the country's most popular tourist lodges have been closed down. The government sends in troops to hunt its own anti-poaching unit, which is hunting a gang of poachers, which is hunting Dumbo and his furry forest friends. And you ask why not?" Robbie shook her head. "Jesus! Do you have any idea what I could do with a yarn like that? I could win a prize."

Hone had watched her performance with amusement. "And is that why you came to Africa, Robbie? To win prizes?"

"No, I came to Africa for the same reason everyone else comes to Africa," she said sarcastically. "To find adventure and romance."

"It would seem you've accomplished that."

"Not yet," she said. "All I need is for you to tell me where Adrian is."

"He'll have my guts for garters if I do."

"I'll have your balls for breakfast if you don't."

"My God what a mouth you have," Hone said.

"So I'll go to confession on Saturday. Quit stalling."

"I'm not going to tell you where Adrian is and that's my final say on the subject," Hone said. "I can't have you going off into the park alone."

"Come with me then."

"I have to stay at the radio. Without me, Adrian has no one to watch his back."

"Please, Stephen."

They locked eyes for a moment, then Hone looked away and started mumbling, more to himself than to Robbie. "I could send one of my chappies . . . no, no, they're houseboys, useless in the bush. Or perhaps . . . no, that wouldn't do either." He snapped out of it, gave Robbie a shrug of helplessness and said, "Impossible."

Robbie shrugged right back at him. "No sweat. I'll just sneak into the park and wander around 'til I find him."

"Or Fisi finds *you*. Out of the question. I can't allow you to do that."

"How are you going to stop me?"

Hone shook his head and said with a deep sigh: "American women are so bloody aggressive."

"Stephen, we're wasting time."

Hone glared at her. Then, with another sigh, he asked, "Can you manage a four-wheel-drive?"

"No sweat."

"You'll use my Toyota," he declared. He took her map and spread it out on the table. "You'll go in here, where it says FGP. It's an isolated forest guard post about halfway between Ark Gate and Wandare Gate. The ranger knows me, and knows the Land Cruiser—I've run supplies to Adrian from time to time and I've bribed the bugger to let me come and go as I please. I use the hooter to let him know it's me. A short blast, then a pause, then two more short blasts. Have you got that?"

"One short, pause, two short," Robbie repeated.

"Good. You'll have to wait until dusk, because my chappie doesn't come on until half past five. And you'll have to give the whole thing up if it isn't still raining."

"What's the weather got to do with it?" Robbie asked.

"Just hear me out," Hone said. "It's a simple post. One ranger in a small shed beside a dirt road. There's a barrier pole across the road, and the ranger can raise and lower the pole from inside his shed with a rope if he wants. If I know my man, he won't want to leave his shed if it's raining. And if your windscreen's fogged, he won't be able to see that it isn't me at the wheel. Just give the signal and he'll put up the pole without coming out of his burrow. Not a complicated plan, but I think it'll work."

"Right off the top of your head, too," Robbie said. "I'm impressed. I'll bet you were one hell of a field commander in your time."

"I had my moments, I suppose," Hone said, pleased.

He spent the next half hour going over the map with her, showing her how to find Adrian once she was in the park. The team's new position wasn't very far from the boundary and he didn't expect she would have any difficulty finding it. When she neared the camp, he said, she was to give the same signal she had used at the guard post. "If you don't," he said, "the lads might shoot the Toyota full of holes, and I'll be in the dog box with my Yank owner again. The bright side to that, of course, is that they might shoot *you* full of holes too, and I would be rid of you."

When he was satisfied that she knew the map, Hone jotted something on a slip of paper. "Give this to Adrian and see he reads it," he said. "I'm changing radio frequencies . . . just in case someone's been listening in."

Robbie folded the paper and put it into her camera bag. "Thanks, Stephen," she said. "You're a sweet man." Then she bent down quickly and planted a kiss squarely on top of his balding head.

Hone flushed and ducked away. "Get out of here," he said gruffly, "before I come to my bloody senses."

Hone's plan worked perfectly. Robbie sounded the horn in the prescribed sequence and the barrier pole was lifted as if by magic. The ranger waved to her from the dry comfort of his shed. She waved back blithely, little more than a blur behind the rain-streaked windshield. It was a few minutes before six o'clock, and it had been raining all day.

The track on the map that Hone had marked for her didn't quite translate into a road. Perhaps it had been a road early in the day, before the rain intensified, but it wasn't a road now. Even with both axles engaged and the gearbox in low, the Toyota was having a hard time gaining purchase in the slick clay.

Robbie had become a resourceful driver in her nearly two years in Africa. There was little alternative. Even in Kenya, one of the most developed countries in Africa, there were few decent roads. Paved Class A roads had potholes and crumbling shoulders. The Class B roads turned into rivers of mud during the rainy season. The Class C roads vanished altogether.

Robbie had never done much driving in her life and had never owned an automobile. Growing up in urban Philadelphia—then living in Newark, Manhattan and London—she had not really needed one. But despite the late start, Kenya had made an accomplished driver of her. She spent most of her weekends in the game reserves chasing the migrating herds, and she had learned to do without roads. She wasn't an expert but she was good. She had that seemingly incompatible meld of caution and fearlessness that is the mark of the skilled bush driver. She could handle just about anything. Anything but this.

The road was like a giant bobsled run. The Land Cruiser, all four wheels locked and spinning, threw up clumps of red mud and slewed from one side of the road to the other. Robbie worked the steering wheel the best she could, but for all the feedback she was getting she might as well have been a child playing driver in a parked car.

She lost it for keeps on a particularly steep downgrade about three miles inside the park.

It was a spot where the road dipped down sharply before crossing a narrow sluice of run-off water and climbing again. She goosed the gas pedal to build enough momentum to take on the hill, and went directly into an uncontrolled slide. When she tapped the brake, the Land Cruiser did a full 360-degree spin and slammed into the opposite embankment, winding up on its side in a ditch which ran along the side of the mountain.

It was over in seconds, but Robbie calmly watched it all unfold in slow motion. She felt completely detached from what was happening, an interested observer but not terribly concerned. She had plenty of time to think about it. She even made up a joke. What did Alice say when she fell down the rabbit hole? "Oh, shiiiiiiiiit!" The Toyota came to rest on its left side, the passenger side. Robbie ended up on her back with both her knees in her face, on top of what was left of the window. She lay still for a moment, taking inventory. Except for a throbbing in one knee, she was all right.

She struggled up to a crouch and tried to open the door on the driver's side—the top side now—but it was badly dented and wouldn't move. Calmly, she rolled down the window and climbed out. Back on firm ground, she tested her bruised knee. When she determined that all of her parts were in working order, she sat down in the mud. And started to shake.

She stayed like that for another moment, then got up and went back into the capsized Land Cruiser to retrieve the map. Out again, she squatted and spread the map across her thighs, hunching over it to keep the rain off. She had to guess as to where she was now, and figured she was no more than two miles from the camp. If she was right she would be there in half an hour, maybe sooner. If she was wrong she didn't want to think about it. It was getting dark, and she was wet, and cold, and she thought she heard a leopard cough somewhere in the woods. She grabbed her camera bag and a flashlight and set off at a brisk walk.

It was fully dark by the time she had covered the first mile. The walk was taking longer than she had estimated. She was wearing flat shoes, but they were leather-soled, useless in the mud. She slipped and fell every few hundred feet.

Hone had told her that about five miles beyond the guard post she would come to a sharp curve in the road, marked by a huge lava boulder on the left and a steep slope on the right. She was supposed to park next to the boulder, sound the horn, and continue the rest of the way on foot. Another fifty yards along the road, she would find a Cape buffalo path tunneling into the forest. If she took the path for approximately three hundred yards, bearing right whenever she came to a fork, she would come to Adrian's camp, a series of three small caves in a line, right beside the path. She couldn't miss it. Besides, Adrian would have heard the horn signal and, thinking it was Hone, would be watching for her.

But Hone had assumed that she would be driving as far as the boulder and that she'd have the twilight to work with. It was a mile and a half from where she left the Land Cruiser to where the road curved sharply. Robbie recognized the big rock easily enough, but finding the buffalo path was something else entirely. She stepped off the fifty yards, probing the bushes with her flashlight, but saw nothing that looked like a major animal path. She went another twenty yards, just to give Hone a comfortable margin of error, then began to backtrack.

She had to retrace her steps again and again before she found the track. When she did, she realized that she had walked right by it several times. She wasn't surprised. She hadn't been expecting the Garden State Parkway, but she had been looking for something slightly larger than a rabbit hole. She had to get down on all fours to enter the tunnel.

But the farther in she went the wider the tunnel became, until she could almost stand upright. After another fifty or sixty feet she broke into the open. She was relieved to be out of the narrow chute. The overgrowth had been dense enough to keep the rain off, but she was prone to claustrophobia and didn't mind getting wet in this case. Besides, she had other, more pressing things to worry about.

It was completely dark now, darker than any night Robbie could remember. When it was overcast in the city, or even in a village, the cloud cover often trapped the ground light and held it close overhead, brightening the sky. But in this place, there was nothing to reflect. Only a blackness so deep, so profound, that Robbie had a feeling of being in some dark and windowless room of the soul, where all her demons scaled the walls and hammered on the door.

She was afraid to switch on her flashlight for fear that it would attract unfriendly mammals, animal or human; afraid not to turn it on for fear she would lose her way. The rain's patter deadened even the sound of her own labored breathing, yet she thought that she heard ominous noises all around her. A Cape buffalo's dry chuff. A mamba's whispering slither. A footfall.

She walked faster, the flashlight's beam dancing jerkily on the path ahead. Then she was jogging, the brambles picking at her clothes and hair. Then she was running, running as she hadn't run since a night when she was fourteen years old and a gang from Oregon Avenue was chasing her. And then she was falling. The ground simply vanished from under her flying feet and she was falling. Falling down into a dark abyss. Falling straight down to Hell. She started a scream but choked on it, and kept on falling.

27

The rain was a thin glue, keeping Adrian Glenton and his men in their caves, stuck in a posture of forced idleness. The downpour came on the heels of a wasted week. They had spent three full days searching the moorlands above the bamboo and had nothing to show for it. No carcasses, no cold camp fires, no unburied feces, no sign at all that Fisi had ever been there. With all the good cover available lower down, Adrian knew Fisi was too clever to come out into the open, but he had to check the higher ground out, if only to be able to shorten his list of possibilities.

Adding to Adrian's frustration was the knowledge that he had run out of time. Having ignored Odongo's command to cease operations, he knew that it wouldn't be long before they sent someone to look for him.

Compared to the rain forest, the moorlands had been easy going. The men had been able to use the Land Rover to cover a lot of ground, and the open spaces had lessened their fear of ambush. All they'd had to worry about were lions, and a snake unique to the high country, a black cobra five feet long, fat as a woman's wrist and both neurotoxic and hemotoxic.

The moorland landscape had been as easy on the eyes and the spirit as it had been on the legs, beautiful even in the mist. There were flat meadows carpeted with *Helichrysums* and *Kniphofia*, everlastings, and red-hot pokers. Giant groundsels grew twenty feet tall on fragile stems and the lobelias wore blue-green flowers along their spikes.

In the mornings, when the fog was thinnest, the team had an occasional glimpse of Mount Kenya on the other side of the valley. Most of them, Adrian included, were willing to accept the Kikuyu tenet that God lived on top of Mount Kenya. Except for Joseph. God used to live there, Joseph said, but he moved to *Ol Doinyo Lengai*, The Mountain of God, in Maasailand after a Dorobo hunter shot an arrow at him. Pythias, of course, was insulted, and didn't speak to Joseph for the rest of the day.

Even closer than Mount Kenya, but more to the south, was yet another holy place, *Mukurweini wa Nyagathanga,* the Garden of Eden. According to Kikuyu gospel, it was there that Gikuyu and Mumbi—

Adam and Eve—had lived. The world's first man and woman produced nine daughters, who became the founders of the nine Kikuyu clans. Joseph's version was somewhat different of course. He thought all mankind was descended from God's three sons: Maasae, Kokoyo, and Kunoni, the respective patriarchs of the Masai, the black race and the white race.

There had been an abundance of wildlife on the plateau: lions, warthogs, a variety of antelope, and buffalo. In the early mornings, the men could see the steam rising off their backs. They also had seen many hyenas, the four-legged kind. Observing them, Adrian was struck by how fitting it was that Fisi had elected to use the hyena as his inspiration and his *nom de guerre*. With its big head, powerful jaws, sloped back, loon's laugh, awkward gait, scruffy fur, and revolting eating habits, the hyena was utterly loathsome to man. It was also, of all the creatures in God's menagerie, the most ambiguous, the most deceptive, and the most misunderstood.

How ambiguous? It was impossible to determine a hyena's sex without dissection; the female's clitoris was elongated, the same shape and size as the male's penis. She even had a sham scrotum.

How deceptive? Because of the cringing lope, hyenas had a reputation for being slow. In fact, they could run forty miles per hour and maintain that pace all night. While it was true that a cheetah could do better than sixty, it was only in short bursts. If a zebra or antelope had a good head start it might outlast a cheetah. If a hyena was on their trail, it was supper time.

How misunderstood? The prevailing image of the hyena was that of a craven scavenger, skulking about a pride of feeding lions, waiting for the leftovers. But chances were the hyenas had made the kill the night before, only to be run off by the lions when morning came. A hyena would, it was true, eat just about anything—from a puff adder to a brother hyena—and it would let others do its killing for it during the day. But with nightfall the hyena became a different creature altogether, an aggressive hunter, a killer that operates in darkness and in packs.

Like Fisi, "The Hyena." Both were wary and secretive animals who hid in holes or in tall grass during the day and came out mostly at night. Both were highly territorial. Both had a penchant for calling cards. The hyena marked its preserve by dropping one of its distinctive white stools, or by "pasting," rubbing its anal glands along a stalk of grass and secreting a pasty substance which had a strong odor, even to humans. "The Hyena" left a tooth behind. Lastly, the hyena ate every bit of its victim, including the muscles, the head, and the bones. Fisi too left little of his victim intact.

Feeling guilty about frittering away three precious days and anxious to make up the lost time, Adrian hustled the team back down into the rain forest. He pushed the men mercilessly the rest of the week, shaving two hours off the already short six-hour sleep period so they could cover more ground. All the men, except for Pythias, were having problems. Tembo, so much older than the others, had trouble with the blistering pace and kept falling behind. Ekali still hadn't adapted to the forest, so unlike his native desert; he had a head cold and the dampness seeped into his joints so that he ached all over. As for Adrian and Joseph, both men were in a constant state of distemper. Joseph was as disgruntled as a leopard with a thorn in its pad, unable to fathom an enemy who would not show himself and fight like a man. Adrian was merely impatient with everyone and everything, impossible to please. He kept looking at his wristwatch for no apparent reason and yelling at them. Pythias began calling him Wasimu, and Tembo and Ekali soon joined in. "Yes, Wasimu. No, Wasimu. Whatever you say, Wasimu." Adrian wasn't amused. *Wasimu* was a Dorobo word for a crazy man.

The terrain, steeper and muddier than the moor, made the Land Rover more of a hindrance than a help, so they hid it in the bush and went back to foot patrols. They traveled light, carrying rifles and food only, leaving everything else in the Land Rover. To save time they ate just one meal a day: *posho,* maize meal mixed with water. But a few days before, they had happened upon the carcass of a freshly poached elephant, and after losing Fisi's trail to the late rain, turned back and had a proper feast: elephant heart stew and fat-laced chops taken from between the ear and eye. After days of mealies, even the tongue was good. Tembo had a way of cooking it that got rid of the rubbery taste and made it more like beef tongue: he boiled it first, then wrapped it in a leaf and shoved it under the fire's coals to roast.

As far as everyone but Adrian and Joseph was concerned, that dinner had been the second best thing to happen to them all week. The best came the next day when the rain did not stop after an hour or two but went on through the night, and through the next day and night, and the next, until even "Wasimu" was finally forced to call a halt and seek shelter.

Adrian was at the fire brewing a cup of bedtime tea when the radio came to life. "Tea Time, Tea Time, this is Aberdare Base, over."

Joseph was closest. With a grunt, he rolled over in his blankets, groped for the hand-set and flipped it to Glenton.

"Hullo, Base. Tea Time here, over."

"Why aren't you set to the new frequency?" Hone asked, dispensing with radio protocol, not ending the transmission with an *over*.

"What new frequency?"

"Didn't you get my message?"

"What message?"

"Women," Hone mumbled, his voice barely audible. Then he said, "I hope you're not too angry with me."

"Why should I be angry with you?" Glenton asked.

"I tried to talk her out of it, but she threatened all sorts of foolish nonsense if I didn't tell her."

Glenton held the hand-set at arm's length, staring at it as if it were broken. The radio was connected to a long wire antenna outside the cave and should be working fine, he told himself, but Hone wasn't making sense. He pulled the hand-set back to his mouth and asked: "Stephen, what the devil are you talking about?"

"Robbie, of course."

"What about her?"

"What do you mean what about her?" Hone said, an edge in his voice. "Isn't she there with you?"

"No, of course not," Glenton said. "Why would she . . ." He stopped. Icy fingers seemed to brush his neck. He took a deep breath, pushed the transmit button again and said, "What have you done, Stephen?"

"You're having me on, aren't you?" Hone said. "This is a payback for my telling her how to find you. Well, it's not at all amusing."

"You sent her into the park?" Adrian asked in disbelief.

"She threatened to go in anyway if I didn't," Hone said, his tone defensive. "You know her. She'd bloody well do it."

"When did she leave?"

"At half past five," Hone said. "She should have passed through the guard post about six."

"For Christ's sake, man! It's nearly eleven!" Glenton said, close to shouting. Joseph was up on an elbow, watching with interest.

"Stephen! Quick! How was she coming?"

"The same way I always do."

Glenton switched off the hand-set and hooked it onto his belt, then he snapped at Joseph, "Go get Pythias. The others are to stay here. Tell them to be on their guard. Well? What are you waiting for, *moran*? Move, damn your eyes!"

A minute later they were on the path, moving quickly but silently through the rain, toward the road. Pythias, with his remarkable night vision, had the lead. Adrian, armed with his shotgun and a torch, came right behind. Joseph, carrying only his spear, brought up the rear.

They didn't get far. No more than two hundred yards down the path, the Dorobo stopped abruptly, nearly causing Glenton to crash into him. "What is it?" Adrian asked in a whisper.

"Our trap," Pythias whispered back. "There is something in it."

Glenton gave a hand signal and the three men approached the pit from different directions. When they were all at the lip of the hole, Glenton held up a staying hand and listened. There was no sound coming from the pit, but the lid of twigs and leaves was broken through.

Glenton aimed his shotgun with one hand, held his torch out to one side at arm's length—if someone shot at it, he didn't want to be in the line of fire—and switched on the light.

Robbie Lewis didn't make a sound when the beam hit her. She sat in a corner of the pit in several inches of rainwater, hugging her knees and blinking up at them, her face smeared with mud.

When Glenton turned the torch around and put the light on his own face, she gave him a weak grin and croaked: "Yo! Adrian."

28

The fire was nearly out and Adrian laid on more twigs to coax it back to life. A woolen blanket had been hung over the cave door to block the light and the smoke hugged the ceiling and drifted toward the back, finally escaping up an invisible air shaft. Adrian sat Robbie Lewis next to the fire and said, "You've got to get out of those wet clothes."

"Before or after you show me your etchings?" she asked through chattering teeth.

"Etchings? What etchings?"

"Never mind." She started to unbutton her shirt.

"Wait!" Adrian yelped. "Just hold on, will you? We'll be out of here in a minute." He turned to Joseph. "Gather up our kit and move it in with Tembo."

"The hell you say," Robbie said. "You don't for a moment think I'm staying here by myself, do you?"

"But—"

"But nothing. I've spent enough time alone in dark holes for one night. This place gives me the creeps."

Adrian looked about. "Really? I think it's rather homey myself," he said. "Besides, it's only for tonight. You'll be going back in the morning."

"Wrong again. We will be going back in the morning."

"Well, yes, of course. You didn't think I'd make you go alone, did you?"

"You're not listening," Robbie said. "You're going back with me. To stay."

Adrian stared at her, then said, "I'm afraid I can't do that, Miss Lewis. I still have a job to do here."

"You've been fired. Sacked. Or haven't you heard?"

He grinned. "For the record, no, I haven't heard. And I don't expect to hear until after I've caught Fisi."

"The GSU is looking for you!"

"Yes, I know. They're spending the night four miles from here. Joseph and I watched them make camp. Fine-looking bunch of lads they were, too."

"It's no joke, Adrian. Come back with me. Please."

"No," he said. "I'm not going to call off the hunt just because Inspector Odongo wants me to. I don't have to listen to him any longer. He's in this thing up to his armpits. He's probably the bloody brains behind the entire operation."

"Don't be silly," she said impatiently. "I checked him out, just as you asked. And I was right. He's as clean as a cat. The original Straight Arrow."

"Then you aren't as good a sleuth as I gave you credit for being," Glenton said, "because I have reason to believe otherwise."

"You're wrong," Robbie said. "Until a couple of months ago, Odongo was one of the Kenya Police's best homicide men. Why do you think he was given a shitty wildlife assignment?"

"I don't know and I don't care."

"I'll tell you anyway," she said, and proceeded to give him a summary of the story Samwel Mbituru had told her, about a whore named Alice Ogwella and the International Casino case cover-up. "Now, does that sound like a rogue cop to you?"

Glenton didn't answer, so she added, "If you're going to worry about someone, you should keep an eye on that ranger of yours—Charles. I saw him talking to the GSU officer."

"I know about Charles," Adrian said. "He can't tell them anything; he doesn't know where we are. And don't worry about the GSU. I'll explain everything to them in due time. I would have done it today but they would undoubtedly want to take us in to sort it all out, and that takes time, time I don't have to spare. When The Hyena gets wind that there are soldiers in the park—if he doesn't know it already—he'll strike his tent and leave. We would have to start all over again."

"Please come back with me," Robbie said, unmoved by his argument. "If you're right, and there really is a conspiracy, who says the GSU wants to question you? They may have orders to shoot first and ask questions later."

"The lads and I can take care of ourselves."

"If you don't come with me, I'm going to file my story."

"That, Miss Lewis, is the least of my worries," Glenton said drily. "I rather suspect we've already lost the element of surprise."

"Fine. Be a smart-ass. But if you don't go, I'm not going."

"Oh yes you are."

"Oh no I'm not."

"You're going if I have to carry you all the way to the game ditch and throw you across."

"Go ahead. But you'll have to do it four times a goddamn day, seven days a week, because I'll sneak back into the park and find you again. And I'll keep coming back until you're so old you can't lift me anymore.

So old you fart dust." She had her fists on her hips, glowering at him defiantly.

Adrian shook his head and laughed. "We'll talk about it later, when you've dried off," he said. He threw her a towel, one of his shirts and a pair of trousers. "Put these on. I'll go help Joseph and be back in a few minutes."

The three caves were in a line, each no more than twelve feet from the next. They were almost identical, not very deep but with enough overhead to stand up without stooping. Adrian and Joseph had the first cave, Pythias and Ekali were sharing the middle one, and Tembo had the last to himself. Adrian and Joseph dumped their things on Tembo's floor and lit a Coleman lantern. Tembo was in the neighboring cave, talking to Ekali and Pythias.

Joseph hadn't spoken a word since they had hauled Robbie Lewis out of the trap, and from the looks Glenton was getting it was obvious that something was upsetting the Masai. He was beginning to get on Adrian's nerves. "Oh, for Christ's bloody sake!" Adrian snapped, finally exploding. "What? *What*? Either spit it out or quit glaring at me!"

"Sometimes I wonder why we came to this cursed forest," Joseph said quietly. "There are no cattle here to steal." He turned his back on Glenton to get a drink from the bucket of water Tembo had brought up from the river. It was cold; cold as the *engare endolu,* the "ax-water" they'd used to numb his penis before the circumciser's knife did its work.

"You know full bloody well why we're here," Adrian said. "That isn't what's bothering you. It's the woman, isn't it?"

Joseph turned around to face Adrian. "She will lead them to us," he said. "They will find her car and track her here."

"You couldn't track a bloody brontosaurus in this rain," Adrian said with a snort.

The Masai did not bother to ask what a brontosaurus was. "You know what I mean. She will bring us bad fortune."

"Superstitious nonsense," Adrian declared. "And besides, what do you suggest I do about it at this hour? It's way past midnight and she is still limping from the fall she took." He felt the same way Joseph did, and the Masai knew it. "Look, I will take her back first thing in the morning, all right?"

"She won't go," Joseph said. "And I don't think you can make her go. She has a power over you."

"What complete rot! If you want to be helpful here, you can quit talking nonsense and suggest something."

"We could kill her," Joseph said hopefully.

Adrian laughed. "No, Joseph, we can't."

The disappointment in Joseph's face was real. He was not feeling all that kindly toward females these days. It all had to do with his situation at home.

Joseph had been in bad favor with his tribal elders even before he chose to join Adrian in this new venture. They were still angry at him for wasting his warriorhood working for an *ilmeek* hunter in the first place. Unless it was for lion, and done with a spear, hunting was a trivial pursuit to the Masai tribe. His elders and circumcision brothers shook their heads sadly and wondered what had become of Joseph ole Kantai, once the most promising and admired young man of his age group. It had been even worse after he went through *eunoto* and became a junior elder but still showed no interest in getting married and settling down, as custom and his elders decreed. Joseph had his reasons. He simply was not ready for the sedate life. He was accustomed, no, addicted, to the excitement of life on safari; going into the bush with Glenton; spending a week or two back in the warrior's *manyatta*, drinking and fornicating with his *moran* brothers while Glenton was in Nairobi getting the next client outfitted; then heading back out into the bush.

And then there was the marriage part of it. The girl to whom he was betrothed was not someone he liked any longer, but his family had given her family many gifts over the years to keep the bargain alive, and if he backed out now, his family would lose more than just its reputation. Joseph had liked the girl well enough when she was younger, but she'd grown quarrelsome and uncomely since her circumcision. In Joseph's mind she was already the *endingi,* the "least favored wife," even though he hadn't even the one yet. When Glenton arrived at the kraal to lure him away yet again, Joseph had been grudgingly gathering a dowry. He had already collected two cows, a steer, a ram, a ewe, several jars of honey, some tobacco, and two sheepskins. The very idea of giving all that away for one loud and homely woman had put him in a belligerent frame of mind when it came to members of the opposite sex.

"We can't kill her?" he asked again, just to be sure.

"No, I'm afraid not," said Adrian.

Joseph pouted for a moment, then asked: "Do you know the story of Oltatuani?"

When Adrian said that he didn't, Joseph told the legend.

Oltatuani was a giant who lived in a cave near Naroosura and stole livestock from the Masai, killing anyone who got in his way. The Masai, who usually feared no man, were terrified of him. But the situation became so intolerable that they had to do something, and so they came up with a plan to eliminate him. They would find the loveliest girl in Maasailand and put her into Oltatuani's cave when he was out stealing cows. When he returned and found her, they figured, he would either kill her or keep her. If he killed her, the girl's father would be compensated with livestock. If he kept her, they would devise a way to use her presence to end the giant's reign of terror.

The young woman they chose was willing to risk her life for the good of all, and her father agreed, so the *moran* put her in the cave and hid in the bushes to await developments.

When Oltatuani returned from his pillaging and spied the beautiful girl, he bellowed and lunged at her. But she merely smiled and pretended to be unafraid. Disarmed, the giant slew one of his stolen oxen, roasted some meat, and tossed a piece to the girl as though she were a dog. They did not speak that first night, and the next morning Oltatuani left the cave and went away. But before he went, he gave the girl another piece of meat and this time he handed it to her. When the giant was out of sight, the *moran* rushed into the cave to find out what had happened. Not much, the girl told them. The warriors told her to try talking to the giant, and went back to the bushes.

In the morning, when the giant returned, he spoke first. "Where did you come from?" he asked in a booming voice. "I am a Masai," the girl said. When the giant asked her why she had come, the girl replied: "I have heard about your strength and prowess. I also heard that you were handsome and brave and that is why I came here to be your wife." Oltatuani fell in love right then and there.

After that, Oltatuani rarely left the cave, not even to find food. One morning, when Oltatuani was fast asleep after a long night of lovemaking, the girl carried his weapons out of the cave and called the *moran,* who killed the defenseless giant easily.

When Joseph finished the story, Glenton said, "Subtle, Joseph. Very fucking subtle." Joseph just shrugged.

"Tembo's let the fire die," Glenton said, picking up a blanket and moving toward the door. "Get it going, will you? I'll be back shortly."

He poked his head into the middle cave just long enough to tell Tembo he would be having company for the night, then went on to the next cave. He paused outside the entrance and called softly: "Hullo. Miss Lewis? I'm back. Are you decent?"

"Yes."

He pushed through the blanket, stepped inside and found himself looking at an inverted pink valentine, the prettiest bare backside he'd ever seen. Robbie Lewis, completely naked, was bending over to step into his one and only pair of clean trousers. "Crikey! You're starkers!"

"You asked if I was decent, not if I was dressed."

"Haven't you any modesty at all?" He tore his eyes away and turned his back. "What are you, one of those hippies?"

"Hippies? Hippies have been extinct for years." She had to laugh. When hippies were poking flowers in the barrels of National Guard rifles, she was dating a man who never left the house without a gun, a wise guy from the neighborhood who collected vigorish for the loan sharks. "Besides, it's only a body," Robbie said, "only my outside. I mean, you cut animals open and look at their insides. Now that's dirty."

"Are you *dressed* yet?" Adrian asked over his shoulder.

"Yeah, it's safe to look now," she said. "You won't turn to stone."

Adrian turned around cautiously. She was just fastening the top button of his shirt. "What was that mark on your, ah, your . . ." He stopped and flushed.

"A tattoo," Robbie said, grinning and patting her left buttock. "A stiletto."

"A stiletto?"

She nodded. "A gang symbol. A folly of youth."

Adrian opened his mouth to say something, but she shook her head and said, "Don't ask. It'll only confuse you." Then she touched the zipper of her trousers and taunted: "But you can have a closer look if you like."

This time, Adrian was more angry than flustered. "Yes, I think I would, actually," he said, calling her bluff. "Purely out of cultural curiosity, of course."

"Of course," Robbie said seriously. Keeping her eyes on his, she undid her trousers and slipped them down just enough to expose the one cheek.

Adrian took a deep breath and lowered his eyes. It was a dagger all right, between two and three inches long and quite elaborately detailed. "Amazing," he blurted.

"Thank you," Robbie said, hitching up her trousers. "Or were you talking about the tattoo?"

Adrian couldn't help it. He laughed. "Christ," he said, shaking his head. "I've never known anyone like you before."

"No, I bet not," she said, still looking into his eyes.

"I, um, brought you an extra blanket," he said quickly, handing it to her. She took it and, without taking her eyes off his, tossed it into a corner.

Squirming under her gaze, Adrian cleared his throat and said, "May I ask you a question, Miss Lewis?"

"Fire away."

"It's rather personal."

"No sweat."

Adrian took another deep breath, let it out slowly, and asked, "Is there something going on between us?"

She nodded gravely and said, "Yes, I'm afraid there is."

He seemed more relieved than anything else. "That's what I thought," he said, "but I wanted to be certain."

Robbie stepped close to him, put one hand on the back of his neck, pulled his face down to hers, and kissed him, slowly and deeply, using her tongue. After a minute, she leaned back and asked, "All straight in your mind now?"

"Yes," Adrian said hoarsely, trying to catch his breath. "Yes, I think so."

"Good. Now don't you think it's time you stopped calling me Miss Lewis?"

Adrian was awakened at dawn when someone skipped a small stone into the cave. It caromed off a wall and hit him on the arm. Naked and shivering, he went to the doorway, pulled back the blanket and saw Joseph standing there in the rain.

Joseph was wearing a Villanova University athletic shirt this morning. He had dozens of the things. One of the hunting clients, a man who manufactured college apparel, had promised to send the gun-bearer a sample of his product line. That had been four years ago. Joseph had gotten a new item in the post every couple of months since. The look on Joseph's face was a mixture of amusement and disapproval. "Did you sleep well, my brother?" he said sardonically. Before Adrian could reply, he added, "Tembo is preparing some food for us," then turned and walked off.

Adrian moved to the fire, stirred the ashes until he got a flame and threw on an armful of kindling. He filled the tea kettle with water and set it on the coals. Then he stood over Robbie Lewis for a moment and watched her sleep, feeling both tender and carnal. She had kicked off most of her blanket and her flank was fully exposed, from her painted toenails to the rounded swell of her hip. The dagger tattoo, done in blue ink with a delicate red outline, looked like a birthmark. Glenton studied it, then got down on his knees and kissed it.

"What are you up to down there?" Robbie asked drowsily.

"Looking at *your* etchings," he said.

"Aren't you freezing?" she asked, sliding her leg back under the blanket.

"Yes." Adrian crawled under the blanket with her and she straightened out to fit herself against him. Her hand, as hot as a baker's glove, came up and cupped his testicles. He grew hard instantly.

"Oh no you don't," she said, trapping his penis between her thighs.

"Why not?"

Robbie laughed and said, "I'm too tired. And I'm starving."

"They're serving food two doors down," Adrian said, "but I'd rather breakfast in this morning." He nuzzled her breasts and began to nibble on a nipple erect from the cold.

Robbie pushed him away and got to her feet, dragging the blanket with her and leaving him exposed on the bed of leaves and grass. Wearing the blanket like a toga, she squatted down by the fire and checked the clothes she'd taken off the night before. Finding them dry, she dropped the blanket and started to dress. "You're lovely," Glenton said, watching her slip on bright red panties.

"Thank you, *bwana*. You're kinda cute yourself."

"I love you, Robbie."

Robbie shook her head. "You don't have to say that," she explained patiently. "You're supposed to say that you'll call me next week. I'm supposed to pretend I believe you."

"I want to marry you."

Robbie, struggling to squeeze into her tight jeans, was so surprised she nearly toppled over. "Marry me? Jesus! This is 1978, not 1958. You don't have to propose to a woman just because you've slept with her once. Don't you know anything?"

"Yes," Adrian said quietly. "I know that I love you and that I want to marry you."

"You're serious, aren't you?" she said in amazement.

"Quite serious," he said stiffly. "And stop treating me like some virgin schoolboy. Will you marry me or won't you?"

Robbie took her time answering. "No."

"We would have to live here in Kenya, of course," Adrian said. "I know I'm being rather arbitrary, but I don't think I could live anywhere but Africa. But we can always pop over to the States every so often. I've never been to America. Should be fascinating."

"I said no."

"And we should probably have a baby right off, don't you think? After all, neither of us is getting any younger and it wouldn't do to put it off for too long."

"Adrian! Read my lips. No. *Hapana*. No way, José."

"You're Catholic, right? We'll have the wedding at Saint Paul's and the reception at the Kentmere Club in Limuru. It's a gorgeous spot and the owner's a friend of mine. So. What do you think?"

"I think I must have been pretty good last night."

"You were bloody marvelous," Adrian said, giving a wicked grin. "And if I may say so without sounding boastful, so was I."

Robbie smiled slowly and said, "You certainly were."

"You'll marry me then."

"No."

"Why not?"

"I tried marriage once. It didn't work out too well. I don't think I'm cut out for it."

"It's rather like the heart shot on an elephant," Adrian said. "Practice makes perfect."

"Yeah, but if you miss you get stomped flat."

"No one is going to be trampled."

"Sez you."

"What could be more simple?" Adrian asked earnestly. "We love each other. I'll admit I'm old-fashioned, and probably a bit behind the times, but I believe that when two people love each other they should be married."

"Hey, you're the one who thinks he's in love, not me."

"If you're not, then you're the best bloody actress this side of London's West End."

"That was lust you saw last night. There's a difference between love and lust."

"Imperceptible at best."

She laughed, still shaking her head. "We'd fight all the time. You're the original male chauvinist pig and I'm . . . well, I'm a little pushy."

"You're a lot pushy," he said, correcting her politely. "But there's nothing wrong with having a dash of spice in a relationship. Love *piri-piri*."

Robbie laughed again. "You're impossible."

"I know, but you'll marry me anyway."

"No, I won't."

"But you'll think about it."

She sighed. "Okay, okay, I'll think about it."

"Super! It's done!" Adrian jumped up and began putting on his clothes.

"Nothing is *done*," Robbie said quickly. "I just said I'd think about it." She was going to say more, insert a few more qualifiers, but the tea kettle was whistling.

"Curry time . . . let's go eat," Glenton said brightly. "We can take our tea with us." He poured out two cups of hot water, dropped a packet of Twinings' Earl Grey into each cup, and handed Robbie one.

Tembo was busy at the fire when they came in. The smell of frying fat filled the cave. The others sat round the fire in a circle. Pythias and Ekali, exchanging a knowing glance, smiled shyly at Robbie, and shifted to make room for her and Adrian. Joseph didn't budge.

Robbie looked into Tembo's skillet, then caught Adrian's eye and put a silent question. "Elephant steak," he answered. "Quite good, actually."

"Yeah, I'll bet," Robbie said. "Got anything else? Eggs Benedict maybe?"

Adrian laughed. "I have some Weetabix. But no cream."

"Get it," she said. "I'll eat it dry." Adrian rummaged in his knapsack, found the cereal, and handed it to her. She ate straight from the box.

The first elephant steak was ready. Tembo picked it out of the skillet with a pointed stick and offered it to Adrian, who, wishing to make peace, said, "Give it to Joseph." Tembo shrugged and passed it over. Joseph took it with a thumb and a forefinger and blew on it to cool it. He was about to bite into it when he stopped, jerked his head at Robbie and asked Adrian in Masai: "Is she circumcised?"

"No."

Joseph grunted and began gnawing on his steak. He used both hands, eating like a wild dog, the grease running down his chin. When he was finished, he got up and left the cave.

"What's Joseph's problem?" Robbie asked.

Adrian shrugged and didn't answer.

"He was talking about me, wasn't he? What did he say?"

"He asked me if you were circumcised."

"What!"

"It's the law of the *moran*. A warrior can't eat meat in front of a circumcised woman."

"I thought you said he wasn't a *moran* anymore."

"He's not," Adrian said, "but he still thinks he is."

"That's no excuse. How would he like it if I asked him if he was circumcised?"

"He'd undoubtedly insist on showing you that he is."

Robbie was quiet a moment, then said, "I thought female circumcision was against the law these days."

"Kenya law, perhaps. Not Masai law."

"I didn't know there was a difference."

"There isn't . . . officially," Adrian said. "But the truth is that the concept of *the nation,* as defined and imposed by the colonial powers, has yet to take hold with most Africans. Their allegiance is to self, family, and tribe, in that order. And there it stops. The Masai are worse than most."

"Any of your guys *not* know English?" Robbie asked.

"Ekali doesn't. Why?"

"I want to test your theory," she said. "He won't know what we've been talking about. Ask him if he's Kenyan."

Adrian put the question to Ekali in Swahili, got a reply, and turned back to Robbie. "He says he's a Turkana."

Robbie turned to Pythias and Tembo and asked, "How about you two? Are you Kenyan?"

"I am Dorobo, missy," Pythias said with a shrug.

"I am a Liangulu," said Tembo.

Robbie said, "Then tell me, Pythias. Who *is* a Kenyan?"

"The Kikuyu, I guess, missy. They rule the country."

"There, you see?" Adrian said triumphantly. "I rest my case."

"So what does that make you?" Robbie asked him.

"I've never really thought about it," Adrian said. "But now that you ask, perhaps we Kenya-born *mzungus* are the true Kenyans. Africans have their tribe. Asians have Mother India. But we whites have no other affiliation to muddy the issue."

"Sure you do," Robbie said. "Most of you are Brits."

"I am not a bloody Brit," he said, bridling. "I've never even seen England. I'm a Kenyan."

"No, they're Kenyans," Robbie said, nodding at Pythias, Ekali, and Tembo. "You are a *white* Kenyan. A relatively small and insular community, sustained by its own legend."

"What in the world is that supposed to mean?"

"Nothing," Robbie said, dropping the subject. She turned the Weetabix box upside down to show him it was empty. "I seem to be finished. Are you ready to go back to Stephen's?"

Adrian grew instantly serious. "I told you, Robbie, I'm not going back with you."

"I know you did, but that was before . . ." She paused when she saw that Tembo and Pythias were hanging on every word. "I thought things were different now."

"Things are different now," Adrian said. "Everything but that."

"Can we discuss this outside?" she said.

"It's pissing outside, and there is nothing to discuss," he said. Then, catching her murderous look, he quickly added, "But we can go outside if you like."

They went outside and stood in the rain. The fog was so thick they could barely see each other at a distance of four feet and they were soaked through in a matter of seconds. He was wearing his bush hat, which afforded him some protection, but Robbie's hair was plastered flat against her head. "This is ridiculous," he said. "Let's get inside."

"Not until we come to an agreement," she said, the rain streaming down her face. "For the last time . . . are you coming back with me or not?"

"For the last time . . . no."

"Come with me and I'll marry you. If you don't, you will never see me again."

"Oh, for God's sake," he said in exasperation. "You don't mean that."

"The hell I don't. You should know me well enough by now to know I never, ever bluff."

"Don't do this to me, Robbie. I can't quit now."

"You mean you won't."

"Can't. Won't. What's the difference?"

"It makes a difference to me. What's your answer?"

Glenton looked at her with anguish. "I love you."

"True or false, that's beside the point. Yes or no?"

He shook his head slowly. "I'm sorry. I can't."

"Shit," Robbie said. Then she smiled brightly at him and said, "Okay. Let's get out of the rain. It's a goddamn frog strangler."

Adrian smiled back tentatively, confused by her sudden mood change. "You were bluffing?"

"You win some, you lose some, and a few get rained out," Robbie said with a shrug. "The only thing I can't stand is a tie." She held out her hand to him. Adrian took it and, hand in hand, they made a dash for their cave.

29

The explosion not only woke Peter Odongo, it rocked him, nearly bouncing him out of bed. "Mary Mother of God, what was that?" he said. He tossed back the bedcovers and padded naked to the window. The night sky was bright with an orange-yellow light that seeped into the bedroom and flickered on the walls and ceiling, chasing away the corner shadows.

"What is it, Peter?" Millicent Ogara asked sleepily. She was sitting up in the bed with the blanket bunched around her waist. Her breasts gleamed like polished ebony in the shaky light.

"A fire," Peter said. "Here in the estate."

"Are we in danger? Should we get out?"

"No, I don't think so."

"Then come back to bed," she said, sinking back into her pillow. But Odongo was already pulling on his trousers. "I'm going to have a look," he said. "It seems to be near my block of flats. And there may be people who need help. I may not be on duty, but I'm still a policeman."

"And I'm a nurse!" Millicent suddenly exclaimed, hopping out of bed and grabbing up her clothing. "My God! Where is my head? What was I thinking of?"

They dressed quickly and rushed downstairs. All over the housing estate, people in night clothes were stumbling out of their flats and into the street, hurrying toward the heart of the fire—some, like Peter and Millie, to see if they could help; others merely curious, not wanting to miss anything.

The closer they got, the more alarmed Peter became, but it was Millie who spoke first. "Peter! It is your building!" Everything above the second floor was completely engulfed in flames. People stood in the windows, waving frantically and shrieking for help.

Peter and Millie arrived just in time to witness a sight neither would soon forget: a young woman, a baby in her arms, jumping from a top-floor window. Halfway down, she let go of the infant and tried to save herself, flailing her arms as if she were a bird that might suddenly take flight. She screamed all the way down to the ground. The baby landed a full second later, never having uttered a cry.

Many of the onlookers screamed and turned away, averting their eyes. But not Millicent Ogara. She began running toward the crumpled figures. Peter did not go with her; there was no chance that either the woman or her child could have survived the fall. Instead, he looked about for someone who could tell him what was going on. There was no one from the fire station at the scene yet, and still no ambulance, but he spotted two uniformed policemen with truncheons in their hands, trying to keep the swelling crowd away from the burning building. He grabbed one, a corporal, and showed his identification. "What happened here, Constable?"

The corporal saluted by touching the tip of his stick to his cap brim and said, "We don't know, sir. We think maybe it was a bomb." He was visibly nervous at having an inspector on hand, but even more relieved that he was no longer in charge.

"A bomb?" Odongo said. "What makes you think that?"

"A number of people say they heard a big explosion," the corporal said, "and it's the only way to explain how the fire got out of hand so quickly."

Watching the building burn, Peter was inclined to agree. "Do you know where the bomb was planted?"

"I think so, sir." The constable pointed up. "Do you see the corner flat on the third floor? The one with the big hole in the outside wall? I think it was there." Odongo nodded. It was the first thing he had noticed.

An ambulance, flashers turning and siren howling, pulled into the street from the Kibera Station Road. There was still no sign of the fire brigade, but it no longer mattered. There was nothing the firefighters could do about it now. The blaze couldn't be stopped, or even slowed. It would rage until it burned itself out, until there was nothing left to feed it.

"We don't know who lives in the flat," the corporal was saying, "but we'll launch an inquiry as soon as things quiet down."

"No need for that, Corporal," Odongo said quietly. "It's my flat. I live there."

At Jogoo House next morning, Peter received a barrage of telephone calls from friends and acquaintances throughout the Kenya Police. His friends wanted to be sure he was all right; the acquaintances wanted to pass on the grisly statistics and fish for gossip. Was he aware that the current casualty count stood at fourteen dead and twenty-seven injured, a majority of them women and children, with six people still missing? Had it been a tragic accident? The kitchen stove perhaps? A faulty propane bottle? No! Really? A bomb? But why? Who would want to harm him?

The Assistant Minister for Wildlife was one of the first to ring. "A terrible, terrible thing to happen," he said. "Do you have any idea who might be behind it?"

"No, sir, I don't."

"Just terrible," the Assistant Minister repeated. There was a pause on the line, then he said, "I tried to reach you at the Central Police Station. They told me you hadn't moved back yet."

"Uh, no, sir, I haven't. I was planning to do that this morning in fact."

"Hmm. Yes. Well. I was a little surprised, that's all."

"I will be out of this office and out of Jogoo House by the end of the day."

"By close of play today will be fine. I can understand how you might have other things on your mind right now."

"Yes, sir. A few."

"So, what do you make of last night?"

"I don't know what to make of it, sir."

"No suspects?"

"No, sir. Not yet."

"No clues at all?"

"No, sir. There wasn't much left besides ashes."

"Well, I'm sure you'll catch whoever is responsible for this outrage. Yes. Well. *Kwaheri,* Inspector."

"*Kwaheri,* Minister."

"Oh, one more thing, Inspector. You won't forget to turn over the ministry's car, will you? You can leave the key with the garage supervisor."

"Yes, sir, I'll be sure to do that."

Peter's last call was from Superintendent Jaynes at the Central Police Station. "You've put the hangman's rope round a number of necks during your career," Superintendent Jaynes noted matter-of-factly, "and all of those men have relatives and friends who might like to see you dead."

"Yes, sir, I know."

"We're doing everything we can on this end."

"Yes, sir, I know that, too."

"It's occurred to me that you might want to head up this one yourself," Jaynes said. "The senior superintendent marked you down for a desk job when he heard you were coming back to us, but I think I might be able to persuade him to give you a go at it . . . given the circumstances and all."

"I'd like that, sir."

Chuckling, Jaynes added: "I realize it's only attempted murder and that you won't have a *corpus delicti* to work with, but I thought you wouldn't mind in this particular instance."

"It's plain murder, not attempted murder," Odongo said coolly, "and I already have at least fourteen bodies to work with."

"You're quite right, of course . . . how stupid of me," the superintendent said quickly. "I'm sorry, Inspector. I didn't mean to make light of a serious situation." He coughed, then went ahead. "I'd been planning to ring you this morning even before I heard about last night."

"What about, sir?"

"That Gichinga chap of yours."

"Oh? What has he done now?"

"The man has a habit of popping up in my daily log. But this will be the last time, I dare say. He's gone and gotten himself murdered."

"What!" Odongo exclaimed, almost dropping the receiver. "How? When?"

"Half past two this morning. In Mathare Valley. He was shot to death."

"Who did it?"

"I don't know. We don't know much of anything just yet; I'm still waiting for the paperwork—ballistics and medical examiner and the like. We do know there was a woman with him. She was killed too. Wrong place at the wrong time, no doubt."

"What was her name?" Peter asked.

"Her name? Hmm, let's see." Odongo could hear a rustling of paper in the background. "Ah, yes, here it is. Kyuna. Mary Kyuna. Why? Do you know her?"

"I think I met her once," Peter said.

"I realize that none of this is your affair any longer, officially speaking, but I thought you would be interested."

"Yes, sir. I am. Thank you."

"So, when can we expect to see you back in the station?" Jaynes asked. "We'll need a statement from you about last night, and I'm anxious to put you back to work."

"I . . . I still have some tidying up to do here," Peter said quickly. "Perhaps this evening, or first thing tomorrow morning."

"Fine," Jaynes said. "That gives me time to work on the senior superintendent. I want you in on this bombing case. I would want you on it even if you weren't directly involved."

"Yes, sir. Thank you, sir. Goodbye, sir." Peter rang off and was out the door, making for the car park. The Ministry of Tourism and Wildlife was going to have to wait a while longer to get its Suzuki back.

It took Peter more than an hour to find the house. The alleys of Mathare Valley all looked alike to him. Without a guide, he was like a rat in a maze. In the end, he found it only by giving up his anonymity and asking. Everyone seemed to know the house where James Gichinga had been murdered.

The front door was gone, but Peter didn't know if it was from this morning's incident or the result of his own entry the week before. A small crowd was milling about outside the shack and people were wandering in and out freely. Odongo shooed them away, brandishing his police card and shouting at them, calling them *tais,* vultures.

What few belongings there had been were gone—looted. The only thing left was the sleeping pallet against the wall, the one the woman had been lying on when Peter first saw her. The pallet was covered with bloodstains, and the wall behind it was stitched with bullet holes that let in fingerlike beams of sunlight.

Peter could only guess what had transpired in this room, but he knew he couldn't be off by much. They had found James Gichinga in bed with his favorite whore—the "best fuck in Kenya"—and had not bothered to make a distinction, hosing down that whole side of the room with automatic weapons fire.

He wasn't sure just who *they* were, but he knew they were connected to the poaching ring. Peter couldn't help feeling a nagging sense of guilt, and no matter how he rationalized, it refused to go away. Gichinga's comrades in crime had tried to get rid of him once before, by putting him in the asylum when a nosy Luo policeman began closing in on him. Peter had known that when he turned Gichinga loose and sent him back to work. Now the man with the sorrowful, scarred face was dead, and an innocent woman along with him.

Peter took another moment to examine the room, then went outside and walked around the shack, studying the ground. But the crime scene team had scooped up everything worth finding. He was back inside the house, staring at the bloodstains and bullet holes and wondering why he'd bothered to come, when he was suddenly aware that he was no longer alone. He turned and saw a boy with no hair standing in the open doorway, watching him with large dark eyes.

"*Jambo, toto,*" Peter said softly. "I'm sorry about your mother."

The boy just continued staring, and after a long moment of silence, Odongo said, "I'm going to catch the men who did it. I promise. I'm going to see that they hang."

"It was his fault that she died," the boy said at last, pointing a steady finger at the bloodstained bed. "Can you hang a dead man?"

"No. But I can hang the men who shot them." When the boy didn't respond, Peter asked, "Where were you when they came?"

"Out," said the boy. "She always sent me out when he was here. If I had been here, I could have helped her."

"No, *toto,*" Peter said. "If you had been here, you would be dead, too." When the boy didn't respond, Peter asked, "What will you do now? Do you have someone you can stay with?"

"I don't need anybody. I can take care of myself."

"You're too young to be alone," Peter said. "Where does your mother come from? Your village? Is there family you can go to? I'll take you to them."

The boy was shaking his head. "I was born here. This is my village. And I told you . . . I can look after myself."

"I'll take you to the nuns," Peter said. "They will take care—"

The boy interrupted him before he could complete the sentence: "I have something to sell you—something you will want. Give me two hundred shillings."

"Two hundred shillings!"

"Okay. One hundred."

"What is it you're selling?" Odongo asked.

The boy put out a filthy hand, palm up, and said: "One hundred shillings."

Odongo took out his purse, fished out a hundred-shilling-note and slapped it into the boy's waiting hand. The boy looked it over carefully, studying Mzee's likeness on the front, making sure it wasn't counterfeit. Apparently satisfied, he stuck it down the front of his ragged trousers, crossed to a corner of the room, and began to pry up one of the floorboards.

When the board was loose, the boy stuck an arm into the hole and came out with a small rectangular object wrapped in a sheet of plastic. He presented it to Odongo with an air of great importance, as though it were the Dead Sea Scrolls, or at least the Magna Carta.

"What's this?" Peter asked.

"I don't know," said the boy. "I saw him put it in there when he thought no one was watching."

Peter peeled off the wrapping and found himself holding a leather-bound notebook with the initials *J.G.* embossed on the cover in 14-karat gold leaf. Thumbing through it quickly, he was disappointed to see that it contained only two short entries—one on the first page and one on the second. The rest of the pages were clean.

Odongo flipped back to the first page and saw a name and address entered in a neat, almost flowery hand. An *x* had been marked through it. The name—Simon Muraya—was not one he recognized at first. Then he remembered. Simon Muraya was the *matatu* driver killed in Glenton's ambush, the man who carried Fisi's product to Nairobi and turned it over to Gichinga. On the next page was the name of the man to whom it was given in turn—Ambrose Nyeusi. Under Nyeusi's name was the simple notation "Customs, Embakasi Airport," and a telephone number. That, too, had been crossed out and beneath it, in different colored ink, was another entry: "Mr. Kaggia. Jacaranda Hotel. Do not telephone."

Ambrose Nyeusi had been an invisible man ever since the superintendent in Mombasa cut him loose. He had not reported back to work at the Nairobi airport, and when Odongo checked with Customs he was informed that Nyeusi had been granted an emergency leave of absence; something about his dying mother. Nyeusi had gone to ground, just as Peter had feared he would.

Odongo put the notebook in his pocket, took out another hundred-shilling note and gave it to the boy. "You were right the first time, *toto*," he said. "It's worth two hundred." The boy didn't argue. The note joined its mate, disappearing down the front of the boy's trousers.

"Now what are we going to do with you?" Peter asked with a smile. "Will you let me take you to the sisters?"

The boy backed away from Odongo until he was standing in the doorway. "You're not so bad," he said. "For a policeman." Then he turned and was gone.

The Jacaranda Hotel was a low rambling building just off Chiromo Road, just past the Westlands roundabout. It was not one of Nairobi's premiere hotels, but neither was it one of those hostels for rats like the places in River Road.

The old Motel Agip, renamed the Jacaranda when it changed hands in 1974, had been built by Agip, the Italian oil company, but the only remaining Italian influence was the Pizza Garden, an outdoor restaurant with a brick pizza oven and a scattering of tables set in miniature *bandas* with grass peaked roofs. The patrons were mostly African, but there were usually some Asians and a few adventuresome and budget-minded Americans and Europeans. Peter went through the Pizza Garden, up the stairs and through a veranda bar, and asked the Kikuyu desk clerk for Mr. Kaggia's room number.

"Mr. Kaggia doesn't want to be disturbed," the man said.

"Government business," Odongo said.

"He's sleeping," said the clerk, unimpressed.

Peter pulled out his police credential, stuck it in the man's face and barked, "You'll be sleeping in a fucking cell tonight if I don't have that number in the next two seconds."

"Two-twenty-three. First floor. Up the stairs and to the right."

"That's better," Peter said. "This Kaggia . . . is he a thin fellow with a beard . . . wears spectacles?"

"That's him."

"Is he really sleeping?"

"I don't know, *bwana*," the clerk said, the very soul of cooperation. "That is what he paid me to say if anyone asked for him. He hasn't been out of his room for days. I have his meals sent up to him."

"Is there a telephone in his room?"

"Yes, *bwana*."

"Warn him and you'll wish you'd never been born," Peter said. He walked away, making for the stairs, then turned and came back. "Better yet, do you have another key to the room?"

"The housekeeper has one."

"Where is she?"

The clerk looked at his watch and said, "She should be just starting on that wing now."

"Let's go find her."

Together, they went upstairs and found the chambermaid, who was cleaning 227, two doors down from 223. The clerk told her who Odongo was and which guest he was interested in.

"Where does he go when you clean his room?" Odongo asked the girl.

"He stays in the room," she said.

"Does he keep the door locked? Is it locked now?"

"Yes, sir. Always."

"Do you use the master key to let yourself in?"

"No, sir. He keeps the latch bolt engaged. What happens is . . . I knock, he asks who it is, I tell him it's me and then he lets me in."

"All right," Peter said, reaching around under his tunic and taking out his service revolver, "let's do it like that."

The girl gaped at the gun, her eyes as round as cricket balls. "No, sir, I couldn't! I'd be too frightened to speak."

"You'll do fine," Peter said gently. "Just say what you always say, then walk away." He looked at the desk clerk and added, "You can escort her."

They got into position by the door to room 223 and Peter gave the maid an encouraging wink and a nod. She looked as if she were about to be sick, but she took a deep breath, rapped on the door twice, and called out in a perfectly cheery voice: "It's me, Mr. Kaggia. Time to clean your room." Then she spun about and started for the stairwell at a brisk walk. The desk clerk almost had to run to catch up.

When the door swung open, Odongo stuck his pistol under the man's chin and chirped, "It's me, Mr. Nyeusi. Time to go to prison."

"How did you find me? They said you'd never find me. It doesn't matter. No! Not one bit! You couldn't hold me before and you won't be able to hold me now. I'm okay. It's you who are in trouble. I don't believe you know who you're dealing with." Ambrose Nyeusi sat on the divan with his feet propped on a low table, alternately bemoaning his fate and showing a brave front.

"That's why I'm here," Peter said. "You're going to tell me who I'm dealing with."

"If you believe that, then you are as stupid as you are reckless," Nyeusi said, taking off his spectacles and wiping them with the hem of his dressing gown.

"As the man responsible for getting the stuff out of the country, I think you know who most of the players are," Peter said, ignoring the insult. "As soon as you tell me, you'll be put in a nice, safe prison cell."

"I don't know what you're talking about." Nyeusi put his glasses back on and glared at Odongo. "I have nothing to tell you. And I will not be going to prison, I assure you. You can arrest me but you can't hold me. I'll be freed in an hour."

"Oh?" Odongo said, a note of surprise in his voice. "I'd have thought you would want to be in police custody. That you would insist on it."

Nyeusi looked at Odongo as if he had lost his mind. "Now why would I do that?"

Instead of answering the question, Peter said, "Here is my offer. Tell me everything you know and I'll take you into custody. If not, I'm walking out of here right now."

Nyeusi was shaking his head, as if maybe he was the one who was crazy. He couldn't believe he had heard Odongo right. "You act as if you're doing me a favor by arresting me," he said scornfully.

"Oh, I am," Peter said. "Because if you aren't in police custody, and soon, you're a dead man."

"You're talking shit."

"Am I? Have you heard about your friend James Gichinga?"

"What abou . . . I don't know any James Gichinga."

"He was shot to death in his bed early this morning. It happened only a couple of hours after someone set off a bomb outside the door to my flat in Jamhuri Estate."

Nyeusi didn't say anything, so Peter went on: "They're rolling up the loose ends. They're going to murder everyone who knows enough to hurt them. I'm rather surprised to find you still alive . . . that they didn't get you last night."

"You're lying," Nyeusi said.

"You don't have to take my word for it," Peter said. "It was too late for the morning editions, but it should have made the afternoon papers." He looked at his watch. "Which were on the street half an hour ago."

"You're lying," Nyeusi repeated.

Peter pointed to the telephone. "Ring someone," he said. "Someone you trust."

"I'm going to call your bluff," Nyeusi said, rising and going to the telephone. He picked up the receiver and dialed the hotel switchboard.

When the girl came on, he said, "Just a moment, please," put a hand over the mouthpiece, and turned to Odongo. "I'd like some privacy, if you don't mind."

"I'll wait out here," Odongo said, sliding back the door to the small balcony. "But be careful who you contact. I wouldn't let my comrades know I suspected anything if I were you."

Peter tried to listen through the glass door, but all he could hear was a low murmur. He saw Nyeusi put down the telephone, plop back onto the divan, and put his head in his hands. The Customs man lifted his head quickly when Peter came back into the room. His face wore a haggard look. "It doesn't mean a thing," he said.

"They wanted to know which station I'd be taking you to, didn't they?" Peter said softly.

Nyeusi didn't answer.

"When you said you didn't know, they told you to keep me here, didn't they?" Peter said.

Nyeusi didn't answer.

"They wanted to know if the door would be locked, didn't they?" Peter said.

Neyusi didn't answer.

"Don't you see what's happening?" Peter said. "They want to get to you before you're inside. And me too. They can plug up all the remaining holes with a single burst of machine gun fire. Quick and neat." When Nyeusi still didn't say anything, Odongo lied, "You should see Gichinga's body. They cut him in half."

After another long silence, Ambrose Nyeusi finally said: "I'm forty-seven years old. I don't want to die in prison. Can we come to an arrangement?"

"I can't make promises," Peter said, "but any assistance you give the Kenya Police will be taken into consideration by the magistrate. Regarding your sentence, I think I can safely say that the degree of severity would depend on the degree to which you cooperate."

"Let's get out of here," said Nyeusi.

30

With what he saw as a fitting touch, Odongo finished his interrogation of Ambrose Nyeusi in the middle of Nairobi Game Park. It was a sound move as well. No one would think to look for them there, and an approaching vehicle could be seen from a long way off. It was merely a coincidence, albeit an ironic one, that he parked within view of a browsing rhinoceros. The rhinoceros was the one the Game Department had named Amboseli, and it was famous in conservation circles for having the longest front horn of any known rhino in the world.

Once Ambrose Nyeusi started talking, revelations spilled out of him like water over a weir. He talked nonstop for two hours, giving dates, tonnage figures, air and sea routes, and transshipment points for Europe, Asia, and the Middle East.

But the names were what dropped Peter's jaw. He couldn't believe his ears. The Patel brothers came as no big surprise; he'd already concluded that Old Delhi Trading was a front for smuggling. Nor did the name of a certain ranger corporal. But others hit Peter like lightning bolts. The warden of Aberdare National Park. An assistant commissioner of the Kenya Police. The Nairobi office manager for a major European airline. The list, salted with the names of well-known KANU party members, went on and on, a veritable *Who's Who* of the Wabenzi.

Odongo was stunned and sickened. The warden was a public servant charged with the safekeeping of the nation's wildlife and a man with whom Odongo had worked closely. He was the one who had recommended Charles Ndirangu for Glenton's team. The assistant commissioner of police was a much-decorated hero, someone the young Constable Odongo had idolized. Was he the officer James Gichinga had seen as he was being packed off to the insane asylum? Was he the one who had rung up the super in Mombasa to secure Ambrose Nyeusi's release? The mystery caller from Nairobi who "ranks a police superintendent, the same way a superintendent ranks an inspector"?

But there were two other names on the list that shocked Peter even more. One was Dada. Ambrose Nyeusi was too low in the order to know for a fact that she was the ultimate power behind The Hyena's poaching ring, but he knew that there was a State House connection of some kind because he'd heard the Patels refer to it often enough. And if it was true, then so was the persistent rumor that the "Sister of the Nation" had used her high position to enrich both herself and her once-impoverished family.

The other name—the one that left Peter feeling as if he'd been kicked in the stomach—was that of the Assistant Minister for Wildlife. Peter did not want to believe it. Not because he admired or respected the minister—there was no love lost there—but because it meant that the "brilliant" Inspector Odongo was not so bright after all. But Nyeusi had no apparent reason to lie. And it did explain some things.

While feeling like a fool, Peter was not fool enough to think that he could move against such powerful people on the confession of a lowly Customs official. Who would take the word of a confessed smuggler over that of some of the country's most prominent men? It would be the International Casino case all over again. Besides, Nyeusi would never repeat his testimony in a court of law. Peter had promised the Customs man police protection, but he knew he couldn't keep him locked up They could get him out with a simple phone call, the way they had in Mombasa. And if they didn't kill him outright, they would silence him by other means. With money, or women, or a beach house like the one in Nyali. Important men didn't go to jail unless more important men wanted them there. But if he could not get the Wabenzis, he could at least go after lesser game.

Odongo rang up the prison from the park's main gate and asked them to send a wagon. All he told them was that he had a thief he wanted locked up for a day or two while he worked up a charge sheet. The van arrived and the transfer was made at the petrol station just beyond the park's entrance. When he had seen Ambrose Nyeusi safely away, Peter topped the Suzuki's tank and drove to the highlands.

The day after his arrest, during the morning head count, Ambrose Nyeusi was found hanged in his cell at the sprawling Nairobi Prison next to the Industrial area. Prison officials were at a loss to explain how he had managed to get the rope into his cell. In fact, they were not quite sure what *he* was doing in there. There was no file of charges against him, and when they checked the wagon driver's logbook, the signature of the arresting officer was indecipherable. When it was all sorted out, more or less, a Prisons HQ stamp *bwana* stamped Nyeusi's file "Suicide" and informed the prosecutor that his caseload had been reduced by one.

Police Inspector Peter Odongo would not hear of Nyeusi's death for another two days. He was in Kikuyuland and much too busy to be monitoring the Customs official's progress through the bureaucratic labyrinth. In truth, Peter didn't give Nyeusi a second thought once he had gotten the information he needed from him.

Peter spent the night at the White Rhino Hotel in Nyeri and reported to the district compound early the next morning. Officially, of course, he was no longer involved in the case, but no one in Nairobi had remembered to tell anyone in Nyeri that. Both the district commissioner and the superintendent of police still believed that Peter had the authority of the Assistant Minister for Wildlife behind him, and they had no choice but to give him what he wanted.

What Peter wanted was a flying squad made up of Sergeant Wakiru—he had been impressed with Wakiru's feistiness that day on the mountain, when he found Adam Mwangi—and a dozen armed constables. He supposed he could have used the GSU, but he didn't trust them; he still did not know who had sent them to the Aberdares or what their orders were. Odongo loaded his men into an open-backed lorry and drove them through a steady rain to park headquarters in Mweiga, where he found the warden and ranger corporal Charles Ndirangu conveniently together in the warden's office and put them both under arrest. When they had been deposited back at the police compound, Peter and his squad drove to Aberdare Ranch to call on Stephen Hone.

Hone had apparently seen them coming. He was waiting for them at the bottom of the veranda steps. "What brings you out on such a grim morning, Inspector?" he asked with no trace of warmth in his voice, his shrewd eyes taking in the lorry and its cargo of armed constables.

Oblivious to Hone's tepid greeting, Peter flashed a wide smile and said, "Good news for once. Would you be kind enough to get Mr. Glenton on the radio for me?"

"May I ask what your news is?"

"I've had a break in the case," Peter said. "A Customs officer who shipped for the poachers . . . who knows everything."

"That's good news indeed," Hone said without enthusiasm.

"And not the half of it."

"There's more?"

"Please, if you don't mind, I want Mr. Glenton to be the first to hear it."

"Yes, of course." Hone just stood there in the rain with his hands in his pockets. He did not invite Odongo inside. He did not say anything more until Odongo cleared his throat and said tentatively, "If you could raise Mr. Glenton for me?"

"It wouldn't do you any good, I'm afraid," Hone replied. "He won't talk to you."

"What do you mean? Why not?"

Hone shrugged. "He has his reasons."

Peter frowned and asked, "What reasons?"

"I'd rather not say."

"I'd rather you did say," Peter said, mocking him, angry now. "In fact, I insist on it . . . as an inspector of police."

"Very well then. Adrian thinks that you are working with Fisi and his chappies."

"*What?*" Peter was dumbfounded. "How could he think such a thing?"

Hone was staring at him, his stony eyes at odds with the rest of his round and ruddy face. "Perhaps it is because Fisi always seems to know what his next move is going to be," Hone said. "Or because everything he tells you, and only you, ends up in Fisi's ear. Or perhaps it's because he knows Charles is one of them and that it was you who put Charles on the team."

The anger slowly drained from Peter's face. "Of course," he said. "I might have thought the same."

"You've an explanation, I suppose," Hone said.

"Yes, I do," Peter said. "I hired Charles on the advice of his warden. I arrested both men not more than an hour ago. And, also thanks to my Customs official, I now know who else has been passing Mr. Glenton's plans to the poachers."

"Who?" Hone asked skeptically, not having any of it, his face still closed and unforgiving.

Peter smiled and said, "You, Mr. Hone."

"*Me?* Why you cheeky bastard!"

Peter let it pass. "You relayed Glenton's daily reports to Nairobi, didn't you?" he said. "Whom did you give them to?"

"To you, of course," Hone said impatiently. "I rang your office and gave them to . . ." He faltered and stared at Odongo, who finished the sentence for him: "To the Assistant Minister for Wildlife."

"Yes," Hone said weakly. "Or that imbecile girl of his." Hone paused, then asked: "This Customs chappie of yours . . . he named the minister?" When Odongo nodded, Hone shook his head and muttered, "I'll be buggered."

Sergeant Wakiru had hopped off the lorry and was walking toward them. Hone pointed in the direction of the approaching Wakiru and the waiting constables and asked Peter: "If you're not after Adrian, what are all the guns for?"

Seeing that Sergeant Wakiru was near enough to overhear their conversation, Odongo said, "I'll tell you later." Then he faced Wakiru and asked, "What is it, Sergeant?"

"Sir, if we are going to be here long, may I get the men out of the rain?"

"They won't melt, Sergeant Wakiru," Peter said.

"Yes, sir. Very good, sir." Wakiru snapped off a salute and trotted back to the lorry.

When Peter turned back, he saw that Hone was wearing a sheepish look. "I owe you an apology, Inspector," Hone said. "Adrian was wrong to jump to conclusions. And so was I."

"I understand completely."

"And I apologize for calling you . . . um . . . what I did."

Odongo grinned. "In the name of my mother, I will accept your apology for calling me a bastard," he said, "but so many people have accused me of being cheeky that I am beginning to think there must be something to it."

Hone laughed and Odongo used the opportunity to sneak a glance at his watch. "My men are getting wet and grumpy," he said. "Do you think you might get Mr. Glenton for me now?"

"I'm sorry, Inspector, but I can't. Really. I don't have a radio."

"No?" Peter said in surprise. "What's happened to it?"

"Some fellow from the GSU came and took it away after my Land Cruiser was found abandoned in the park," Hone said. "He reminded me that the park was out of bounds, and then had the nerve to suggest that I'd been in contact with either Fisi or Adrian—what he called 'illegal elements.' From his manner, I couldn't tell which one he considered the worse."

"I see," Peter said, completely confused, not seeing at all. "And how did your car come to be abandoned in the park?"

"The road was slippery and it overturned."

"I meant what were you doing in the park."

"When the GSU man asked me that question," Hone said, "I told him that the car had been stolen."

"Oh," Odongo said, still not sure what Hone was talking about, but anxious to get back to the subject. "Then perhaps you could tell me where Mr. Glenton's camp is."

"That is no good, either," Hone said. "Adrian has alarms and traps all round the camp. If one of your chappies were to trip one off, it could start a war. I've stumbled into one or two myself, and I know where the bloody things are."

"What do you suggest then?" Peter asked.

"I suppose I'll have to take you in," Hone said.

"Would you?" Peter said.

"Why not?" Hone said as if to convince himself. "I can't let Adrian have all the fun, now can I? I'll get my rifle and we'll be off."

As Hone started toward the house, Peter called out after him: "You never said what you were doing in the park when you overturned your car?"

Hone stopped and turned. "Oh, it wasn't I," he said, a smile lighting his cherubic face. "Robbie pranged the bloody thing on her way to Adrian's camp."

"Miss Lewis is with Glenton? What is she doing there?"

"I'll tell you about it on the way," Hone said. "It's a strange story. But then love stories usually are."

"Why did you become a hunter?" Robbie asked.

"To make a living."

"The real reason."

"What do you want me to say?" Adrian said. "That hunting is man's oldest known skill and his most basic instinct? That hunting is necessary to a man's soul?"

"I don't know. Is it?"

"Perhaps. Man can launch other men into space. He can do all sorts of modern miracles. But if he loses the ability to hunt his own food he will lose his soul, and his bond with God. Or is your real question how can I murder sweet little animals?"

"How can you?"

Adrian laughed, then sighed. "It's no more wrong to kill a wild animal than to slaughter a steer for beefsteak. The meat is never wasted; I give it to the nearest village. It's all a matter of killing the animal fairly, with sporting rules, and with dignity."

Robbie's face showed her skepticism, but she didn't give voice to it. Instead she asked, "So, were you a good hunter?"

"Yes."

"How good?"

"Not the best, but one of the best."

"He said modestly."

Adrian shrugged. "False modesty is not a virtue."

"He said philosophically."

The fire was crackling, the lantern was lit and the cave was warm and cozy. They had just finished making love for the second time that morning and were lying naked on their bed of grass and leaves. Adrian had propped a spear outside the cave door as a warning to the others to keep out.

"What made you a good hunter?" Robbie asked.

"Why are you asking all these questions?"

"I'm just trying to learn more about you," she said.

"A bit late for that, don't you think?" he said, running a hand down her belly and palming her mound.

"You're a great piece of ass, Glenton, but there is more to life than sex."

"Not bloody likely," he said, sliding a finger into her.

Robbie let him play. She loved his hands, loved how they felt on her skin—even if they were rough and cracked. They were not the hands of a gentleman, but they were the hands of a gentle man. "What made you a good hunter?" she asked again.

"Seriously?"

"Seriously."

"For starters, I know animals," Adrian said. "I had good teachers—my father, and Pythias and his brother Damon, and their father. I can take one look at a track and tell you how fresh it is . . . whether the animal is male or female . . . how fast it is moving . . . sometimes even its mood. I can pick one animal out of a herd and follow it as the herd moves. I can . . ."

"How do you do that? Follow a specific animal when it's in a herd?"

"By the size and pattern of the footprint," Adrian said. "An animal's footprint is as unique as a human fingerprint."

"What about people?" Robbie asked. "Did you know people as well as you did animals?"

"I knew what I wanted in a client," he said. "I tried to take on only real sportsmen, people with enough time to do it right. I had serious clients and I made certain that they got serious trophies. All I asked of them in return was that they be on time and pay attention. That's the trick nine times out of ten, wouldn't you say?"

"I'd say it sounds like hunting with Hitler. Did any of your clients actually *like* you? Did you get along with them?"

"Certainly," he said. "Why wouldn't I?" When Robbie just laughed, he bristled and said, "I mean, I didn't excuse their boneheaded errors or falsely stroke their egos, but I didn't drink their whisky or chase after their women, either. I did what I was paid to do. I led them to decent-size trophies and advised them on how best to take them. I suppose I could have been a more charming dinner companion, but if it was a bloody house pet they wanted, the pubs were full up with hunters who would have been more than happy to oblige them. Besides, I've never subscribed to that silly idea that the client is always right. In my experience, the client was seldom right."

"How do you tell a good client from a bad one?"

"I tried to screen them in advance, but you can't always spot a rum one. As my father likes to say, if there is a flaw in your character, Africa will find it."

"Gee, it's too bad I missed a chance to be your client," Robbie said wryly. "Sounds like a barrel of fun."

"We had fun," Adrian said defensively. "But a safari was serious business. The client was investing a small fortune by the time he arranged his passage to Africa, outfitted himself and paid for the licenses and the white hunter. And he bloody well wanted something to show for it. Something he could hang on the wall back home."

Robbie just grunted and Adrian couldn't tell whether it was a reaction to what he was saying or to what he was doing to her with his fingers. "Listen," he said earnestly, trying to make her see, "it all came down to a professional code of conduct. Either you had one or you didn't, and if you didn't you were no more than what you Yanks call a bullshit artist, one of the Hollywood Hunters who hang about the pubs."

"And *Bwana* Glenton had a code."

"Bloody well right I did. As I saw it, the professional hunter had a twofold responsibility. One was to the client, to see that he got good shots at good game. The other was to the animal being hunted, to see that it was taken fairly and cleanly, with a minimum of pain and indignity. Surely you understand a code of conduct—or don't journalists know about such things?"

"Sure. Shine a light into the dark corners of the globe and always tell the truth. Give people the truth and it will make them free."

"Why do you sound so cynical? Don't you believe it?"

"Yeah, I believe it. In theory anyway."

"But not in practice?"

"In practice, too. Right up until I got to Africa."

"You mean you don't tell the truth about Africa?"

"Not really. None of us does. When we try, it doesn't get into print."

Adrian stopped stroking her and propped himself up on an elbow so he could see her face. "Why is that?"

"Because the truth isn't very palatable to our editors," she said. "In fact, it scares holy hell out of them. They're afraid that if they print the truth they might be accused of racism. You can't write off an entire continent . . . especially a black one."

"And why should you write off Africa?"

"Because things are getting worse, not better. This is a doomed continent, Adrian. Doomed. It's the saddest damn thing I've ever witnessed, but that doesn't alter the truth of it."

"It's not all that bad," Adrian said, a little surprised by the raw emotion in her voice. "Is it?"

"Yeah, it is," Robbie said. "You've got bush wars going on everywhere: Ethiopia, Somalia, Rhodesia, Namibia, Angola, Chad, Mozambique, the Sudan, you name it. Africa is the most fertile continent on the planet, yet most of these countries can't feed themselves. They're all in debt to their eyeballs and would go into the toilet tomorrow if not for foreign aid and the World Bank. And their infrastructures are as weak as their economies. Roads, bridges, buildings, whole damn towns; everything is falling apart. And their leaders! Don't make me puke.

They make speeches blaming all of their problems on the legacy of colonialism even as they're putting their countries up for sale by signing so-called friendship treaties with one or another of the major powers, giving away natural resources in return for military aid to keep themselves in power. Graft starts at the top. Zaire's savior, Mobutu, has three billion dollars stashed away in a Swiss bank account. That's billions with a *B.* Even the few who aren't personally corrupt do more harm than good. Take a so-called good leader like Nyerere—*Mwalimu,* the Teacher. Visiting editors love him because he's brilliant and charming and can joke in English. But he's run Tanzania right into the ground with his half-assed socialism. There aren't too many Gandhis out there. Leaders today are no better than those old tribal chiefs who let in the colonizers for some colored beads. And while they're getting rich, their people live in shit. Well, that just won't wash anymore. They can't go on blaming colonialism forever. These goddamn clowns have had power for a generation, and look what they have done with it. There isn't a country in black Africa that's as well off today as it was on the eve of independence ten or fifteen or twenty years ago. Not one."

Robbie was not saying anything that Adrian had not heard before, or much that he hadn't thought himself at one time or another, but he was taken aback by the passion and bitterness in her voice. He didn't quite know what to say in reply. "You sound like Pate . . . my father," he said finally. "Perhaps you'd agree with him on a solution as well. He thinks that the wogs should simply admit that *Uhuru* was a big mistake and get down on their knees and beg the Europeans to come back and run the place for them."

"Of course I don't," she said. "Freedom, even when it's more illusionary than real, comes before anything else. As for your father's idea, that is nostalgia, not a solution. There is no solution. That is why I say Africa is doomed. That is what makes it so damned sad." She paused, then asked, "Or do you agree with your father?"

Adrian shrugged. "Sometimes," he confessed. "Other times I think Africa should go completely native. Expel all *mzungus* and Asians. Bar tourists. Get rid of the autos and the office buildings and the videocassette recorders and the discos and anything else associated with the modern world."

"That is romantic crap, Adrian, and you know it."

He laughed. "I suppose it is," he said. "But sometimes I find myself thinking that Africa is God's cruelest punishment for eating that bloody apple. He expelled us from the Garden, but here in Africa we've been permitted to dwell on the edge, close enough for the occasional glimpse inside. Close enough to see what we once had, what we've lost."

"It wasn't lost," Robbie said. "It was pissed away."

To Adrian's disappointment, she had left the bed and was putting on her clothes. He wasn't quite sure how the talk had turned so serious so quickly, but it had spoiled any hopes he might have had for yet another go at her. He couldn't seem to get his fill of her. With a sigh of self-pity, he reached for his trousers.

"Well, if things really are as bad as you seem to think they are," Adrian said with a smile, "perhaps we should live in America when we're married."

Robbie, fully dressed now, laughed and shook her head at his persistence. "I don't think you would like it there," she said.

"Why not? Perhaps it's better there."

"Not better . . . different," Robbie said. "The things that seem to be important there are not very important here."

"Like what?" he asked.

"Who's the center square on Hollywood Squares?"

"What?"

"Who's Mr. Clean?"

"Who?"

"Who's Roseanne Rosanadanna? Or the Coneheads?"

"That isn't quite fair," Adrian said. "You can't expect me to know every famous American. Two can play at that game, you know. Who's Sonny Mehta? Who's Angela Rippon?"

"Sonny Mehta is a Safari Rally driver," Robbie answered promptly, "and Angela Rippon is a BBC news reader."

"Bloody hell," Adrian muttered. "I keep forgetting that you lived in London."

"Besides," Robbie said, "you can't get Weetabix or Bovril or Marmite in the States."

"Who needs them?" Adrian said with a laugh. "We'll live on love."

"No elephant steaks," Robbie said.

"What! No McDumbos with ivory arches?" Adrian exclaimed, feigning shock. "Now that would be a bother."

Robbie started to laugh, then stopped abruptly, her eyes going wide with surprise. At the same time, Glenton heard the blanket rustling behind him. He turned, expecting to see one of his men, ready to curse whomever it was for not announcing himself. Instead he found himself face to face with Inspector Odongo and two rifle-toting police constables. Close on their heels was Stephen Hone, pushing his way into the cave. Behind Hone, standing in the rain and surrounded by another group of armed policemen, were Joseph and the others.

"*Et tu,* Stephen?" Adrian said softly.

"It's not what you think, old sport," Hone said.

"I come to raise Caesar, not to harry him," Odongo said, smiling.

"Two-thirds of a pun," Robbie chimed in. "Pee-euu."

"Will someone please tell me what is going on?" Glenton said, his voice starting low and escalating into a bellow.

"We've come to help you bag The Hyena," Odongo answered, making a sweeping gesture with his arm to indicate his police escort. He glanced quickly at Robbie, then back at Adrian and said, "But only when you're fully dressed and ready to go, of course."

Adrian looked down and, red-faced, zipped his fly. "And just what makes you think I need your bloody help?" he asked unpleasantly, trying to cover his embarrassment.

Odongo merely grinned and said, "Because you don't know where Fisi is camped and I do."

31

According to Ambrose Nyeusi, the poachers were camped at the top of the Gura Giant Falls, in the southeastern quadrant of Aberdare Park, and would be there for another two to three days. From a tactical standpoint, the campsite had its pluses and minuses. The noise of the falls—the Gura River dropped three hundred meters in three cascading steps—would muffle the sound of an enemy's approach, but the site was surrounded by a wild tangle of woods and lay only a short distance from the Karimu Circuit, a looping dirt road.

After studying a map and consulting with Pythias, Adrian decided not to use the roads at all. "They're certain to have lookouts posted on the Circuit, and at key junctions on other roads," he said. "We'll have to go through the bush."

Hone agreed, and Odongo, no expert in such matters, went along in spite of his worry that his policemen would find the march rough going.

It was Joseph who suggested using a ruse to cover their movements. It worried him that the team had been in the same spot for three days, and he feared that someone was watching them. He had scouted the GSU bivouac at dawn to confirm that they hadn't moved, that they too were sitting out the steady rain, but he was still uneasy. "The Hyena has a man watching these caves," he announced flatly. "I can smell him."

Adrian had worked with Joseph for too many years to take his friend's concern lightly. If Joseph was worried then they should all be worried. "Do you have anything in particular in mind?" he asked.

The Masai's plan was simple and inspired. Adrian and his team would be taken away in irons, as if Inspector Odongo and his constables were arresting them. They would leave the park and head south to the village of Tusha, then take Track Eight back into the park, reentering at the Kiandongoro Gate. They would leave their vehicles at the fire-spotter's station just inside the gate and strike out overland. "It's a good four or five miles through very bad bush," Joseph said in conclusion, giving Odongo a questioning look. "Will your people make it?"

"They will if my boot is in their backsides," Odongo assured him.

Adrian was holding out both hands to let Odongo slip on the handcuffs, just to make it look good, when he saw Robbie Lewis attaching a wide-angle lens to a camera body. "What do you think you're doing?" he asked Robbie, dropping his hands before Odongo could cuff him.

"What does it look like I'm doing? I'm working," Robbie said. "Go on . . . put on the cuffs. It will make a great snap." She raised the camera, sighted on him, and said, "Say cheese."

"You're not coming on this safari, Robbie," Adrian said.

She lowered the camera, smiled sadly, and said in a voice full of mock pity, "Jesus, you'd think a guy would eventually get tired of being wrong all the time."

"You're the one who's wrong if you think I'm joking," he said.

Robbie's smile quavered, and then died. "You're putting me on," she said. "I mean, not even you would have the balls to let me get this far and then tell me I can't be in on the grand finale. Right? Tell me I'm right, Adrian. While you've still got teeth."

"We haven't time to argue," he said. "You are not coming and that is that."

"That is not that," she retorted. She turned on Hone and Odongo. "Don't just stand there. Tell him."

Peter shook his head. "Sorry, Miss Lewis, but I have to side with Mr. Glenton. It would be much too dangerous."

"He's right," Hone said, piling on. "You can't go."

"I'd like to see anybody try to stop me . . . What the hell! Hey! HEY!" Adrian had taken the handcuffs from Odongo and had snapped one of the grips onto Robbie's left wrist. He quickly grabbed her other wrist, spun her around roughly and shackled her hands together behind her back.

"Get these fucking things off of me!" Robbie raved. "You can't do this to me! Goddamn you, Adrian Glenton! I hate your guts! I'll hate you as long as I live!"

"And may that be a good long time," Glenton said calmly. Then he lifted her off her feet in a bear hug, kissed the tip of her nose, and tossed her over his shoulder and carried her out of the cave.

The roar of the falls masked the noise made by Odongo's constables, and a good thing it was too, Adrian decided. The policemen stumbled through the forest like wounded elephants, thrashing about and cursing and making enough noise to raise the dead.

Odongo's squad was down to ten. One man had dropped out after only a mile, too played out to go on. Another had quit only a few miles later. Stephen Hone was no longer with them either. Adrian had persuaded him to take Robbie back to Aberdare Ranch and make certain she stayed there. They could have used the extra gun, but Stephen's legs were no longer those of a young bucko. He would not have lasted the course and both men knew it. Robbie provided a convenient excuse to take the old man off the hook without shaming him.

Of Odongo's group only Sergeant Wakiru, the oldest of the bunch, had come through the trek in relatively good shape. The others were huffing and puffing, out on their feet. They were going to need time to catch their breath. "Why don't you rest your lads while I do a recce," Adrian suggested to Odongo. To his surprise, the Luo had weathered the march quite well.

Peter glanced back over his shoulder and saw his men far behind, strung out along the trail. "I guess they could use a blow," he conceded, a little embarrassed. "Our training isn't what it once was."

"They're all right," Glenton said graciously. "We didn't lose as many as I expected." He and Odongo were near the head of the file, momentarily out of earshot of the others. Adrian took the opportunity to say something that needed saying. Now it was his turn to be embarrassed. "Stephen told me about your little chat," he said, "and I'm sorry for suspecting you and for not giving you benefit of the doubt. I believed right from the start that you were all right. I should have trusted my instincts."

"No harm done, Mr. Glenton."

"Please, call me Adrian."

Odongo nodded. "No harm done, Adrian."

Leaving the main party sprawled in the underbrush beside the trail, Glenton collared Joseph and Pythias and set out to find the poachers' camp.

Pythias, the bush magician, found it in fifteen minutes. It would not have taken him even that long if Adrian had not insisted on caution, watching out for sentries on the trails. The camp, a collection of camouflaged army tents, was across the river in a bankside clearing, less than forty yards from where the Gura suddenly dropped out of sight.

"We'll have to find an upstream ford and go at them from the other side," Glenton said, almost shouting; anything less would have been lost to the thunder of the falls. Joseph just nodded, saving his voice. Pythias, his job done, didn't reply at all, leaving tactics to those who knew more about it.

"Where are their lookouts?" Adrian asked. "On their side of the river only? Or do you think it's a trap?"

"You tell me," Joseph answered with a shrug. "You're the one who decided to trust an uncircumcized fish-eater."

Adrian knew what Joseph was thinking. They had gone from the caves directly to the Kiandongoro Gate, stopping in Nyeri only long enough to drop Robbie Lewis and Stephen Hone at the Outspan Hotel, where Hone could borrow a car. Odongo had gone in with them, to use the loo. He had only been gone for a few minutes, but he was the only one who had been out of Adrian's sight long enough to have passed a warning to Fisi.

He pushed the idea from his mind. He had falsely accused Odongo once, and that was enough. His gut told him Odongo was all right. Robbie vouched for him, too, and despite his japes about her sleuthing skills, she was nobody's fool. There came a point where a man simply had to decide to trust people.

Adrian raised his field glasses and studied the camp. He had to wipe the lenses first. A delicate mist, spray from the falls, was in the air, and it, more than the light rain, left a wet film over everything. From what he could see, there was not much activity. Three men, all Somalis, were sitting round a fire smoking cigarettes, shielded from the rain by a canopy made from a tarpaulin propped up by four slender poles. Their rifles—German G-3s, the same as those used by the General Service Unit—were stacked within arm's reach. The smoke of their fire was lost in the mist.

At the other end of the camp, another Somali was sitting out of the rain under a leafy tree, scraping an elephant tusk with a hunting knife. On the ground beside him were five more tusks. A fifth man, a Kikuyu by the look of him, was kneeling at the river's edge, cleaning out some pots. Glenton kept the glasses on this man, wondering if he was The Hyena. He doubted it. There was nothing in the least remarkable about him. Amos Mwangi had said that there were one or two other Kikuyus in the gang. Besides, Fisi did not sound like the sort of man who would volunteer to do the washing up.

Adrian glassed the tents, looking for some sign of life. There were six tents in all, each capable of sleeping four or five. Odongo's snout, the Customs officer, had put the gang's membership at twenty-three, counting Fisi. Figuring that Fisi probably slept alone, it worked out about right. But where in the hell were they?

As if on cue, seven men walked out of the woods and into the camp. Two of them carried a dead leopard on a pole. It was one of the biggest leopards that Adrian had ever seen, as large as the one he had shot at Shaba in his second year as a professional. "Jesus Christ," he mumbled, "look at the size of that cat!" He gave the glasses to Joseph, who looked, grunted, and handed them back without comment, unimpressed. It wasn't as if it were a lion.

Glenton put the glasses back up just in time to see half a dozen men emerge from the tents to greet the party. One man tied one end of a rope to the leopard's back legs, tossed the other end over a tree branch, and hoisted the carcass off the ground. Another man promptly began to skin the animal. Adrian panned the crowd, searching for Fisi. And, suddenly, there he was, coming out of the tent nearest the riverbank, dressed in fatigues, a hyena-skin cape, and bright yellow stockings. It had to be him. He was a huge man for a Kikuyu, as tall as any of his Somalis and as burly as a wrestler. Adrian's hands shook, the way they always did when he found himself face to face with a particularly outstanding trophy.

Confirming the man's importance, the Somalis made a path for him, stepping aside deferentially as he walked toward the hanging carcass. He reached up to touch the leopard, stroking the beast's fur as he might a woman's hair. His own hair, done up in dreadlocks, reached halfway down his back. Adrian could not see his face.

Adrian passed the glasses to Joseph. "There's our boy," he said. "Have a look." The Masai looked, adjusted the focus, and looked again.

"He's a big one, isn't he?" Adrian said.

"The larger the man, the larger the target," Joseph said as he handed back the binoculars.

Adrian raised the glasses, reset the focus, and immediately exclaimed, "Bloody fucking hell!"

"W-What?" Pythias said quickly, alarmed by Adrian's tone of voice. He had not asked for a turn with the binoculars. If The Hyena were to turn around and their eyes met . . . especially through the glass that magnified things . . . he shuddered at the thought. To meet Evil's eye was to give it a window into your soul. The Dorobo had a healthy respect for Kikuyu magic.

"One of the Somalis just cut out the leopard's heart and handed it to Fisi," Glenton said without taking his eyes away from the glasses. "Now ask me what he did with it."

"All right," Joseph said, humoring him. "What did he do with it?"

"He took a big bloody bite out of it!" Glenton's voice said that he didn't quite believe it.

"*Wasimu*," Pythias mumbled. "He's crazy."

"Maybe he's just hungry," said Joseph.

Pythias gave the Masai a look of disgust. "You're crazy, too," he said. "I'm beginning to think that everyone in this forest is crazy but me."

Adrian wasn't listening. He kept the binoculars trained on the back of Fisi's head, willing him to turn around so he could get a good look at his face. "Turn, damn you," he said under his breath.

It was as if The Hyena had heard. He suddenly went stiff and pivoted slowly, gazing toward the river . . . across the river. He seemed to be staring right at Adrian. His mouth and beard were black with blood from the leopard's heart. And his eyes! Pythias had been right! Even from this far away, Adrian could see the piercing eyes of a madman, an African Rasputin.

"Keep still," Adrian warned. "He's looking our way." He saw The Hyena close his eyes and lift his head, sniffing the air. Then Fisi laughed and started for his tent. The Somalis, apparently used to such eccentric behavior, paid him no mind. Someone had produced a bottle of the local liqueur, a sticky concoction called Kenya Cane, and was passing it around.

Adrian didn't lower the glasses until Fisi was back in his tent. "For a moment there, I was afraid he'd spotted us."

"No man could see us in this cover," Joseph said.

"No *man,* maybe," Pythias said. "But a hyena . . ." He left the thought hanging in the air.

Adrian nudged Joseph. "What do you think, *moran*?"

"No sweat," Joseph said blithely. He had little use for Robbie Lewis, but that hadn't stopped him from adding one of her pet expressions to his collection of Yank colloquialisms. "The forest will give us good cover to the camp's edge. Then we form three assault lines, one on each flank, and go in on your signal. They have the advantage in men and weapons, but we have surprise and terrain. With their backs to the river, they have nowhere to run and nowhere to hide."

"Shouldn't we give them a chance to surrender?"

"If they were Kikuyus maybe," Joseph said, "but not the men of Somaliland. It would be too risky. My Samburu cousins have told me that they are brave warriors, that they are not afraid to die."

Joseph was probably right, Adrian thought with a sinking heart. Somalis seldom ran from a fight. "Your plan sounds all right to me, but let's see what Odongo thinks of it. It's his show now, not mine."

They made their way back to the main group, where Adrian told Odongo what they had seen, and briefly outlined Joseph's battle plan. Odongo heard him out, keeping his eyes on Joseph all the while, then shrugged and said, "All right, we will do it Joseph's way. Only a fool would try to tell a Masai how to fight."

A slow grin cracked Joseph's face. "And only a greater fool would question the intelligence and wisdom of the Luo," he said.

Odongo's motley army was on the devil's doorstep, in the woods at the edge of the camp, near enough to hear the murmur of voices. To Glenton's surprise, and great relief, there had been no traps or sentries along the feeder trails. Not one. A minor miracle.

Joseph had scouted the way, ready to cut a Somali throat if he had to, and secretly hoping he would. But there had not been a Somali handy. Even so, he'd asked Adrian to "look down at the earring." In order to look down at the earring a Masai *moran* had to turn his head nearly ninety degrees. Adrian knew what the proverb meant: watch the rear.

Was Fisi so confident that he believed there was no need for outpost security, Adrian wondered? But then why shouldn't he be? What had *Mbwa Kali* done to make him feel anything less than in complete command of the situation and the park? Just what had the Great White Hunter really accomplished? One botched ambush, one dead Somali, one live Somali minus a few fingers, and one tiny cache of captured goods. It wasn't much to show for weeks of bum-breaking effort, of living no better than the animals they were trying to save. All the while, the poachers went merrily about their bloody business, butchering every horn-heavy elephant or rhinoceros unfortunate enough to attract their attention. Merely thinking about it made Adrian angry, and his anger helped to exorcise his fear of the fight to come.

The men were in position and waiting on Adrian's signal. Odongo had divided his force into three squads: two units of six men each, led by himself and Joseph, and a four-man team under Glenton's command. Adrian's squad consisted of himself, Pythias, Ekali and Tembo. He had insisted on keeping his own boys with him, thinking he'd better be able to watch out for them. As for assignments, Joseph had given himself the vital middle sector, the short leg of a block-letter U. The others would attack from the flanks, with the Gura River serving as a natural ally, closing off the fourth and final side of the box. Adrian's squad had their own rifles—his own personal arsenal and the two automatic rifles that Odongo had donated to the cause—and were better off than the constables, who were armed with carbines. The fact that the poachers enjoyed such an advantage in fire power made the element of surprise all the more important.

From his hiding place in the bushes, Glenton had a clear view into the camp. Two of the poachers were still working on the leopard. They had the pelt fully off now and had taken it out of the rain. They sat by the fire under the tarp with the hide across their laps, scraping the underside of the skin to remove the flesh and sinews. They chatted with their comrades as they toiled, enjoying a good laugh about something. Adrian counted a total of seven men at the fire.

The rest of the poachers, including The Hyena, had returned to their tents. Adrian was doing sums in his head, trying to account for them all and knowing he was going to come up a handful short, when five men suddenly walked out of the woods and into the clearing. Adrian's heart skipped a beat. For one panicky moment he thought they were Joseph's men, that Joseph had rushed his fences, springing the ambush prematurely. Then he realized that these were more of The Hyena's men. They had come right through Joseph's position. He didn't know how they could have missed tripping over Joseph and his men.

The new arrivals, all of them Somalis, were empty-handed except for their rifles. They went over to the fire and began talking with their comrades, no doubt explaining their failure to bring home a prize. The others just laughed and pointed at the leopard's pelt.

Adrian heard Joseph's voice inside his head, as clearly as if the Masai were standing next to him. "Do it! Do it now! While they're bunched together!" He reached for the silver whistle hanging on a cord about his neck—he'd finally found a use for the thing—and blew; a single, piercing blast that cut through the constant background noise, the hum of the falls.

The signal touched off a chain reaction. The bush itself seemed to become a living beast, a green cobra with a hundred tongues of flame, spitting fire. The Somalis at the campfire, caught by surprise and taking the full brunt of the first two volleys, panicked. Those who survived the fusilade—four of the twelve—did not even make a grab for their weapons. One man bolted for the woods, straight at Adrian, who waited until he was six or seven paces away before giving him both barrels of the Holland and Holland, almost cutting him in two. The three remaining men ran for the river, instinctively trying to put as much ground as possible between themselves and the guns.

By now, the rest of Fisi's men were pouring out of their tents, and they came out shooting. Automatic rifle fire began to drown out the staccato pops of the police carbines. Shouts and curses, in half a dozen different languages and dialects, filled the air, adding to the uproar.

Suddenly, above the din, Glenton heard a familiar voice yell: "Men of the Kenya Constabulary! On my command! Charge!" An instant later, Peter Odongo rushed out of the forest with his squad hard on his heels, firing from the hip as they ran. A moment after that, Joseph, undoubtedly inspired by Odongo's remarkable act, burst from the bush with a war cry of his own—"Fear me, Somali dogs!"—the team's M-16 in one hand and his long Masai spear in the other.

Before he knew quite how it happened, Adrian was on his feet and joining in the assault. The distinctive boom of his shotgun echoed above the din as he loosed first one bore and then the other. He was completely calm now, no longer afraid. It was just another control shoot, a job that had to be done. He was Karamojo Bell in a herd of elephant, potting them one by one. Unlike the others, he stood rooted in one place, paying no mind to the bullets that were kicking up dirt all around his feet, and dropped four moving targets in rapid succession, working like a well-oiled robot. Swing, lead, shoot. Swing, lead, shoot. Reload. Swing, lead, shoot. Swing, lead, shoot. Reload.

Caught up in the heat of the moment, Adrian wasn't aware that his team had followed him out into the clearing until he heard Tembo's cry: "*Bwana*! I've been killed!"

The Liangulu was on the ground directly behind him, four long strides away. He was lying on his back, craning his head to look down the front of his dirty overcoat. The hole in his coat, just above the groin area, was the size of a lion's paw print. "Bloody hell, Tembo," Adrian said, kneeling beside the old man and gently pushing his head down. "Oh, fucking hell."

Working in a fever, Adrian unsheathed his knife and cut a strip from Tembo's coat, intending to use it as a compress. But when he unbuttoned the coat and pulled it open, he could see that Tembo was right . . . he *had* been killed. It was just a matter of time, minutes at most. The wound was terrible. The bullet had tumbled going in, leaving a fist-size hole in the lower abdomen, two inches below the navel. Adrian covered it anyway, applying the compress with one hand while he cradled the old man's head with the other. He tried to keep his eyes on Tembo's eyes, away from the wound. The makeshift compress was already soaked with blood, as soggy as a sponge.

Adrian was dimly aware that the shooting had tapered off. He looked up. The clearing was littered with fallen men, but the eye of the storm had passed them by, heading for the river. "Tembo, listen, do you hear? It's *kwisha*. It's all over," Adrian said, trying to comfort the old man. "You'll be getting out of this place soon, *mzee*. I promise." But when he looked back down, he saw that his lies were wasted. Tembo had already left.

With a shaking hand, Adrian gently straightened the old man's floppy earlobes and closed the glassy eyes. He was not familiar enough with Liangulu beliefs to know what became of a man when he died, but he knew exactly where Tembo had gone. To an elephant graveyard.

Adrian got to his feet and retrieved his shotgun. He had to break it open to see if it was loaded. He couldn't seem to remember. His mind was numb. All he could think of was the surprise in the old drunk's voice. "*Bwana*, I've been killed." First Chege and now Tembo. Adrian could not think of two more harmless souls. How could he have led them into such a bloody balls-up? How had it come to this?

Adrian snapped the shotgun shut and looked for something to kill. The action had shifted to the river's edge where the Somalis were making a last stand. Despite the drop in fire volume, there were still pockets of resistance up and down the riverbank. But Odongo's men seemed to have the upper hand. Adrian saw two Somalis kneeling in the mud, their hands on top of their heads, trying to give themselves up to anyone who passed by. He saw another man break for the trees and get halfway before being killed. For the most part, the poachers seemed to realize that the river itself wasn't an option. The current, swollen with run-off from the rains, was too strong.

There were exceptions, however. One man had waded as far as the middle of the stream and looked as if he were going to make it across. Seeing this, another poacher plunged in, only to be knocked off his feet and swept toward the falls. A second man tried. He too was bowled over and carried off. The man in the water had to be incredibly strong. Struck by a sudden thought, Adrian groped for his field glasses. And then he was sprinting for the Gura, trying to aim the shotgun as he ran, bellowing: "FISI! FISI, YOU BASTARD!"

The Hyena, almost to the opposite bank, did not hear the curse, but he did hear the shotgun's first report. He turned, saw Adrian, and raised his own rifle.

Adrian fired again and missed again. He couldn't believe it! He could not remember ever having missed so simple a shot before, much less twice in as many heartbeats. He went to one knee, digging into his pocket for more shells, his eyes fixed on the target.

The Hyena fired one shot from a G-3 automatic rifle. The round struck Adrian high on the right arm, above the biceps, a glancing blow that missed the bone but still packed enough of a wallop to dump him onto his backside and make him let go of his shotgun.

Cradling his arm, Adrian sat up just in time to see Fisi raise and sight the rifle for a second, more leisurely, shot. His mind was calm and clear, unclouded by false illusion. So this is it, is it? he mused. With all the miles and miles of bloody Africa out there, I am going to die in the Aberdares. Somehow, he'd always thought that it would be the Masai Mara. If he had any regrets, besides accepting Odongo's offer of a job, it was that. That and the fact that he would never know what a life with Robbie Lewis might be like. Contentious and equally short, he imagined. But never boring.

But the second shot didn't come. Instead, The Hyena was lowering his rifle. No. Dropping it. He needed both hands to grab the shaft of the spear that had pierced him through the trunk. Adrian turned his head, "looking at the earring," and saw Joseph standing a few feet behind him. "You promised him to me," the Masai said accusingly. "Or had you forgotten?"

Confused, and not especially elated—he still had not adjusted to the idea of his own survival—Adrian looked to the river. Fisi was swaying, fighting to keep his balance in the current. And then he toppled over, making a splash as he went down.

Adrian struggled to his feet, and he and Joseph began to trot along the bank, following The Hyena who was bobbing downriver on his back, the shaft of Joseph's spear still sticking up out of his torso like the mast of an Arab dhow. Their last glimpse of him was a brief flash of yellow stockings as he tipped and went over the waterfall.

Adrian and Joseph looked at each other for a moment and then embraced. Adrian stepped back and said, "Tembo is dead."

"So is the Turkana," Joseph said.

"Oh no, not Ekali," Adrian said in a whisper. "How about Pythias? Is he all right?"

"*Aiya*. I think he stayed in the forest."

"Thank God for that," Adrian said, exhaling with relief. "And Odongo?"

"He is unhurt. He was a lion." It was the highest praise a Masai could bestow. "Here, let me see your arm."

"It's nothing," Adrian said.

"Okay, dipshit, you're a lion too," the Masai said with a laugh. "Now let me see it." He took Adrian's arm, examined the wound and grunted. He tore two strips from Adrian's bush jacket and went to the river to soak them. When he came back, he used the larger cloth to wash the upper arm, then wrapped the smaller one around a slender stick and began to swab out the wound itself. It stung, but Adrian took care not to show it. That would be like "kicking the knife," flinching during circumcision.

Peter Odongo came over while Joseph was playing Florence Nightingale.

"I'm happy to see you all in one piece, Peter," Adrian said. "How bad is it?"

"Bad enough," Odongo said. "Are you wounded?"

"Only a scratch," Adrian said. "How bad?"

"Two of your men are dead."

"Yes, I know. How did your lads come through?"

"Four dead, four wounded," Odongo said. "I lost Sergeant Wakiru."

"Sorry, I know you thought a great deal of him."

"He was a good man," Peter said quietly. "They were all good men."

"Yes. Yes, they were."

"There," Joseph said, tying off the crude bandage he had fashioned from the larger strip of cloth. "I know you *mzungus* believe that your ancestors were monkeys, but do not swing in the trees for a few days."

Adrian didn't smile. He was looking at the river, at the spot where it fell out of sight. "Do you think there's a path down to the bottom of the falls?" he asked.

Joseph shrugged. "Probably."

"What is at the bottom of the falls?" Odongo asked.

"Fisi," said Adrian.

"Did you see him go over?"

"Yes, Joseph and I both saw it."

"Then he's dead," Peter said.

"Yes, I know. But I'd like to bring in the body."

"I'll send some constables to look for it," Peter said.

"I'll want to go myself," Adrian said. He looked at Joseph. "What do you say, *moran*?"

Joseph shrugged again. "Sure, I'll go. If you think you can make it with that arm."

"Don't worry about me. I'll make it. Want to come along, Inspector?"

Peter shook his head. "I have to radio Nyeri. We need a doctor, and transport for the dead and wounded." He took a map from his tunic pocket and gave it a quick look. "The nearest dispensary seems to be in Kiandongoro village. We can set up a temporary field headquarters there."

"Have someone ring Hone and ask him to meet us there," Adrian said. "And he can, um, bring Miss Lewis along if he likes."

It took them nearly an hour to make it to the bottom of the Gura Giant Falls. There was a trail of sorts, but Adrian had to take it slowly because of his arm, with Joseph helping him over the more treacherous sections. For the last hundred yards, they had to communicate by hand signal because of the noise.

It took them the better part of another hour to conduct a thorough search. The pool at the foot of the waterfall was as long as it was wide, a roiling white cauldron of foam and spray. Adrian left it to the more nimble Joseph to check the edges of the pool on foot while he studied the opposite bank through the binoculars. The results were identical. No trace of either Fisi or the other two men Glenton had seen go over the falls.

They slowly worked their way downstream until they came to the tail of the pool where the gorge narrowed and the Gura regained its shape. Adrian's arm was throbbing, and he wasn't looking forward to the climb back to the top. He caught up to Joseph and was about to suggest that they start back when the Masai came to a stop, grabbed him by the arm—the sore one, of course—and pointed.

Adrian followed Joseph's finger with his eyes, and found himself looking at the carcass of a spotted hyena, lying half in and half out of the water. The beast's eyes were wide open and its lips were pulled back in a snarl, showing the tearing teeth. The carcass appeared to be fresh, less than a day old.

Neither man said a word. They stood there staring at the thing, avoiding each other's eyes, until Adrian put his mouth next to Joseph's ear and said, "A coincidence. Nothing more."

"Yes," said Joseph.

"I mean, there's no spear wound or anything like that," Adrian said.

"No," said Joseph.

There was another long silence. Then Joseph said, "Give me your knife."

"Hullo?"

"Give me your knife."

"Oh. Yes. Of course." Adrian unsheathed the Randall and gave it to him.

Working rapidly, and without fanfare, Joseph rolled the hyena onto its back, punched a hole in the stomach wall just above the scrotum, and sliced the carcass open from belly to brisket. Then he cut free the heart, pulled it out and threw it as far as he could into the pool.

32

The period that immediately followed the breakup of what the Nairobi newspapers were to call The Hyena Pack, once they finally got around to doing the story, was hectic and full of uncertainty. For Adrian and Peter. For an entire nation.

While Glenton and Odongo had no way of knowing it at the time, the events in the Aberdares were being overshadowed and rendered insignificant even as the final shots echoed through the park's fog-shrouded peaks and valleys. For the editors of the *Nation* and the *Standard* and the other major newspapers, a story that would have been page-one news on any other day was no more than an afterthought, a paragraph or two in the daily crime report. The foreign press didn't bother with it at all, not even Robbie's magazine, which had the inside story.

But Glenton knew nothing about that when he and Joseph got back to the top of the Gura Falls only to find everyone gone except for a policeman who'd been left behind to guide them to the Karimu Circuit road, where a lorry was standing by to take them to Kiandongoro village.

Odongo had established a temporary field headquarters at the village dispensary. The yard was swarming with constables and Field Force rangers. Four prisoners—a Kikuyu and three Somalis—sat out in the rain, chained together at the neck. The dead were laid out in two parallel lines. Glenton counted nine bodies in one row, all poachers, and half a dozen in the other: four of Odongo's policemen, including Sergeant Wakiru, and his two, Tembo and Ekali. Pythias was there too, sitting in the mud, cradling Ekali's head in his lap.

A crowd of villagers had collected on the fringe of the yard, kept from coming closer by a police cordon. Adrian and Joseph heard one of the village women call out to one of the policemen: "It is true what we've heard? Is The Hyena really dead?"

"Yes, he's dead," the constable said.

"Which one is he?" another villager asked, pointing at the two rows of dead. "May we see him?"

"His body is not here," the policeman said. "I think it was lost." When the people heard this they started murmuring among themselves.

Adrian finally found Odongo in the dispensary itself, a cinderblock bungalow with a tin roof. Dr. Ramanujam of Nyeri hospital was there with his head nurse, as were the district commissioner and the police superintendent. Dr. Ramanujam's nurse was attending to the less seriously wounded—a group that included three of the four policemen and two of the four poachers—while the surgeon himself readied the worst cases for transfer to the district hospital.

Odongo was standing with the DC and the superintendent of police. "Did you find Fisi?" he asked when he saw Adrian.

"No," Adrian said. "How are things here?"

"My man should make it, but the doctor is not sure about those two," Peter said, nodding toward the two poachers being carried out on litters. "I can't say I give a fuck."

"What is the tally?"

Odongo took out his black notebook. "Four dead and four wounded for us," he said. "Twelve poachers killed, including the three you saw go over the waterfall, and eight captured, four of them wounded. If my count was correct and there were twenty-three in all, three managed to escape."

Adrian nodded. "They probably scarpered into the woods."

"Splendid work, Glenton, simply splendid," the district commissioner said, snatching up Adrian's hand and pumping it enthusiastically. It wasn't until he saw Adrian wince that he noticed the wound. "What's this?" he cried. "You're hurt!"

"It's nothing," Adrian said. "I've had thorn scratches worse than this."

"Doctor, come quickly!" the district commissioner called across the room. "Mr. Glenton needs tending!"

Ramanujam came over and made Adrian strip to the waist, then untied Joseph's dressing and had a look. "It's not very serious," he confirmed. Even so, he cleaned the wound with a disinfectant and put a proper dressing on it.

"Wounded in the nation's service," the commissioner said dramatically. "Yes, indeed! A splendid job!"

"Right sentiment, wrong man, commissioner," Adrian said. "It's all Inspector Odongo's doing. He found their camp."

"I have already congratulated the inspector," said the DC, "but I wanted to congratulate you as well. Odongo tells me you and your team played a crucial role. Nairobi will be pleased. I am pleased. The superintendent is pleased."

In fact, the superintendent looked anything but pleased. Here was a mere inspector, and a Luo at that, getting credit for solving the most pressing police problem in his district. "My only regret," he said sadly, "is that four of *my* men had to die for the inspector to accomplish *his* mission."

Adrian quickly came to Odongo's defense. "Considering we were outnumbered and outgunned, things could've been a bloody sight worse." The superintendent merely shrugged. That wasn't what his report was going to say.

A moment later Stephen Hone bustled into the dispensary. "Ah, here you are," he cried, clapping both Adrian and Peter on the back.

Adrian peered over Hone's shoulder at the empty doorway. "Where's Robbie?" he asked. "Didn't she come with you?"

"Why no, she didn't," Hone said. "She left for Nairobi the minute she heard the big news. But she knows you're all right, and she sends her love."

"Oh." Adrian tried not to show his disappointment. Get the story and bugger off, was that it? Perhaps that was all she'd been after all along. He tried to dismiss the thought as uncharitable, but it refused to go away entirely.

Joseph, who had been waiting outside, was beckoning to him from the doorway. When Adrian went over, the Masai said, "Pythias would like to go now. And he wants to take Ekali's body with him. Back to Turkana."

"How does he plan to get it there?"

"He says that if you'll give him his wages, he's found a *matatu* willing to take them."

"Tell him I'll be right out." Adrian went back to where Odongo and Hone were chatting. "Peter, Pythias wants to take Ekali home. Will you release the body to him?"

"Of course. He can have it whenever he likes."

"Good. Oh yes, and I'll need ten thousand bob."

"Ten thousand shillings! Mother of God! What for?"

"Wages. It's been exactly a month. That's five thousand for me and a thousand for each of the boys."

"You want it *now*?"

"Three thousand of it, at least. One each for Joseph and Pythias, and a thousand for Ekali. I want to send Ekali's pay to his father. And while I'm on the subject, Chege had a wife and four children. I realize he wasn't official, but I'd like his widow to get Charles's money. Is that a problem?"

"No, it's a fine idea," Peter said quickly. "But I don't have that kind of money with me." He turned out his pocket to make his point. "And until the proper forms are submitted and approved, I won't have any money for any of you. Heaven knows when you'll have it. You were right about the bureaucrats."

"Bugger the bastards. Three of my boys are dead because of that bloody crook minister of yours."

"Keep your voice down," Peter said, glancing over to see if the district officials had overheard. "Your people weren't the only ones who died today, you know. Do you think Sergeant Wakiru's wife and children will get his salary any sooner?"

"That's your problem, not mine," Adrian said.

"Oh, for God's sake," Hone snapped. "I have ten thousand in the strongbox at home. Take it, Adrian. The government will reimburse me. Only stop this bloody bickering. You sound like an old married couple." The two offenders stared at Hone and then at each other, and grinned sheepishly.

When Hone left to get the money, Adrian went outside to let Pythias and Joseph know what was happening. "Please tell the *jumbe* how sorry I am about his son," he told Pythias. "I will come and tell him myself as soon as I can."

When the Dorobo just nodded, Adrian said, "You are going to stay in Turkana, aren't you?"

"Yes," Pythias said. "Do you think it's wrong?"

"I think nothing could be more right."

"I will have to let *Bwana* Wilkinson know."

"I'll get word to him," Adrian said. "You just go on and don't give it another thought. You can leave as soon as *Bwana* Hone gets back here with the money." The instant he mentioned money he remembered the fifty thousand shillings he had taken from the *matatu* driver in the ambush at the Ngweno *shamba*. It was in his knapsack, still wrapped in butcher's paper. He had forgotten all about it. He could meet all his obligations and give each man a bonus besides.

"I was planning to ask you to take Ekali's salary to his father," he told Pythias. "But now that I think about it, I'm not so sure that would be the right thing to do. Do you think the chief might feel insulted?"

"Yes," said Pythias. "I think he would."

"I was afraid of that," Adrian said. Then he grinned and said, "I have another idea. You take the money."

"Me? No, no, Adrian. That wouldn't be proper."

"It's better than proper. It's perfect. Ekali would want you to have it. He would want you to use it to buy yourself a bride. A wife as fine as Nimonia does not come cheaply."

Pythias's face turned darker. Then he gave a shy smile and nodded.

Adrian clapped his hands once, imitating Ekali's father, the *jumbe*, and said: "Good. It's settled." Then he turned to Joseph. "What about you, *moran*? What are you going to do?"

"I'm going home to Maasailand," Joseph said. He paused, then said: "There's a proverb. *Mepal oloitiko isirat lenyena.* Do you know it?"

Adrian nodded and said, "The zebra does not despise its own stripes. It means a man should not abuse his traditions."

"I have been thinking that maybe the elders are right," Joseph said. "Perhaps it is time for me to settle down to a normal life." He looked at the two rows of bodies. "Besides, I'm getting too old for this shit."

By the time Stephen Hone returned from the ranch—only to learn that he'd made the trip for nothing—a miracle had happened: the rain had stopped and the sun was out. Weak, but out nonetheless. It was the first bit of sun they had seen in weeks. Adrian lifted his face to its warmth. As he did so, he noticed that the Kenya flag flying over the dispensary was at half mast. "Is that for our benefit?" he asked Hone, pointing to it.

"Haven't you heard?" Hone said, giving him a queer look.

"Heard what?"

"Why do you think Robbie shot off to Nairobi like that?" Hone said. "Jomo Kenyatta died this morning."

Nairobi was dressed in mourning. The public statues were draped with black crepe. Shops, black-bordered photographs of Mzee in the windows, were locked and shuttered. In Uhuru Park the banners and bunting, hung for the coming Independence Day celebration, were cruel reminders of how quickly things could change. Even the beasts in the Nairobi Game Park were said to be grieving; rumor had it that at the exact moment Mzee died, a male lion in the park roared once and fell over dead for no apparent reason.

To Adrian, who hadn't put foot in the city for more than a month, not since the day he had set off for Rumuruti to recruit Damon and Pythias, Nairobi would have seemed different in any case. Everything looked oddly unfamiliar to him. He could not remember the name of this building, that street. It was as if he were a tourist on his first visit. It couldn't simply have been the time away. He was used to spending long stretches in the bush; he'd been gone a month or more on a dozen different safaris. He didn't know what it was.

Adrian did not see much of Robbie that first week back. She was putting in fifteen- and sixteen-hour days to feed the voracious appetites of her editors. Her magazine was doing a "crash cover" on the subject "Whither Kenya?" after the loss of Africa's leading political figure. Thus far, Robbie said, the story was an upbeat one. Contrary to some predictions of strife and chaos, the transition seemed to be going smoothly. The more moderate elements of the ruling KANU party appeared to have the upper hand, and, with the whole world looking on with interest, they'd decided to demonstrate how democratic they could be by allowing the Vice President to succeed Kenyatta even though he was Kalenjin and not Kikuyu. He was, however, a good party man who could be counted on to remember who had put him into the State House. It seemed that there was to be none of the typical African rhapsody of coup and countercoup. One could almost hear the nation's collective sigh of relief.

As for Adrian, he was unemployed once again, but he was by no means idle. He spent most of his first day back making courtesy calls.

The first was to the Nairobi South B housing complex in the Eastleigh district, to see Chege's widow. He had planned all along to give her Tembo's wages—as far as Adrian knew, Tembo had been the last of his line, with no surviving family of his own—but when he was confronted with the poverty in which she and her children lived, he ended up giving her half of what he'd taken from the dead *matatu* driver and most of his own salary as well.

His next stop was the Muthaiga Club, to let Pate know he was back. To his astonishment, he found his father weeping in front of the television set in the lounge, watching the Voice of Kenya's broadcast of Mzee's lying-in-state.

"The man was a giant," Pate snuffled. "The rest of that lot are nothing but bloody pygmies. It is the end of an era, Adrian. *Our* era." Adrian did not think it was the right time to remind his father that he had spent the last twenty years calling Jomo Kenyatta "that bloody butcher," and holding him directly responsible for the excesses of Mau Mau.

The next morning, Peter Odongo telephoned Adrian at home to ask if he wanted to go to State House to view the body.

"It's by invitation only," Adrian said.

"We have been invited," Peter said with a laugh. "And by no less than the new President himself. It seems that you and I are national heroes."

That afternoon, Adrian and Peter queued up to pay their last respects to the only president Kenya had ever known. He was laid out under the State House chandelier, on a polished wooden table draped with purple cloth, his head resting on a white pillow. He had on his favorite blue pinstripe suit and there was a red rose in his buttonhole. His jewel-encrusted fly whisk was in his right hand. A man in the queue had told them that dignitaries from around the world were in town for the funeral, everyone from Idi Amin to Prince Charles.

Back outside, they were talking about how dignified Mzee had looked when Adrian nudged Peter and pointed to a removals van that was pulled up to the side of the house. Dada, all in black, was berating the driver about something. "The new lord of the manor isn't wasting any time, is he?" Adrian said. "It looks as if the Queen Bee has been asked to change hives."

Peter, glaring in Dada's direction, merely grunted.

"So what's going to happen, Peter?" Adrian asked as they continued down the driveway toward the car park. "I mean with your investigation and all?"

"Nothing is going to happen," Peter said bitterly. "I've just learned that my only informant died in prison. They said that he took his own life. I wonder."

"Your Customs chap?"

Peter nodded. "I have nothing without him. To pursue the matter any further *would* be an act of suicide. Mine."

"So that's it then? Case closed? The warden and Charles get to carry the can for the whole sorry lot?"

"I'm afraid so."

"At least with Dada gone they won't have so many toys to play with," Adrian said. "Speaking of which, how do you think the transition is going?"

"The new president should have been a Luo," Odongo said. "We are the second largest tribe, and it's our turn." Then he sighed and added, "At least it wasn't another Kikuyu. I don't know. It's too early to tell, but the fact that it has been a peaceful transition is cause for hope I suppose. Perhaps it's a sign that we have matured as a nation, as a people."

They walked on without speaking for a moment, then Peter said, out of the blue: "I am going to be married."

Adrian stopped and slapped him on the back. "Well, good for you! Who's the poor girl?"

"A nurse. I met her here in the city, but she comes from my home village."

"Ah, yes," Adrian said with a grin. "That small fishing village on the Kavirondo Gulf. Somewhere near Kisumu."

Peter grinned back. "We call it the Winam Gulf."

"Well, I think it's super," Adrian said. Then he cleared his throat and said, "I'm going to be married myself."

Peter merely nodded, not in the least surprised. "I must call Miss Lewis and congratulate her."

"You might want to hold off on that a bit," Adrian said quickly. "She, um, hasn't actually said yes yet."

"All right. But let me be the first to hear. After all, I was the one who introduced you."

"That's right, you did," Adrian said with a laugh. "Not exactly a promising beginning, was it?" It wasn't until they were back to the Land Rover that a sudden thought struck him. "That makes all of us," he said wonderingly. "Odd, isn't it?"

"What is?" Peter said, not following.

"We're all to be married. You, me, Pythias . . . even Joseph, if I'm any judge of men. All of us who are left." Adrian glanced at Peter, cocking an eyebrow. "Do you think it means something?"

Odongo thought about it for a moment, then shrugged and said, "I can't imagine what."

A week after Mzee's funeral, both Adrian and Peter were back at State House, in the garden this time, summoned for a special ceremony in their honor. With both Robbie and Millie looking on, they received a medal, pinned on by the new head of state himself, for service to the nation's wildlife. Both men seriously considered declining the award, but in the end they did not. They couldn't think of a way to explain such a boorish act without leveling accusations they couldn't prove.

It was a small ceremony, a family affair. Besides Adrian and Robbie and Peter and Millicent, the senior superintendent of the Central Police Station was there. So was the Assistant Minister for Wildlife, drinking from the President's fountain of praise. The Assistant Minister, looking cool and confident in his vanilla suit, even made a short speech, full of plaudits for the brave work of Police Inspector Odongo and Good Citizen Glenton, proud of *his* team.

Reporters and photographers from the Nairobi newspapers were there too, and in case they hadn't made the observation on their own, one of the President's aides helpfully pointed out to them that here was a perfect example of how black and white Kenyans could work together for the good of the nation. Wasn't this proof that the spirit of *Harambee*, of one nation "pulling together," was alive and well? That Jomo Kenyatta's legacy lived on?

When the ceremony was over, the President asked everyone to come inside for coffee. "I have another small surprise for Inspector Odongo," he said, exchanging conspiratorial glances with the Assistant Minister and the senior superintendent.

When they were all settled in his office, the President reached into his desk drawer and took out a set of officer's insignia. "You are officially promoted to the rank of senior superintendent, as of today," he said, smiling broadly as he crossed the room to pin the pips onto Peter's dress uniform. Everyone applauded. Peter just stood there, looking stunned. It was an extraordinary tribute, a jump of three full grades.

"A new posting comes with it, of course," the President said, still smiling. "I'm putting you in charge of an entire district." He named a town in the Northern Frontier District infamous as a center of bandit activity. "You've proven that you can handle the difficult jobs."

"I'm very grateful, Mr. President," Peter said, finding his voice at last. "Thank you, sir."

"You can thank me for the promotion," the President said modestly, "but the posting was the Assistant Minister's idea. With your senior superintendent's full agreement, of course."

"Of course," Peter echoed, giving the two men a curt nod and a frozen smile. They stared back with mocking eyes, their silent laughter filling the room.

Adrian spent most of the following week moving house. At Robbie's request. "I want you to move in here," she said one morning after he'd spent the night at her house in Muthaiga.

"Poor thing," he said with mock pity. "Can't bear to be away from me for even a few hours."

"I just want to get you away from Little Miss Hyphen."

"Philippa?" he said. "She's just an old friend."

"If she were *old* I wouldn't mind. She has the hots for you and I want you out of that cottage."

"Nonsense. Besides, I couldn't possibly consider living in sin. Think of my reputation. No, it wouldn't do at all. I am afraid you'll have to marry me first."

"I never buy a product until I've thoroughly checked it out," Robbie said. "You get the small closet. The one by the window is mine."

Then it was Adrian's turn to play the jealous lover. A week after he moved in, he confronted her. "All right, then. What about this Markson chap?"

"Who?"

"Don't play the bloody innocent. John Markson. You had dinner with him."

"Oh, him. He's a source. A wildlife type. I interviewed him for the poaching cover. Speaking of which . . . the bastards have bumped it again." The subject rankled. Kenyatta's death had pushed her wildlife story back a week. Then the Shah had fled Iran one step ahead of a lynch mob, which had bumped it another week. And next week's cover would be Iran again. She recognized the signs well enough. Her editors became evasive whenever she asked about rescheduling it. Her big story, her scoop, was dying a slow death. Adrian was unsympathetic.

His attitude was that since she didn't have enough proof to tell the full
story anyway, it didn't really matter. Easy for him to say.

"Don't switch the subject," Adrian said. "He took you to Bobbe's.
Candlelight. Wine. The whole bloody bit."

"I told you, he's a source. I needed to talk to him and dinner was the
only time he could see me." Her eyes narrowed suspiciously. "Wait a
minute. How do you know where we went? How do you know I had
dinner with him at all?"

Adrian grinned. "Alan Bobbe told me, and Markson himself confirmed it when I saw him in his office this afternoon."

"You went to see him just because I had dinner with him? Jesus
Christ, Adrian! How embarrassing! What did you do, beat him up?"

"Of course not. That's no way to land a job."

"A job!"

Adrian nodded. "It seems your young man and I are going to be
colleagues. Starting Monday week. I thought as long as we were sharing
a woman, we might as well share an office."

"What!" Robbie squealed. "Wait a minute! I want to make sure I've
got this right. The Great White Hunter is going to work for the Wildlife
Society?"

"Mmm-hmm."

"That's great! How did this happen?"

"I'm not quite certain," Adrian said with a laugh. "From what I
gather, some conservation poobah saw the press account of that silly
medal business. He read how a former hunter had used his donkey's
years of experience in the bush to stop the killing of helpless animals,
and about how bloody marvelous I am. He rang yesterday morning
while you were at the office to ask if I had ever given any thought to
working the other side of the fence."

"And?"

"And I need a job. You've been good enough not to say anything
about who has been filling the chop-box around here, but I thought it
was time I began earning my keep."

"What kind of work will you be doing?"

"From the sound of it I'm to be a combination consultant and
fairground freak," he said with a laugh. "I'll advise the Society on
anti-poaching methods and go about giving speeches at fund-raising
dinners in the U.K. and the States, where the money is. Public speaking
isn't exactly my cuppa, I know, but they seem to think that the sermon
will be more convincing if it comes from a reformed murderer of
animals."

"You're not very good at lying, Adrian," Robbie said.

"Who says I'd be lying?"

"Oh? *Have* you reformed?"

He shrugged. "All I know is that I've seen quite enough killing. Of any sort." Then he chuckled and added, "To quote Joseph ole Kantai, that great Masai philosopher: I'm getting too old for that shit."

Robbie, watching him closely, didn't crack a smile. "So you're content then?" she asked.

"It's a job that will keep me in the bush a good part of the time. That's all I ever wanted."

"But you'd be giving up hunting."

"I'd already given up hunting. That was decided for me, remember?"

"You know what I mean," she said. "You could find a way if you wanted to."

He shook his head. "I would have to leave Kenya. As the old saying goes: what you gain on the swings you lose on the roundabouts." He gave her a puzzled look. "Why? Do you think I *should* go back to hunting?"

"Not at all. I'm just trying to find out if you're at peace with this. If you've worked it out in your own mind."

Adrian started work two weeks later. Surprisingly, life went on much the same; he had a light schedule until the new year, mostly a matter of getting to know the people he would be working with. Robbie also had some free time. The holiday season in the States was always a slow news time, and except for a quick trip to Rhodesia for a war update, she was home with Adrian.

They spent a quiet Christmas. They had dinner with Pate at the Club and exchanged gifts in the lounge. The following day, Boxing Day, they drove to Maasailand, bearing Christmas gifts for Joseph. Adrian brought a skin, the biggest lion he had ever shot; Robbie brought a Temple University sweatshirt. Half expecting to find Joseph married, they took along a few wedding presents as well; blankets and pots and baskets, and some costume jewelry for the bride.

Instead, they did not find Joseph at all. He was not in his *manyatta* and no one in the *engang* had seen him for days. They did find his former fire-stick elder, who informed them that Joseph would not be getting married. He had severed his engagement his first day home from the Aberdare Forest, after first giving what he had saved in dowry to his family to make up for the gifts they had given the young woman's family. And where was Joseph now? Adrian asked. In the feasting camp with the new generation of warriors, the elder said in disgust. He had announced that the *morani* were fifteen years younger than he was, and that there was much he could teach them.

Adrian and Robbie left their gifts in Joseph's hut and returned to Nairobi. They were to get their wedding, only a few days later in fact, but it wasn't Joseph's.

Peter Odongo and Millicent Ogara were married in Luoland but with none of the usual Luo trappings. There simply wasn't time. The newest senior superintendent of police had to be on seat in his new post by the first of the year.

Traditionally, the Luo marriage rites were both lengthy and complicated. First a "bridewealth," the number of cattle the man had to pay the woman's family, had to be worked out, a process that sometimes took months. When that was settled, there was a mock fight between the couple's friends in which the bride was "captured" and carried off to the bridegroom's *pacho*. After a few weeks, the couple would visit the woman's *pacho* to pay respects to her mother and a feast was held. At this point the would-be husband handed over a number of cows as the first installment of the bridewealth. After that, the woman lived with her parents, permitted to visit her beloved for a short time whenever he added a cow to the bridewealth. When the entire bridewealth was paid off, a proper marriage ceremony, the *riso*, was conducted, followed by a feast, and the man and woman were fully married at last.

Peter and Millie cut straight to the end of the process. The *riso* and feast were held at her family homestead. Thanks to an advance on the pay increase that accompanied his promotion, Peter was able to pay the bridewealth all at once. Both sets of parents, ashamed of having unmarried children so advanced in years, were so relieved to see them married off that they lodged no protests. The wedding feast was a memorable affair. Adrian and Robbie came and Robbie did a dance round the fire that half delighted, half scandalized, and wholly mesmerized the Luo. The very next morning, despite a crushing hangover, Peter loaded his and Millie's valises and wedding gifts into his new Range Rover—one of the perks that went with being a senior district official—and started north.

It was late on a wet March afternoon, in the first week of the long rains, when Adrian was called upstairs by Robbie. "I'm in the bedroom," she yelled down. "Hurry!"

"You are a naughty bit of fluff, I must say," he called as he took the stairs two at a time. But when he walked into the bedroom, Robbie was at the window, not on the bed. "Come look," she said, drawing back the shades.

He looked, and saw a caravan of Mercedes-Benzes pulling into Dada's driveway. "What's this, the bloody Wabenzi Ball?"

"There's the Assistant Minister," Robbie said, "and I'll bet the three Asian gentlemen are the infamous Patel brothers."

"Who's the other African?" Adrian asked. "I think I know him from somewhere." He went to the closet for his binoculars and came back for another look. "I'm almost certain I've seen him before. Here, have a look."

Robbie took the glasses. "He does look familiar. Wait a minute. Wasn't he at the medal ceremony? That's it. He's one of the President's aides."

They watched in silence as the men filed into the house, then went downstairs and had a gin-and-lime sundowner.

As for Peter Odongo, stuck out in the bush as he was, it was a couple of months before he heard the reports of renewed poaching activity in the Aberdares.

Author's Endnote

This is a work of fiction and, with the exception of a few historical figures, its characters are the inventions of the author. For literary purposes, I have taken liberty with one vital date. The late Kenya President, *Mzee* Jomo Kenyatta, died on August 22, 1978, rather than in December of that year.

More than a decade after the period in which my story is set, the assault on Africa's wildlife continues. If anything, the situation has worsened. According to recent surveys, the elephants of Kenya are being poached at a rate of 150 a week. The elephant population, estimated at nearly 140,000 in the early 1970s, has declined by more than 85 percent, to about 16,000. Some conservation experts put the number even lower, closer to 11,000. Things are equally desperate for the black rhinoceros. Africa's black rhinoceros population, estimated to be 60,000 in the early 1970s, has dropped to merely 800.

One final statistic: as this novel was being completed, more than a hundred game wardens, park rangers, and wildlife officials were being investigated by the Kenya authorities, under suspicion of corruption and collusion with poachers.

In recent months, the Kenya government has taken some dramatic steps to address the issue. President Daniel arap Moi has issued orders to park rangers to shoot poachers on sight. He also has appointed a person of integrity—Richard Leakey, the former head of the National Museum and the son of renowned paleontologists Louis and Mary Leakey—as Director of the Kenya Wildlife Department, which has reverted back to its previous semi-autonomous status. It is a beginning.

—N.P., September 1989